HEART OF
WOOD & STEEL

Maxine Taylor

This is a work of fiction. All characters, organizations, and events portrayed in this novel are either products of the author's imagination or are used fictitiously. Any resemblance to actual events, locales, or persons, living or dead, is coincidental.

ISBN: 979-8-9942858-1-7

Cover illustrations by Jacquelyn Romney
Interior illustrations by @mothdeity
Printed in United States of America
Independently published

For the sisters of my heart who have been with me every step of this journey.
Osea yao faémo.

NYMPH ISLAND OF TEGADONA

THESSALIA
REALM OF THE OREADS

POLARIS
MOTHER MOUNTAIN

GRANTINE
MOTHER MOUNTAIN

VENDARI
MOTHER MOUNTAIN

MARINTHIAN OCEAN
REALM OF THE OCEANIDS

DRAINED HELENA
MOTHER LAKE

CHAFO
MOTHER LAKE

LACUSTRIS
REALM OF THE NAIADS

APONYX
CITY OF MAN

VALA
MOTHER LAKE

FIDDLEWOOD
MOTHER OAK
(DECEASED)

BRYNA'S SEEDLING

THE DRYAD
HOLLOW

THORNEWOOD
MOTHER OAK

SYLVANWOOD
MOTHER OAK
(DECEASED)

EURYALEA
REALM OF THE DRYADS

N
W E
S

Aponyx
City of Man

The Spire

The Ey8aphee

The Foothills

The Central Quarter

The Terraces

The Silos

Bracknell Manor

To the Thornewood

The Thorn

There is a thorn that hides within
The softest fronds of ferns
She guards the bush from greedy hands
And ones that don't take turns

Her stem bursts forth with power
Her barbs could make you blush
She stares you down, shielded by shadows
Daring you to touch

Her poisoned bite is subtle
At first, it feels like love
She'll have you seeing stars mid-day
Chasing butterflies and doves

But her kiss is death, ever so slow
Seeking nothing but retribution
On men who take with greedy hands
And deserve no absolution

Chapter One

It was only quiet in the Thornewood on execution days.

For Eryna, however, they were the only days that tasted of freedom.

Dirt kicked high into the air as she sped through the forest on light feet, outpacing the rapidly rising sun.

Good. I cut it too close last time.

"Eryna!" a distant voice called. Apparently, her Dryad sisters realized she was missing a full ten minutes sooner than last execution day. It didn't matter. She wouldn't stop now.

Eryna picked up her pace, a smile playing at her lips as her fingers grazed a patch of soft ferns. Her lungs burned with glee and crisp morning air. Her heart pounded louder, her feet faster against the pine-littered earth even as her long yellow hair snagged on some nettles. Still, she wouldn't stop. Hair grew back, but moments were lost forever if they were missed, and she wouldn't miss the flaming towers today.

She skidded to a stop nearly colliding with the trunk of her favorite redwood. Catching her breath, she eyed the still dark sky through the colossal canopy.

"Minutes to spare." She smiled, pleased with today's pace. It might've even been a personal record. She backed up several paces, ready to launch herself at the tree when a quiet whimper caught her attention. She froze.

Not today, not now, she thought, straining all her senses to make sure she wasn't mistaking it for the natural sounds of the Wood.

A small animal whimpered in pain again, not a sound so much as it was a feeling beneath Eryna's feet. She groaned.

Definitely real. What terrible timing.

"Eryna, I know you're out here you reckless sprite!" her sister's distant voice echoed. Now it was *really* terrible timing. But from the sound of it, her sister was miles off. There was still a little time before Eryna would be captured and dragged back home to watch the execution, but only just. She glanced at the sky again. A halo of light now rimmed its edges. The sun would break the horizon in a matter of minutes—no more than ten.

The animal cried again, and this time, she couldn't ignore it. Who was she kidding? She never ignored a cry for help. It was in her very roots to mend the wounded.

She shut her eyes and sighed, "This better be quick."

Eryna turned toward the sensation. The deeper she moved through the forest, the stronger the soil hemorrhaged sorrow, fear. It intensified as Eryna navigated the trees until she found herself at the lip of a sudden drop; a trap her sisters set for humans. She peaked over the edge. A small, furry orange face looked up at her and whimpered.

"You again," she scolded, and the little fox tucked its snout beneath its paw. The soil beneath Eryna churned to shame and embarrassment. "How many times have I rescued you from this hole?"

The fox whimpered again but avoided her gaze. Eryna sighed and grabbed a nearby willow reed. Concentrating, she channeled the earth's energy into the reed. It lengthened and stretched until it reached the injured animal. The fox bit down on the reed and Eryna pushed her energy back, back, back into the soil. The reed shrank, gently pulling the fox from the trap. Eryna laid it out on a patch of soft moss and poked and prodded it with an assessing hand.

"Three broken ribs, a broken leg, and then some. Think I should let you heal naturally this time. You might learn a lesson or two," she said. The fox whipped a pleading gaze at her, eyes wide and watery. She pursed her lips, relenting. "Fine. But you must promise you'll remember this trap. This is the third time you've nearly become mulch."

The fox barked and placed its head in Eryna's palm, its fur radiating gratitude. Warmth seeped from Eryna's hands, and as she concentrated, each broken bone reset, and each strained muscle knit together. After the last bruise dissolved, the fox leapt up and bound off into the depths of the forest, out of sight.

"You're welcome!" Eryna shouted after it, but it was long gone. She scoffed and mumbled to herself, "Not like I had anything else to do." She looked up at the sky. She had five minutes, maybe, if Gaia looked on her favorably. She also hadn't heard her sister in a few minutes. She had to be closer. No more time to waste.

Sweat beaded on her white birch tree skin as she sprinted back to the redwood and started her climb, once again challenging the sun. As Eryna braced her foot against a thick knot, her hip shook with a sudden foreign buzz, and she paused her climb.

Her eyes fell on the rectangular metal object in the silk bag at her waist. She'd discovered it yesterday lying in the dirt around where her sister Dera had found the trespasser. The odd vibrating started three hours ago but she'd chosen to ignore it, too afraid to examine it anywhere near her sisters. Human objects were strictly forbidden. She should have turned it in the second she'd found it, but curiosity was a sharp hook. She'd heard of these human communication objects, but she'd never imagined holding one. If her sisters discovered she had it, they would not only confiscate it but probably punish Eryna in the most severe manner they could think of—like uprooting black walnut trees for the rest of her long, long life—pesky invasive things.

The buzzing stopped. She looked up at the last hundred feet of her climb and spied the blue of dawn. One minute left to sunrise. Maybe two.

"Eryna of the Thornewood, I swear to Gaia…" The grumbling voice was so close now, it was unmistakably Dera.

Eryna's freedom was almost gone. She'd lost precious time to that pesky fox and that strange object. She wouldn't lose any more.

Her arms trembled and she grunted as she pulled herself harder, higher, faster until she broke through the canopy and into the open air. She settled on a sturdy branch and inhaled deeply, absorbing the rare silence into her lungs, into the very sap of her bones. She'd made it, but barely. The metallic buzzing tickled her skin again, but she ignored it with every nerve in her body. These morning escapes were rare. She wouldn't miss a second.

She stared unblinking as the sky melted into a rich blue, dissolved into a pale yellow, then plunged into a fiery orange as the sun peaked its crest over the eastern horizon. The cumulus clouds transformed into tufts of molten gold above the canopies of the Thornewood forest.

The distant glass and steel towers of the human city of Aponyx stood like small, pointed peaks against the warming sky. A few towered unfathomably high over the world below, unyielding in their grandeur just like the humans who'd built them. Her sisters called the city a monstrous display of stolen power. They weren't wrong. But at the right time of day, at just the right angle, it was breathtaking, radiant.

One structure stood above the rest: an immense spire that tapered off to a sharp point. Its glittering body caught the light and blazed to life, like a flaming waterfall.

Eryna leaned forward as if she could get closer, touch the tower, see the humans in the city below as they began their day. But this was as close as she'd ever get.

The sunrise must be brilliant from there, she thought, settling into her favorite daydream, picturing herself standing inside that sharp tower. This time, a boy stood next to her, their fingers brushing.

She'd never been close to a human boy, but her sisters' stories of when humans and Dryads once lived peacefully were fossilized in her mind like a leaf in stone. That time was long gone before Eryna was born from the Mother Oak.

Her hip vibrated again. Eryna bit her lip and finally withdrew the rectangular object. It was smooth, light, with a few small silver shapes raised along the outer edge that clicked when pressed. One side was silver with small glass circles in the corner. Eryna flipped it to the other side and gasped, her heart lurching.

It was one long piece of glass that glowed with a face.

A human boy.

He was most likely a young adult or adolescent. It was hard to tell with humans, sometimes. His hair was dark as night, short on the sides and longer on top. The strands were tousled as if he'd just run his fingers through it. His mouth was half-open, his smile playful and mischievous as a raccoon yet vicious and unforgiving as a wolf. His full lips pushed his cheeks high, crinkling his dark brown eyes at the corners.

She tilted the object left and right, flipping the boy onto his head and back down, wondering how to shake him out, but he didn't move. He must either be stuck in there by some sort of curse, or he wasn't really in there at all. Only his likeness.

She couldn't tell if he was handsome or not. His features were certainly symmetrical and proportional, but after decades of observing the trespassing humans, she found that their attractiveness wasn't distilled down to facial features alone. It was often in the way they carried themselves. In the way they moved. In the way energy rippled from them or didn't.

Two vibrant circles at the bottom of the object caught her eye. One red, the other green.

She moved her finger toward the green circle.

"Eryna!" Dera's voice echoed up at her from the ground, startling her. The object slipped through her fingers, but she swung low and recovered it just before it fell out of reach. She blew out a breath of relief then tucked it back into her bag. *Hades*, she cursed. Time was up.

"I know you're up there!" Dera called again.

"Who is this Eryna you speak of? I know of no such nymph," Eryna replied, smiling to herself as she descended the tree, nearly free-falling.

"*Faémona*, if you aren't down here in ten seconds, you will be stuck mending the trap nets for a year," Dera threatened as Eryna's feet hit the earth with a soft bounce. Ignoring the sour nickname, she smiled wide at her vexed sister, whose arms would have switched sides if they were crossed any harder. Her textured brown skin like the bark of the sweet birch tree flushed with frustration.

"I'm already always on mending duty," Eryna said as she pried her sister's arm from its locked position and threaded it through hers. "Bit of a weak threat, if you ask me."

Dera rolled her eyes but softened into her as they walked through the moss-covered pines toward the *Domecowé*, the sacred center of the Thornewood.

"Yes, well, that's what happens when you're the youngest," Dera chastised. Eryna wilted.

"I've been the youngest for a hundred years. I should be trusted with more than petty traps by now."

"You forage," Dera offered.

"Everyone forages."

"You coordinated the winter solstice festivities this past season."

"Only because Althea made me. I couldn't exactly tell our clan leader to go touch moss, could I? Besides, she knows I detest winter."

Dera stifled a laugh.

"How about...you tend to the wounded."

"Tough competition for that job when you're the only remaining healer in your clan," Eryna snorted. Silence fell between them. Then Eryna glanced at Dera thoughtfully. "Come to think of it, I could use that as leverage with Althea. Thanks for the idea."

Dera turned and faced Eryna.

"Responsibility is earned, *faémona*, not extorted."

Eryna wrinkled her nose.

Faémona. "Little sister," in the language of the Dryads.

It'd been a nickname she bore from the time she was pulled from the great hollow of the Mother Oak, and one she couldn't shed as there were no others below her to pass it to. Eryna's gaze narrowed.

"Have I not earned responsibility these hundred years?"

Dera sighed and gently squeezed Eryna's shoulders. "In some ways, yes. But days like this where you pine after the human city when you should be helping us prepare for the execution, no. You have not."

The execution. Dread wrapped around Eryna like a suffocating vine. Another day, another trespasser caught searching for the sacred Heart of the Thornewood Mother Oak. The humans knew what happened if they breached the border between Aponyx and Euryalea— the Dryads' promise of execution had loomed over them for seventy-five years now.

So why didn't they stop?

Eryna's eyes found the ground, her lips turned down at the prospect of watching another human life go to waste.

"I know you don't like the executions," Dera said, dipping her head to catch Eryna's gaze.

"Hasn't it been long enough since the war?" Eryna asked, her voice quiet. "Can't we stop the cruelty?" The executions never made sense to her, especially when she knew there was once a time of peace between humans and Dryads. A time where they even mingled their communities, fell in love, kissed—

Dera cleared her throat.

"Cruel is destroying lands and stealing the Hearts of our Mother

Oaks. Cruel is murdering entire clans of Dryads." She softened after a moment and sighed. "We're trying to protect what little we have left. Come. The execution is about to start. We cannot be late."

They trotted quickly through burbling creeks, past clusters of apple, cherry, and peach trees, and through the wild strawberry patch.

As they finally crossed the tree line into the *Domecowé*, Eryna bristled at the turn in the atmosphere. The air was charged with electric excitement and anticipation that only execution days brought about; a stark difference from the calm silence she'd been steeped in all morning.

Eryna and Dera briskly walked toward the colossal Mother Oak rooted at the center of the clearing and knelt. They placed their palms on her millennia-old trunk in greeting.

"Mother, for this day of life, we thank you," they said in unison. Eryna lingered a little longer, thanking her mother for the small amount of freedom she'd experienced that morning. Then she joined the others.

"*Osea yao faémo*," she greeted her sisters and was immediately pulled into conversation.

"I can't wait to see him. I hear he's the youngest trespasser in decades," Mori exclaimed.

"I hear he was closer than anyone to finding the third Heart," Oihane replied.

"I hear he's handsome. As far as humans go, anyway," Maya whispered as if it was a scandalous secret.

Eryna scanned the clearing for the trespasser. They were usually held nearby, sometimes tied to the Mother Oak, depending on how much of a flight risk they were. She always tried to catch a glimpse of them before the execution, if only to see a living human in such close proximity. While she'd never dishonor her culture and disobey her sisters, a small part of her fantasized about freeing one of the more handsome ones.

Maybe they would fall in love at first sight—a phenomenon she'd once heard in a human fable a sister told. Maybe he'd whisk her away to Aponyx or the Mainland. They would find a cozy dwelling in the woods, have a few children, and live a happy life until he grew old and she…didn't. The fantasy ended there. It was an impossible life that would never be.

A loud *boom* rattled the forest floor. She turned to see Althea at one of the ceremonial drums.

It was time.

"Sisters, sit," Althea said, silencing the Dryads.

She stood above them all, regal, and stoic. Her long orange hair waved gently around her shoulders, her brown maple-bark skin shone in the dappled sunlight, and her short silk dress donned soft ferns, toadstools, and baby tooth moss. Even without her laurel crown, she was clearly their leader, as her most remarkable trait was her commanding green eyes. Vibrant green eyes were the mark of a Dryad, but Althea's emanated centuries of life and wisdom. Where humans grew old, weak, and sickly in age, Dryads, like trees, only strengthened. Althea was not only the oldest of all the Dryads, but the strongest. The most alive.

She was also the least pliable.

At her command, everyone sat in a half-circle facing the Mother Oak. But Dera remained standing. Eryna gazed up at her, brows folded in question. Dera smiled down at her tightly, then turned and walked to meet Althea at the base of the Mother Oak. Eryna tensed.

There was only one reason for Dera to be up there.

Althea clasped her hands behind her back. "Bring the boy," she said.

Two sisters, Mori and Ilana, disappeared behind the Mother Oak. When they returned, they had *him* in hand. The trespasser.

The chatter had been right. He was handsome, despite being disheveled and caked in dirt. He was tall, though not much more than her sisters. He was light skinned with pale yellow hair and looked similar in age to the boy in the object. He was the youngest trespasser she'd ever seen. They were typically less boy, more man. This one was closer to her in maturity than any in her lifetime.

That foolish fantasy of love suddenly nagged at her, but she shoved it aside. It was useless to entertain. Humans were all monsters; greedy men set on stealing Euryalea's last functioning Heart. Eryna and her sisters' lives were safer without them.

But when the boy met Eryna's gaze, she froze. Blue as the petals of a Forget-Me-Not, his eyes were puffy and red. They screamed of innocence, of regret. Usually, the eyes of trespassers held a possessiveness, a greed, a desire to pilfer and obliterate and ruin anything that wasn't or refused to be theirs. He lacked that entirely. His eyes were clear, earnest, and held a certain wonder.

He was not like the others. Eryna's stomach clenched.

Mori and Ilana set him on his knees next to Althea. She glanced down at him, but he didn't meet her gaze. Instead, he lifted his eyes to the sky, as if seeking final solace in whatever higher power his faith resided.

"We gather to witness repayment for what was once stolen from our people," Althea started. It was her usual speech, always spellbinding, just as she was. "As our cousins of the Fiddlewood and Sylvanwood were returned to the dirt before their time at the hands of humans, so it is for any human intruder who wishes to steal the last Heart of Euryalea. This is our promise."

"This is our promise," the Dryads chanted back. They started a low, slow hum, patting a steady beat against their thighs as Althea struck the drum, producing another thunderous *boom*.

"This trespasser was found in the Thornewood searching for our Mother's Heart when the moon was at its highest. As we told the humans seventy-five years ago, the moment they cross into Euryalea, they forfeit their lives to us. A warning they refuse to mind."

"I wasn't looking for the Heart, I—" he protested like many of those before him, but the hum of the Dryads drowned him out, their voices louder, the beat quicker.

The boy closed his eyes in resignation. A tear cut through his ruddy cheek. He silently muttered to himself—words that would be his last. Eryna couldn't look away, couldn't stop wondering about his life in Aponyx. Surely someone so young would be missed.

Althea pulled the stone knife from her waist, its sharp edge rust-stained with decades of human blood. She held it high.

"Let us remind them once more!" she exclaimed. Eryna's sisters yelped excitedly, and the hum of the Thornewood Dryads climbed higher and higher, louder and louder until it was a howling, stormy wind.

Another *boom* from the drum reverberated through the air, and Eryna's hip suddenly buzzed.

It wasn't from the drum.

The object at her hip glowed, the boy's face smiling that wolfish smile through the netting of her satchel. She shielded it before anyone could see.

"Sister Dera," Althea beckoned. Eryna's head shot up in time to see her flipping the hilt of the stone knife toward Dera.

Dera, please. Look at him. He's innocent, Eryna silently begged, staring at her sister with wide, pleading eyes. It was futile. Dera had lived through the humans' betrayal of the Dryads; her soul was just as stained as the knife in her hand. Eryna glanced between the boy and Dera. Her sister's face was unrecognizable. It was no longer warm and kind. It was cold. Distant. Uncompromising. Eryna could do nothing but watch as Dera placed herself behind him, braced a hand on his head, and set the stone knife at his neck.

His eyes screwed shut. His lips stilled.

"Blood paid for blood spilled," Althea chanted.

"Blood paid for blood spilled," the Dryads echoed violently. All but Eryna.

The boy took a deep breath.

It stopped short in his chest.

He coughed, and blood sprayed onto the sisters closest to the front, spurting from the wound in his neck. Many shrieked in delight, others howled and jeered, but Eryna remained silent, her gaze lingering on Dera's smile, the blood trickling from the stone knife in her shaking hand.

The boy collapsed. His face blanched as he drained of blood. His blue eyes opened. Eryna couldn't help herself. She looked right at them.

Then his struggled breaths ceased, and Eryna swore she felt the moment his soul left his body and dissolved into the soil, back to the earth, like a star winking out; the way all souls of living beings inevitably would.

Flora or fauna.

Human or Dryad.

In the end, they were all the same.

Chapter Two

Two dozen bonfires blazed high and bright around the Mother Oak. Eryna's steps were slow and even, matching the pace of the roaring drums as she roamed around her dancing sisters. Their movements were feverish and primal. A Dryad was born from the Mother Oak with dance written into her heart.

Except Eryna's body couldn't catch the beat. Every motion felt awkward and forced. Her airy dress of willow reeds and ranunculus and delphiniums was unusually stifling. Her circlet of mourning dove feathers and pink chiffon roses weighed on her head like a stone. Everywhere she looked she saw the boy's Forget-Me-Not eyes finding hers with his last breath. She could barely stand to walk on the soil, let alone dance on it, as the sensation of his soul slipping into the ground still coated her feet. Eryna swallowed the last dregs of berry wine from her cup, but it soured on her tongue. She eyed the empty vessel. How could last season's wine have already turned?

She scanned the two hundred faces before her in search of Dera, but it was nearly impossible to see through the smoke, the heat, and the crowd. Then she was suddenly crushed against a warm chest.

"Don't be so glum, *faémona*," the light voice sang as arms like an ash tree rocked Eryna back and forth.

Oihane.

She permanently spoke in song and moved in dance. Eryna gave a half-hearted smile and swayed with her.

"Who's glum?" Eryna asked, her lips pushing into a false smile. "You couldn't possibly be talking about me."

Oihane sighed and pulled Eryna toward a stump laden with wooden cups that overflowed with berry wine. She tore Eryna's empty cup from her hand, tossed it over her shoulder, and thrust a new one forward.

"You're right. Moping around the bonfires like a wounded pup is a clear sign you're having a wonderful night."

Eryna glared at Oihane.

"I am not moping," she grumbled. Oihane raised a skeptical brow, and Eryna relented with a sigh. She was indeed moping, even if she hadn't realized it.

"Humans aren't worth it, Eryna. They're monsters. That boy had it coming the moment he crossed the border, and he knew it."

"It isn't about the boy—"

Oihane pushed Eryna's wine to her lips, cutting her objection short.

"Well, whatever has you down, get over it. Drink! Dance! Be merry!" Oihane raised her arms and twirled in a circle, then clasped Eryna's shoulders. "Celebrate the fact that we are *alive,* and we still have her Heart." Oihane signaled to the colossal tree at the center of the bonfires. Its thick trunk was strong and solid, her full, leafy crown high and vibrant; she was their mother, their life bringer. Every Thornewood Dryad was delivered earth-side through her.

"I know you don't remember much of the war time," Oihane continued. "You were only a sapling then and we shielded you from it as best we could. The executions were our only solution. Without them, we'd be long gone like our cousins. They work, *faémona.*"

Eryna's wine soured again, and this time she knew it wasn't the drink. She was over a hundred years old. Just because she was the last Dryad born didn't mean she was *still* the sapling her sisters treated her like. But a hundred years was considered adolescence as far as the Dryads were concerned.

Eryna nodded and sipped the wine to douse her bitterness. After a breath, she smiled, a weak expression that barely reached her cheeks.

"You're right," she said. "I must have just eaten some spoiled wheat or something. I'm not feeling like myself. I should go rest."

Oihane warily eyed Eryna. After a moment, her features melted into a sympathetic smile. She kissed her on the forehead and rejoined the ruckus, leaving Eryna at the edge of the celebration. Swiftly, Eryna tread to the Hollow where she and a group of Dryads had made their dwellings and collapsed into her eucalyptus tree.

Silk stuffed with pampas grass and soft white pine needles cradled Eryna's fatigued body. The distant clamor of the bonfire celebration became a steady, soothing rhythm, each drumbeat putting more distance between her and the execution. She closed her eyes, trying to think of something else. But every time Eryna stared at the back of her lids, empty blue eyes stared back.

She quickly gave up on sleep and gazed at the night sky through the thick pines, finding her favorite nymph constellations: Mafa, the Oread warrior who fought in the Titan wars; Kazia, the wayfaring Naiad who discovered their nymph island of Tegadona; and Ardian, the Dryad who loved a dying man so much, the gods transformed him into a tree for her. He was gone now, of course, having been part of the Fiddlewood. But Eryna had seen his tree once, back when she was twelve or thirteen, when the Fiddlewood was still—

Buzz. Buzz. Buzz.

Eryna shot up, heart pounding, blood pulsing in her ears. She glanced down, and the bright white glow of the metallic object shone back at her. She'd nearly forgotten about it. It hadn't come alive since the execution.

Eryna scanned her immediate area. None of her sisters were in sight, the drumbeats still heavy with no signs of ending.

She was alone and would be for a while.

Carefully, she examined the object. The same boy with the same wolfish grin smiled back at her, and the same red and green circles hovered just above his chest. Eryna studied the circles. They were different compared to the boy, flat and unnatural. It was as if they existed within the glass, and posed a question: yes, or no?

But why was this question being asked? And which was yes, and which was no?

Green could be "yes." It was the color of the earth at its most fertile, and the soft moss on which she loved to daydream.

Which would make red "no." It was the color of fire, and the mark on the belly of the black widow warning curious observers to stay away.

But green could also be no. It was the poisonous emerald tree boa, or the dart frog whose slick secretions could kill even the strongest of beings.

Which would make red yes. It was juicy ripe strawberries in the heat of summer and the morning song of the cardinal.

Yes. Red was most certainly the correct answer to whatever question was being asked. Eryna touched the red circle.

The object stilled. The boy faded to black.

Eryna's heart sank. Maybe she should've picked green.

She stared at the object, willing it to vibrate once more, to give her a second chance to answer the question. But it stayed dark and silent.

Minutes passed and Eryna continued to stare at the object.

Her lids drooped. Her head lolled. Her shoulders curved forward and she decided to give in to sleep. Her head had just hit the silk when—

Buzz. Buzz. Buzz.

Quick as a viper's strike, she sat up and clutched the object tight.

She touched the green circle without hesitation. The glow dimmed but didn't completely fade, and in the boy's place was a short word in the human language: *Brody*.

A name? A place? An object?

"Hello?" a tiny voice called. It spoke the human tongue and was warm and most definitely male. The sound of it conjured the image of the boy's wolfish grin. Wide, charming, withholding. It had to be him.

Her head swiveled in all directions in search of prying eyes. She found none.

"Hello?" he asked again. He sounded so small, so far away. Eryna brought the object closer to her face to see where the voice came from. She pressed her ear against a small row of holes, and this time, it was as if he was right next to her. "Tyler? Are you there? Dude, answer me. We're coming to get you."

Eryna jerked back, startled. But curiosity was a snare, and she was nothing more than a fresh spring rabbit. She brought the object to her ear once more.

"Hello?" she replied, thankful the Dryads were well practiced in the human language. *To know our enemy, we must understand the language of our enemy*, Althea always said during Eryna's lessons.

"Oh my gods," the boy whispered. Eryna heard rustling and muffled chatter. She waited. More chatter. Waited some more. Even more chatter. She could only make out three words: "one of *them*."

The voice returned.

"You still there?" he asked.

She should've ended it then. She'd already gone too far the moment she decided to take the object. But Eryna didn't know how to stop whatever this thing was, and she couldn't shake the desire to hear more of the wolf-boy's voice.

"Yes," she replied, cursing herself for giving in.

"Good. I'm glad," he said, and she hadn't realized his words made her smile until her cheeks were already pressed high against her eyes. She shook it off as he spoke again, "Is my friend Tyler there? Blue eyes, blond hair, tall and a little awkward like a bean stalk?"

A sharp pain struck Eryna's chest.

Friend.

The boy they executed earlier had friends; friends who were worried about him.

It was one thing to see the humans as intruders, trespassers, aggressors. But to know them as beings with people who loved them the way Eryna loved her sisters was something else entirely. She was once again at this morning's execution. His eyes flashed to hers. This was too much. It was all too much.

Eryna stood, object in hand.

"Can you still hear me?" the boy in the object asked.

"Your friend's not here," she replied, scanning the area for something, anything to stop the object and end this conversation.

"Where is he?"

"He's…" Eryna pulled the metal from her ear and pressed all the small silver shapes. They did nothing but make more shapes and colors appear. "Stupid object of Hades' creation," Eryna quietly cursed as she fumbled with it.

"What happened to Tyler? What did you do?" The boy's voice took an accusatory tone that set Eryna's teeth on edge.

"I didn't do anything!" Eryna argued back, surprised by her own reaction. She hit the object—a "phone," he'd called it—against a tree but it was surprisingly durable.

"Sorry. I'm sorry," the boy apologized. "I didn't mean to offend you. We're just concerned about him, and his parents are worried sick."

Eryna paused. This needed to end now. Eryna fell to her knees and scoured the ground until she found a heavy rock the size of her palm.

Perfect.

She laid the phone on a stump and raised the rock overhead.

"Please," the boy said, almost begged, as if he knew what was about to happen. The crack in his voice gave Eryna pause. "Just tell me if you know where he is. Is he…is he dead?"

Eryna inhaled a deep, shaky breath. She shouldn't answer that. She shouldn't have even said hello in the first place, but it was too late now.

"Your friend is gone," she said, as she brought the rock down on the phone. Glass splintered beneath the stone. All was silent. All was still, the cicadas and distant drumming now her only companions.

Eryna stood over the broken phone for several minutes, watching. Waiting. It didn't buzz again. The boy didn't reappear.

There was no way she would sleep tonight.

Chapter Three

Eryna tread the trail back to her favorite redwood, the shattered phone a weight in her silk bag. She'd surely be called home as soon as her sisters returned to the Hollow for the night and noticed she was missing. But Eryna was determined to discard the object as far from them as she dared.

She settled on her usual sturdy branch and pulled it out. Weighing it in her palm, she glanced at it a final time, waiting for it to come to life. It never did.

She chucked it into the night. Even in darkness, she could see it arc out toward the deep forest. The disgruntled yelp of a coyote echoed up at her, and she winced.

"Sorry!" she called.

The full moon washed Eryna's pale birch skin in a layer of silver. She gazed toward the distant lights of the Aponyx skyline and wondered which of the colossal steel structures the blue-eyed boy—Tyler, the wolfish boy had called him—had seen up close. Maybe he even lived in the tall one that caught the sunrise like a flame. She bet he'd seen the sunrise from there at least once. She suddenly envied those blue eyes and the human things they'd seen.

A rustling below drew her attention. She turned in time to spot a great horned owl soaring between branches. As she followed its path, her gaze caught on the distant corpse of the Slyvanwood's Mother Oak.

The bare, crooked limbs of the once great tree sprawled high and wide, towering over everything. Eryna's spine prickled as she studied the husk of a forest that was once the abundant Slyvanwood. Not so much as a termite lived there now. Not since its Heart was stolen over two centuries ago.

The Sylvanwood Mother Oak was the first casualty of the humans' betrayal led by Martin Blackwell — a Mainland-born man who created Aponyx four centuries ago. He was said to be tall, dark, and handsome, and could charm the roots right out from under the Dryads' soles.

It made him the perfect hunter.

After gaining the trust of the Dryads, he came with friends to enjoy a bonfire night. Once the Dryads were full of wine and limp from dance, they stole the Heart right out of the Mother Oak's cavity.

It took all of two months for the Dryads to turn to mulch once it left Euryalea's borders; hardly a blink, in the life of a Dryad.

The Sylvanwood died with them.

Each tree, each bush, each weed and insect and soft bodied animal that lived within the domain of the Sylvanwood, died.

The northern Fiddlewood was next. Eryna was fifteen when it happened.

By the time they came for the Thornewood's Heart, the Dryads were ready. By then, it was known that the humans had found a way to exploit the Hearts for their own use. Humans were no longer friends and lovers. They were a fungus, an invasive species. Something that needed to be purged.

So, the executions began.

Eryna studied the Sylvanwood Oak, her sharp silhouette like an inverse lightning strike, lashing out against the sky in rage, in grief. Every time Eryna saw its nakedness, she understood the rot her sisters carried.

But what if the new generation of humans entering Euryalea came to make a truce, not steal the Heart? Hadn't it been long enough to attempt peace?

In that moment, Eryna decided that if she ever discovered a trespasser, she would give him a chance to explain. It was the least she could do.

Finally exhausted, Eryna leaned back and let her mind drift away on the breeze. She revisited the conversation with the boy and recalled something she'd paid no mind to before.

We're coming to get you, he'd said, which meant he was intent on coming here, to the Thornewood.

Worry wove a complicated web around her as she saw the boy's wolfish smile, the ghost of his warm voice still in her ear. Part of her desperately wanted to witness him in person, but she knew the moment he crossed that border, he was a dead man.

Please, Gaia, keep him far from here, she prayed as her heavy lids shut.

Chirp. Chirp chirp.

Two taps pricked Eryna's forearm. She groaned and turned from the sensation, exhausted to her very pith.

Chirp.

The taps pecked at her shoulder, and she shrugged them off, her mind slow, unready to wake. She'd only closed her eyes for a moment.

A tug on her hair got her attention, and three urgent, annoyed *chirps* echoed in her ear canal. Eryna startled awake. She blinked sleep from her eyes and opened them to the dim light of dawn, not yet sunrise, but no longer night. She'd rested longer than she anticipated. There was still time to get home.

As her vision sharpened, she came face to face with a small finch staring pointedly at her. Its head tilted to the side. Eryna smiled.

"Hello, friend," she said, giving the bird a soft stroke. Urgency radiated from its feathers. "What's wrong? Am I in trouble?" she asked. While Dryads and animals spoke different languages, Eryna found there were many ways to communicate with all beings, and they could always find a way of understanding each other. The finch bristled, as if to say "no."

"But there *is* trouble?"

Chirp. That was a yes, Eryna decided.

"Is it my sisters?"

Another shake of its feathers. Another "no." Eryna relaxed an inch, then nodded to the little bird.

"Show me, then."

The finch dove down toward the ground. Eryna descended the redwood as quickly as she could without sprouting her own wings and taking flight. She hit the ground with a force that made her knees buckle.

"You could slow down a bit, you know," Eryna chided. The bird doubled back, hovered in front of Eryna and released a single, ear-piercing *chirp*. Eryna raised her palms in surrender and stifled laughter.

"You're right. I'll simply move faster."

Eryna kept pace with the bird until it stopped on the branch of a particularly low hanging willow and stayed there.

Eryna seethed. Ten feet in front of her sat a steep plummet to the bottom of a pit that a certain fox loved to get stuck in. A small groan escaped it. Eryna's gaze shot to the finch, and she crossed her arms, vexed beyond belief.

"No," she contested. "I said I wouldn't help that little monster again and I meant it."

Eryna turned and started home, but the finch was immediately in her face, herding her toward the pit with aggressive wing flaps. She raised a hand.

"Thank you for alerting me to trouble. I do appreciate it, but it's time that fox learn."

Eryna tried sidestepping the bird, but its chirps grew louder, its wing flutters more aggressive. Eryna retreated backward and stumbled toward the pit. At the last second, she regained her balance, but not before glimpsing the reason the finch so adamantly pushed her toward the hole.

Oh, Gaia.

Eryna's throat constricted as she caught sight of dark hair. Dark eyes looked up at her, and her heart raced.

It was not that pesky fox at the bottom of the trap.

It was the boy from the object.

Only he was no longer in the object. He was a full-sized human being, and he was here in the Thornewood.

Chapter Four

Eryna pressed her body tight to the ground.

Gaia, please say he didn't see me, she prayed, but she knew it was too late. He'd looked right at her.

"Someone there?" he called out. Eryna refused to so much as breathe. She could wait it out. He would fall asleep or pass out and she could leave unseen.

Suddenly, all she'd decided earlier about giving trespassers a chance seemed absurd. She never actually expected to meet one. Even if he wasn't there for the Heart, what would she do? Send him back to Aponyx? It wouldn't be long until her sisters found her—and him.

The boy cleared his throat.

"You know I can see you, right?" he said, his voice landing somewhere between laughter and irritation. Eryna cursed her long hair dangling over the edge of the trap.

Slowly, she peered down at the boy. He sat crammed in the corner propped against the dirt wall, one arm limp, the other resting on his abdomen. He wore a pair of dark blue pants— "jeans," she believed the humans called them—and a long-sleeved top that looked like it was one soft as a feather prior to acquiring a crust of thick, dried mud.

Heat prickled across her body as his eyes roamed her face, her textured skin, her deep wavy hair, her silk floral dress. Every inch of her felt the trail of his gaze.

"Hi." He smiled. It was the same edacious grin she'd seen in the phone, only this time, Eryna knew for certain he was handsome. Very, very handsome. "Mind helping me? Pretty sure I broke my collarbone."

Eryna clutched the dirt to steady her nerves and held the boy's gaze with fierce intensity, refusing to give into his charm. The Dryads had an old tale about a rabbit who was once tricked into helping a wolf. It didn't end well.

"Our kind doesn't help your kind," she replied, her voice tight and foreign in her ears.

Where the Dryad language was round and lyrical on the tongue, the human language was sharp and caught in the throat like a dry corn kernel. The boy's brow rose, his mouth quirked to the side.

"And our kind doesn't ask for help from your kind, and yet, here we are," he replied. "Look, I don't want any trouble. I only came to find my friend."

"I told you your friend was gone. You should've stayed away," Eryna said flatly. The boy stilled.

"That was you?"

She didn't reply. She'd already said too much. He was a trespasser, and there was only one way trespassers got out of the Thornewood: by the sharpened edge of a stone knife. Eryna stood and started toward the Hollow.

"Wait!" the boy called. Eryna refused to turn back no matter how much she wanted to. "Please," his voice trembled. "I mean it when I say I don't want trouble. I'm just trying to find my friend. But you're right. He's clearly not here. I just need help out of this hole and then you'll never see me again."

Eryna fought against the pull of his plea, her steps slowing. If she got him out now, he might make it to the border. She could ask the forest to protect him, to shield him from her sisters…No. He wasn't worth the punishment; the lifetime of being *faémona* with no real responsibilities or privileges; a cycle she would never break.

A soft, heart-wrenching cry broke out of the pit.

"Please," he said, voice brittle and hoarse. "I'm in so much pain."

Eryna closed her eyes and heaved a deep, abject sigh.

Curse this stupid, stupid boy.

She stormed to the trap and glared down at him. His face was buried in his palm, his shoulders shook, and right then Eryna knew she was about to do the stupidest thing she'd ever done, Mother Oak forgive her.

She grasped a willow reed and lengthened it until its lance-shaped leaves brushed the boy's cheek. Startled, he looked up at Eryna. "Grab it," she ordered. He obeyed. She lifted him from the trap, and he collapsed at her feet, sucking a breath between clenched teeth.

It was time to go. Eryna had done more than enough. It was time to point him toward Aponyx and be on her way.

A thought paused her in her tracks. *I really* should *turn him in.*

She should take him straight to Althea like a proud cub. Her sisters would. Even though she hated the executions, turning him in would win her favor with her sisters, or possibly more.

They would be proud of her.

But she couldn't ignore that primal urge to heal, to help as she watched him struggle, his face twisted in anguish. She dropped to her knees and pushed him to a seated position, the two of them now only a foot apart; the closest she'd ever been to a human.

"Thank you," he said, smiling, though it looked more like stifled pain. Still, Eryna's muscles liquified at the sight of it, and the way he kept his eyes on her made it feel as though they were the only two beings in the Thornewood. The boy swallowed, and Eryna watched as the knot in his throat bobbed.

"I should probably start running if I want to make it out alive, huh?" he said, and before she could think, before she could shut her big, Hades-damned mouth, she blurted, "I can heal you."

What in Gaia's name was wrong with her?

The boy raised a brow.

"Are you just saying that to keep me from escaping?"

To her surprise, she laughed. It would be a good tactic for sure. She mirrored his expression.

"Who said I'd let you escape in the first place?"

The boy choked, the sound so quiet she barely caught it, and Eryna laughed harder. After a moment, he laughed, too. It was a nice sound that sunk into her bones. Slowly, she hovered her hand over where his shoulder met his neck.

"May I?" she asked, meeting his gaze, awaiting permission.

His eyes searched hers as if looking for deceit, but she possessed nothing for him to uncover. For reasons beyond understanding, she wanted to help this boy. He nodded.

Eryna's fingers met his skin. The small hairs on her arm rose with violent quickness, like the air around them was suddenly electrically charged. He was warm, and his blood rushed like spring river rapids; his pulse hammered in the leaps and bounds a jackrabbit, his nerves frantic and untamable as lightning.

Healing a Dryad was a calm, predictable process, reliable as the maple tree. Eryna had never touched—let alone healed—a human before. The deluge of new senses was overwhelming. She inhaled deeply to breathe through it and sent a wave of nerves from her fingertips into his skin, probing for anything broken or out of place.

He was right. His collarbone was all but shattered to dust. Beyond that, his other shoulder was dislocated, his hip fractured, his kidney hemorrhaging, and his body was littered with bruises.

"The legends about Dryads are true, then" he said, breaking her concentration. She refused to look at him. No sense in making this interaction more intimate than it already was.

"Humans have created many legends about us. Some are bound to be true."

"I just didn't expect you to be so beautiful."

She looked up this time. He'd shortened the distance between them by several inches, his lips lifted at the corner in a mischievous smirk. She leaned back, widening the gap.

"Are you attempting to charm me out of killing you?" she asked, averting her gaze to his shoulder. He kept his eyes on her. Her face burned under the concentration of his stare.

"Is it working?" he asked, his smirk splitting to a full smile. Eryna stayed silent and stoic. She liked the way it made him squirm. "Why heal me just to kill me?"

"Maybe I like my prey fresh." Eryna glanced at him and flashed an impish smile before returning to the task at hand. She kept her healing slow and steady. A few bruises dispersed at her command. His hip bone gently fused together. His kidney returned to normal function.

"What if I'm not prey?" The boy inched closer, his breath tickling her cheek. She glanced at him, his lids heavy, his stare dark and teasing. "What if I'm another predator?"

Gaia, this boy is proud of himself.

Clearly, his flavor of charm worked on human women, but Eryna didn't seem to have the palate for it.

He was mostly healed now, save his collarbone and shoulder. No use in dragging it out any longer. In a single breath, she yanked her nerves back and popped his shoulder into place at the same time as she fused his collarbone. He yelped and fell to the ground, clutching his fresh shoulder. Eryna smiled.

"You're all predators. That's why we kill your kind." She stood and pointed a firm finger to the northwest. "Aponyx is that way. I'd start running if I were you."

She gave the boy one last, quick look before her mind had time to build a lifetime of fantasies around him. Then she started toward the

Hollow, praying that if she ever saw him again, it wouldn't be with a stone knife at his throat.

"At least tell me your name," he asked, grabbing her wrist. Eryna froze. Her heart shot to her throat. She could barely breathe, barely think. He'd touched her. Willingly. "I'm going to die anyway. Call it a last wish." He shrugged.

She shouldn't oblige. She really, really shouldn't.

"Eryna," she murmured. The boy lit up, eyes bright, smile wide.

"Nice to meet you Eryna…" he paused. "Do you have a last name?"

"That's a human thing."

"Dryads don't?" Eryna shook her head. "Well, if you could choose, what would it be? It feels strange to only know you by one name. Like you're a celebrity or something."

"Celebrity?" Eryna repeated slowly, learning the motions of the foreign word. He laughed.

"I realize that reference probably doesn't land with you. Still, what would it be?"

What a strange question to ask at a time like this. He should be running for his life back to the protective borders of his city right now.

And yet, Eryna couldn't help but entertain it. Surnames were quintessentially human. Dryads had no need, for they were all the same; all sisters born of the same Mother Oak, or cousins born of neighboring Oaks. But, given the choice, it might be interesting to have one.

"I guess…Thorne. Since I am of the Thornewood."

The boy perked up, his wolfish grin returning.

"I like it."

He slid his hand into hers. A small gold ring engraved with the letter "B" pressed into her palm. She hadn't noticed it until now. He gave her hand a tight squeeze and shook it. "Nice to meet you, Eryna Thorne. I'm Brody."

Same as the word on the phone. It was a name after all.

"Brody," she repeated, tasting his name on her tongue. It was smooth, round, and sweet like a fresh apple, but felt incomplete. "What's your human last name, Brody?"

His lips parted, then shut, then parted once more as if weighing his answer. He opened his mouth again, but a distant shout cut him off.

"Eryna!"

They jumped, and Eryna pulled her hand out of his like it burned with the heat of a hundred bonfires.

Dera. Her sisters. They were looking for her, and by the sound of it, were minutes from finding her. Possibly seconds.

"Go. Right now," Eryna urged, shoving Brody in the direction of Aponyx. He shook his head, eyes wide with panic.

"I'll never make it."

Eryna shoved him again, his heart hammering violently beneath her palms.

"You have to try."

But it was too late. Dera broke through foliage first.

"Eryna, there you are. We've been looking everywhere for—"

She stopped. Her eyes landed on Brody. Then flicked to Eryna. Then back to Brody. Mori and Ilana arrived seconds later.

"Oh, Gaia," Mori breathed.

"Sweet Mother Oak." Ilana threw a palm to her chest.

Dera stepped forward.

"Eryna, what's going on?" she asked.

Eryna's heart ferociously beat beneath her breastbone, threatening to crack it in half.

"I...I..." Before she could muster an explanation, it all got so, so much worse.

"What have I missed?" Althea asked as she joined the small gathering. She looked from Brody, to Eryna, to the sisters. She glanced at Brody once more, her gaze landing on the small golden ring. Then she smiled.

Smiled.

"Gather the sisters," she said to Mori in their mother tongue. "We have another execution on our hands. Go."

Mori was off at once, slipping through the trees with haste.

Brody looked at Eryna, clearly lost.

"What did she say?" he asked, but no answer arrived at her lips. If she told him the truth, it would only make it worse.

"You should've run," Eryna whispered, so quiet only he could hear.

Althea looked at Dera and Ilana and nodded toward Brody. Before he could so much as move, they had him by the arms and marched him forward. He looked over his shoulder at Eryna.

"What did she say, Eryna? What's happening?"

She simply lowered her eyes to the ground to keep from looking his direction, his voice fading with the distance.

Coward, she cursed herself. She should've told him. He had a right to know. But if she didn't say it out loud, it felt like there was still hope. Maybe she could change her sisters' minds.

Just Eryna and Althea remained.

"I'm proud of you, *faémona,*" Althea said, cupping Eryna's face. The gesture was ingratiating and gentle, as if everything Eryna had ever done before this moment hadn't been worth Althea's time or attention. "Capturing them isn't easy. Maybe you are ready for more than I give you credit for. We will talk later."

Eryna smiled politely and retreated a step out of her grasp. She should be dancing with joy at Althea's words, at finally being the subject of her acclaim. Yet, guilt rotted beneath her skin, spoiling the praise from her leader.

"It was easier than I thought it would be," she replied, looking away in hopes Althea wouldn't spot the lie. "Although, I don't think he was here for the Heart."

Eryna instantly knew it was the wrong thing to say. Althea softly smiled, sadness diluting the expression, and placed a palm on Eryna's chest.

"You are too soft, *faémona*. You give humans too much credit. They are always here for the Heart. Always."

And Eryna bit her tongue. It wasn't the time to argue.

"Will we have another execution tomorrow, then?" Eryna asked instead.

Althea tucked Eryna beneath her arm and ushered her in the direction of the *Domecowé*.

"No, sweet child. Within the hour."

Eryna tensed.

Within the hour? Executions never took place the same day. There was always a minimum one day's notice for the sisters to gather.

Eryna looked up at Althea, questioning. "Why the urgency?"

Althea gave Eryna's shoulders a light, proud squeeze.

"Because dear Eryna. You've captured a Blackwell."

Chapter Five

A Blackwell.

He was a *Blackwell.*

Eryna paced back and forth in the eerily vacant Hollow, cursing herself out for being so naive.

Dark hair, dark eyes, tan skin. It was a perfect match to the description of the Blackwells. How had she not made that connection earlier? She'd witnessed decades of trespassers who matched that description, but none who carried themselves with the same confidence and charm. And while she was sure her sisters could've pegged him as a Blackwell with their eyes closed, it had to have been his ring that gave him away. She'd never seen such a ring. It was no doubt the mark of a powerful human family; *the* powerful human family of Aponyx.

"You'll burrow to Ekatan if you keep pacing like that," Dera said. Eryna looked up.

"This doesn't feel right," she started, then clamped her mouth shut before more regrettable words spilled out. But she had to say *something.* She couldn't shake the heavy stone in her stomach, the dry lump in her throat. She couldn't be so forward with her other sisters, but this was Dera. Dera would listen to her. Dera would see reason.

"What doesn't?"

"This!" Eryna wildly gestured in the direction of the *Domecowé*. "The execution. It doesn't feel right. It never feels right. I truly don't think he was here for the Heart. There must be another way, some punishment that doesn't end in death. We shouldn't have to kill every human we come across."

Dera studied Eryna with sympathetic eyes. Then she pulled her into an embrace and stroked her hair with loving fingers.

"There is so much I love and envy about your youthfulness." Dera sighed. "You see the world with such hope. You could stare down the maw of a mountain lion and see the cub within. But sometimes I wish we hadn't fostered it so much." Eryna looked at her, surprised. Dera had never spoken to her like this. "Sometimes I wish we'd let you see the world's ugliness; let you witness our cousins turn to nothing but petals, the squirrels, the lynx, and the eagles of the other Woods turn to skeletal husks. And while I'd never, ever wish for you to have felt the violent hands of greedy men taking what they want from you, sometimes I wish you knew the brokenness that followed.

"Every scar Euryalea bares, every burden we carry is because of *that* boy's ancestor. Even if he is innocent, he must answer for the sins of his forefathers. I have faith one day you'll understand." Eryna did understand Dera's sentiment. Still, it couldn't be the only solution.

Light footfalls moved behind Eryna, and she turned to find Oihane swaying as if her excitement couldn't be contained within the confines of her body.

"It's time," she sang. Eryna's limbs were suddenly heavy, leaden. Oihane tightly grasped Eryna's hand and held it all the way to the *Domecowé*.

Immediately, something was off.

The chant had already begun.

The steady pounding of hands on thighs was already loud and fast.

Eryna spotted Althea at the base of the Mother Oak as usual. Her gaze drifted right. Brody was on his knees, head bowed, eyes locked on Eryna.

She looked away.

She couldn't see him like this. Instead, she skimmed her sisters in their half-circle. Everyone was present. Everyone. They had started the execution ceremony without her. But why?

Suddenly, Eryna noticed something she hadn't before: Every one of her sisters was watching her. Not Althea. Not Brody.

Her.

Eryna looked at Oihane, whose smile was so wide her dimples turned to craters.

She looked at Dera, who gave her a reassuring nod and pressed a soft kiss to her cheek.

"You'll do great," she whispered.

Do great?

Then all at once, it was clear.

Eryna's blood chilled. There wasn't enough air in the forest to fill her lungs. She couldn't think beyond the racing pulse in her ears, her heart hammering out a rapid *beat, beat, beat* that matched the rhythm of her sisters' drumming.

This couldn't be happening. This couldn't be real.

And yet, it was. It was an ambush.

Althea beat the drum, letting out a violent *boom*, and Eryna's knees almost buckled. The energy of this execution was noticeably more feral, more blood-thirsty than any other. Her sisters wanted every last drop of his blood drained.

Oihane and Dera pulled Eryna forward. Everything inside her screamed *no, no, no*. Acid singed her throat. Her whole body clenched. But no matter how much she resisted, her legs moved until she was directly in front of Althea. *Traitorous limbs.* Eryna looked at her sisters a final time in hopes someone might recognize her fear, offer to take her place, but all she saw were ravenous grins, ferocious faces hungrily eyeing Brody.

Althea nodded at Dera and Oihane.

Oihane squeezed Eryna's arms and whispered, "You've got this." Then she slipped away to join the rest. Dera smiled at Eryna and guided her in a steadying breath. Then she held out the stone knife.

"I can't do this," Eryna whispered, her throat swollen with anxiety.

Dera nodded, soft and sorrowful.

"You can and you must. I believe in you." Dera grabbed Eryna's hand and placed the stone knife in her grip. "Remember what we talked about."

Dera joined Oihane and the others, leaving Eryna in the center of the ceremony flanked by Althea and Brody. Althea approached Eryna, hooked a finger under her chin and lifted it to meet her gaze.

"Make us proud, *faémona*. Bring honor to every Dryad lost."

She gave Eryna a small push. Four steps later, Eryna stared down into Brody's eyes. For a moment, she wondered if the streaks on his cheeks were from fresh tears. She saw none. His face was nothing but peaceful. He studied the knife in her hand.

"Is Tyler's blood on that?" he asked. She glanced down at rusty layers staining the edge. She nodded. Brody's throat bobbed. "Was it you?"

She shook her head, unable to manage words through her quivering lips.

"Have you done this before?"

She shook her head again. Brody lifted his gaze to meet hers, his chin high and shoulders back.

"Then I'm glad to be your first," he said, mustering a painfully pitiful smile. Even in the face of death, this boy was charming.

Eryna looked deep into his eyes, willing him to see how much she didn't want to do this. But, like Dera said, she must. There was no other choice.

Brody's smile fell and he looked down at the knife.

"Go on. Get it over with."

Eryna's fist closed around the hilt. She stood behind Brody, braced his head with one hand and held the knife to his neck with the other. He trembled beneath her grip. She took a deep breath.

"Blood paid for blood spilled," Althea thundered.

"Blood paid for blood spilled," the Dryads chanted.

The *Domecowé* went silent. The breeze stopped. The cicadas and the birds ceased their singing. It was as if the entire forest held a collective breath to witness this moment. Everyone and everything was watching her.

Eryna's arm shook as she urged it to move, to slice the knife across Brody's neck, but it wouldn't happen.

She couldn't do it.

She couldn't do it.

She *wouldn't* do it.

Brody leaned the weight of his head into her palm.

"Do it, Thorne," he said. "Just do it."

Eryna bit her lip so hard, the copper tang of blood trickled onto her tongue as she searched for the will within to kill this boy. She would find it. She had to find it.

She could do it.

She could do it.

She *would* do it.

Eryna tightened her grip on his head. "I'm sorry," she whispered.

Her muscles tensed. Her shoulders straightened. Energy filled her arm, her hand ready, her mind absolute.

She took another deep, steadying breath.

Suddenly, a loud metallic rattle echoed through the forest. It was like the sound of an arrow slicing through wind, only sharper, faster, and more deadly.

Eryna glanced at Althea for clarity.

But Althea was looking down at her own chest. A red wetness quickly spread across the white eagle feathers of her top. She fell to her knees, then to her side.

For one single, silent heartbeat, every Dryad watched and waited to see what happened next. Althea didn't move. She didn't breathe. Ilana and Mori rushed to the leader. Another metallic rattle sounded, and Mori collapsed.

Then the Thornewood erupted with more metallic rattles.

Dryads screamed, ran, and collapsed in a vicious cycle.

Two hands pulled Eryna to the ground and pressed her firmly to the earth. Brody's voice was in her ear, his body pinning her down.

"Stay down. Don't move."

Another metallic rattle sounded.

Then another.

And another.

She'd never heard such an atrocious noise before, but she knew what made it. *Guns*, Eryna realized. She'd been taught about these monstrous human weapons in her lessons.

"Brody, what's happening?" Eryna asked, but he didn't answer. He only repeated that she needed to "stay down."

Ilana's face was suddenly on the ground in front of hers, cold and unmoving. Eryna wiggled an arm free and reached out to her sister, no pulse, no warmth. At least she went quick.

The injured, the broken, and the almost dead could be healed. Death, however, was too far gone. Death was irreversible. Death was final.

A piercing scream shattered Eryna's ears, and as she searched for the source, she realized it was her own voice. Tears turned the dirt beneath her cheek to mud, and with all her might, she squirmed and fought, elbowed and wriggled her way out from under Brody.

"Thorne don't!" he shouted, but she didn't listen. She didn't care. She threw herself into the chaos on the hunt for Dera and Oihane. A sharp pain sliced through her thigh, and she screamed, the sound violently ripping out of her. But there was no time to stop, to acknowledge or tend to the wound. Her energy was better saved for her sisters. She pushed on, a lamed fish swimming upstream with no heading.

She stumbled over a crouched figure and looked down to see Maya huddled over a body, shaking the sister violently as if she could force her soul back into her body. Her shoulders trembled; her chest heaved. Dread permeated Eryna as she looked at the face of the sister on the ground.

It wasn't Dera.

Guilt tainted the relief that washed over her. It might not have been Dera, but it was still one of her sisters. Every step Eryna took had a different sister pulling on her arm, begging to be healed or to heal another. Eryna quickly healed the wound of one sister—Terra. She was hardly finished before being pulled toward another, Nyessa.

She was not so lucky. But Eryna could at least make her comfortable as she slipped away.

She'd just closed Nyessa's eyes when she was grabbed again. Dera's face hovered in front of hers. Eryna dissolved into sobs.

"Are you hurt? Are you okay?" she asked, frantically scanning her big sister.

"I'm okay. You?" she asked. Eryna nodded.

"Fine, I think. Just a flesh wound. Where's Oihane?" Eryna changed the subject, hoping Dera wouldn't notice her thigh and what was obviously *not* just a flesh wound.

"She made it through the Hollow and is on the run. I think she's safe." Dera grabbed Eryna's hand. "We need to hide."

Eryna dug her heels in.

"I'm needed here. I need to save as many as I can."

"You cannot save them if you are dead. You'll be needed later. The most important thing right now is to protect you—"

Another metallic rattle shook them. It was close. Too close.

They looked down.

Blood bloomed across Dera's side.

"No!" Eryna screamed, her throat raw. Dera collapsed, and Eryna cradled her body. She tried to work quickly. Dera was losing so, so much blood, but she was still breathing. She was still alive. She could heal Dera, she could save her and…

Suddenly, a dark shadow loomed over them. Eryna looked up.

Brody stood over her, a large rock raised overhead. He bit his lip.

"I'm sorry, Thorne," he said.

And then at once, everything was black.

Chapter Six

$\mathcal{S}$hadows and lights were the first thing Eryna noticed.

Her cheek rested against a cold, smooth material and her skull throbbed as if a knife was lodged in it. Her body jostled and she hissed as her thigh suddenly burned like hot coals were sewn beneath her skin.

Where the Hades am I?

She tried to move, but her limbs weighed with sleep. She cracked an eyelid and strained to clear her vision. But flashing lights and shadows made her dizzy. Another excruciating throb sliced through her head and down to the pit of her stomach. She wretched. Acrid bile burned her throat, her mouth, her nostrils. Then a strange material was pressed to her lips.

"Hold this," a voice said in the human tongue. It was familiar, but unclear through the groaning in her head as she wretched again, clutching the thin crinkling material to her face. All she could taste and smell was stomach acid and last night's pig roast. She wretched another time. A hand rubbed soothing circles on her back.

"I'm getting you somewhere safe," a warm voice said. Through her stupor, Eryna could've sworn it was Brody, but that wouldn't make sense. Last she saw him, he was on his knees, and she was about to…to…but there was a sharp, metallic rattle.

Althea collapsing.

The forest floor covered in her sisters, in blood.

So much blood.

And Dera. Eryna was in the middle of healing Dera, who was losing too much blood to stay alive without her help.

But then he was there, looking down at her. *Brody.*

Everything after that was an abyss. Until now. Until here.

More lights and shadows passed in the form of large, towering giants. She could only manage to look for a moment before the motion unsettled her again. She clamped down on her jaw, her glands swelling and salivating, begging to purge the final contents of her stomach. She tried to push through, to hold onto what little fuel she had left in her body.

She failed. Miserably.

Her jaw unhinged like a snake and a final wave of stomach acid shot from her mouth into whatever receptacle she held. She took a shuddering breath and leaned back into the cold material, letting it sooth her clammy skin. Her head lolled to the side.

Through watering eyes and hazy vision, she saw Brody's silhouette next to her, one hand on a thin wheel in front of him, the other resting on her thigh.

Then consciousness slipped through her grasp.

Arms slid under Eryna's body. A cool breeze played on her skin and the smell of night settled in her nostrils. But it was an unfamiliar scent. Fresh pine and decaying wood didn't hang in the air. It still smelled like a mild summer night, but was tinged with sour scents, sulfurous and burnt.

Eryna opened her eyes, her vision still blurry. She could only see lights. Some lights moved. Some lights didn't. Some stretched impossibly high in vertical towers that touched the dark endless sky. There was so much electricity in the atmosphere Eryna could almost taste it, tingling on her tongue.

Then the cool air turned warm and artificial. The bright lights were gone, replaced by softer ones. Eryna blinked, making a concerted effort to clear her sight so she could take in her surroundings, but everything was so hazy, so sideways, and stars swam across her vision.

A soft chime rang out and they moved into what sounded like a room made of metal. A sudden force pressed Eryna down into the arms holding her. Uncomfortable pressure built in her ears, and she screwed her eyes tight. The arms gave her a squeeze.

"First time in an elevator, I'm guessing," a voice said, chuckling. This time she knew for certain it was Brody.

Her eyes flew open.

She could barely make out his dark hair and wolfy grin, but sure enough, it was him. Pressure pounded in her ears, her head, and her vision wavered. Black crept in at the edges until she had to close her eyes to keep another wave of nausea at bay.

The metal contraption stopped. The pressure stopped. For a fleeting second, she was weightless; caught between the sensations of falling upward and downward. They moved again, and there were two voices now. Him and someone female.

Bless Gaia, someone female.

"Why are you here?" the female voice demanded. Even through dulled senses Eryna could tell the girl was furious. "And why do you have that *thing?* You can't just walk around with a demon in your arms, Brody, what are you thinking?!" Clearly, Eryna was not a welcomed guest. The girl sighed. "Get inside before anyone sees you," she ordered. A door shut behind them.

"Do you have a spare room she can use for the night?" Brody asked.

"Even if we did, I wouldn't let that monster use it," the girl said. "Neens, please."

Neens?

And humans made fun of Dryad names.

"Why can't she stay at your place?" she asked. "It's not like your palace lacks space."

"They don't know I brought her back with me. And I have a few things to take care of before my father gets back, but I promise I'll come for her first thing in the morning."

"Yeah, because you're so good at keeping your word," the girl scoffed. Then she went quiet for a moment. "Did you find Tyler?"

Brody didn't respond, but Eryna felt his muscles move against her cheek, as if shaking his head.

"Is...is he...?" she asked, unable to finish her sentence, but Eryna knew exactly what she was asking. Brody nodded.

"No," the girl said, her tone curt and final. "Now that thing definitely can't stay here, and I'm not in the mood to do you any favors. Tyler wouldn't be gone if you...if..." she fumbled for words. The anger in her voice seemed to choke her. The girl huffed, and light clacks made it sound as if she was pacing. "Besides, I don't want it in the house. Derrick will kill her if he finds out. He might even kill *you*."

"I know, I know. I'm going to try and make it up to your family as best I can, but please, Jenin. I can't take her home with me. She needs someone to be there when she wakes up. Just put her in a room no one will go into. Only until the morning."

The silence was so thick, Eryna thought she might have blacked out again until the girl groaned.

"Fine. This way."

The girl's clacking steps were sharper, more pointed than Brody's, the sound harshly tapping across Eryna's aching skull. A door opened, and moments later Eryna was laid on something soft and airy. A warm touch brushed hair from her face, then retreated.

The quieter, heavier steps—Brody's—grew more distant until he reached the spot Eryna mentally placed the girl in the room.

"I'll buy you some time, but you better be back first thing in the morning," she said. The door opened.

"I'll try," he replied. "I'll be back once I know what to do with her."

Brody's steps strode off, away from the room. The girl frantically clacked after him. "Wait, you said you'd be back by morning," she accused. "You can't leave me with her, Brody! Gods, you're so infuriating, you little lying piece of shit!"

The door shut, choking off all sound besides the quiet sigh of the material around Eryna as it settled into place.

One minute of silence.

Two.

Three.

Four.

After five minutes, Eryna realized no one was coming back.

Wherever she was, however far from home, she was utterly alone.

Chapter Seven

A splintering, fiery pain tore Eryna from a dreamless sleep. Cold sweat plastered her hair to her forehead. The soft, unfamiliar material around her was too thick, too suffocating. She turned on her side and her thigh screamed in agony. She sat up, hissing through her teeth, and looked down.

Someone had put her in a large cotton shirt and short human pants that ended just above a bandage tightly wrapped around her thigh. She wilted.

It was real.

The chaos, the blood, her sisters dying in front of her.

It was all real.

Which meant she needed to be with her family to heal the sisters who might've survived and help bury the ones who hadn't. She wasn't sure where she was right now, but all she needed was the open sky to find her way home.

Brody wasn't there. Brody had left her in this place, wherever or whatever it was, but it didn't matter. All that mattered was getting home. Her eyes fell on a walnut door on the far end of the room. She bolted, her thigh smarting fiercely with each step. There was no time to heal herself, and she was far too weak. She would have to do it later once she was safe and had regained some strength.

She grasped the handle. It didn't budge.

They must have locked her in. Eryna pounded the wood.

"Someone, help!" she shouted, though she wasn't certain her cry for help would fall on friendly ears. Eryna pounded the door and aggressively jiggled the handle. "I need to get out of here. I need to get back to Euryalea!"

Suddenly, forceful hands and thick cotton cut her off. Her own hot breath pressed up into her nostrils. Eryna screamed, but her voice died in her throat.

"Are you crazy?" The female voice from last night asked. "You can't say stuff like that here." Eryna kicked and squirmed, but the girl overpowered her and forced her to sit on the edge of a soft surface covered in cotton and linen—a bed, she assumed. The girl looked her square in the eyes, her moss-colored irises flaring.

"I'm going to remove the sock and you have to promise you won't scream." It wasn't a promise Eryna could keep, but she'd do anything to get home. She nodded. The girl ripped the cotton from Eryna's mouth but clamped a tight palm over her lips.

"I promised Brody I would keep you alive until he came back, and as tempting as that promise is to break, I don't go back on my word. No one can know what you are or that you're even here. You need to stay in this room. Do you understand?" the girl asked, brows hitched high. Slowly, Eryna nodded.

"Good," the girl replied. She hadn't yet removed her hand. That was a mistake. Eryna sunk her teeth into the girl's palm, and she retracted, cradling it tight to her chest. "Ouch, you psychotic monster!"

Eryna bolted again. She vaguely heard the *click clack* of the girl's footsteps cross the room, but there was no time to look back. The door might be locked, but maybe she could break it down. Only a few more steps, a few more hops, and she would be there.

A heavy sigh sounded behind her, and as she turned to look, Eryna saw the girl with a heavy steel trinket in her hand.

The next thing she saw was the floor, then nothing at all, and darkness took her again.

It was night when Eryna woke.

"Well, that was stupid," the girl huffed from where she sat frustratedly folded in a large velvet chair. Eryna leveled a sour gaze at her. Snide responses tingled her tongue with their acid, but she bit them back. Precious time had already been wasted. Banter would only waste more. Eryna sprang from the bed but was yanked backward and fell to the floor with a yelp, landing squarely on her wounded thigh. Her wrists were bound and tied to the bed by a rough rope. She shot the girl a nasty look.

"Like I said," the girl said. "You can't be roaming around this place. People here will kill you if they know what you are. Specifically, Derrick."

Eryna silently eyed her wrists, barely listening. She gave the rope a light tug. The twine was strong and tight. No wriggling free. Still, there had to be a way of escaping these bonds. She sat on the edge of the bed and finally took in her surroundings. The room was large and spacious with a light marble floor, four navy walls, and large glass windows that stretched to the ceiling. Walnut furniture adorned the space but didn't overcrowd it. A table here, a chest of drawers there. A few heavy trinkets sat atop surfaces, one of which made the soft spot on Eryna's head throb as she eyed its steel form.

The girl picked up a silver tray and placed it on the bed.

"I don't know what demons eat," she said. On the tray sat a bowl with handfuls of grass and dirt, rose buds, and a fistful of pansies. There was also an apple and a bouquet of calendulas, foxgloves, and lilies. The array was almost certainly meant as an insult, but Eryna was pretty pleased. There was plenty to pick from.

She popped a rosebud in her mouth. The girl's jaw clenched and Eryna tried not to laugh. As she reached for the apple, the rope dragged over her bandaged wound, and she cringed. The girl eyed it.

"I'd have a doctor come look at that, but I don't think anyone here knows how to work with your...*kind.*"

She practically spat the word. Eryna glared and took a bite of apple. It was sweet and crisp, and the moment it hit her tongue she realized she couldn't remember the last time she'd eaten. Had it been hours or days since the execution? She took a few more bites, chewed on a few pansies, and energy slowly reentered her body. She closed her eyes, and at the pace of a slow inhale, she knit the shattered bone, torn muscle, and broken skin of her thigh back together. Then she cleared the damage in her brain and smoothed the bumps on her skull. She was as good as new by the time she was down to the apple core. She looked at the girl and chuckled at her slack jaw and wide eyes.

"Where am I?" she asked, draining the last juices of the core. The girl clamped her jaw shut and straightened. "Aponyx," she replied. Eryna scoffed and nodded toward the window.

"Clearly. But what part? Central Quarter? The Terraces? The Skirts?" She rattled off the names of the Aponyx sectors she'd heard about.

"Does it look like you're in The Skirts?" The girl growled. The Skirts was the most dilapidated of Aponyx's sectors and bordered the Fiddlewood, the northern-most wood of Euryalea. By the grand buildings outside she was positive she wasn't in The Skirts. Still, it was worth asking just to see the look on the girl's face.

"Guess not." Eryna grabbed a calendula stem and bit the flower clean off. "Is this Brody's home?"

The girl stood and looked down at her. "No, it's not, and where you are isn't important. You won't be here long. Brody should be here soon, thank Gods. For now, you're in the safest place you can be."

"Unless you kill me," Eryna replied.

The girl rolled her eyes then clacked her way to the door. Eryna glanced at the girl's feet to see the source of such a sharp sound. She wore deep blue shoes that looked silk-soft and extremely uncomfortable as they sat propped up on four-inch sticks.

"As much as I would love to, it won't be me who kills you. At least not until Brody comes back and decides what to do with you."

As the girl opened the door to leave, Eryna's abdomen flared with urgent pressure. She scanned the room but saw no good spots to relieve herself. She didn't want to go next to the bed, but she would if it was her only option.

"Where should I relieve myself?" she called, not quite sure what the humans called that type of thing. The girl stopped and sighed. She clacked her way back to Eryna, untied her lead from the bed and gave it a small tug.

"Come on. I'll show you the bathroom," she said. Eryna followed her to a door where they entered a sparkling white room. It had a strange glass box with a silver spout on the ceiling, a large white bowl that looked like a spot for bathing, and a small white bowl that held a few inches of water. There was also an all-white surface with two smaller bowls and spouts, behind which was the purest silver glass Eryna had ever seen.

She gasped.

She drew close to the glass and leaned forward, her fingers skimming the pale white textured skin in the reflection.

She'd never seen her own face in such detail.

Her light-yellow hair was tattered and tangled, streaked through with dried blood. It was littered with twigs and dirt and a few remaining chiffon roses from her circlet. Her brows arched high over her large, upturned emerald eyes lined in thick lashes. Her nose struck a straight arrow down the center of her face and pointed to full pink lips. She tilted her head to catch the light at different angles.

The girl scoffed, and asked, "Never seen your face before?" Eryna shook her head, eyes still tracing her features. The girl tensed. "You're joking. You've actually never seen your face before?"

"In ponds and puddles. Never like this," Eryna replied.

Then the pressure in her abdomen pushed hard and she remembered why they were in the bathroom. She looked around. While she had to relieve herself, she was also incredibly parched. She eyed the small bowl with the water in it, reached down, cupped her hand and—

Eryna's hand was slapped away before she could grab water to drink.

"What the Hades are you doing? That's not what that's for. Ew. Disgusting." The girl grimaced and strode toward the tall surface. She turned the spout on one of the bowls and water streamed out of it. "If you want water, you can get it out of the sink. But *that*," she pointed at the bowl Eryna almost drank from. "The toilet is where you go."

Oh. Eryna's face flushed. How was she supposed to know?

Silently, the girl turned her back, and Eryna took that as her sign to proceed.

Once done, the girl showed her how to clean her hands in the "sink." As Eryna did so, she caught the girl curiously assessing her in the "mirror" like she was a complex puzzle. The girl's mouth twisted, and she crossed her arms and sighed. "I didn't want to do this, but I just know that if someone sees you, *I'm* going to be the one in trouble, not Brody." She pulled out a small brown bottle the size of her palm and thrust it forward. "Here. Drink this and maybe you'll look a little less like a damn tree."

Eryna eyed the bottle skeptically and read it.

BEAUTY PERFECTING TONIC
FOR SMOOTHER SKIN AND AN EVEN TONE

Eryna shook her head. "I like the way I look. Birch trees are sacred."

"That's all good and well until someone sees you and realizes the forest monsters have come to the big city."

"But I was brought here against my will," Eryna protested.

"Doesn't make a difference to me. Won't make a difference to them." The girl stepped closer with the bottle outstretched. "I don't know what it'll do or how long it'll last, but it's better than doing nothing."

Hesitantly, Eryna eyed the bottle again. Then she looked at the girl through a narrowed gaze.

"How do I know I can trust you?"

The girl shrugged.

"You don't. But it's this or probable death, so I guess weigh your options."

Eryna's jaw off set as she studied the bottle. She didn't want to change the way she looked. She loved her pale, textured skin, her hair the color of birch leaves just before they turn in autumn. It might not even be tonic at all, but poison. It could very well kill her.

But it might also buy her some safety, and that was everything if she was going to get home. If something about her changed enough to pass as human, she could simply walk back to Euryalea, free as a bird.

Before she could change her mind, Eryna grabbed the bottle and drank it. She cringed as the oddly thick liquid slid down her throat. It was far too sweet, like overly ripe grapes, and had an undercurrent of rot, as if the sweetness was meant to cover up the taste of something decaying and amiss. Eryna hesitated, wondering if it really was poison.

But then her skin tingled, her scalp itched, and the girl's eyes widened as they fell on her. Eryna looked at the mirror.

Her skin smoothed to a creamy beige and her hair warmed to a soft honey color. Her pulse raced as her Dryad-self disappeared in front of her own eyes, and she pleaded to Gaia that the tonic was finished, that it wouldn't take more of her.

Not my eyes, please, not my eyes, she begged. Thankfully, the changes had stopped with her skin and hair, and her eyes remained vibrant and green. That still didn't prevent Eryna's heart from breaking as she stared at the person looking back at her.

She was unrecognizable.

She was *human*. And she didn't like it one bit. Her eyes were all she had left of herself.

"Well, I certainly didn't expect that," the girl said. Then she tugged on Eryna's lead. "Come on. I have to get to dinner."

Eryna tried to glance at the mirror again, to see her Dryad eyes one more time and assure herself that she was still Eryna of the Thornewood. But the girl promptly shut the bathroom door. Eryna couldn't stop staring at her smooth, beige hands, as the girl tied her back to the bed and made for the exit. The skin was soft as a peach and completely foreign. What would her sisters think if they saw her now?

Eryna's chest lurched.

Her sisters.

"What happened to the Thornewood?" Eryna called after the girl, who froze with her fingertips on the doorhandle.

"Why would I tell you? By the way, that was my last bottle of tonic, so be grateful I wasted it on you, demon."

Then she left.

"Wait," Eryna called after her "Please, just tell me!"

But there was only silence. Eryna suddenly felt alone in every way possible. She yearned for the mirror again, to stare at her eyes all night. They weren't just the last connection she had to herself; they were the last connection she had to her home.

With nothing to do but wait, she cracked the closest window she could reach for air, but the sour scent of the human city only made it harder to breathe in this artificial place.

Moving lights drew her attention to a tower across the way, momentarily distracting her.

BLACKWELL TECHNOLOGIES PRESENTS: SCENT PERFECTING TONIC!

Blackwell Technologies? Eryna thought. She examined the empty tonic bottle in her hand. It was also a Blackwell Technologies product. Was this what the Blackwells did? Make magical tonics? Did it have to do with why they wanted the third Heart?

The moving image displayed a woman spritzing something onto her neck. She smiled wide, the expression uncomfortable and forced, painful even, as if the mist burned her skin. Unable to stand looking at her smile, Eryna glanced toward the city below. Her legs instantly went weak. Everything looked miniature, like ants bustling along trails. The next highest towers barely skimmed the height of the one she was in.

And in that moment, she knew exactly where she was.

Her favorite tower. She'd always wanted to escape the Thornewood to stand in this very spot. Now she wanted nothing more than to escape this tower to get back to the Thornewood.

I will see it again, she promised herself. *At any cost.*

Any.

Chapter Eight

Everything in this room was dead.

The marble floor had been chipped from its mother rock; the walnut furniture ripped from the forest. The cotton bedding had been pulled from its plant, refined, and spun; the down stuffing stripped from the limp bodies of ducks.

It was a lifeless tomb, save for the poor excuse of greenery atop a nearby table—a sansevieria that hadn't been watered or seen proper sunlight in Gaia knows how long. It was better than nothing but provided Eryna no comfort. Even its clay pot was dry and baked and dead.

Sleep didn't just escape her, it avoided her entirely.

And where was Brody?

The girl had said Brody would be there "soon." Eryna had since passed the time detangling her hair, strand by strand, and he was still not there. That was four hours ago.

She glimpsed her beige hand and startled. An ache broke in her chest at the lack of texture on her skin, at the honey-colored locks she ran her hands through. She grieved for her old self, for her sisters, for her home.

Then Eryna had a thought: if something happened to the

Thornewood, would she die even this far away?

It had to be a good sign that she was still alive. The third Heart of Euryalea, the Heart of the Thornewood Mother Oak, must still be out there. There had to be life left in the Thornewood, yet. There was still hope.

If only she could break free of her bonds.

Eryna had already checked the area around her ten times over for sharp objects. There were none. She'd also tried twisting her wrists free, only to get a nasty rope burn. She'd even contemplated chewing her hands off, but decided she rather liked having hands and planned on using them in the future, if she had one.

The only items remotely within reach were a small table, a window, and the sansevieria.

Eryna gasped.

The plant. The clay pot.

How had she not thought of it before?

Eryna snatched the plant from the table and, though it broke her heart to destroy its home, dropped it. The clay shattered, a curved shard landing at Eryna's feet.

Bless Gaia.

She worked through the rope. It fell to the floor with a quiet *thump*. Eryna twisted her wrists, examining the burns. She willed the skin to regenerate, the burns to disappear. They barely faded. She was too weak to fully heal. She needed to eat more, but first, she needed to get out.

Eryna rushed to the door but remembered it was locked. She scanned the room and her eyes fell on the steel object the girl had used to knock her out, a small rust-colored streak staining its blunt end.

That'll work.

She snatched it and brought it down on the door handle. It gave way immediately. The door creaked open. She peaked her head out and stared down the cavernous hall. It stretched as far as she could see.

Getting out would prove more difficult than anticipated.

Stealthy as a panther, she moved through the dim space on slow, light feet, the only sound a loud *tick* and *tock* of a large ornate clock down the hall. There were so many doors. Eryna stopped in front of one marked with the word "Gym." Such a strange word. Short, no primary vowels most human words contained. Ever so quietly, Eryna opened the door. It was a large, cold, and dark room. A thick black material covered the floor, and there were shiny metal contraptions of all shapes and sizes that looked like they could be torture devices.

Not a way out.

Eryna shut the door and moved on, passing unlabeled door after unlabeled door. The hall hinged left and took her down another long corridor. She passed a door that seeped with warmth and smelled of cedar. She pressed her palm to it and thought maybe it was a sign; maybe this was the one that would lead her out and back to the forest.

She was promptly disappointed. It was nothing but a cramped box lined in cedar planks, a basin of hot coals tucked in a corner. She lingered less than a minute.

Further down was a large black door with a bar for a handle—the most unique door she'd seen so far. It led her into a strange room with large, cushioned chairs on raised steps facing a white sheet. Shelves of brightly colored boxes sat under a sign that read "candy," and a little red and yellow machine sat under one that read "popcorn." This room was certainly intriguing, but it wasn't a way out.

Eryna stepped back into the hall and her eyes caught on double doors down the way, cracked open a foot or so. The room was dark. She tiptoed over and glanced in. It was large and magnificent, with a black and white marbled floor, a high domed ceiling, dark green paneled walls, endless shelves of books, and several large tables, desks, dressers, and a massive bed. It screamed of abundance.

It was also an absolute disaster.

The bed was crumpled and looked as though it hadn't been

adjusted in days. Wrinkled clothes piled high in a corner. Whole rows of books littered the ground below empty shelves. A lingering hint of spiced sandalwood and tobacco hung in the air, but the warm scent was overpowered by stale dust.

Eryna's heart leapt to her throat as her eyes landed on a framed image of three boys: one was Brody, the other was a yellow-haired boy she'd never seen, and the third was the boy they'd executed a few days ago. Tyler.

"Can I help you?" A voice asked from behind her. Eryna turned and when she saw the source of the voice, she froze.

A tall boy with fair skin, fair hair.

It was Tyler.

No, it couldn't be him. She'd seen him die, *felt* him die.

She searched his eyes. They were a mix of green and brown, like the moss that coated the Thornewood, like that girl's eyes.

Not Forget-Me-Not blue.

It was the other boy, then. The one she didn't know.

His hair was short and hung in wild waves around his face. He stood straight and tall, held up by an easy confidence, but a heaviness pulled at his shoulders. His blue linen shirt was wrinkled, his skin dull and tired, his under eyes bruised. His cheeks glowed bright pink as if he'd had too much wine.

His head tilted to the side, his moss-colored eyes narrowing. Eryna couldn't tell if the tight press of his full lips was due to irritation, or if it was just the way they naturally set.

Him and the girl were clearly related.

"Can I help you?" he repeated, and Eryna suddenly realized she'd been silently staring at him for close to a minute.

"I was looking for a way out," she replied. The boy's eyes narrowed further, and he scanned her up and down. She was suddenly very thankful for the tonic and that she'd spent the time detangling her hair. His gaze lingered briefly on the faint red marks on her wrists, and his lips quirked into a slight smile.

"I see. Well, it's not in there," he said, bobbing his head toward the room. His room, most likely. Then he reached toward Eryna's face and, before she could react, plucked out the single chiffon rose she'd tucked behind her ear. He spun the micro stem between his fingers and twirled the flower, watching it intently.

"Rose of Sharon," he remarked. "My mom used to love these. Didn't realize there were any left in the garden."

Pulse racing, Eryna watched the petals dance as he twirled the flower. The boy paused and glanced over her shoulder. Eryna followed his gaze.

"What are you doing?" The girl called from down the hall, arms crossed, seething. Her expression looked as if she'd sucked on a lemon wedge. The boy chuckled.

"Didn't realize you were so bad in bed, Jenin, you had to hold them hostage. I found this one trying to escape." He signaled to Eryna and laughed harder, obviously finding himself more humorous than the girl—Jenin—did. He walked toward Jenin and shoved his hands in his pockets, taking the flower. Eryna cursed herself for not retrieving it seconds earlier.

Jenin punched the boy in the shoulder.

"Shut up, Derrick, it's not like that."

Derrick. Eryna froze. A memory resurfaced from when Brody carried her into this place. *Derrick will kill her if he finds out she's here,* Jenin had said. Eryna studied the boy through a new gaze, straining to see the threat he posed. Surely Jenin hadn't meant him. He lacked the aura of a killer. Yes, he seemed a little put out, but not violent. If anything, he just seemed sad.

"Oh? Then what's it like?" he pressed.

"None of your business, perv." Jenin stormed past Derrick and threaded her arm through Eryna's, giving it a tug. "Let's go. This part of the house is far too dull."

Jenin pulled Eryna down the hall, but before they could get more than ten steps, Derrick trotted ahead and walked backward at a matched pace.

"Wait a minute. What if she doesn't want to hang out with you anymore? What if she found someone more interesting?" Derrick smiled at Eryna, all teeth and dimples. She eyed it wearily, though something light flitted around in her stomach.

Jenin rolled her eyes.

"You'd have to actually be interesting for that to happen."

"You can't be that much more interesting if you have to hold her hostage," he offered, shrugging. Then he looked at Eryna. "I never caught your name, actually. What is it?"

"Don't answer that," Jenin urged.

"Eryna Thorne," Eryna replied, defiantly.

"Alright you got her name, moron, now leave us alone," Jenin said, scrunching her face. She dragged Eryna down the hall back toward the prison of a room. Derrick stopped following them, but before they turned the corner, he called out, "If you get bored of my sister, Eryna, you know where to find me."

Eryna glimpsed his smile before they disappeared down the hall. Jenin remained silent until they were back in the room. She shut the door then pressed an ear up against it. She scowled at Eryna.

"I told you to stay in this room," Jenin whispered, her voice choked as if she would erupt if she spoke any louder.

"You can't lock me in here like a caged bird," Eryna challenged. Jenin looked down at the broken handle and fumed.

"Well not now, I can't!" she whispered furiously. Then she pressed her fingers to her brow and sighed. "Brody will be back soon, and you'll be out of this place."

"You keep saying that, but I'm starting to wonder if he's coming back at all. Besides, I don't care about Brody. I have to get back to my family in the Thornewood. I have to get home!"

"They burnt it to the ground!" Jenin shouted.

Eryna stilled. Silence between them swelled like a stormy wave before crashing violently against the shore. Jenin slid her fingers to her temples. "They set fire to the Thornewood shortly after Brody got you out. Euryalea is dead. The Dryads are dead. There is no home. There is nothing for you to get back to."

Eryna studied Jenin, desperately seeking the lie in her mossy eyes. It had to be a lie. Eryna was still alive, which meant the Thornewood must still be alive. It *must* be.

"That can't be true," Eryna murmured, more to herself than Jenin.

"Well, it is. I'd say I'm sorry, but your 'family' has claimed the lives of more members of mine than the ones left living, so I really have no sympathy for you."

Pressure built behind Eryna's eyes as a single image flashed in her mind: Fire. Hot, crackling, roaring fire as burning leaves rained down around them like brightly glowing feathers while Brody carried her away. It was a faint memory, but it was there, real as the ice-cold marble beneath her feet.

Her sisters. *Gone.*

The *Domecowé* and her Mother Oak. *Gone.*

The Hollow. Her redwood. Her foxes and finches and owls and wolves and rabbits and raccoons.

Gone, gone, gone.

"Why did Brody bring me here?" Eryna asked, anger flaring in her heart. He hadn't saved her from death; He'd cheated her out of it and now she was forced to live in a world without everyone she'd ever loved.

Jenin sighed. "I don't know. I guess we'll find out once he comes back. But if you have any shred of self-preservation, you need to stay in this room, and stay away from Derrick," she said.

"Why? He's nicer than you. Maybe he'll help me out of this prison."

Jenin scoffed.

"He is nice. To *humans*. Us Ashfords hate your kind more than the Blackwells. That boy you killed a few days ago? His name was Tyler. He was our cousin, and Derrick's best friend."

"I didn't kill him," Eryna shot Jenin a look so sharp, it could've sliced her to ribbons. Jenin waved her off.

"It doesn't matter. You're all the same to us, and if Derrick finds out what you are, he won't hesitate to kill you. Which is why you need to stay here until Brody comes back. Please. I don't feel like cleaning up your blood and explaining to my father how a demon got into our home."

Then Jenin slipped out the door without another word. She didn't tie Eryna up and she couldn't lock the door.

She didn't have to.

Eryna crawled into bed, the ache in her chest settling like a rock so deep, she could barely breathe. She turned the brief memory of the Thornewood on fire over in her mind, willing it to be false, but she could smell the smoke. She could taste the anger and death in the air. She could hear the screams of her sisters.

Eryna might still be alive, which meant the Heart was likely still safe, but what was the point of getting home now if it was just her and an empty husk of a forest?

No sisters, no animals, just Eryna and a torched Mother Oak that no longer produced Dryads.

She would live alone until she died alone a thousand or more years from now, wandering a broken Euryalea until Gaia finally called her home to Elysium.

Chapter Nine

Sleep finally caught Eryna. It was a deep sleep, a dark sleep, and one she happily embraced until she was so rudely torn from it by two voices.

"Where the Hades have you been?" Jenin accused. She sounded small and distant, like she was in a faraway realm.

Eryna sat up and blinked her heavy lids. Based on the angle of the sun, it was early morning. When had she fallen asleep? Hours ago? Days? Life had become a wheel, no end or beginning. She was simply crushed beneath it one moment, then ripped up and thrown back toward the ground the next.

"I had some things to take care of," Brody replied, his voice as small and distant as Jenin's.

He's back. Eryna's heart raced, and she glanced around the room. She was alone but could somehow hear the two of them. She got out of bed and followed the noise toward the bathroom.

"You promised you'd be back by morning *two* days ago!"

Two days. It'd been two days since that awful morning.

"I said I'd be back when I knew what to do with her," Brody replied. It was as if he was inside some sort of tunnel. Eryna looked up. High on the ceiling was small metal rectangle with slits through which warm air wafted. She climbed on the counter and rose up on her toes as far as she could to get a closer listen.

"What's there to do besides kill her?" Jenin asked. Eryna scoffed. She'd hidden some of the clay shards beneath the bed for that exact reason. "I don't like the look on your face right now, Brody. You're up to something."

Eryna leaned closer. She stopped breathing so she wouldn't miss a single word.

"They never found the third Heart," he said.

"I knew it!" Eryna gasped, and nearly slipped off the counter but quickly righted herself.

"They checked the Mother Oak, and it was empty. We think they hid it somewhere."

What?

Eryna had never heard of the Heart being removed from the Mother Oak. She didn't even know it was possible. And how was the Mother Oak still alive without the Heart? How was *she* alive?

"You want to see if she knows where it is? That's a stupid plan. She'll never tell you," Jenin said. She was right. Even if Eryna knew where it was, she'd sooner die and be reunited with her sisters than tell him.

"Maybe not yet but give it time."

"She's tried to jailbreak three times already. I doubt you'll be able to keep her here long enough."

"You of all people know how charming I can be," Brody replied, and Eryna could almost see the wolfish grin on his face. Her blood boiled at the implication that he could woo her into betraying her family and home. This was a different Brody than the one she'd met; the one who stroked her back and told her it would be okay while she vomited. Then again, if those moments were all she had to base his character on, she barely knew him at all.

"First off, we were ten," Jenin replied. "Second, you think you can charm that demon into staying here, with humans—people she hates—then pry the location of the Heart out of her? Are you out of your mind? If your father finds out..."

"He won't find out. And she's not a demon. She had multiple chances to kill me, and she didn't. I think she's softer than the rest." Eryna cringed at the term "softer" and how easily he'd spotted that vulnerability. Gaia, was she paying for that softness now. "You and I are the only ones who know what she truly is. We'll just have to give her a backstory, make her look like one of us."

"I already took care of that."

"What do you mean—"

"Don't worry about it. Do you hear yourself? This plan is delusional!" Jenin nearly shouted.

"My father moved the other two Hearts to our place so he could be closer to them. They're dying. He's getting sicker, and I know your father is, too. The future of our families depends on this. We *need* that third Heart. Delusion is all we've got, Neens."

Eryna paused.

The other two Hearts were still alive, and they were in Brody's home.

Suddenly, her chest pounded, her hands trembled, and for the first time since the execution, she felt a glimmer of true hope. She had to get those Hearts. If she could take them back to Euryalea, maybe she could restore the Fiddlewood and Sylvanwood. Maybe, if all three Hearts were back in Euryalea, the Mother Oaks would produce Dryads again, and all three forests would heal.

There would be life once more. She wouldn't be alone. She just had to escape this prison and steal the Hearts from the Blackwells' home, all without being killed. Somehow.

Then she had an idea.

Brody wanted to charm the location of the third Heart out of her. She could play that game, too. She could be equally as charming as he was. After all, he *had* called her beautiful and she knew it wasn't a lie.

Humans had always found nymphs attractive. It's what drew them to the nymph island of Tegadona in the first place.

But with an agenda of his own, Brody wouldn't be so easily deceived. It had to be a sport; he had to feel like he was chasing something. According to her sisters, human men always did.

Eryna hadn't realized Jenin and Brody had stopped speaking until footsteps approached from down the hall. She hopped off the surface and glanced in the mirror, pinching her cheeks until they turned a soft shade of rose. Then she sucked on her lower lip until it swelled and she smiled.

It was time for the games to begin.

Chapter Ten

Eryna walked out of the bathroom to find Jenin and Brody already in the room. Brody's jaw fell open the second he saw her.

"You...you look...," he stuttered, not a single coherent sentence finding his lips. If she hadn't overheard his conversation with Jenin, she might've blushed or smiled at him. Instead, she simply looked at him, neutral and cool.

"You're back," she said. Not a question or exclamation. A statement. He scanned her, opened his mouth, but still nothing came out.

He glanced at Jenin. "How?"

"Beauty Tonic. That, and the damn demon healed herself," Jenin replied as she set down a fresh tray of food.

"She's not a demon, Jenin, quit it with that."

Eryna caught Brody's sideways glance at her, as if gauging her reaction. She didn't acknowledge it. Instead, head high, she grabbed a chair from the corner of the room, dragged it to the table and sat. There was more on the tray than flowers and dirt this time: berries, apples, pears, toasted breads, and pastries. Eryna grabbed a strawberry and popped it in her mouth, the flesh soft and the juice rich. She looked at Brody, raised her brows, and waited for him to speak.

His lips parted and a question formed between his brows. After another moment of stupefied silence, he sat next to her, leaning his elbow on the back of his chair.

"I'm sorry I couldn't come sooner. I was held up. I know I owe you an explanation," he said. He looked at her, his dark eyes clear and sympathetic. Ever so slightly, he leaned in. The air around him was electric, and if she were more of a fool, she'd be drawn in like a fly.

"Why did you bring me here?" she asked as she grabbed another strawberry. This time she slowly bit it in half. Brody eyed her lips as she licked juice off them.

"You spared my life, I spared yours."

Spared her life? He thinks he *spared her life* by making her a hostage? Eryna wanted to scream. She wanted to chuck the tray of food across the room. She wanted to flip the table and beat Brody over the head with a chair. Instead, she dramatically glanced at the floor, then looked up at him through thick lashes.

"You think too highly of me if you think I spared your life on purpose."

Brody grabbed one of the berries off the tray and popped it in his mouth. "You could've killed me the second we met. You didn't. You healed me. You saved me." Brody shrugged. "I don't know what else to call that."

"It was the decent thing to do."

"In all my life, I haven't heard of a single time a Dryad let a human go because it was 'decent.' You also hesitated during the execution." Brody gently gripped Eryna's hand. He ran his thumb across her skin, and she fought against the prickling sensation that ran up her arm. "I owe you my life twice over, Eryna Thorne. This was the only way I could think to repay it."

She pursed her lips and let a whisper of her true feelings show.

"Leaving me in peace to heal my sisters and my home would've fulfilled that debt."

"I know," he said, the words quiet and sullen. His gaze fell, as if he couldn't look at her when he spoke. "They were only supposed to rescue me, but I...I had no idea what would to happen to your sisters and your home. I mean it."

He finally met her eyes and held them so intently, it seemed almost genuine. Eryna almost believed his performance.

Almost.

He might've been ignorant of his peoples' plans, but it changed nothing. Not to mention, she knew for certain now that he was after the third Heart. Still, if she played this right, she could undo his mess. She could save all of Euryalea if she found the two Hearts that the Blackwells possessed.

She would beat him at his own game.

Eryna sighed and pulled her hand from his.

"I'm grateful you spared my life. Truly. But what am I supposed to do now? I have no home, no family. I have nothing left. I have nowhere to go."

Brody made a show of thoughtfully nodding and scrubbing his chin with his hand. Then he perked up like he'd suddenly been struck by brilliance.

"Stay here with us. We could teach you how to belong."

Jenin snorted under her breath from where she leaned against the wall. Eryna glimpsed her picking dirt from her nails as if completely disinterested in the conversation. But from the tension in her shoulders, the tilt of her head, and the way she checked the same nail four times, she knew she was listening, and listening carefully.

"Belong where?" Eryna asked, feigning a dumbstruck tone. "In *Aponyx*?"

"Why not?" Brody smiled. "We just need a large supply of that beauty tonic, which shouldn't be a problem seeing as I'm the son of Blackwell Technology's CEO. Besides, you said it yourself. You have nowhere to go. Let Aponyx be your home, at least for a little while. We're all off to university in the fall anyway. But if you stay the rest of the summer, you can acclimate to human life, and then go anywhere you want. We can help you."

Eryna pretended to consider the idea, as if Brody was granting her some magnificent gift of a new life; a fresh start, something too good to be true. It *was* too good to be true, but he didn't need to know she knew that.

"You would do that?" she asked, bright-eyed.

"Of course. It's the least I can do," Brody said, his wolfish smile returning as he gently placed a hand on Eryna's knee, his "B" ring glinting in the light. He drew circles on her skin with his thumb, and she pushed against what it stirred inside her.

Jenin scoffed louder this time and Brody glanced her way.

"Something you'd like to share with the class, Jenin?" he asked. She glanced up from her nails and narrowed her eyes.

"As a matter of fact, yes. Have you both completely lost it? She'll never pass for human. Any halfwit could sniff her out like a bloodhound. What if the tonic wears off? What if her tolerance increases? What then?"

Brody glanced between Jenin and Eryna and nodded thoughtfully. "The tonic is mine to worry about. Leave that to me." Then he smiled, a crooked, mischievous expression. "As for fitting in, however, she'll have you to help her."

Jenin nearly choked. Her arms crossed tight over her chest, and she stared at Brody with such disgust, such disdain, if looks could kill he'd have been vaporized.

"That's not what we agreed to."

He stood and walked toward Jenin.

"Please, Jenin? It will be fun! Think of it as a project."

Eryna bit the inside of her cheek to keep from asserting that she wasn't a project, but a living, breathing being.

"A project would be figuring out how to turn a pug into a poodle. You're asking me to make that *thing* human. She's not a project. She's a monster. She's beyond help. She'll never belong in our world, and you're an idiot to think otherwise."

"I have ears," Eryna cut in. Jenin looked at her, brows raised.

"I sure hope so because you need to hear this, too. This. Won't. Work. Isn't there another nymph realm that will take you in? The Oreads? The Naiads? Wouldn't they happily accept a refugee Dryad?"

"No," Eryna lied. They would absolutely take her in, but if she wanted to save Euryalea, she had to stay here. For now, this was her place. Except, as Jenin's eyes narrowed on her, Eryna realized Brody might not be the hard one to trick.

"You're lying," she challenged. Eryna swallowed hard and dug deep for another lie, not that it would be hard to find one. Humans knew nothing of nymph relations and cared very little to learn.

"We sought refuge once before. Because humans were—are— relentless in their pursuit of our Hearts, the Naiads and the Oreads labeled us 'untouchable.' They refuse to open their realms to us. They think you'll follow after and destroy their Hearts and homes, too."

It was only a half lie. It was true the other realms were hesitant to assist in the early days of the war. But it took barely a decade for them to abandon their fear and rally around the Dryads however they could. However, Aponyx's rapid growth made reaching each other more difficult these days.

Jenin pressed her tongue to the inside of her cheek. Then, silently, she opened the door to leave. Brody cut off her exit, shutting the door with a single hand.

"Jenin, please. We both need this," Brody insisted, his words slow and loaded with more than words alone. Eryna watched as they stared at each other. On the surface, it looked like an intimate moment, but Eryna knew it was a silent conversation. His gaze begged as if to say *we can't afford not to do this.* Her gaze narrowed as if to say *I will hate you forever for putting me in this position.*

Eryna watched and waited, hoping Jenin would give in, because if she didn't, it would make stealing the Hearts almost impossible. Eryna needed to assimilate, and she wasn't sure how she would do that without Jenin's help.

Jenin closed her eyes and sighed.

"Fine. She can stay here," Jenin conceded. Brody all but leapt out of his shoes and hugged her, spinning her in a circle. She wriggled out of his arms and pointed one strong finger at Eryna and the other at Brody. "But if you guys blow this and we all end up dead, I will find you in the afterlife and drag you to Hades with my bare, ghostly hands. Got it?"

Brody laughed and batted her finger away.

"We won't, I promise." He looked at Eryna, eyes wild and beaming. "This is great! We'll start immediately, especially since the Hunt is tonight. It'll be the perfect place to introduce you into society."

"That's tonight?" Jenin gasped. Eryna perked up.

"What's the Hu—"

A bell rang through the halls so loud it could surely be heard miles away. Brody sauntered to Eryna and took her hand.

"Ready for your first human test?"

Eryna looked at Jenin, and then Brody, hoping one of them would offer more information than that.

"What test?" she asked.

Brody smiled.

"Breakfast."

Chapter Eleven

This place was a labyrinth of doors and corridors. Eryna laughed at her earlier naiveté thinking she could escape. She never would've found a way out.

She, Jenin, and Brody had gone through three doors, down four halls, and up two sets of stairs to get to the "breakfast room." Surrounded by windows and a domed glass ceiling was a thick chestnut table piled high with food. It was set for eight, but only one person was seated: Derrick.

He sat sideways in the chair, arm slung over the back of it, ankle propped over his knee. His head hung down, and Eryna thought he might be sad or possibly even crying. But as she drew closer, she saw a familiar metal object in his hand. It was a phone. His thumb tapped and slid against the glass, shapes and colors moving at his will. He looked up and smiled wide when he saw Eryna.

"I wondered if I'd see you again," he said. Eryna returned the smile, but before she could respond, Derrick's eyes laned on Brody and his expression fell.

"Didn't realize you were coming today," Derrick said. Brody smiled and nodded toward the food.

"Do I ever miss a weekend breakfast at the Ashford's?" he replied. Jenin rolled her eyes and blew past the boys, heading straight for the table. Eryna trailed her but couldn't help shrinking a little at the tension hanging in the air between the boys, the angst rippling off Derrick.

"Don't you have your own house to eat breakfast at?" Jenin said. "Or is chef Brenna starving you?"

Brody sat, grabbed a plate, then dug into a tray of swirled golden-brown pastries smothered in a white frost. They looked sticky and filling and absolutely delicious. The Dryads had pastries of their own, but she'd never seen one like this.

"Brenna will always be number one, but she doesn't make Saturday morning cinnamon rolls quite like your chef does." Brody put three on his plate, took a bite and groaned, melting into his seat like warm butter. He shook his head. "Phenomenal. Every time."

Derrick chuckled, the tension diffusing slightly, and Jenin stifled a smile as they began filling their plates. Unsure where to begin, Eryna carefully eyed the spread. Some of it was familiar: bowls of berries, stone fruits, halved citruses, thinly sliced pork belly and links, soft flaky rolls, toasted breads, and bouquets of lilacs, marigolds, and roses.

But much of it was unfamiliar: The sticky brown pastries and small beige disks that looked fluffy as a cloud. There were pitchers of colored liquids, and a mess of something yellow and white with melted bits of orange throughout. It smelled like some type of egg. Eryna loved eggs, but she'd never eaten them like this.

She started with what she knew. A spoonful of berries, an apple, and a couple slices of pork belly. She reached for the marigolds, then paused. While a marigold was light and crisp, it could take a bitter turn if it wasn't fresh. She plucked one from the stem and chewed, deeming it suitable. She grabbed a fistful and put them on her plate, satisfied with her spread.

It wasn't until she glanced up that she realized flowers weren't a common human cuisine. Heat rose to her cheeks as Jenin, Derrick, and Brody stared at her, all frozen mid-bite. Jenin's jaw tightened, and Derrick's brow lifted. Brody, however, was open-mouth smiling like he found it to be the most entertaining thing he'd ever seen. He stood, plucked a marigold of his own, and chewed it.

"I forgot those were edible. Not as good as the cinnamon roll, though," he said, smoothly changing the subject. He grabbed Eryna's plate and put one of the pastries on it.

"Try it." He encouraged. Eryna took a bite.

It was warm and sweet and melted the second it hit her tongue. Cinnamon and sugar and almond and orange zest overwhelmed her senses and oh, Gaia, it was one of the most wonderful things she'd ever tasted. She immediately stuffed another piece in her mouth. It was just as delicious as the first, maybe more. "Oh," was all she could say.

"Right?" Brody laughed, digging into his own roll. The four of them ate in silence for several minutes. Eryna eyed the empty seats.

"Where is everyone else?" she asked, pouring herself a glass of the red liquid. She assumed it was wine and questioned why humans drank wine with breakfast. But when she took a sip, it was bright and tangy and fresh. Cranberry juice, Eryna realized.

Jenin scrutinized the table settings.

"Our father doesn't usually join us for breakfast," she said.

"Try never," Derrick grumbled. Jenin shot him a look and continued.

"Our mother passed a few years ago, so it's really just us."

"Tyler was always here, too, until he…" Derrick trailed off, eyes trained on his plate. The air in the room shifted to a wintery ice and Eryna's throat clenched as she thought of the blue-eyed boy. The cranberry juice in her mouth turned metallic and tasted of blood. "Those disgusting savages got what they deserved. I'd have burned the whole realm down myself if father had let me go."

"Derrick," Jenin warned. Brody looked away as if wishing he

were anywhere else. Eryna sunk in her seat and tried to evaporate into nothingness.

"We can't just move on with our lives as if nothing happened, Jenin."

"It's what we've always done. People in our family die all the time. We were closer to him than others, but our world can't stop turning just because his did." Derrick opened his mouth to protest, but Jenin glared at him. "Conversation over. You're ruining my appetite talking about *them*."

Eryna sensed Jenin had said those final words to put an end to the conversation, but she could feel their sharp edges. She silently stared at her plate, watching Dera kill the boy over and over again. She glanced up briefly and caught Derrick staring at her, his expression unreadable. Eryna cleared her throat, desperate for a subject change.

"So, what animal do you track during the Hunt? I'm a decent hunter," she said.

The three of them broke into laughter, cleaving the tension from the room altogether. Eryna glanced around, clearly not understanding the joke. Brody dabbed his mouth with a bit of thick cotton.

"The Hunt isn't for an animal. It's for keys," he said. He leaned in, as if begging for her to ask more. She obliged.

"What sort of keys?"

"All kinds! It's a scavenger hunt we host every summer at Blackwell Manor. Our family hides keys around the grounds, but only one is the prize key. Once it's found that person needs to find the door it opens."

"How long does it last?"

"Four weeks, but there are only three days when the Hunt actually occurs, and we don't announce it until the day of."

Eryna waited for more, hoping there'd be another element to this hunt, but it seemed Brody was done speaking. It was rather underwhelming.

"That's it? You just find a door?" she asked.

"You've clearly never been to Blackwell Manor," Derrick added. Brody nodded in agreement.

"There are hundreds of keys, and hundreds of doors. Some keys open doors, some don't, but only one key opens a door that has an invaluable prize behind it."

An invaluable prize.

"What's the prize?" she asked, unable to keep the question to herself. She already knew it wouldn't be the Hearts, but she couldn't wrangle her curiosity with the way Brody spoke slow and low, like telling his favorite story around the bonfire. He leaned across the table and smiled.

"That'd spoil all the fun, wouldn't it?" Brody winked, and heat climbed the back of her neck.

"Rumor has it, it's over half the Blackwell fortune. Or some say it's the missing royal jewels from the Mainland, or even a potion from a witch on the Southern Continent that grants the drinker eternal life," Derrick said, his voice thick and mysterious, playing off Brody's energy. Then Jenin shattered it with a snort.

"In all likelihood," she said. "It's a lifetime supply of Blackwell Tech's tonics, which is a stupid prize. Besides, whatever the rumors are, in the ten years the Hunt has been around, not a single person has won. It's just an excuse for the high society of Aponyx to have elaborate parties, get drunk, and hook up in private rooms at Blackwell Manor."

This is perfect.

In fact, it was so much more than perfect. Eryna thought she'd have to risk death to sneak into Brody's home and search for the Hearts, but now she had a reason to be there and snoop around. She was so close to the Hearts it was as if they were at this very table with her, beating alongside her own. Eryna hadn't realized she was smiling until Brody looked at her and said, "That's the spirit. Think of it as your entrance into Aponyx society. Now that you've decided to stay and all."

Derrick perked up, eyes bright and clear. "You're staying? That's great!"

"She's not staying here for *you*, dimwit. She's my guest, and completely off limits so roll your tongue back in your mouth," Jenin said as she reached across the table and pushed her brother's jaw shut. He chomped at her hand, and she slapped him.

Eryna giggled. It seemed siblings acted like siblings everywhere, no matter what type of being they were.

Just then, Brody stood, tossed his cotton cloth on the table, and stretched. "Well, I have to get going. We have some last-minute preparations to take care of. Jenin, thanks for getting Eryna settled." Before he left the room, he flashed them a smile so fiendish, Hades would be proud. "See you all tonight. Let the games begin."

A moment later, he was gone. He had no idea how right he was. The games were indeed about to begin.

"Jenin? Derrick? Anyone home?" A distant voice echoed. Derrick tensed. Jenin almost jumped out of her seat. They looked at each other.

"He's home," Jenin whispered, a hollow look in her eyes that Eryna couldn't pin down. The siblings stood, faster than a frog snatches a fly.

"I have to run a couple errands. Meet you two in the foyer at seven. We'll go to Blackwell Manor together," Derrick said, and before the girls could respond, he slipped through a side door.

Jenin grabbed Eryna's arm and maneuvered her some distance away from the breakfast room. Then she circled Eryna like she was cornered prey, looked her up and down, and sighed.

"We might as well go shopping since you're staying, you masochist. We both need outfits for tonight, and it's time you look a little less…feral." Jenin smiled, and Eryna realized she hadn't seen Jenin smile a single time since meeting her.

It was terrifying.

Chapter Twelve

Thin, ropey cords sliced deep into Eryna's forearms, cutting off her circulation as no less than twelve bags dangled like pendulums from her arms. They burst with the same basic clothes, and though she hated every piece, she stopped protesting after Jenin demanded she accept her generosity even though the clothes were being "wasted on an unappreciative heathen."

If Eryna learned anything from shopping, it was that she especially hated jeans. Who allowed such an item to exist? Nothing was comfortable about the thick denim compressing her soft thighs and lower belly as she walked. She also couldn't catch her breath beneath her tight white t-shirt, and her feet throbbed from the ankle-high boots Jenin had squeezed her into. It was all so suffocating and confining.

Eryna missed her flower circlet. She missed the way flora and freshly harvested silk trailed over her skin, nature against nature. None of this synthetic fabric. Though, she didn't mind the dark "sunglasses" that shielded her eyes from the late afternoon light. They allowed her to take in the world around her without being so obviously new to it all. And, Gaia, it was so much to take in.

Bright lights were inescapable, sounds assaulting and unfamiliar, and thousands of humans filled the paved walkways lined with "shops." Each shop begged people to enter and buy their goods, wear their clothes, taste their food. There was scarcely a surface of this world that didn't have a moving image displaying some BLACKWELL TECHNOLOGIES product or service that promised to make the buyer happier, prettier, smarter, sexier, or thinner.

Metal contraptions—Jenin called them "cars"—maneuvered the open pavement. Some looked pristine and new, some rusted and aged; some were sporty and round, and others were rather large and boxy and packed with humans. No matter the size and shape of the vehicle, they were all loud, abrasive, and emitted off-putting, burnt smells.

And while this intense new world overwhelmed Eryna to tears more than once, she couldn't get enough of one thing: the towers. Glass and steel behemoths twisted and stretched high up to the heavens, dwarfing her in the shadows of their splendor. This close, the towers were more magnificent than she ever imagined. If the giant sequoias of the Eastern Thornewood made her feel like an ant, Eryna might as well have been a flea compared to the towers.

"People live in all of these?" she asked Jenin. Jenin followed her gaze upward.

"Some. Most are office buildings where people work."

Work. Another concept Jenin had explained. Sitting for eight or more hours in a day to do a job for someone else seemed soul-sucking. No wonder the humans were always searching for products and services that made them feel less like what they were and more like what they wished to be.

Such strange beings, humans, Eryna thought, and she was drowning in them. Humans of all different shapes and sizes and colors filled the sidewalks. Some, like Jenin, were slender women in tall heels clacking along the pavement, and some were mothers pushing younglings in little wheeled seats. But most of the humans on the street were men. Men in well-fitted suits walking with intense purpose, men in jeans and short-sleeved shirts scanning the stores as they walked, and groups of young men hollering and hooting at whatever jokes or discussions they were engaged in. And what all those men had in common is that whenever Eryna and Jenin passed, they stared. Shamelessly. While the looks never lasted more than three seconds, three seconds was plenty for Eryna's skin to crawl.

A handsome man in a nice suit looked her up and down as he passed. He smiled. It wasn't a friendly smile.

"Why do the men stare at us like that?" Eryna murmured, leaning into Jenin. Jenin kept her face straight ahead, sunglasses on, expression cold.

"If you have to ask, you clearly didn't look in the mirror hard enough yesterday." Eryna couldn't be sure, but it sounded as though Jenin had almost complimented her.

"I don't like it," Eryna replied.

"Well, they'll do it with or without your consent so you might as well get used to it."

It was then that Eryna noticed something else: When a man passed by a woman, the man would look. The woman wouldn't, and if she did, it was only a passing glance.

"Why don't women look at men the same way?" Eryna asked.

Jenin's silence and lack of wit made Eryna certain she'd asked a question Jenin might not know the answer to. Jenin's shoulders pulled back a little tighter, her head a little higher.

"Why should we? Something we're missing?" she replied, and before Eryna could ask more, Jenin veered her off the main stretch of pavement and back into the Ashford's building.

The door to the "penthouse" opened without Jenin even touching it, and they entered a grand circular entryway. Giant vases filled with dried willow reeds decorated the space, along with dozens of white candles and lush flower arrangements of hydrangeas, orchids, lilies of the valley, ranunculi, and king protea. The marble floor shone like a mirror beneath windows that stretched overhead in a dome, and warm afternoon light filled the room. A woman in a simple blue dress greeted the girls. Jenin dropped her bags on the floor, along with all but one of Eryna's bags.

"Please have a guest room made up. This is Eryna. These are her clothes and toiletries. She will be with us for the remainder of the summer," she said. The woman nodded, and Jenin clacked away. Eryna hustled to follow. Jenin stopped in front of white double doors and threw them open.

Clearly, she wasn't a fan of color. Her paneled walls were white, her floor a light wood, possibly maple. Her bed was a creation of creamy silken sheets and tan fur pillows, set in a light beige upholstered frame. Her desks and tables were white, but their surfaces were barely visible as they were topped with large art pieces and a generous amount of greenery. Eryna was pleasantly surprised; there was a lot of life in this room.

Jenin spilled the contents of Eryna's bag on the bed, then looked at the small clock on her wrist. A "watch," Eryna had once heard them called.

"Sit," Jenin said, pointing to a chair in front of a large table and mirror surrounded by white electric bulbs. Eryna sat, eyeing the array of brushes and colored tubes and powders and glass bottles in front of her. She wanted to touch them all, test them, but before she could, Jenin turned the bulbs on and nearly blinded Eryna. Then she pinched Eryna's chin and turned her face toward her.

"Hm," Jenin said, scrutinizing her. Jenin's face soured and she made a sound of disgust. "It's annoying how pretty you are when you look human."

Jenin rummaged through Eryna's new cosmetics, then plucked from her own collection. It was a strangely intimate activity, allowing Jenin to dab cold liquids and loose powders on her skin as she assessed her like an artist does a painting. After a few minutes of silence, Eryna asked the question she could no longer hold in.

"What is Brody to you?"

Jenin's mouth turned down, but her gaze remained focused on Eryna, brushing a pale pink dust on her cheeks.

"Please don't tell me you're interested in Brody. He's nothing but bad news," she replied. Gaia, did Eryna already know that. But that wasn't an answer.

"I don't understand why he brought me to you. You hate Dryads, so why does he trust me with you? And why go along with it? What's in it for you?"

Jenin paused so briefly, Eryna might not have noticed it if her brush hadn't faltered mid-stroke. She set the tool aside and grabbed a large comb from the table. She stood behind Eryna and looked at her in the mirror, eyes sharp.

"What's in it for me is that I'm being nice to a good friend. That's all we are. Unlike the thousands of girls in this city, Brody's charm doesn't work on me. He isn't my type. He's one of my little brother's best friends, and as such, is also a brother to me."

Then Jenin tightly yanked her hair back with a comb and Eryna yelped. She caught Jenin stifling a smile in the mirror.

"I'm just trying to understand human relationships. I've only been around my sisters," Eryna said between hair tugs. "I was born to and raised by all females. I've never been around men."

Jenin pulled and smoothed Eryna's hair back into a sleek, yet bouncy ponytail. Then her brows rose.

"I have to assume you're not counting the men you've killed," she scoffed.

"I haven't killed anyone." Eryna glared at her.

"Still, you were around them."

"But I never interacted with them. I only saw them from afar. Many of my sisters are..." Eryna paused for a breath, her throat tight as she realized she had to adjust that sentence. "*Were* old enough to have had relationships with humans before the war times, so I've heard things.

But Brody's the only human boy I've interacted with. And your brother."

Jenin tied off Eryna's hair with a tight elastic and shot her a sharp look.

"You stay away from my brother."

Eryna lifted a brow at Jenin's immediate feistiness.

"I have no interest in your brother." She hardly knew the boy. He might've been attractive but looking at him made her feel as though she was looking at Tyler. Silently, Jenin walked to her bed and laid out the luxurious black dress they'd picked for Eryna. Then she faced Eryna squarely, expression serious.

"It's not just my brother. Stay away from all the men in this city. How long have you lived without them?"

"A little over a hundred years."

"Holy gods, you're old." Jenin blanched a little, then continued. "Well, you've lived plenty long without men. Don't start now."

"Why?"

Just then, Jenin's door opened. A tall man dressed in a crisp black ensemble complete with a black bow at his neck walked in. His hair was short, blonde, and peppered through with gray, but his face seemed strangely young for him to be as old as his hair suggested. His bright blue eyes were wide and ready, as if perpetually waiting to be shocked by what someone was about to say.

Jenin's entire body froze at Eryna's side.

"My darling girl," the man said. "I haven't seen you and your brother in days. I've looked everywhere for you both."

Jenin's throat bobbed as she swallowed hard. Then she smiled at the man, the hollowest, forced smile Eryna had ever seen.

"We've been busy. We missed you, father. When did you get back?"

The man stepped closer, and either Eryna was seeing things, or Jenin ever so slightly angled herself between her and the man.

"I got back this morning. Figured you'd be at breakfast, but when

I got to the breakfast room, no one was there." Then he looked at Eryna, and the second his eyes met hers, a shock ran through her body. She wanted to crawl under Jenin's bed and wait for him to leave. He wasn't particularly tall, but his energy was assaulting and heavy.

"Hello," he said. "I don't think we've met. I'm Damian Ashford."

The man outstretched his right hand, and Eryna thought back to how Brody greeted her when they first met. Eryna clutched his hand tight and gave it a firm shake. His brows rose.

"Nice grip. And you are?"

"This is Eryna Thorne," Jenin cut in. She could've faceplanted from how hard she tripped over her words. "She's a guest of Brody's from the Mainland, but I offered for her stay with us this summer."

"Oh? Well, we're lucky to have you, then. Though I wish my lovely daughter would've asked me first. Where are you from?"

Eryna opened her mouth to speak, unsure of what she could possibly say, but Jenin was quick with a response.

"Meedra," she said, and Eryna tried not to look puzzled. She'd never heard of Meedra, but then again, she didn't know much about the human continent of Anthropogas, or what the humans call the "Mainland."

"Jenin, darling, it's rude to speak for others."

"Sorry. She's just very shy. Like most Northwesterners."

Jenin's posture was confident, but what her father couldn't see was the way her thumbs constantly circled each other behind her back. This was the most unsettled Eryna had seen her.

Briefly, Damian's face pinched tight, and Eryna finally saw the familial relation. Then he relaxed, his expression once again bright and effervescent. The change was so eerily quick, Eryna's skin prickled.

"Meedra, you say? Such a small town. This must all be very different for you then. Let me know if there's anything we can do to make your stay more comfortable."

"I will, thank you," Eryna replied.

Damian turned toward Jenin and approached on slow, sure steps. In a few long strides, he towered over her. "I noticed shopping bags in the foyer. I thought we'd discussed excessive spending."

Jenin inhaled a shaky breath, and Eryna couldn't seem to slow her own heart rate down as it beat furiously in her chest, absorbing Jenin's anxious energy, uncertain of what would happen next.

"Yes, father. I'm sorry. We needed outfits for tonight, and I wanted to gift Eryna new clothes and a few personal items. Hers got lost in transit."

Damian stared down at Jenin for a moment, his gaze so heavy, Eryna swore it could have squashed Jenin into the ground. Then he looked at Eryna and smiled, the expression unnatural.

"My daughter's such a wonderful hostess. She's always had a big heart. Again, welcome to Aponyx." Damian turned to leave, and as he reached the door, he called back. "See you kids tonight."

The moment the door latched shut, the tension burst like an infected wound. Jenin looked at Eryna, her expression once again cold and unfeeling. She nodded toward the dress, shoes, and bits of gold jewelry on the bed, and handed her another bottle of Beauty Perfecting Tonic.

"Take the tonic. I was only able to get one. We'll get more from Brody tonight. Get dressed and don't ruin your hair or make up. I'll meet you in the foyer in forty-five minutes. I'd like to finish getting ready alone." Jenin walked into her bathroom and shut the door.

As Eryna dressed, she couldn't help wondering if humans were always fearful of their fathers the way Jenin and Derrick seemed to be. It took no more than ten seconds to decide that wasn't the case.

This man must be a particular brand of frightening.

Chapter Thirteen

The problem with meeting Jenin in the foyer was that Eryna had no idea how to get there. After she dressed, she started in the direction she was certain they had come earlier but hit a dead end. She'd need to pay more attention to the layout if she had any hope of escaping when it was time.

She wandered the halls, fumbling with the chain of her "purse" hoping to recognize a piece of art, a door—*something*. Eventually, Eryna ended up in an empty hall with one door glowing softly with natural light.

A way out?

Possibly. It was the best hope of one she'd had since leaving Jenin's room. She walked as quick as the strappy heeled shoes allowed and came upon a glass door that led to a lush garden. Eryna burst into the open air, almost falling to her knees at all the plant life around her. She quickly steadied herself. Jenin would end her if she ruined her new dress.

Tall cypress trees and carefully pruned laurels lined a gravel path, the empty spaces between them filled with hydrangea topiaries and overgrown rose bushes in blushing pinks, sky blues, buttery yellows, and sunset oranges. Ivy-covered wrought iron archways towered overhead; the vines just low enough for Eryna to skim with her fingertips. As she did, the leaves perked up. Then she asked the ivy to tell the rest of the garden she was there.

Suddenly, hibernating rose buds erupted all around her, and violet allium and periwinkle aster sprung from the soil. Scarlet ladybugs buzzed through the air, and a rainbow of butterflies flitted from flower to flower. The soft sound of distant flowing water called to Eryna, and she followed the tug. As she passed through an archway, white clematis bloomed across the brick. Just as Eryna reached where the path opened wide, her heart stopped.

Towering like a titan over a trickling fountain and neatly arranged couches was an exquisite wisteria. Its fronds rained lavender blooms as it gently swayed in a light breeze. Eryna practically ran to it. She placed a palm on its trunk.

"Hello, beautiful," she whispered in the language of the Dryads, the language all nature understood. The vine creaked and moaned like Eryna had just woken it from a long slumber. Its blooms swelled, and Eryna felt words spoken directly into her heart.

I haven't been visited in some time. Thank you for coming.

Eryna smiled.

"Then I will visit often," she replied. "I'm in need of a friend."

Just then, two tiny feet perched on Eryna's shoulder, and three bright *chirps* sounded in her ear. Eryna glanced down and saw a small finch cock its head. It wasn't a kind of finch she'd seen before. It was smaller than the ones in Euryalea, and a little duller, but most definitely a finch. Eryna held a finger to it as a perch.

"Is there something you need?" she asked. When she stroked its feathers, it radiated excitement at being spoken to and touched. Eryna chuckled. "Attention, perhaps?"

The little bird shook its feathers and gave two more affirmative *chirps.*

"Well, then, I'm happy to oblige." Eryna smiled. Then she realized the luck she'd stumbled upon. Plant life was stationary, but birds traveled, and far. "Have you seen Euryalea recently?"

The bird looked at her sideways, then shook its head, and looked out toward the balcony where Aponyx sprawled for miles.

The city was all it knew. This bird had never seen the true natural world. Eryna's heart sank.

"I understand," she said, and gave the bird another stroke. "When I go back home, I'll find a way to take you with me. You will love Euryalea."

The finch leaned into her touch, and with a grateful *chirp*, flew off into the city. She watched it for a minute, wishing she could sprout her own wings and fly home, far from this place. But she needed those Hearts. Without them, going home was pointless.

"Were you just talking to a bird?"

Eryna turned to see a smiling Derrick leaning against the brick arch. His disheveled waves had been neatly styled, the bruises under his eyes gone, and his black ensemble of crushed velvet hugged his body tight. She hadn't noticed earlier how muscular his arms were, the breadth of his shoulders, the way his torso tapered down to a solid waist.

He looked good.

She swallowed, trying to clear the dry patch in her throat.

"Do you not talk to birds?" she asked, certain he'd interpret it as a joke. His musical laugh confirmed as much.

"Only when I need a weather report, I suppose."

"Ah, yes. They are good for that. So long as you don't ask a crow."

Derrick pushed off the wall, clasped his hands behind his back and walked toward Eryna slowly, his steps fluid, graceful. He tilted his head.

"Why not a crow?"

"They're quite the tricksters, you see, blessed with the gift of knowledge and the curse of truth. They know everything that ever was, is, and will ever be, and must tell you if you ask. But there's always a price." Eryna shrugged as if the answer was obvious, because it was. This wasn't just common knowledge amongst the nymphs, but the witches and the faeries and the old gods and all other magical beings. It always surprised Eryna how scarcely humans understood magic.

"What kind of price? Gold? Souls?"

Eryna laughed, and it startled her. The last time she'd laughed like that was with Dera. Her heart rippled in agony at the thought of her sister, but she pushed the feeling down. This was no time to cry.

"Only Hades and psychopomps deal in souls. Crows are more…" she pursed her lips, searching for the right word. "Specific. The price they require depends on the question asked. They may desire a strand of your hair, or three of your fingernails, or to borrow your left eye every third full moon of the year. There's no knowing the price until after you've asked the question."

Derrick stopped a few feet from Eryna, body heat radiating off him. His eyes narrowed, his lips quirked to the side, and a dimple cratered one cheek. He looked her up and down, but it wasn't uncomfortable. It was a look of curiosity, fascination.

"That doesn't seem fair," he criticized.

"It is to them."

"You certainly know a lot about crows."

Before Eryna replied, she paused, knowing she must tread carefully.

"My family taught me about a lot of things," she said.

"Do you have a big family?"

Eryna silently nodded. She turned and walked beneath the wisteria to keep from lingering on the subject. Derrick matched her pace easily.

"Do you miss them?" he pressed.

That rippling pain once again bubbled up and pressure built behind her eyes, but she swallowed the sorrow. She couldn't cry in front of Derrick, and definitely not while wearing all the cosmetics Jenin had put on her. Jenin would kill her for that alone.

"Very much," Eryna replied.

"I'm sure they miss you as well," he said. Then he paused and looked at her. "I just realized I don't know where you're from."

Eryna silently thanked Jenin for having already fabricated that lie.

"Meedra."

Derrick's brows rose. "Interesting. I've never met anyone from Meedra. It's tiny, isn't it? What's it like to live there?"

Eryna couldn't answer that. He was asking too many questions. She had to shift the focus off her.

"Nothing like Aponyx," she said. Then she glanced around the terrace garden. "This is magnificent. Did your father build this?"

"No." The word flew out of his mouth quickly. He took a breath. "It was my mother's creation. She always said Aponyx was too unnatural for her. She built this garden as an escape."

He silently took in the terrace. As he did, Eryna swore his eyes swam with distant memories, and she wished she could follow him there if only to see the happiness this beautiful nature had once inspired. He cleared his throat and his gaze dropped.

"I'm sorry about this morning. I didn't mean to get so passionate. I could tell you were uncomfortable. You're not from here so it's probably confusing, but my cousin was murdered a few days ago by the neighboring Dryads and, well...I haven't really been in a great place."

He looked over Eryna's shoulder at the wisteria, then at the ground again, and everywhere except Eryna. It was clear he was being earnest. She gave his arm a gentle squeeze and he looked at her with apologetic eyes.

"I understand more than you know," she said.

Just then, his pocket buzzed. He fished out his phone and pressed it to his ear. "Yeah?" He paused, listening to the voice. "Yeah, she's with me. We'll be right there."

He put his phone away, smiled, and offered Eryna his arm.

"My sister would like us to 'hurry up or else you'll be walking the whole way there like peasants,'" he said, twisting his voice into a mockery of Jenin's. It was an impressive impression. Eryna chuckled and took his arm, thankful for the support as she was still acclimating to the heels.

As they entered the foyer, Eryna spotted a very impatient but very exquisite Jenin. Her black, floor length dress was simple and elegant with an edgy flare. The strapless bodice cut a straight line across her chest, and a slit exposed her right leg all the way to her hip. She donned tiny golden earrings and soft black gloves up to her elbows. Her hair was glossy and straight down to her mid-back, and her eyes were smoked out with black kohl and thick lashes that enhanced their green-brown color. It also intensified her glare.

"Good evening, Jenin. I'd say you look lovely, but you'd have to take off your lizard skin first," Derrick greeted, snickering.

"When I said forty-five minutes, I meant forty-five minutes," she replied in her own greeting.

"My fault," Derrick replied in place of Eryna. "I caught her on her way and wanted to show her Mom's garden."

Jenin stiffened, her jaw tight and arms crossed, like she was caught between exploding or smacking someone. Surprisingly, she did neither.

"Well, now we're late."

"If we leave now, we'll still be half an hour early," Derrick countered. Jenin tapped her foot impatiently.

"Yes, well, you know how I like to be early. Whoever said it was fashionable to be late clearly wasn't a firstborn daughter."

Derrick rolled his eyes but smiled. Jenin turned her full attention on Eryna, and Eryna immediately wanted to shrivel up. Being caught under Jenin's scrutinizing gaze was like being dissected while awake.

But then Jenin smiled. It was a poor excuse of a smile, her lips tight and barely lifted at the corners, but a smile, nonetheless. She waved a vague hand in Eryna's direction.

"I did good. I'm happy with this."

Then she walked out the door. Derrick and Eryna followed, but before they crossed the entryway, he pulled her aside.

"I'm sure you'll hear this a lot tonight, but I want to be the first to tell you. You look beautiful," he said, then took up her arm again. As they passed a mirror, Eryna had a single moment to study herself.

The black floor length dress Jenin had picked for her was quite flattering. The top was modest and long-sleeved on the left, and rather exposing on the right, leaving her arm bare and a half circle cut out of the torso. Like Jenin's dress, the skirt had a slit that flashed Eryna's leg and sparkly black heels each time she walked. Her simple gold earrings looked like falling leaves in autumn, and her sleek ponytail exposed her long, elegant neck.

But what caught Eryna off guard, what Jenin had done best, was that instead of dulling her emerald eyes, she'd enhanced them. Glittering light pink eyeshadow and thick black lash paint made her eyes sparkle like true gems. She worried for a moment her eyes would give her away, but she looked at herself again and realized there was no possible way anyone would know what she was.

When humans thought of Dryads, they thought of wild tree-women romping around the forest scandalously dressed in scraps of florals and greenery. With the tonic, this make up, these clothes and accessories, she saw the simple illusion for what it truly was.

She didn't just look beautiful and human.

She *was* human.

Chapter Fourteen

Even a century of life couldn't have prepared Eryna for Blackwell Manor.

Jenin and Derrick had mentioned it was in The Terraces, the wealthiest neighborhood of Aponyx. While Eryna had no context for the term "neighborhood," she figured it meant the dwellings closely neighbored one another. But the structures they passed were nowhere near each other, and she'd hardly call Blackwell Manor a dwelling.

It was a fortress.

The luxurious black vehicle in which they rode came to a stop at the gaping mouth of a long brick walkway overflowing with attendees in their nicest dresses and what Jenin called "suits." At the end of it, the manor stood tall and proud against the darkened evening sky, all black brick and straight edges and thick pillars and sharp, yet delicately carved eaves, stacked five windows high and as wide as Eryna could see. She was sure it stopped somewhere, but from where she sat, the manor was an endless horizon.

Glass and steel towers were one kind of wonder, but they were sleek and new. Blackwell Manor looked aged and haunted and lovingly cared for, as if the original owners had built it hundreds of years ago and refused to die so they could keep it exactly as it was. She needed to see more. Eryna reached for the car handle, but Jenin batted her hand away.

"Never get your own door. Someone else will do it. It makes for a better entrance," she murmured, plucking a piece of fuzz from her glove. Derrick exited the front seat and opened Eryna's door. He offered her a hand, and she took it, his skin warm and soft against hers. He eased her out onto the brick path. Jenin cleared her throat.

"Hello?" she called to her brother, irritated. He glared at her. Eryna dropped Derrick's hand and walked a few steps toward the magnificent manor, light radiating from each of its bay windows. Sharp heels clacked behind her and stopped at her side.

"No welcome orchestra this year? Disappointing," Jenin commented. Then she threaded her arm through Eryna's and nodded at her brother. "Go ahead, Derrick. We have women things to discuss."

Derrick scowled at his sister but didn't protest, adjusting his cuffs as he joined the crowd on the brick path. Jenin and Eryna followed at a slowed pace. Jenin tilted her head toward Eryna.

"Don't forget what I said. Stay away from Derrick," she warned. Eryna rolled her eyes. She wanted to tell Jenin she had no interest in being around Derrick, but because she knew she'd get a reaction, she prodded a little.

"I'm curious," Eryna said. "What is it about me you find so threatening? Worried I'll slit his throat in the night like my sisters did your cousin?"

Jenin tensed at Eryna's side but shielded it with a single exasperated laugh.

"Don't forget who has the upper hand." Jenin exaggeratedly sighed and patted Eryna's arm like she was scolding a child. "As annoying as it is, I'm looking out for *you*, not him. I mean it when I say he'll kill you if he knows what you are. And while I'd wear your blood proudly, I don't need it staining my freshly manicured nails. Besides, Brody would be pissed."

Surprisingly, Eryna believed it. She got the impression Jenin felt herself above lying.

"Then I'll try my best to stay away. I can't promise he'll do the same."

"Well, you have to. At least until he tires of your novelty. Derrick is like a puppy, and you're a shiny new toy. Your shine will wear off, and he'll move on to the next. It's what all men do."

Eryna narrowed her eyes, ready to ask if men were truly so bad as Jenin made them seem, when they caught up to Derrick and stepped into the black and white tiled entry of the Manor. Her mouth fell open and air left her lungs in such a rush, nothing remained but a small gasp. It was the most impressive thing she'd ever seen.

As they crossed the threshold, the Manor domed high overhead. The entryway was lined with five stories of creamy marble balconies, works of art painted on the walls and ceiling, and larger than life candelabras resembling goddesses and nymphs. At the center of it all was a large staircase that rose two stories high.

Eryna craned her neck in all directions looking for Brody, but it was impossible to see in this sea of black and white, at least five hundred bodies deep.

Men dressed in fine white suits carried trays of tiny food and heavily poured glasses of wine and bubbling liquid. Eryna observed as guests plucked glasses and food from the trays, hardly acknowledging the people carrying them, then deposited their waste on the next passing tray. The chatter was loud, the energy vivacious, and elegant music echoed off the cavernous hall, wrapping around Eryna like a hot breeze at the peak of summer.

But what intrigued her most of all was the people. Though she'd seen her fair share of humans while shopping, there was a clear difference between the average human and these attendees. Everyone wore a fitted black suit or opulent black dress doused in finery. Thick strands of pearls and brilliant diamonds hung from necks and adorned fingers. Gold watches and silver links flashed at wrists. And everyone carried a purse.

"Is it common for men to carry purses, too?" Eryna asked Jenin, who was scooping two glasses of the bubbly drink from a tray. She didn't offer either to Eryna. Instead, she downed one in a matter of seconds and discarded the empty glass, then clutched the other one tight and scanned the crowd with shifty eyes, like a rabbit hiding from a fox.

"Yikes, Neens. Slow down." Derrick chuckled.

"*You* slow down," she replied, side-eyeing her brother. He grabbed his own pair of bubbling glasses. He offered Eryna one. She gave him a grateful smile and took it. He raised his in a salute. She mimicked him and they both drank.

Eryna's lips and tongue were immediately greeted by tiny fizzing bubbles. The drink was strange and refreshing and tasted like a dry wine. As she swallowed, it bubbled up to the inside of her nostrils. She shook her head, the sensation startling.

Derrick laughed.

"Never had sparkling wine before?" he asked, his voice bright and humored. Eryna shook her head and licked the lingering taste from her lips. She went back for a second sip, knowing what to expect this time.

"It's lovely," she said. Derrick nodded in agreement.

"It is but be careful how much you drink. Those bubbles take it straight to the head."

"Noted," Eryna replied before another sip.

"And no, it's not common for men to carry purses," Derrick said, eyeing the crowd. "But during the Hunt, it's how people store the keys they collect. The first night of the Hunt is exclusively a hunt for keys. People have an hour to collect as many as possible before the party begins, and undiscovered keys are removed. No doors will be opened until night two."

Eryna looked down and realized both Derrick and Jenin lacked purses of their own.

"Do you two not participate?"

"Absolutely not," Jenin said. "Like I said this morning, there is no prize. No one has ever won. It's pointless playing."

"There is too, a prize," Derick challenged, and Eryna caught a small flicker of hope in his eyes. It faded quick. "But we're Brody's best friends. It would look rigged if we won. Besides, we have more than enough. We don't need endless riches and eternal life."

"Everyone here has more than enough," Jenin grumbled.

"Well, if it isn't the Ashford misfits." A sharp female voice said from behind Eryna. Jenin rolled her eyes and Derrick plastered a forced smile to his face.

"Hi, Sierra," they said in unison. Eryna turned to see the person who caused such a reaction. The girl was almost as tall as Eryna, with thick dark hair that cascaded around her face in waves past her chest. The straps of her black dress crossed over her breastbone in an X and hugged her curvy body tight all the way down to her satin black heels. Her dark brown eyes and soft pink lips popped against her warm brown skin. She looked Eryna up and down in a blatant display of disgust and raised her thick brows.

"And you are...?" she drawled.

"Eryna Thorne. Visiting from the Mainland," Eryna replied. Assuming it was the official human form of introduction, she extended her hand like Brody and Damian had done to her. Sierra glanced down at her hand and squinted.

"Ew," was all she said. Eryna lowered her hand, more than a bit embarrassed. She looked at Derrick, who gave her an encouraging smile and mouthed *don't worry about it.*

"Seriously, Sierra, could you be more of a bitch?" Jenin asked, then drained her sparkling wine down to the dregs.

"Seriously, Jenin, could you be more of a lush?" Sierra retorted. Then she turned her attention on Derrick. Her scowl faded, she flashed beautifully straight white teeth, and her brown eyes sparkled. "I'm having an after party tonight. You should come. We have plenty of space if you need to stay the night."

Jenin rolled her eyes, and Derrick forced another smile and shoved his hand in his pocket.

"Thanks for the invite, Sierra, but Jenin and I are sticking with Eryna tonight. She's our guest for the summer. It'd be rude of me to ditch her."

Sierra's face fell as she glanced at Eryna again, this time less disgusted, more disdainful. Eryna smiled. She couldn't help it. Sierra looked at Derrick again and schooled her face into a sultry gaze.

"Well, if you suddenly realize you're in the mood for better company, we're down the street. I guess you two could come, too," she said, glancing at Jenin and Eryna. "By the way, Jenin, my cousin Heston is back in town tonight. He said he'd like to see you."

"Tell him I'd rather eat a bowl of glass, but thanks," she said, grabbing a third sparkling wine.

Sierra rolled her eyes and turned back to Derrick. She smoothed his collar and brushed his neck with her thumb.

"You look good."

Then she left and melted into the crowd.

"Ugh. She's so annoying," Jenin groaned.

"Who is she?" Eryna asked, her eyes lingering on the spot where Sierra had grazed Derrick's neck. She didn't realize she was staring until he spoke.

"Sierra Lundal. Her father, Jerry, is Mr. Blackwell's lead scientist at Blackwell Technologies. Our three fathers are best friends. Because of that, we're all expected to be as well."

"She's a royal pain in the ass, is what she is. Literally," Jenin cut in. "Her father is a cousin of the royal family on the Mainland, making her a marchioness or whatever."

"If her father is royal, then why is he Mr. Blackwell's scientist?" Eryna asked. She didn't know much about the human royal family, but she knew enough to find it odd he wasn't getting special treatment in

Aponyx. Jenin and Derrick exchanged sideways glances, something that looked more like a knee-jerk reaction than intentional.

"Aponyx operates a little differently than the Mainland," Derrick said. "We're still under the jurisdiction of the royal family, but Aponyx is the land of opportunity. Jerry may have royal blood, but he chose to take the job as the head scientist of Blackwell Technologies and desires to be treated like a scientist, not a royal. And we respect it. Aponyx values hard work and brilliance."

"And greed and power," Jenin said under her breath before taking a sip of wine.

"Besides," Derrick continued, "Blackwell Tech has been around Aponyx for a long time. Mr. Blackwell is a bit more...seasoned in Aponyx society."

"What does that mean—"

"Ladies, gentlemen. Welcome to the tenth annual Blackwell Hunt." A loud, bewitching voice boomed over the crowd. Every head turned toward the stairs, and every eye fell on a tall, handsome dark-haired man in a sharp black suit. He posed on the landing with his arms spread wide, like he was ready to perform on this elevated stage. The people burst into raucous applause. The man eyed the crowd as if waiting for something, as if he was unsatisfied with a thousand hands clapping for him.

He waited.

And waited.

The applause escalated. Attendees yelped and shouted and hollered with excitement. The man finally smiled, wide and proud and hungry. Like a wolf. The resemblance was uncanny.

This had to be Mr. Blackwell.

It was like staring into Brody's future, though not as far as Eryna would've imagined. Mr. Blackwell was aged but not much, his skin still healthy and taught against his high cheeks, and his hair had very little gray.

He hardly looked like a dying man.

He bowed, straightened, and threw a hand to his chest.

"Thank you. Really, I don't deserve it." He waved off the crowd, even blushed a little. Eryna tried not to roll her eyes, his pretense so painfully obvious. But clearly everyone ate it up. They idolized him, the son of the son of the son of the man who built Aponyx.

Mr. Blackwell lifted a hand and the crowd hushed.

"As you know, the Hunt is my heart. My favorite project I've ever worked on, and it has been an absolute honor to have hosted you these last nine years. But I must make an announcement. This year, I am stepping down."

Attendees erupted with gasps and exclamations, curses and cries. The people were absolutely beside themselves.

"No!"

"How could this happen?"

"We look forward to the Hunt all year."

"We come all the way from Kendrea for this!"

Mr. Blackwell raised a hand, but this time it took more than a minute for the crowd to settle, though settle they did.

"Please. I'm not finished. I am stepping down, because I'm passing the Hunt baton to a new host, one I'm certain you will welcome with open arms. This year's host and the official Hunt host for the foreseeable future is none other than my pride and joy, my baby boy— and yet, somehow he's a man now—Brody."

Brody appeared next to his beaming father. Chest puffed, smile wide, he towered high and proud over the attendees.

And they loved him. Gaia, did they love him.

Brody raised his hand, and Eryna swore the ground shook with the force of applause. Young women dissolved into tears, screaming at the top of their lungs like they were in the presence of Apollo in his prime. Eryna couldn't help but throw a startled look toward Jenin, who returned it with a head shake and an eye roll.

Brody smiled, scanned the crowd, and winked at a young woman nearby. The poor thing fainted. In that moment Eryna finally understood who and what he was to this city, these humans. He wasn't just some boy stuck in a metal object or caught in a trap. He wasn't just some human Eryna saved. His father was king of this city, and he was their crowned prince. He was the bright and shining future of Aponyx.

"Thank you, everyone. Needless to say, I feel very welcomed as the new host," Brody said, and it took him two full minutes to rein in the screams of the crowd, specifically the young women. He chuckled, and a few sighs flitted across room. "This year, the prize for the Hunt is unlike anything you've ever seen before. It has the power to make your dreams come true. It can grant you true love. It can make you filthy, filthy rich…as if anyone here needs more of that. It is priceless, timeless, and is all yours if you find the right key and the right door."

Eryna suddenly found herself absorbed in what he was offering. She wanted her dreams to come true, her dreams of reviving her sisters and restoring Euryalea. She wanted true love, the kind that existed between sisters who knew each other better than anyone. And she wanted to be filthy rich, rich in happiness, rich in the comforts of home, rich in an abundant realm. Maybe she didn't have to trick the Hearts out of Brody at all. Maybe she could play along with the Hunt, and maybe she could actually win.

A light hand touched her arm and she turned to find Jenin at her shoulder. Eryna's thoughts must have been carved into her face.

"They're empty words, Eryna," Jenin whispered. "They say shit like this every year to drum up the crowd. There is no prize. Only promises the Blackwells can't keep. Don't get caught up in it. You're smarter than that."

Had the wine gone to Jenin's head and suddenly made her soft? Or maybe it was some trick to keep Eryna from playing the game and winning the prize.

That must be it.

Jenin didn't care about her. She hated her and all nymph-kind.

She'd said so several times since Brody dropped Eryna with her two days ago. There had to be something for Eryna in that prize, or at the very least, Eryna could use the Hunt to search the Manor for the Hearts.

It was decided, then. Eryna would play.

"Ladies and gentlemen of Aponyx, it is time for the tenth annual Hunt to begin in three..."

Brody started the count. The crowd shuffled, tensed, and attendees readied their bags.

"Two..."

Eryna eyed the closest corridor and pulled on all her Dryad grace to weave and slink past the crowd, situating herself right at its archway. She thought she heard Jenin call out her name, but it was so faint, she decided she'd imagined it.

"One. Let the Hunt begin!"

Chapter Fifteen

If Eryna weren't preternaturally light-footed, she would've drowned in the tsunami of attendees that flooded the corridors. As it was, she was already halfway down the hall with some much needed space between her and them. The only issue was that she had no idea what to do. Would these keys be out in the open? Were they hidden? Did they blend in with the surroundings?

While Eryna's excitement had fueled her, she realized she hadn't thought this plan through.

"There, try the planter," a voice behind her said. Derrick.

Eryna stopped at a small table pressed against the wall. Sitting atop it was a large pot filled with an expansive pothos, its vines spilling over the side of the table. Eryna felt around in the dirt, apologizing for the intrusion, and found nothing.

"Under it," Derrick said, gingerly peaking behind a large painting. Eryna lifted the planter and there sat a small brown key. Her heart leapt to her throat.

And then it was gone.

"Thanks!" A young boy called, snatching the key as he sprinted past.

"Hey!" Eryna set after him, but Derrick stopped her.

"Forget him. There are plenty more. Let's go this way."

Derrick turned down the hall and felt around the papered walls. At least twenty other participants were doing the same. Eryna followed suit, the juniper green paper silky smooth to the touch. She looked at Derrick.

"I thought you don't play," she remarked.

"I don't. But seeing as you decided to, I figured you'd want an assistant. You're fast, by the way. I had to sprint to keep up with you." He smiled and ran his fingers through his hair, sweat beading at his hairline.

"Thanks," she said, her face toward the wall so he wouldn't see her blush. She reached a red velvet curtain and plunged into its folds. Skin met metal.

She grabbed the object and pulled her hand back. In her palm sat a thick pewter key, its neck long and solid, its head adorned with a deep red velvet bow and golden tassel. She beamed at Derrick.

"Nice." He smiled back, then grabbed her purse and held it open. Eryna popped the key inside.

"That way." She pointed toward a fork at the end of the hall. As they moved, Eryna glimpsed the action in adjacent corridors. Players stormed down the halls in mobs. Couples ran hand-in-hand. Solo participants sprinted and muscled past each other. People swiped keys, spilled plants, and knocked over what looked to be priceless artifacts. There was shouting, screaming, cackling, and lively chatter. The air was a symphony of loud crashes, cheers, and the constant shattering of glass.

It was utter chaos.

They turned the corner and came upon a hall of marble statues toppled over and crumbled to bits. Eryna saw a short round woman with brown hair quickly fleeing the scene and guessed she was the culprit.

"This happens *every* year?" Eryna asked, unable to shield her disbelief. Derrick nodded, laughed, and kicked a chunk of marble with the toe of his shiny black shoe.

"It does. Don't worry, they're all props. The Blackwells are on the board of a movie studio, and they provide the decor for the Hunt. The true artifacts are in storage."

"That's good," Eryna said. She wondered what a "prop" and "movie studio" were and tucked those words away to ask Jenin later. As they picked their way around the crumbled marble, Eryna scanned the ground. Her eyes fell on a piece of marble so small it could have easily been dismissed as debris. She bent down to examine it, and pride rippled through her.

A marble key.

She plucked it off the ground and put it in her purse.

"So," Eryna started as they moved into a large stretch of balconies that overlooked the main entrance. "How far apart are you and Jenin? You seem similar in age."

If she was going to spend this time with Derrick, she might as well use him to learn more about Jenin and Brody and Blackwell Manor. The more she knew, the more it might help her locate the Hearts.

"Only about a year and a half apart. She acts like she's ten years older, though. Our mom wanted us to be close in age so that we always had someone to have our back," he said, skimming his fingers beneath a table's edge. Eryna drug her fingers across the bars of a balcony hoping a key might fall out.

"You're close, then?" she asked. He shrugged.

"As close as any siblings, I guess. We used to be a lot closer, but when our mom died, Jenin sort of stepped into that role. It put some distance between us." He spoke the words nonchalantly, but Eryna felt the undercurrent of heartache.

Not paying attention to her feet, she tripped over the corner of a rug, lifting the edge. A simple brass key sat beneath it. She picked it up and put it in her purse. When she looked up, Derrick was smiling at her.

"You're good at this," he said, dimples pressed deep into his cheeks. Heat flushed up the back of her neck and she glanced at the floor.

"I'd hardly call tripping a skill," she said. He chuckled, then held out his arm to steady Eryna as they descended the grand staircase.

"Would you say Brody is your best friend?" she asked.

"Tyler was my best friend," he answered. Eryna swallowed.

"Oh. I'm sorry."

"Don't be," he said. But he had no idea how sorry she really should be.

They checked the candelabras and shattered glass vases on the first landing, the ornate floral arrangements now trampled to mulch.

"I would consider Brody my next closest friend," Derrick continued. "Though we're not exactly on the best terms right now and..." Derrick's voice trailed off and he waved a dismissive hand. "Doesn't matter. He's still my best friend. But Tyler was family. We understood each other, you know?"

Eryna nodded.

"I do."

They were back in the entryway, the room nearly empty compared to half an hour ago.

"Is it just Brody and his father living here?" she asked. Derrick nodded.

"Yeah. His parents didn't want more kids, and his mom died around the same time ours did. Only a few months apart."

"Hm," Eryna remarked, glancing around the room. This empty, the manor seemed impossibly large. Living in such a place with only one other person was unfathomable. "Sounds lonely."

"He fares just fine. He's hardly ever alone if you know what I mean." Derrick laughed and raised his brows at Eryna. From the way young women had screamed and cried earlier, Eryna picked up on Derrick's meaning. She laughed but couldn't help the strange jealousy that tightened around her like a vine. She had to change the subject.

"What about through there?" She pointed to an open archway.

They entered a ballroom where honeyed music was being plucked on strings. The room was a sea of moving bodies, couples twirling, and groups chatting in corners.

"This is where the party is. Nobody comes here unless they're not participating or the Hunt is over," Derrick remarked, scanning the crowd. Eryna looked at him and smiled.

"What better place to hide keys?"

His brows rose, his mouth turned down in thought.

"I like the way you think, Eryna Thorne," he said.

They scoured every nook and cranny, table, and chair in the room. Eryna came upon an elaborate gold mirror and as she was about to move on, she spotted the key. It was thick and gold, the ornate head an artwork of curls and loops. She pinched its neck with two fingers and gently pried it from the frame. She turned to show Derrick, and at the same time, he held up a white and red bejeweled key he'd found. They smiled at each other.

He held up a flat palm, and Eryna, uncertain what to do, slapped her palm against his, hoping that was right. He smiled wide and flicked the key toward her. She snatched it out of the air and dropped both keys into her purse. Eryna counted them.

"Five keys. That feels like enough, right?" she asked. Derrick glanced into her purse. He was so close she could feel his warm breath on her chest like soft feathers against her skin. Their eyes met, and a riot of flapping wings tickled her stomach.

"Who's to say? Some could open doors, one could be the prize key, or none could open anything at all. It's what keeps people coming back."

"What is?" she asked. He stepped closer, scanning her face.

"Hope."

He leaned in, and Eryna fought the desire to let him. She sidestepped, and as she did, her hip knocked into a table, sending a potted plant crashing to the ground. They looked down. A vibrant green key sat in the soil, looking as if it'd been cut from a leaf. Derrick examined it.

"Pretty," he remarked, then looked at Eryna. "Almost the same color as your eyes." He held it out by its head. Eryna reached for it, and as her fingers closed around the key, he gently grasped her hand.

"Dance with me?" he asked.

Of course. The response was on the tip of her tongue, but she stopped herself. Jenin would kill her. But she loved dancing, and she wanted to know how Derrick moved, how he felt the rhythm, how he might hold her—

"Thorne, there you are!" A loud voice exclaimed. She and Derrick turned to see Brody walking toward them, his wolfish grin playing at his lips. He eyed the green key in Eryna's hand.

"Oh good, you're playing. I was hoping you would. Sorry, I've been a terrible host. I was looking for you but kept getting stuck in conversations and whatnot." He waved a passive hand. Then he scanned her and stopped, eyes wide. The knot at his throat bobbed.

"Gods, you look…" he smiled, less wolf and more doe. Soft. Bashful. "You look amazing."

"Thank you," she replied.

Just then, he startled at some internal thought and slipped his hand into his breast pocket and pulled out a shiny black key. The metal work on the head formed an ornate "B," and a small black bead was clasped around its neck.

"I like my favorite participants to get a head start. It's not the prize key, but it will give you an advantage." Brody smiled. He held her gaze a moment longer.

"Brody, son! I need to you to meet someone," Mr. Blackwell's voice echoed from halfway across the room. Brody's smile fell.

"Duty calls," he said. "Find me before you leave."

Brody made to walk past Eryna but stopped at her side. He turned toward her, his lips hovering a hair's breadth from her ear.

"Don't let the show from earlier fool you. There's only one

person I'd like to spend my night with if I could," he murmured. She looked at him, his eyes warm yet serious. He briefly glanced at her lips. "You really do look breathtaking tonight."

As he slipped away, Eryna felt the cool press of metal in her hand. She studied the black key, then put it in her purse. When she looked up, she realized Derrick had slipped away at some point during that conversation. In his place stood a wobbly Jenin.

"I tooooldd you not to play, you demonnnn," she scolded, but it was impossible to take her seriously. Eryna knew the feeling from nights she drank too much berry wine. Eryna linked her arm with Jenin's and started toward the large table of food.

"Come on," she said. "Let's get some bread in you."

As they crossed the room, Eryna slyly pulled the keys from her purse one by one and stuffed them into her cleavage. She dropped the purse on a passing table and made a note to remember where it was.

No one knew when the next Hunt would be, and Eryna was too impatient. Derrick had said no doors would be opened until then. That didn't mean doors *couldn't* be opened before.

Because if Eryna just so happened to forget her purse and not realize it until she got back to the Ashford's, she would have to go back for it, and right away. She couldn't risk losing her keys. And by that time, everyone would surely be gone. She would be alone with Blackwell Manor.

Chapter Sixteen

"Let's get you home," Derrick said as he and Eryna slid a limp Jenin into the back seat of the car.

"Buh ay don wanna go hoommmee," she slurred, an intoxicated smile pulling at her lips. After the Hunt finished, the ballroom spun into a flurry of chaos. The bodies packed in tight, swaying and twirling to the deafening music and rising chatter. Eryna was tempted more than once to find Derrick for that dance, but Jenin kept finding wine, and Eryna made it her personal mission to keep her close.

As the ballroom clock chimed two in the morning and she found Jenin carrying someone's fur coat and calling it her "new pet," Eryna knew it was time to go. She'd spotted Derrick across the room, cornered by Sierra. It took two seconds to convince him it was time to leave.

Eryna and Derrick situated Jenin across their laps like a heavy, inebriated blanket.

"Home, please," Derrick said to the driver.

Eryna settled her head against the seat and gazed out the window at the passing lights in the night. A rare kind of silence settled around them, thick and peaceful. It was the kind of silence that felt like one large, infinite inhale, and was the most at ease Eryna had felt in days.

As they crossed from the Terraces to the Central Quarter, Derrick turned to Eryna.

"She isn't usually like this, you know," he whispered, as if speaking any louder would burst their sacred bubble of quiet. Eryna shrugged.

"Everyone overdoes it sometimes," she whispered back.

Derrick's face soured briefly, but he shuttered it and gnawed his cheek.

"It wasn't just tonight. It's happened more frequently the last couple months."

"Oh," she replied, but something in Eryna wanted to know more, if only because, with the way Derrick eyed her expectantly, it seemed like he wanted to say more.

"What changed?" she asked.

Derrick shook his head.

"At first I thought it was a new habit she picked up at university this year, but from everyone I've talked to, she wasn't like this."

"Are you worried about her?"

Derrick ground his jaw, like he was swirling words around in his mouth before deciding whether or not to say them. He sighed.

"I'll always worry about her. The same way she'll always worry about me. We're blood."

Eryna smiled softly, her heart constricting in her chest as Dera came to mind, Oihane, the rest of her sisters.

Derrick turned toward the window and once again slipped under the blanket of silence. Eryna eyed him, mentally tracing the strong muscles of his neck, the sharp cut of his jaw, the soft curve of his ears. She ran her gaze down the dips and edges of his profile, slowing down as he ever so slightly licked his lower lip, then chewed it.

"I was going to find you for that dance, but I didn't want to leave your sister," she said, surprised by her words. She had no intention of speaking that thought aloud.

Before he could reply, Jenin stirred on their laps.

"Mmmm cookies sound nice," she mumbled. Eryna and Derrick looked at each other and broke into stifled laughter. He smiled and shook his head.

"I'm glad you stayed with her. I should have, but I was busy avoiding Sierra." Then he held out his hand the same way Brody and Damian had when they'd first greeted Eryna.

"Next Hunt, then?" he asked, not so much a question as it was an offer. Maybe this gesture was more than just a greeting? An agreement? Hoping she was right, Eryna shook his hand like she'd done before.

"Next Hunt," she said, smiling. Eryna hadn't realized they were still holding hands until the car stopped in front of the Ashford's tower, or what she'd overheard someone call "The Spire."

Derrick opened the door and scooped Jenin into his arms. Eryna shook off the lingering heat from Derrick's hand and straightened.

It was time.

She made a show of searching the floor, the seats, and murmured, "Oh no."

Derrick looked at her.

"Forget something?" he asked.

"My purse. I can't find my purse!" Eryna said, feigning exasperation.

"We can get it tomorrow. I'm sure it's somewhere safe—"

"My keys are in it," she cut Derrick off. She needed to get out of there before he made her wait until tomorrow, or worse, decided to come with her. "I can't lose those keys. I don't want anyone to steal them. If they haven't been stolen already. I'll be right back."

Eryna shut the car door just as Derrick said something, but whatever it was, it would have to wait.

"Back to Blackwell Manor, please," she said to the driver. He nodded, but he didn't remain silent this drive.

"Just so you know, miss, the Manor closes its doors at three. They refuse to let people back in once the party is over."

Eryna ground her teeth and narrowed her eyes, but she figured this man was simply being courteous. It was probably what Derrick was attempting to tell her before she shut the door in his face.

"I'll have to try," she said, and that was that. The driver remained silent the rest of the way to Blackwell Manor.

Chapter Seventeen

Eryna quickly tread the brick path back to the manor, determined to be in and out in less than fifteen minutes. She just needed time to get her bearings, to assess the situation while alone. The previously open and inviting front doors were now sealed tight. She jiggled the handles, but they didn't move. She knocked. No one answered.

"My name's Eryna Thorne. I'm a guest of Brody's. I forgot my purse and would like to get it, please," she said, knocking again. The doors cracked open and an older man peaked his head out.

"The Manor is closed," he said, and was about to shut the door in her face when she braced a palm against it. She was getting into Blackwell Manor however she could.

"Please. I'll be quick, I promise."

"I'm sorry, madam, but the rules of the Hunt are inflexible. No person is to be let back into the Manor besides the Blackwells and trusted friends unless it's a Hunt day. We don't want people having an unfair advantage."

"But I am a trusted friend. I'm Eryna Thorne, a guest of Brody's."

"Yes. You said that earlier. And yet, if you are a guest of the

Blackwell's, why are you not staying on the premises?"

Eryna tried her best not to scowl at him. It was a fair point. She could tell him to ask Brody, but she didn't want to be followed during her search, and Brody would certainly follow her.

"I'm staying with the Ashfords. Please, I just want my keys."

The man pursed his lips, assessing her for a moment. Then he straightened.

"I'm sorry," he said, the shut the door in finality.

Eryna groaned and just about kicked the door with her sparkly black heel but didn't want to hurt her toes. She started toward the car.

Curse that driver for being right, and curse that stupid doorman for not letting her in. Besides, Brody had given her a key specifically for an advantage. Eryna didn't buy that the Blackwells enforced the Hunt be played by the rules. She turned around and glanced at the Manor, its dark façade more imposing than welcoming now that it was empty and asleep.

There had to be another way in.

She scanned the walls and saw a thick vine that climbed up to the third-floor balcony on the east wing. It was her best bet. Her dress and heels would get destroyed. Jenin would surely kill her now.

She turned off the path and walked along a gravel trail that wove through bushes and birch trees and tall, tapered cypresses. It took her deeper into the grounds, and suddenly she realized she'd lost sight of the Manor. There was not a single light illuminating the path, nor could she see any distant lights from the Manor. She was in complete darkness and was completely lost.

It was no time to panic. She was raised in the wide-open woods, for Gaia's sake. Deep night in the woods was much scarier than this, with its natural predators and unpredictable paths. Every couple decades, the Thornewood decided to rearrange itself, and night was its favorite time to do so. But this was unfamiliar territory, in an unfamiliar world, and just as anxiety clutched Eryna's chest, she brushed against a fragrant orange tree. She grasped one of its branches.

"Point me toward the Manor, please," she whispered. Its blooms released fragrant citrus, and as Eryna inhaled, she felt a pull on her right.

That way, then, she thought.

Eryna followed the pull until she met another orange tree. She did the same, only this time, the pull was forward. Another orange tree sent her left, a fourth sent her left again, and a fifth sent her forward.

She still couldn't see the Manor. Eryna questioned the motives of the playful orange trees, and as she turned to find a more trustworthy cypress or oak, something *buzzed* at her chest. It was a similar vibration to the Tyler's phone, only she didn't have one of those on her. All she had were keys.

The keys.

She reached into her cleavage and checked each key for the sensation. She found the culprit and pulled out a key with thick ironwork in the shape of a "B."

It was the key Brody had given her. It ferociously hummed like a live electrical current ran through it. She marched forward, led by the mounding sensation until she arrived at a large hedge. Only, there was nowhere to go. It was a dead end.

Or maybe…

Eryna searched the hedge and noticed a small light at the base of it. Unsure if what she was about to do was silly or brilliant, Eryna shoved her arm into the hedge. Branches scraped her skin like the needled claws of a cat. She fumbled and searched and moved her hand until the key fit perfectly into a small hole. She turned the key, and it *clicked.* She retracted her arm and stuffed the key back in her cleavage. The hedge pulled away from the wall, attached to a thick metal door. It swung wide, revealing a dark tunnel. She stared down the gaping maw of the cave-like structure.

Eryna stepped inside, and the moment she did, the door shut behind her. The clack of her heels echoed off the damp walls, and a minute later, two pinholes of light appeared at the end of the tunnel. She sped her steps, and as she reached the light, she looked out the holes, which were covered in a thin gossamer. On the other side of the tunnel was the grand ballroom.

Relief coursed through her veins and her heart rate spiked. She pushed against the wall, and it gave way. She stepped into the darkened ballroom and as she closed the door, she saw that she'd come through the smiling portrait of a young woman. If Eryna hadn't known any better, she'd say her painted eyes looked normal. It was a perfect illusion.

The disaster that was the ballroom when she'd left an hour ago was now sleek and pristine. There were no banquet tables, no shattered glasses or spilled wine or piles of tossed food. The floors had been washed and waxed, all plants and decorations restored to their original states, and it smelled like fresh pine. Hades might work hard, but Gaia, does the Blackwell staff work harder. Then Eryna realized something.

"Oh, no," she muttered.

Everything had been cleaned and removed from the room.

Including her purse.

Maybe she could ask a staff member where it might be? She didn't exactly need the purse, she had all her keys, but if she returned without it, Derrick and Jenin would ask too many questions about how she had her keys but not her purse.

"Looking for this?" A voice asked from the open archway. She leapt out of her skin, her soul momentarily leaving her body. She turned to find a smiling Brody clutching her purse, leaning coolly against the wall. He was no longer in his suit, but a more relaxed cotton shirt and soft cotton pants that hugged tight at his ankles.

"Didn't want to lose my keys," she replied.

Brody opened the purse and glanced inside. His smile doubled.

"I don't see any keys in here."

Heat filled every inch of Eryna's cheeks, and she was grateful he couldn't see her blush in this darkness. He pushed off the wall and drew nearer. Eryna shrugged.

"Seems like I'm too late, then. Someone stole them."

Brody stopped two feet from her and smirked.

"Judging by the fact that you're in my house and all doors are locked and guarded, I doubt that. Without that key I gave you, it's impossible to get in here during the Hunt weeks."

Eryna ran through every lie she could think of.

I found an open window in the back.

I bribed one of the staff members to let me in.

My Dryad powers let me teleport.

Each caught in her throat because she knew he wouldn't buy them. Brody chuckled.

"Don't be embarrassed," he said. "We give that key out for a reason. In the ten-year history of the Hunt, you're only the second person to figure out how to use it. You're smart, Eryna." He held out her purse, and she took it.

"Thanks," she said. His gaze lingered on her. She could feel the heat of it rippling across her skin, her lips, her eyes. Then he turned and walked away, leaving her suddenly cold. He looked back at her.

"You coming?" he called.

She joined him at the base of the grand staircase where he stared toward the top—his elevated stage from earlier. Looking at it now, Eryna realized it wasn't a stage but a pedestal. One that both his father and the people of Aponyx had put him on. He turned to her.

"So, did you want to look around? Search for any doors? I'm happy to help, you know," he said. She did want to look around, but she wanted to look for the Hearts, and Brody couldn't help with that.

"I just came for the purse. Thank you, though."

"Hm." Brody stared at her for a moment, perplexed. Then he lifted a brow and smirked, drawing within a foot of her. "You know, this is the first time we've been alone since the Thornewood."

Eryna rolled her eyes. Maybe it was his mention of the last time she was home, and her sisters were alive, but something about his words struck deep, reminding her of who and what he was: a hunter that needed a chase.

"You're right," she said. "Between you destroying my home, kidnapping me, then abandoning me for two days, it seems we haven't gotten a moment alone. I think I'll be going now. Good night."

Before her confidence could slip, she walked toward the door.

"Wait, Eryna. Dammit." Quick steps pattered behind her. Brody reached her side in a matter of strides. "I'm sorry. I really am trying to make up for all that. I really do think you'll like it here. At least, I know I would like you to be here. All I was trying to say was that I'm sorry we haven't had more time alone. I'd like to get to know you better."

As they reached the door, Eryna stopped and looked at him, arms crossed. She narrowed her eyes and met his gaze.

"You have a very strange sense of logic, you know."

Brody gave a breathy laugh.

"Yeah, I've been told that before."

Then he reached up, and before Eryna could move from his grasp, his fingers pulled a stray leaf from her hair, brushing her temple and cheek as he did so. He stopped at the bottom of her chin and tilted her head up slightly. Their lips were inches apart. A chilled sensation ran through her, and for a moment she wanted to lean in.

But she didn't. She couldn't give in so easily. It was just a game to him, the way it was just a game to her. There was nothing real between them, and there never could be. Not when she had a realm to restore.

"I should get back to The Spire," she said. Brody nodded.

"I'll walk you out, then."

They crossed the brick path in silence, and just before they reached the car, he pulled out a bag. Within it, glass clinked against glass.

"I meant to give you this earlier, but you never found me before you left. It should be enough tonic to last a couple days. I'll try and swipe some more tomorrow."

She put the bag in her purse.

"Thanks," she replied. Brody opened the car door and helped

her inside. He held onto her hand.

"I thought having you stay with the Ashfords was a better idea than staying here, but I'm starting to get a little jealous. If you ever need a change of scenery, you're always welcome at Blackwell Manor."

Eryna tilted her head, deliberating, trying to play it cool. In reality, she was rejoicing inside. An open invitation to Blackwell Manor was exactly what she needed.

"I'll think about it," she replied.

Then he pressed a soft, lingering kiss to the back of her hand and shut the door.

"Get what you need?" The driver asked as he set off to The Spire.

"I did," she replied.

When she was certain he wasn't watching, she smiled to herself as she removed each of the keys from her cleavage and put them back in her purse.

She would have those Hearts in no time.

Chapter Eighteen

Left at the gray door.

Right at the painting of the night sky.

Right again at the...Athena statue? Isn't it supposed to be right here?

Eryna groaned, then backtracked to the painting. Maybe it was a left instead of a right?

When she'd arrived back at The Spire around three forty-five, a staff member waited for her in the foyer to show her to her new room. She'd tried as best she could to memorize the way, but she was so exhausted, she was barely lucid. When she opened the door, her eyes were on the bed one moment, her face in the soft cotton the next. It wasn't until the breakfast bell rang that she woke with a start and quickly changed out of her dress.

She would've slept through breakfast if she wasn't absolutely ravenous and needed to fuel up. Her plan was to eat, find a way to Blackwell Manor and spend the day searching. She was certain Brody would be off doing something else, and even if he wasn't, it was a big house. It couldn't be hard to escape his notice.

Finally, Eryna found the stairs that led to the breakfast room.

She expected Jenin and Derrick to be halfway through their

meals with how long it took her to get there, but so far it was just Derrick. He smiled at Eryna as she walked in, though his expression faltered. He chewed the inside of his cheek and stifled a laugh. Eryna tried not to think anything of it.

"Morning," he said brightly, tucking into a heap of eggs and sausage on his plate. "Get your keys?"

Eryna sat and added two of the fluffy circular cakes to her plate and drizzled them with maple syrup. She nodded.

"I did. I'm surprised no one took them."

"I'm surprised they let you in."

A moment later, a very disheveled Jenin graced them with her presence. Dressed in a thick gray cotton top with a hood and matching gray pants that dwarfed her petit frame, she silently trudged in and sat. Dark sunglasses covered her eyes. Derrick smiled.

"Good mor—"

"Don't," she cut him off, holding up a hand. He bit down on his lips, quelling a chuckle, as did Eryna. Jenin grabbed a plate and piled it with every item on the table. She took a large bite of eggs. "How bad was I last night?" she asked, looking at Derrick. He nodded at Eryna.

"Don't ask me. She was the one who babysat you all night."

Arms crossed, Jenin stared at Eryna. At least Eryna assumed she was staring. It was hard to tell through her sunglasses.

"What's wrong with your face?" Jenin asked, snickering. Derrick elbowed her. Eryna froze. She glanced at her reflection in her knife and gasped. Thick black smudges ringed her eyes, lipstick smeared up toward her cheek, and wrinkles from the cotton sheets were imprinted across the entire left side of her face.

"I look like a raccoon got into a patch of berries," she said, grabbing a cotton napkin and wiping her lips.

"Yeah, if a raccoon had poor grooming skills," Jenin said between giggles, unable to control herself. This time, Eryna couldn't help but laugh, and Derrick joined.

"What are we all laughing at?" Damian asked from the doorway. The laughter died immediately. All the air was sucked out of the room, replaced by a flash flood of tension.

"Father," Derrick and Jenin said in unison, their startled voices pitching higher. Derrick continued, "You don't usually join us on Sundays."

Damian strolled into the dining area.

"Can't I have breakfast with my family on any given day? Or must I stick to a schedule?" he asked. He bent down and kissed Jenin on the cheek, then mussed Derrick's hair. The two of them smiled politely, but from the rise of Jenin's shoulders and the clench of Derrick's jaw, they were clearly uncomfortable.

"Good morning, Eryna. Looks like you had a good night," Damian said, smirking as he filled his plate. "How was your first Hunt?"

Eryna briefly turned to hide her blush but refused to shy away from him as she spoke. He seemed like the type who enjoyed making people uncomfortable, and she wouldn't give that life.

"I did have a good night. I wasn't expecting it to be so grand," she said.

"If there's one thing the Blackwells do well, it's the Hunt. Find any keys?"

"Six. Derrick helped."

Damian bit into a crispy piece of buttered toast and smiled.

"That's my boy. Way to show some hospitality. And speaking of hospitality, I'd like to throw a little dinner party tonight in honor of you as our guest. I've already extended a few invites. The Lundals said they would love to come, and Brody as well, though unfortunately his father can't make it. Oh, and the Lundals' cousin, Heston Perry."

"Father, no," Jenin objected, slamming her hands on the table. Derrick stared at her, wide-eyed.

"Jenin, dear. He's staying with the Lundals for a couple weeks. It would be rude not to invite him."

"Then disinvite the whole family. Better yet, cancel the dinner party altogether. Eryna doesn't even want one. Right, Eryna?" Jenin turned to her and stared. Of course, Eryna didn't want a dinner party, she had plans of searching Blackwell Manor. Except she felt put on the spot, and words came out of her all mangled.

"It's a generous offer, but…well…I—"

"See? She's just too polite to say it," Jenin insisted.

"Jenin," Damian said her name hard and sharp, like he was trying to slice her in half. "Enough. What did I say about speaking for others? Besides, preparations are already in motion. It's done."

So much for my plans, Eryna scoffed in her head.

Jenin ground her teeth but said nothing. Damian finished his plate, stood, and looked down at her.

"The Perry boy's infatuated with you. The sooner you accept that, the better. I'm only thinking of your future, my sweet girl."

He kissed the top of her head, then glanced down at her plate. He patted her hair.

"Watch how much you serve yourself. People notice how much you eat."

Damian lightly touched Jenin's nose, and once he was out of sight, she angrily swatted her face with a sleeve, like trying to rub off her father's lingering touch.

Bile singed Eryna's throat and the hairs in her nose. Who was Damian to comment on how his daughter chose to fuel her body? Who she is to accept the advances of?

Ready to burst from the anger coursing through her body, Eryna tried to transmute it, to lessen the weight as it pressed hard on her chest. Anger was a crushing boulder, but humor was light as a feather. She dramatically cleared her throat.

"On second thought, maybe I shouldn't wash my face," Eryna said, signaling to her eyes. "I can dress as one of the Furies tonight and you can tell Sierra it's time to answer for her crimes."

Eryna smiled, hoping Jenin would bite, but Derrick bit first.

"What crimes should we say she's committed? Crimes of fashion? Crimes of being a nuisance to society?" He laughed.

"Which Fury comes for those who've committed the crime of being a spoiled brat?" Jenin cracked a smile. Then she stood, sighed, and walked toward the door. "Come on, Thorne. If we're having a dinner party tonight, we can't have you looking like you haunt the place."

Chapter Nineteen

Clack. Clack. Clack. Clack.

Eryna's heels tapped out her quickened heartbeat as she paced at the foot of her bed.

"Again," Jenin demanded from her spot atop the linen duvet, clutching a silk pillow.

"My name's Eryna Thorne, I'm from Meedra, the northwestern edge of the province of Noridas," Eryna replied.

"Don't say 'the province of Noridas.' Just say Noridas. Everyone knows it's a province."

"Right. Got it." Eryna nodded.

"And what is life in Meedra like?"

"Quiet. Cold. A small fishing town where it rains most of the year."

"And your parents?"

Eryna nervously ran her fingers along her dress. It was a simple silhouette, a single tube that fell around mid-calf and slipped perfectly over her curves, topped with grass-thin straps. The berry wine color was deepened with a top layer of thin, charcoal chiffon that ruched the entire length of the dress. It was so rich she could almost taste it. That was if she could taste anything besides the acrid bile from her nervous stomach.

"My father's Aaron, he's the captain of the ship Helios. My mother, Anissa...fishes hairless?"

Jenin covered her face with the pillow and collapsed backward.

"An heiress. She's a *fishing heiress*, Eryna. Gods."

Eryna pinched her brow.

"Gaia, I'll never get this right."

It was hopeless. She would die tonight, simple as that. They'd been practicing this backstory for hours and she still couldn't get it.

Jenin slid off the bed and replaced the pillow.

"Well, you have to. Your life literally depends on it. You have the advantage here. No one's been to Meedra, except for supposedly Brody when he 'met' you. He'll have to come up with that story on his own...since *someone* won't answer their phone!" Jenin yelled that last part at her phone as if Brody's face was plastered to it. "For now, you could say unicorns fart rainbows in Meedra and they might believe you, but you need to pick a story and *stick to it*. Memorize it. It's who you are here."

"I know, I know," Eryna grumbled. "If my mother is a fishing heiress, won't everyone wonder why they've never heard of her?"

Jenin waved a dismissive hand.

"There needs to be a good reason Brody invited you to Aponyx. You can't just be a common person from one of the smallest towns on the Mainland. You need to be worthy of a Blackwell's association. Besides, there are thousands of heirs and heiresses on the Mainland. Not even the royal family knows them all, which is good, seeing as we'll have to fool a member of it tonight."

Eryna paused. Her stomach lurched.

"What? Who?"

Jenin's expression soured.

"Heston Perry. He's a duke. His great-grandfather is King Elias Perry of the Mainland."

Eryna's jaw tightened so hard, her cheeks ached. She groaned.

"That's it, I'm not going tonight. I can't fool your human royalty. They're going to know, Jenin. This isn't going to work. I'm dead. I'm dead. I'm so dead."

"Look at me," Jenin said, clapping Eryna's shoulders. "You'll be fine. Heston is a narcissistic idiot. He doesn't listen when anyone speaks unless it has to do with him. Just get your story straight for my father and the Lundals, and if you feel yourself slipping, pretend to be sick and excuse yourself."

A small knock on the door sounded.

"Dinner, Miss Jenin," one of the staff members said. Eryna's pulse spiked, her entire body tensed. Jenin squeezed her shoulders again.

"You got this," she said.

The large double doors of the dining room came into view. Everyone must already be in there, Eryna guessed, for the hall was entirely empty except for one person.

Brody. He saw the girls and perked up. Against Eryna's wishes, her heart stuttered at the sight of his wolfish grin.

"Hey!" Brody greeted. "You guys ready—"

"Where have you been?!" Jenin seethed. "We've spent *hours*..." she paused, her gaze shifting about the hall. "...Hours discussing Eryna's life in Meedra and how you two 'met.'"

Jenin accentuated the last word with narrowed eyes. Brody's expression lit with delight.

"Have you? Good. I would have joined you, but I was busy getting more..." Brody's eyes shifted about like Jenin's. "...*product*. There's enough to last a month, maybe more. It should be in Eryna's room after dinner."

The tonic, Eryna thought, thanking Gaia. While her skin remained soft and human, she'd felt the effects of the last tonic wearing off earlier. She'd set out another bottle to take before dinner, right next to the door where she would see it and remember to...

Eryna's heart stopped.

She'd forgotten to take the tonic.

A light shove brought Eryna back to the present where Jenin finished filling Brody in on the backstory.

"Go. I'll be there in a minute," Jenin insisted.

"Wait, I need to go back to my room, I forgot to—" Eryna protested, but Jenin nudged her again.

"There's no time, you're already late and now you're ruining my entrance."

"But—"

"Go!"

"Don't worry, Thorne, I got you. Let's go," Brody said, guiding Eryna toward the double doors, his arm solid and steady against hers. She didn't realize her hands were trembling until Brody's warm fingers curled around hers.

"Hey," he said. Eryna glanced at him. His eyes were soft and reassuring, his smile kind. He gently squeezed her hand. "Just look at me if you need help. You're not alone in this. I'm here, okay?"

Eryna took a deep breath and nodded. She would get through this dinner. She had to. All she needed was to remember her backstory, convince royalty that she was human, and pray the tonic wouldn't wear off mid-dinner. Only then would she make it out of this night alive.

Chapter Twenty

The double doors opened. At once, six people stood and stared at Eryna. Her arm involuntarily tightened against Brody's. He returned it with a reassuring squeeze.

"Our guest of honor. Welcome," Damian greeted from one end of the table, his smile tacky as days old sap.

Eryna swallowed hard.

"Thank you," she replied. Damian signaled to Derrick, who smiled wide, dimples deep in his cheeks. His eyes briefly fell on her and Brody's linked arms, no more than a cursory glance. Still, a strange warmth stirred in Eryna, but her nerves prevented her from giving him more than a weak smile in return.

"You already know my son, Derrick. Have you met his friend Sierra Lundal?"

Eryna looked to Sierra, seated next to Derrick. As much as Eryna disliked her, she couldn't deny Sierra looked fantastic. Her glossy dark hair swam around her face in waves, and her light-yellow dress brought out the dark bronze in her skin. She was as gorgeous as any of Eryna's sisters if it weren't for her permanent expression set like she'd just smelled something foul.

"We've met," Eryna replied. Damian continued down the line.

"This is Jerry Lundal, our lead scientist at Blackwell Tech."

Jerry donned a well-fitted, maroon suit. He was tall with vaguely beige skin and muddied brown hair combed into a short coif. He looked equally as young as Damian and Mr. Blackwell, though his dark brown eyes were more tired and strained, their edges ever so slightly wrinkled.

"His wife, Parvati Lundal."

Parvati stood tall and straight, her spine like an iron rod. She wore a simple black dress with tight sleeves. Her dark hair was half up, and her dark bronze skin glowed. It was no guess where Sierra got her beauty.

Eryna made eye contact with Parvati and immediately regretted it. Her eyes were cold and hard as boulders that could crush her with a single stare. Eryna might've been the guest of honor, but the room revolved around Parvati.

"And finally, Heston Perry, Duke of Promar."

Like Jerry, Heston was tall and vaguely beige with muddied brown hair. He wore a white suit decorated in all manner of medals and ribbons. His smile appeared kind, but it immediately put Eryna off. Something about his gray-blue eyes sparkled with entitlement. The two seats at his sides were empty, one clearly meant for her.

Wonderful.

Eryna smiled at everyone as best she could.

"Lovely to meet you all." She turned to Damian and tried to stomach looking him in the eye. "Thank you for hosting. It's an honor to be your guest."

He signaled to the seat between Heston and Parvati. Eryna's stomach sank.

"Please, sit," he said.

Still frozen in the doorway, Eryna might not have moved if she hadn't been linked to Brody. He guided her to the seat, and as they arrived, Heston bowed so dramatically low, his head almost touched his knees.

"Please, allow me," he said, pulling out her chair. Brody released her arm and she sat. Heston eased the chair forward until her stomach squeezed against the table.

"Thank you," she said to Heston in a tight voice, then scooted the chair back. Eryna looked down.

Why were there so many utensils? And plates? And cups? Who needed this many items to eat a single meal?

Brody stopped behind the other seat next to Heston and Damian cleared his throat.

"Jenin is seated there," he said. Brody nodded and moved to the open chair next to Sierra. "Speaking of, where's my daughter? We're all quite hungry and can't wait all night for her to finish her hair."

On cue, the doors burst open. Jenin marched in, her steps commanding. Everything about her appearance was soft, feminine, innocent. The thin chiffon sleeves of her light pink dress puffed at the shoulders, and the open back was held together with a white silk bow that matched the one in her hair.

And yet, everything about her manner was boisterous and edged in angst. She strode the perimeter of the room, a small white paper stick lodged between her lips. She ignored Heston's assistance and slid into the open seat. She leaned forward and touched the tip of the white stick to the flame of a candle. She inhaled slowly, the end of the stick burning bright, and red. Smoky tobacco filled the air.

Jenin melted into her seat, crossed her legs, and pinched the stick between her middle and forefinger. Damian looked enraged, his jaw clenched and skin blotchy.

Jenin looked around innocently. "Oh, dear. Were you all waiting on me?" she asked as she puffed smoke out the side of her mouth. The cloud billowed around Damian. He flinched like someone had punched him in the face. He looked at his daughter with such ire, Eryna worried he might leap across the table and strangle her.

"Jenin, dear. You know this is a smoke-free room," he said, the words short but polite. The staff had just served the first course, a salad of mixed greens, soft cheese, berries, and a honey dressing, but no one touched it. Everyone was locked on the exchange between father and daughter.

"Oh!" she exclaimed brightly. "I'd completely forgotten. My apologies, father."

Jenin puffed on the stick again with a long, crackling inhale as the tip smoldered like a hot coal. Then she plunked it in her father's glass of sparkling wine, and it died out with a loud sizzle. Damian said nothing. Every mouth hung open except Parvati's. She seemed utterly unfazed, or if anything, humored. Derrick, however, looked ready to throw himself between the two of them.

Jenin glanced around the room and raised her brows.

"Everyone suddenly lose their appetites?" she asked.

The clink of silver on porcelain rang out seconds later. The entire room sat in silence as the second course—a creamy, chilled cucumber soup—arrived. Eryna was grateful for silence. Silence meant no one was asking questions. She glimpsed the soft skin of her hand and sighed with relief. The tonic was still working.

"So, Eryna. Where are you visiting from?" Heston asked, breaking the silence. Dread filled Eryna's stomach as the attention of the room shifted to her, but this question was easy.

"Meedra," Eryna replied between sips of soup. Maybe if she kept her mouth full, she could lessen her chances of messing up.

"Ah," Heston said, as if reflecting on a fond memory. "I'm ashamed to say I've never been to Meedra, but I do adore Noridas." Eryna practically fell into her soup, she was so relieved to hear he'd never visited her fictional home. She took several more relaxed sips, filling her time as Heston droned on. "My childhood summers were spent on the Conch Peninsula. It's my favorite. It has the best beaches, all fine white sand. None of the rocky, muddy beaches like the ones in Corrigan and

Kendrea. At least once a year I spend a weekend four-wheeling in the Dunes between Noridas and Promar. Have you been?"

Eryna silently shook her head, mouth full of soup.

"Oh, you must! It's really quite a spectacle. The sand transitions from the white sands of Noridas to the red sands of Promar, and the Dunes between are pink." Heston leaned into the table and smiled what Eryna assumed was his most charming smile. It might work on human girls, but to her, he looked like a snake rearing back, ready to attack. "I hear you're here through the summer. I'll take you to the Dunes on your way back to Meedra if you'd like."

"That's nonsensical. She'd have to go past Meedra to get to the Dunes," Jenin chimed in, loudly slurping her soup. Eryna swore she heard Jenin call Heston an "idiot" under her breath.

"We could make a trip out of it," he said, brushing off Jenin's comment. "I could show you where I won my first fencing tournament, or where my first horse was born, or where—"

"Heston, dear, enough about yourself," Parvati coolly cut him off, her voice strong as stone but smooth as polished marble. She looked at Eryna, then at Brody, and her eyes shone with something like a challenge. Eryna sensed she should fear such a look. "Brody, how is it you ended up in Meedra and met this young lady? Seems like such a silly little place to visit." Parvati turned to Eryna. "No offense," she apologized, but her tone savored of every offense possible. It seemed Sierra didn't just get her beauty from her mother.

"I was on my university tour," Brody answered.

"You pick a school, yet?" Heston cut in. "I went to Burnstad."

"Yes, actually. Garrison," Brody replied.

"Ah, rivals then." Heston raised a brow and jokingly pointed his knife at Brody, who politely laughed.

"Nice choice," Damian commented.

"Great school," Jerry agreed.

"Me too!" Sierra squealed, touching Brody's shoulder. She

looked at Derrick. "Aren't you going there, too?"

"I am." He nodded through a smile that barely reached his cheeks. Sierra beamed at the two boys.

"Oh, this is going to be so fun. We'll go to all the parties together and—"

"I'm still speaking, darling," Parvati said, no louder than a passing comment, but the room silenced as if she'd screamed it. She brought the conversation back to Brody. "From what I recall when I visited Meedra, there were no universities nearby. That was many decades ago, though. Have things changed?"

Eryna paused, spoon halfway to her mouth. Every drop in her stomach spoiled.

She's been to Meedra.

She glanced sideways at Jenin, who returned it. They both looked at Brody. He smiled his usual wolfish grin.

"I was touring Zeutan University at the time. It isn't close, per say, but I met a student who said I needed to visit Meedra for the best fried flounder in the eight seas, and I have a soft spot for fried flounder. I met Eryna while she was at a restaurant with her family. We chatted about her summer plans, and I asked her to spend the rest of summer here." The lie was smooth, rolling effortlessly from his lips like he'd practiced it a million times. Maybe he had.

"Just like that? You invited her here knowing hardly anything about her?"

"We spent a couple days together. See she...well...her parents..." Brody faltered and quickly glanced at Eryna.

"My father captains the Helios, and my mother is a fishing heiress. Meedra is just so small, you see, and my parents wanted me to experience life outside of its borders," Eryna added.

"A fishing heiress? Interesting. What kind of fish?" Parvati took a long sip of wine but kept her eyes on Eryna.

"All kinds, but mainly cod."

"I didn't realize there were cod in that part of the Marinthian Ocean. I thought Meedra was known for its flounder?" Parvati tilted her head.

Eryna nearly choked. But she took a deep breath and tried to recover.

"You're right. I misspoke. I meant flounder, but there are plenty of cod, too, if you know the right spots." Eryna smiled the kindest, most light-hearted smile she could.

"Right. Well, that's a lovely story. So then are you two...?" Parvati pointed a fork between Brody and Eryna. Derrick and Sierra perked up.

Eryna looked at Brody, questioning. She wasn't quite sure what Parvati meant, but from the way everyone in the room held their breath, she guessed the question was whether they were romantically involved. Brody looked at Eryna and smiled.

"Yes," Brody said at the same time Eryna replied, "No."

They narrowed their eyes at each other.

"Yes," Eryna answered again at the same time as Brody's "no."

"Well, which is it?" Sierra asked, annoyed.

Soup gone, Eryna had nothing left to occupy her mouth besides a large glass of wine. She grabbed it and drank like her life depended on it.

"It's complicated." Brody shrugged. "I'm going to university next year and Eryna is traveling for a year."

Eryna momentarily glanced down at her lap and caught sight of the tips of her fingers.

They were white.

She choked on her wine then coughed it down.

Several seconds later, the white had reached her knuckles.

The tonic was fading. Fast.

She shoved her hands beneath her napkin, heart hammering in her chest. She had to get out of the room, but she couldn't just get up and leave.

Parvati cleared her throat. Eryna looked up to see everyone's expectant faces. Clearly, she'd missed a question.

"Sorry, what was that?" she asked through a cough.

"I asked where you'll be traveling during your skip year?" Parvati said.

"I..." Eryna clutched the napkin tight. Her pulse raced in her ears, and an uneasy numbness climbed from her stomach to her throat, compressing her chest like it was trying to squeeze the life out of her. She tried to swallow, to clear her mind, but all she could think of was getting out of this room.

"Ek..." she started, then remembered the humans knew Ekatan by a different name. "The Southern Continent," she managed to get out.

She looked at Brody for approval, but he shut his eyes as if trying to shield disappointment. It wasn't until Damian replied that she realized her mistake.

"Interesting. Why there?" he asked. "Isn't that Hecate's realm? Just a lot of witches and questionable beings?"

"Well, I..." She had no way around this one. She wasn't thinking straight, and she'd completely forgotten humans hated and feared the Southern Continent, its lands unconquerable, filled with magical beings of all kinds.

"Hey!" Jenin shouted, and the clap of skin-on-skin echoed throughout the room.

One second, Heston's suit was white and crisp. The next, dripping in red liquid. Wine rained from the tips of his hair, down his face, and over the bright red welt of Jenin's hand on his cheek.

"Jenin Anastasia Ashford, that is *enough*!" Damian shouted. "Apologize at once."

"Not in a million years."

She made to exit the room, but Damian grabbed her wrist. Hard.

"Jenin, dear, apologize to the Duke right now." Damian's grip tightened. Jenin whimpered but remained firm.

"*He* owes *me* an apology," she gritted out. Then she tore her wrist away and stormed off. It was the perfect opportunity for Eryna.

"I should go check on her," she offered, rising.

"Sit!" Damian commanded. Eryna froze. The whole room froze. He took a deep breath and calmly continued, "Let her cool down. You are the guest of honor. This is your night. No need to have you chasing after my dramatic, selfish daughter."

"He's right. I'll go," Derrick said, and before Damian could stop him, he was gone. Eryna sat back down, and as she did, she noticed the white skin migrating past her wrist. She pulled the napkin higher but wasn't sure how much time was left before she could no longer cover the evidence of what she truly was. Minutes at most.

Next to her, Heston dabbed his face with his napkin, then dabbed his suit.

"I'm so sorry, your grace," Damian apologized, red heat filling his cheeks. "We'll send the suit out for dry cleaning immediately."

Heston waved him off and chuckled.

"No need, sir. I have my own team for that." Then he smiled at Eryna, elbowing her lightly. "Apparently not every girl likes to hold hands. Good thing I enjoy a nice cabernet. If this had been a pinot, I might've called for an execution."

He laughed. The whole room laughed, except Eryna, who could only smile politely. She kept turning over in her mind what could have possibly caused such a reaction from Jenin. She glanced down and the softness of her forearm had suddenly turned textured and barky. Arm shielded by the napkin, she shot up.

"If you'll forgive me, I must excuse myself. I'm not feeling well. Thank you for the lovely dinner, Mr. Ashford," Eryna said to Damian. He nodded.

"It's me who must be forgiven. This dinner didn't turn out how I'd hoped. Maybe we'll try again when my daughter isn't feeling so…rebellious."

Eryna gave him a polite smile, then rushed out of the dining room. It took her less than two minutes to find the way to her room, and in that time, the white had reached past her shoulder.

"Eryna!" Derrick's voice called from behind her as she strode down the hall. She glanced back and saw him smiling as he trotted after her.

She sped up.

He couldn't see her like this. It would be over if he did. She'd be dead, and Euryalea would be gone forever.

"Eryna, wait," he called out again.

"Not now, Derrick," she replied, feeling awful for how rude she sounded. She scurried into her room and slammed the door shut just as Derrick caught up. She locked the door.

"Sorry, I think the soup made me sick. I don't feel well," she said through the door, hoping it was a good enough excuse to satisfy the bewilderment she'd glimpsed on his face. It was silent for a moment, and Eryna worried he might've left. Then she heard him sigh.

"Okay, well, I hope you feel better. Let me know if you need anything," he replied, and as his footsteps faded, Eryna sighed in relief. She grabbed the tonic off the table, slid to the floor, and guzzled it down.

She'd have to be much more careful about taking the tonics before they wore off. She'd survived another day as a human, but there was no telling how many more she would have to endure before she found those Hearts. She needed to hurry. From that moment on, she decided, every hour spent not searching Blackwell Manor was an hour wasted. And she was done wasting time.

Chapter Twenty-One

Eryna stripped out of her dress, threw on comfortable black clothes and tied her hair out of the way. Agile and no nonsense was the aim. She needed to move quick and blend into the shadows.

She dumped her keys out of her purse and stuffed them in her pockets. Now it was just a matter of getting to the Manor. The plan was to go down to the street and hope the Ashford's driver was parked out there. It wasn't a foolproof plan. It wasn't much of a plan at all, if she was being honest, but it was all she had.

She opened the door and immediately collided with a hard chest, falling to the ground. It wasn't until she blinked several times that she realized she was staring down at a beaming Brody pinned beneath her. He laughed.

"I came to see how you're feeling, but from the looks of it, you've made a full recovery." A mischievous grin hung at the edge of his lips. His body was warm beneath hers. Eryna couldn't seem to move no matter how much she knew she should. The most she'd ever touched a human was when she healed Brody in the Thornewood. Now they were practically enmeshed.

Brody adjusted his head on the floor. He looked at her sideways and bit his lower lip.

"I can stay like this all night if you want. I don't mind," he said. His brown eyes intensified. Heat flashed through Eryna, and she scrambled to a stand and brushed off her clothes. Really, she was trying to brush *him* off her clothes. She had to focus. She had places to be, Hearts to find, a realm to restore.

"Sorry about that," she said, holding out a hand. He took it and stood.

"All good, though I'm interested to know where you were going in such a rush," he said. Then paused. His expression changed, eyes wide, mouth agape like his brain had finally kicked in. "You were gonna go door hunting, weren't you?"

"What? No." Before he could spot the obvious lie in her stupefied expression, she walked away. Only, the elevators were the opposite way. She silently cursed stupid Brody and his stupid smile for ruining her plans once again. He caught up and elbowed her lightly.

"Yes, yes you were." He was practically glowing. She bit her tongue, fighting back curses. He grabbed her hand and directed her toward the elevators. "Okay, I'm in."

"Absolutely not. You're not allowed to help me," she protested, ripping her hand from his grasp.

"Why not?"

"That's cheating!"

"It's not cheating."

"It's your house. You're the host."

"Exactly. My house, my rules." He smiled. "Besides, I only helped hide the keys. I don't know where the prize is, and I have no idea what keys you have. It'll be as much a surprise for me as it is for you. All these years, I've never played."

Eryna crossed her arms, regarding him warily.

"Sure, I doubt that. No human girls begged for your help in exchange for a kiss or something?" The words came out greener than intended, tinted with envy. Brody caught her tone. Slowly, he stepped toward Eryna, a sly smile on his face.

"My father never let me participate. But today's not a Hunt day, and I want to spend time with you. I don't even need a kiss, but I wouldn't say no to one. Especially from you." He was only inches from her now. Eryna was tall, but Brody was taller. His heavy gaze burrowed into her.

Then he was suddenly on his knees.

He clasped her hands tight and stared up at her with wide, pleading eyes.

"C'mon, Thorne, please?"

"No, don't do that," Eryna said, trying to tug him off the ground. He wouldn't budge.

"Technically, I don't have to ask. It's my house, after all. But I'm asking because I don't want to force you to spend time with me if you don't want to."

Eryna weighed her options. On one hand, she couldn't hunt for Hearts with him around. On the other, she could use him as her personal guide to learn the Manor's layout for the next time she was there alone. Unfortunately, the second option was the smarter, more strategic choice. *That damn Blackwell.* Eryna heaved a sigh.

"Fine."

"Yes!" Brody nearly leapt into the air with excitement. He grabbed Eryna's hand and pulled her toward the elevators. "This will be great."

"What will be great?" Derrick's voice sounded. Where had he even come from?

"We're searching for doors. Come on!" Brody shouted.

"Right now?" Derrick asked, quickening his steps to match their pace. *Not him, too*, Eryna thought. It was enough to have Brody following her all night, but now Derrick? Her plan was unraveling quicker than one of Oihane's dresses on a rowdy bonfire night.

Oihane.

Eryna's heart throbbed, an ache that reached so deep, it felt as though a fist had closed around her spine from the inside and squeezed. She missed her sister so much she could curl into a ball and cry right where she stood. She also missed Dera's quiet strength, her arms always ready to embrace Eryna when she needed a hug, and Gaia, did she need a hug. It was a foul fate that her sisters were gone, the Thornewood was ashen mulch, and here Eryna was hiding amongst the humans, hand-in-hand with a Blackwell, the very family at the root of her peoples' destruction.

As they entered the elevator, Eryna glanced at Brody. He pulled his fingers through his dark hair, an easy smile on his lips as the two boys chatted about something Eryna cared little to pay attention to. He threw his head back and laughed at Derrick's response. Eryna examined him further.

He was so carefree, so unburdened by the weight of the world, and so...powerful. Unjustifiably so.

Eryna thought back to him welcoming the crowd at yesterday's Hunt. Their world revolved around him, yet they were entirely ignorant of how his family and his people had just decimated *her* family and *her* people. Or more likely, they just didn't care, and loved him all the more for it.

A grime coated her skin at the thought, like she'd rolled in dirt and couldn't wash it off no matter how hard she scrubbed. A stark realization hit her that the last time she'd been in full control of her fate was when she'd discovered Brody in that trap and made the mistake of not ending right there.

Or...was that not true, either?

Was she even in control then?

Whoever killed her sisters had to have been waiting during the execution. They were too prepared, there were too many deaths for it to have been an impulsive attack. It had to have been planned.

And Brody had been the bait.

Suddenly, it all made sense why he'd kept talking when he should have been running. He had always been in on it. Always.

Every smile he'd given her spoiled and rotted in her mind. Every compliment, every gesture, every moment she'd thought he'd done something earnest turned to ash on her tongue. Furious flames sparked within her, spreading quick and untamed like the fire that had consumed her home forest. Smokey hatred singed her throat as she watched him— the boy who stole everything from her.

Now, more than ever, she knew she had to get those Hearts at whatever cost, and keys and doors were just an excuse. She had a new plan to steal more than the Hearts of Euryalea.

She needed to steal Brody's heart. Then she needed to destroy it.

Brody glanced at her and caught her stare. He playfully narrowed his gaze.

"What?" he asked.

Eryna smiled and gave his fingers a soft squeeze.

"Nothing," she said. "Just happy to be here."

His smile widened and he tucked under his arm. She leaned in and pressed her cheek to his shoulder. He smelled of fresh leather and warm spices and a touch of cedar wood. It was infuriatingly delicious. He stroked his thumb over her shoulder, and even through her clothes, everywhere he touched was like a poisonous fire on her skin.

In her periphery, she saw Derrick eye them. He shoved his hands in his pockets and leaned against the wall.

"Should I call the car?" he asked.

"Oh, no," Brody said, mischief tinging his voice. "*I* drove tonight."

Derrick's face lit up. "Oh, gods yes," he said. As they exited to the street, Eryna saw a sleek black vehicle like a hawk with its wings tucked, and she knew she was in for a different kind of ride than the one to Blackwell Manor yesterday.

Chapter Twenty-Two

Eryna wasn't sure whether to laugh, cry, or scream.

Never in her life had she moved so fast. She didn't know *anything* could move so fast.

A hand touched her knee and gave it a gentle shake.

"You can open your eyes now," Brody said, chuckling. She cracked a lid and glanced around; the world was finally motionless. Her leather jacket made a sticky peeling sound as she pulled away from the deep seat. Silently, slowly, she looked at Brody. All she could do was breathe.

"Fun, right?" he asked, smiling. Brody winked and gave her hand a squeeze. "Take all the time you need," he said. Then he opened his door and stepped out. Eryna's door swung wide, and a hand covered in a white glove reached toward her.

"Miss Thorne," a voice greeted—the man who'd shut her out of Blackwell Manor. She took his hand and met his gaze, unable to keep the smugness from her expression. He bowed his head. "My apologies for not letting you in before. We run a tight ship around here during the Hunt. I hope you understand."

"Apology accepted," Eryna replied as he helped her to wobbly legs. She held onto him longer than she liked. Then Derrick was suddenly at her side, supporting her arm.

"I got you," he murmured. She knew she shouldn't hold onto him like this, especially now that she needed to focus on Brody. But she was so weak, and he was so steady. He smiled at her. His smile really was so nice.

Another arm slide across her back and lightly tugged her in the opposite direction, breaking her grip on Derrick.

"Thanks, man, I got her," Brody said.

I'm not a toy to be fought over. Eryna rolled her eyes, then trotted several steps out of both their reaches.

"Where should we start?" she asked, marching through the open doors. The Manor was alive and buzzing, and every staff member greeted Brody with genuine smiles as they moved in a choreography of tasks. Some carried bed sheets piled as high as their chins, some had stacks of books, some had trays of food, and others had armfuls of metal bits that looked like they fit into a large mechanism.

Why so many things if no one else lives here? Eryna wondered. She looked back at Brody.

"I thought it was just you and your father here," she remarked. He nodded.

"It is. But he's moved a lot of his work here, so some of his colleagues are around."

"I thought no one but family and trusted friends were allowed in the Manor during the Hunt?" she asked, throwing a pointed look at the man in the white gloves. Brody caught up to Eryna, placed a hand on her lower back, and steered her toward a corridor just off the entry.

"True. But technically they fall under the 'trusted friends' category. And anyway, they're not allowed to play."

"Hm," she remarked.

Well, that's going to make things more difficult, Eryna thought. It was one thing when it was just Brody and his father she had to worry about.

But trying to search the place with Mr. Blackwell's colleagues around posed an obstacle she wasn't prepared for. Eryna set that thought aside for later. Tonight, was about learning her way around the place.

They entered a massive space with people rapidly milling about, dressed in white. One stirred a large pot over a contained flame, another chopped vegetables, and another rummaged through a storage area. The aromatic scent of caramelized onions and garlic engulfed Eryna, a mix of nostalgia and curiosity bursting in her chest. She fought the urge to peek into the pot to see if she recognized what they were making.

The person in the storage area turned around, saw the three of them, and smiled brightly.

"Ah, just in time," she said. She was a rather short and soft woman with round rosy cheeks and light blue eyes, her hair stuffed under a large white hat. She swatted the person stirring the pot out of the way and disappeared behind the counter. When she rose, she held a metal sheet containing several round biscuits dotted with brown chunks.

From behind, Derrick murmured in Eryna's ear, "We have the cinnamon rolls, but the Blackwells have Brenna's chocolate chip cookies."

Eryna intently watched Brenna, actively ignoring the warm ripple Derrick's voice sent down her spine. Brenna gingerly transferred the cookies to a plate, poured three glasses of creamy white liquid, and shuffled over to the tall table where they stood.

"Fresh from the oven," she said. Her eyes lingered on Eryna for a moment, then slid to Brody.

"This her?" she asked. He nodded.

Brody had told Brenna about her?

What had Brody told Brenna about her?

Brenna eyed Eryna again, then gave her cheeks a gentle pinch.

"Brody Martin Alexander Blackwell, she's even lovelier than you let on," Brenna squealed and embraced Eryna. At first, Eryna wasn't sure what to do. But then Brenna squeezed tighter, and Eryna couldn't help hugging her back, concaving onto the woman's shoulder like a wilted lily.

Eryna knew she needed a hug, but she didn't realize how starved for comforting touch she truly was. Pressure built in her chest, her eyes burned, and her throat tightened. She held Brenna close and tried hard not to cry, but she couldn't help the single tear that slipped beneath her lid without permission. Brenna pulled away and held Eryna at arm's length.

"Hope I'll be seeing much more of you around here, dear," she said. Then she looked at the boys. "What trouble are you getting into tonight?"

Brody grabbed a couple cookies from the plate, took a bite of one and handed the other to Eryna. It was warm and bog-soft. She immediately took a bite, and a tangle of warm sugar and browned butter and bittersweet chocolate melted on her tongue. It was even better than the cinnamon roll. She caught Derrick dunking his cookie into the white liquid, so she mirrored him and took another bite. The flavors burst in her mouth once more, this time coated in what she realized was cold, creamy milk. She devoured it in seconds.

"We," Brody replied through a full mouth, "are door hunting."

"Are you now? With Miss Thorne's keys, then?" Brenna asked as she crossed her arms and looked exaggeratedly interested in the topic. "I'm guessing your father doesn't know?"

Brody shook his head vehemently and stuffed the rest of the cookie in his mouth.

"No, and if you tell him, I swear I'll run off to the Ashford's for every foreseeable meal," he said. Brenna grabbed a towel and repeatedly whipped it at Brody. He crossed his arms and hiked up his leg to block her attack, laughing through tight lips and a full mouth.

"Don't mess with me, boy. You wouldn't dare miss a meal of mine. It's hard enough I lose you to *them* every Saturday morning," Brenna said, looking at Derrick through narrowed eyes, though a smile played on her lips. "If I could just get that chef of yours to give me that blasted cinnamon roll recipe…"

Derrick grabbed another cookie and beamed.

"He might say the same about your chocolate chip cookies," he chirped, taking a bite. Brody enveloped Brenna in a hug and kissed the top of her head. It was a tender moment, and Eryna had to shove her fluttering heart deep into her chest and remind it to stay put.

"Bren Bren, you could never lose me. Thanks for the hunting fuel, but we're off. We have doors to find!" he said, grabbing another cookie. Then he took Eryna's hand and pulled her from the room. Eryna stretched to swipe another cookie off the plate as she was tugged away but missed. Brenna rushed to shove one in her hand and gave Eryna a wink as they rounded the corner out of sight.

Eryna liked her. A lot.

Brody, Derrick, and Eryna stopped at the base of the grand staircase. Brody nudged her.

"Let's see them, then," he said. She knew he meant the keys. She dug them from her pocket and displayed the seven keys in her open palm. She eyed each one: The pewter key from the curtain, the marble key from the hall of statues, the brassy key from under the rug, the bejeweled key from the lamp, the golden key from the mirror, the green key from the planter, and the thick iron Blackwell key.

Brody plucked the Blackwell key from the pile and put it back in Eryna's pocket.

"Obviously, we don't need that one," he said, muttering to himself. "Okay, there are six keys here, and three of us. Let's each take two. Then we'll pick a hall and try our keys. We'll narrow them down quicker," Brody suggested, looking between Eryna and Derrick. She considered suggesting they split up to cover more ground so she could secretly search for the Hearts, but she was certain they wouldn't let her out of their sights tonight. So, Eryna nodded.

"Sounds good to me," she said.

"Same," Derrick agreed. He looked at Eryna. "Your keys. You

pick first."

Eryna scanned the keys in her palm. The pewter one with its red velvet bow and large golden tassel called to her. She put it in her pocket. Then she chose the marble one, its body shiny and smooth. Brody signaled for Derrick to go next, and he picked the green and bejeweled keys. That left Brody the gold and brassy ones.

"Where do we start, then?" Eryna asked, scanning the enormous expanse of balconies, halls, and the sweeping staircase. Brody shrugged.

"Wherever you want."

A small hallway off the second-floor balconies caught her attention. She pointed at it.

"There."

She looked to Brody as if he might know whether that was the right place to start, even though he'd already assured them he knew nothing. He smiled and gave a single deliberate nod.

"Then we'll start there."

His gaze ticked back and forth between Eryna and Derrick.

Then his eyes narrowed.

A conspiratorial grin spread across his face.

"Race you there," he challenged, and before either of them could reply, he was gone.

Chapter Twenty-Three

"Let's go, Thorne!" Derrick excitedly shouted as he took her hand. She couldn't help the competitive fire that surged within her.

"Don't forget, I've outrun you in heels before," she challenged. Heat in her steps, grace in her long limbs, she picked up her pace and made it halfway to the corridor before Derrick had even made it to the top of the stairs. She rounded the corner to find a lackadaisical Brody lounging against a door, repeatedly flicking the brassy key in the air.

"What took you so long?" he chided, but the rapid rise and fall of his chest betrayed him. Eryna rolled her eyes and smiled, joining him at the door. He glanced over her shoulder.

"Sure you should let him see you run so fast?" Brody muttered, a flash of concern crossing his expression.

"Don't worry, I kept my pace human-speed," she replied, chuckling.

"Gods, you're quick," Derrick huffed as he joined them moments later. "I haven't worked out in a couple weeks, but I didn't think I was *that* out of shape." He wiped his forehead with the back of his hand and ran his fingers through his hair. Eryna followed the movement with her eyes, curious how soft his hair might feel between her fingers.

Brody laughed.

"You need to stop skipping leg day, bro." He clapped Derrick on the shoulder, then pointed to a door. "Eryna, start here with your two keys. Derrick take the next door over. I'll take the one across the hall. Then we rotate. That way we'll have a chance to try our keys in each of the doors."

"Yes, captain!" Derrick mockingly saluted, then sauntered down the hall.

Eryna faced the door in front of her and tried the lock. Not a match. Her keys also lacked that buzzing she'd previously experienced. While she wasn't sure it was exclusive to the Blackwell key, she had a feeling it might not be.

Next, she thought, and walked to where Derrick was lining his keys up.

"Nothing?" she asked, the keys very clearly not a fit.

"Nothing," he replied, and moved to the next door, but not without flashing her a smile that sent a flutter up her core.

She held her keys up to the next lock. Not a fit, and no sensation.

"Nothing?" Brody asked as he arrived at her side.

"Nothing," she replied. She brushed against him as she moved to the next door, and when a small exhale escaped him, she smiled to herself.

In a matter of minutes, they'd finished searching the hall with no success. They moved to the next hall.

And the next.

And the next, until they'd searched the entire second floor.

Then the third.

"Statistically speaking, we *have* to come across a door that works with one of your keys soon," Brody groaned, leaning against the grand staircase. Derrick glanced at his watch.

"It's been two hours. Let's finish tomorrow," he said, scrubbing his hands over his face. Eryna agreed through sagging shoulders and a drowsy mind. Brody shook his head.

"I have to work the next few days and then we prep for the next Hunt. Tonight's all I've got." He looked at them with wide, pleading eyes. "Just one more hall, please?"

Eryna and Derrick looked at each other, clearly ready to call it quits. She'd seen enough of Blackwell Manor tonight to know its general layout.

"Please?" Brody begged. Eryna shifted on her feet and sighed, hoping that one more hall would satisfy Brody.

"Fine," she said, but pressure in her abdomen caught her attention. "I need to use the bathroom first, though."

Brody almost leapt with excitement and pointed to a hall beneath the stairs. "Down that way to the right. Meet back here in five," he said.

She trotted off and quickly found what she needed. Thank Gaia, they left that room unlocked. As she left the bathroom, Eryna glimpsed a painting down the hall of a young boy who looked like Brody seated in a chair, a beautiful young woman behind him, her hand on his shoulder. It was the same woman who's painting she'd come through in the ballroom.

There was pure joy in his face as he gazed up at the woman. When Eryna looked at her, she saw an immediate resemblance in the cut of her jaw, the mischievous sparkle in her eye.

It had to be Brody's mother.

Eryna drew closer, needing to get a better look to confirm her suspicions, when suddenly, her pocket vibrated.

She froze.

To her right was a large door made of thick mahogany. Eryna reached into her pocket and plucked out the key.

It was the pewter one with the velvet bow.

"Brody," she called, his name catching in her throat. He didn't come. He probably hadn't heard her. "Brody!" she shouted.

Seconds later, steps bounded toward her, Brody's voice echoing ahead.

"What's wrong? Are you okay—?" he stopped short as him and Derrick rounded the corner. His eyes fell on the key in her hand. "You found one," he breathed. She nodded.

"I found one."

The boys hurried to her.

"Hey, that was the first key you found," Derrick remarked, smiling at her.

"Technically, second," she countered, returning the smile. She thought back to the Hunt, the two of them scouring the papered walls and crowded halls together.

"Wait, what happened to the first?" Brody asked, glancing between Derrick and Eryna.

"Jordan Denny stole it," Derrick replied.

"What a dick. Can't say I'm surprised, though," Brody remarked. Then he looked at the key in Eryna's hand. "Go ahead. Open it."

Eryna stared at it, its frenzied current pinging across her skin. She held it out to Brody. "Do you want to do it?" she asked. After all, he was the one who'd grown up with this tradition.

To her surprise, he curled her fingers over it and guided her to the door. He wrapped his arms around her waist and settled his chin on her shoulder. His lips brushed against her neck.

"This one's all you," he said into her skin. Intense excitement burst through Eryna's chest like a daffodil through spring soil. Her head went light and fuzzy, and she told herself it was from the key and nothing else. She reached forward, her body wracked with electricity so strong, she wondered if Brody could feel it, too. She glanced sidelong at Derrick and caught his eyes burrowing into the spot where Brody's arms were clasped around her.

The key found the hole with a soft *click*. A sharp pain struck her chest, her stomach violently churned, and air fled her lungs. She gasped, nearly dropping the key, but a second later the pain was gone. Brody tensed behind her.

"You okay?" he asked, but she assured him with a nod. She twisted the key twice until the door gave way to a black void. Eryna couldn't see more than an inch inside, but Brody moved them into the pitch dark. Derrick entered behind them.

Then the door shut tight, drowning them in darkness. The air was still and stale like it hadn't been disturbed in ages. The room was quiet and the ground stodgy beneath their feet, muffling their steps.

"Hello?" Derrick called into the void, startling Eryna an inch off the ground. Her shoulder knocked into Brody's chin and his teeth audibly clashed. She gasped.

"Oh, no, I'm so sorry," she fussed, but Brody held her tight, laughing into her neck, his breath warm everywhere it touched.

"Don't worry about it," he said.

"Where are we?" she asked. This was his home. Surely, he knew all the rooms.

"Not sure. I'm hardly ever in this wing."

Eryna hoped her eyes would adjust to the dark, but they didn't. "Are there lights in here?"

"I'm on it," Derrick said, his footsteps trailing some distance away.

Brody, however, remained still. He pulled Eryna close, drawing her deeper into his broad chest.

"We should help him look," she suggested, the words weak and halfhearted.

"He'll manage," Brody said, slowly dragging his lips up her neck to a soft spot behind her ear. "If he doesn't, the dark can be fun, too, you know," he murmured. It took every fiber in her body to fight the tremor that shot through her as his thumbs traced her waist, up to her ribs and back down. Sparks spread across her chest. Her core tightened. Her heart flapped with the rapid beats of a hummingbird. Her head went so light, she worried it might float off her shoulders. She tried catching her breath, but it repeatedly escaped her lungs, as if mocking her.

Brody reached down, interlaced his fingers with hers, and whisked her away until her back gently connected with something solid, the two of them now chest-to-chest. They stood there like that in the darkened silence for several seconds, just breathing, assessing the feel of each other as the heat between them built with each passing moment.

And it was time to stoke the fire.

Eryna needed those Hearts. Brody was her best bet of finding them.

She ran her palms up his chest, hooked them around his neck, and pulled him close until her lips met the shell of his ear. "Show me what kind of fun you humans have in the dark, then," she whispered. His fingers tightened on her waist, digging deep into her hip bones. Her body blazed, her core going taught as he hovered his face in front of hers.

"I've wanted to do this since the moment we met, Thorne," he whispered. He leaned forward and brushed his soft, full lips against hers but stopped there, like he was waiting for her to make the final move. Her heart flapped harder and higher until it lodged itself in her throat.

She'd never kissed someone before.

After hearing her sisters' many stories, she'd dreamt of her first kiss for decades, but she never thought the day would actually come. She had no idea what to do, but many of her sisters claimed it was as natural as breathing.

Eryna closed her eyes and prayed to Gaia she would do this right. She *had* to do this right.

She leaned forward.

Her lips found his, like a key in a lock, and—

The room blazed to life, the lights blinding and abrasive.

Brody groaned and burrowed his forehead into Eryna's chest. He straightened and sighed.

I'm sorry, he mouthed. Eryna smiled and shook her head, but it was impossible to shield her chagrin. She wanted that first kiss.

Desperately.

Brody scanned her face, then quirked his lips to the side. "We're not finished here, Eryna Thorne," he whispered, and pressed a warm, lingering kiss to her cheek before pulling her toward the front of the room.

It was a large, cavernous space with a wooden stage framed in thick red velvet curtains. A hundred seats fanned out across the floor and up into a second level balcony. The walls were adorned in an intricate gold pattern, and the domed ceiling was painted like the sky at every stage: dawn, day, dusk, night, and all the twilights in between.

"The old theater," Brody remarked as he hopped up on the stage and explored in long, eager steps. "I knew it was somewhere over here, but that must've been a side entrance."

"It's beautiful," Eryna breathed, her eyes traversing the night portion of the painted sky. A single constellation stood out to her: Ardian. Her heart swelled, and she thought of home.

Then her vision blurred, but she blinked it away. She really needed to get some sleep.

"I'd heard about the grand plays in Aponyx from..." Eryna scraped her hazy mind for a lie, having to remind herself that Derrick, who was now making his way her direction, didn't know her true nature. "...my...my fami—"

Suddenly, her head pounded and pain tore through her chest. Her stomach soured and dark spots clouded her vision. Her legs wobbled, the world tilted, and the last thing she heard was someone shouting her name.

Chapter Twenty-Four

Eryna's mind woke before her body.

Her limbs were stiff as bamboo, mouth dry as soil in late August, lids heavy as stones. A cool rag dabbed her forehead, and voices she didn't recognize mumbled around her.

There was a hard knock on the door. The wood creaked open.

"Can I see her now?" A female voice asked. Jenin.

When did I get back to The Spire? Eryna wondered.

"Give her a few minutes, Miss Ashford," someone replied.

"Screw that, I'm coming in."

The light clacks of Jenin's heels drew nearer until the edge of the bed depressed at Eryna's side. She cracked an eye to find Jenin glowering at her.

"When I said pretend to be sick, I didn't mean actually get sick."

Jenin's voice was sharp, irritated. But even through the haze of waking, Eryna heard genuine concern. She patted Jenin's hand, and to her surprise, Jenin didn't retract.

"You're not the only one who likes to make a scene," Eryna said, her voice crispy and harsh, like it hadn't been used in days. "How long have I been out?"

Jenin glanced at her watch. "A day and a half."

"What?" Eryna shot up in bed and scanned her hands, her arms, touched her face. Her skin was silky smooth and flush. There's no way her most recent dose of tonic lasted a day and a half.

"Relax, I was able to slip you...*medication* when I visited earlier. Had to shove it down your throat. You haven't missed much besides Brody and my brother holding vigil outside your door."

Eryna glanced over Jenin's shoulder toward the door. Jenin snorted.

"I made them leave a few hours ago. Brody's father called looking for him and my brother needs to focus his attention elsewhere."

Eryna rolled her eyes but stopped short as a person in an official looking uniform arrived bedside.

"Feeling okay? Any light headedness, shaking, nausea?" he asked, flashing a bright light in her eyes. Yes, her head was light, and yes, she was a little nauseated from sitting up so quickly, but it was nothing food, water, and sunlight couldn't fix. Eryna shook her head.

Jenin shooed him away. "Thank you, Dr. Bennett. You can go," she said. Once the man was gone, she brought out a small rectangular box and a plate of cookies.

"Brody left these for you," she said. Eryna's heart involuntarily fluttered. She took a cookie then studied the box, curiosity gripping her like talons. She tore open the lid and inside sat a phone with a note.

Jenin will show you how to use this. Call me the moment you wake up.
-Brody

Eryna handed Jenin the box and showed her the note. Jenin rolled her eyes.

"Gods, it's like being with a child," she grumbled as she took the phone and held a button on the side until it lit up. For the better part of thirty minutes, Jenin pointed out various functions and symbols and explained their meaning. She showed Eryna how to "call" someone to talk, and how to "text" someone to send a message in written word.

Brody must have set the phone up with his and Jenin's information, as they were the only names in there. She found it strange that Derrick's was missing, seeing as she was staying at the Ashford's, but it's possible he forgot. She'd find Derrick later and get his information, too.

After Jenin had Eryna call and text her multiple times to make sure she understood how to work the phone, she stood.

"I'll have them bring you something more substantial than cookies. You're skinnier than I am right now, and I can't have that," she said. It was her second failed attempt at shielded concern. Eryna chuckled.

"Hey, Jenin," Eryna called. "It was nice of you to check on me." Jenin squinted at her.

"Don't get used to it, demon," she replied, wrestling the slight smile that spread across her lips before she shut the door.

Eryna picked up the phone to call Brody.

Why was she suddenly nervous? Why did the idea of talking over the phone feel so intimate and exciting and uncomfortable?

A few rings, and he didn't answer. Relief spread through her, followed by a pit of sadness. It went to "voicemail," but Jenin hadn't prepared her for that other than saying voicemails were "useless when she could text instead." So, Eryna hung up and tried again.

He still didn't answer.

He must be busy with something, she thought. Jenin had said his father needed him today. She opened her texts and sent one to him. She kept it simple.

I'm up. Thank you for the phone and the cookies.

A soft knock sounded on the door, and moments later a woman entered with a tray of food. Eryna barely waited for her to set it down before inhaling half of it. Once full, she assessed her body, searching for sickness or injury that might've caused her to faint, but all she found was fatigue.

If she could reach nature, if she could be around some flora and fresh air and more than just confined human life, it might help.

Then it struck Eryna.

The terrace garden.

She quickly dressed and made her way there, heading straight for the wisteria. As she stepped through the brick arch, her feet faltered.

Lounging on a couch underneath the wisteria was Derrick. Shirtless.

Eyes shut, his face was turned toward the sun like a lazy, resting lynx. Eryna couldn't keep from eyeing the strong curves of his muscles, the warm tint in his skin. She couldn't rip her gaze from the steady rise and fall of his chest, wondering what might happen if she were to get closer, reach out and touch him. He looked so serene, so harmless. She really should leave him be, let him enjoy this moment of peace.

But a small flicker of pink caught her eye.

Pinched between his fingers was the chiffon rose he'd pulled from her hair a few nights ago. He twirled it, repeatedly rolling the micro stem along his thumb.

"Jenin, if you've come to bully me into helping you rearrange your room again, please kindly take a walk off the roof," Derrick said without opening his eyes. Eryna involuntarily giggled then clamped a hand over her mouth. So much for leaving him be.

Derrick's eyes shot open. He sat rod straight. His entire body stilled, but the rise and fall of his chest nearly doubled in pace.

"You're up," he breathed. Eryna nodded.

"I'm up."

He eyed her carefully, like she could faint again any moment and he was ready to catch her.

"Good. That's good. You feeling okay?" he asked, grazing the couch with his hands as if searching for something.

Eryna bobbed her head, deliberating, and walked toward him.

"Tired. But I'd rather not sleep. I've done enough of that for a bit." She really was exhausted. The food helped, but just barely. Her legs were still weak, her body heavy on her feet.

"Woah, woah, woah," Derrick said, and Eryna's world tilted again, only this time it stopped before she was on the ground. Derrick's warm arms scooped her up and pressed her against his bare chest. He set her on the couch in the direct sunlight. Her body drank it in, starved of fresh air and summer heat.

"Thanks," she said. He settled next to her and pulled on a white t-shirt. She closed her eyes and leaned into the cushions. "Is that what happened in the theater?"

"Mmhm," he replied, and she wondered if he'd been the one to catch her then, too. "One moment we were talking about plays, the next you were limp. Were you not feeling well?"

Eryna thought on it for a moment, replaying the night in her mind. Nothing felt off except...the pain in her chest, the nausea, the breathlessness as she unlocked the theater door. It was the only moment she could think of. That and she hadn't had a second of true rest since her arrival in Aponyx.

"I suppose so. I think I'm just exhausted from..." Eryna feigned a yawn to pause for the right words. The truth was out of the question. "...traveling. I haven't slept much. I need to slow down."

Except slowing down was the last thing she could do. She had to find the Hearts, and fast. The sooner she did that, the sooner she could get home. But she could barely open her eyes, let alone sneak into Blackwell Manor. Eryna tilted sideways and her cheek connected with soft cotton. Derrick's warmth seeped through the material as she settled against his solid chest. She shouldn't be curled into him like this, but it was just so comfortable. So easy. Still, Eryna didn't want to give him the wrong idea.

She tried pulling away, but Derrick pulled her in tight, and Gaia, did she like the way it felt. She looked up at him and gave him a soft smile, unable to fight how much she enjoyed it. He reached across her face and tucked an errant strand of hair behind her ear.

"Then we'll take it easy for a little while, huh?" he said, smiling. She nodded, unable to argue.

"You still have my flower," she remarked. He nodded and displayed it in his palm. They studied it together.

"I can't believe how fresh it is still," he said. He sounded more intrigued than suspicious. Still, she wondered if he found it curious.

"They survive long after being cut from the stem," she said, just in case. "You can actually propagate these, you know."

He stilled under her. She looked up and caught intense hope in his eyes as he stared at the flower. She nudged him. "You said your mother liked these?"

He nodded.

"Her favorite." His voice was so quiet, it was almost lost to the breeze. Eryna could barely remain upright, but maybe if she dug her hands in the dirt, connected with the Earth, she could find some magic within herself. She picked up the flower.

"Show me where they used to grow," she said.

He helped her to a small patch of dirt that held a young rose bush. She knelt, set the flower aside, and shoved her hands into the dirt until they connected with the roots of the roses. They shrunk from her, but she assured them with her touch that she was simply moving them, not disposing of them. They relaxed and allowed her to easily pry them from the soil. Eryna's body tingled, like her limbs had been asleep for weeks and were just now waking. Except she knew it wasn't her limbs—it was her life force.

She was nature, and nature was her.

Small surges of energy coursed through her veins. Every second her hands spent in the dirt was a second of new life being breathed into her. After adjusting the bush, she was left with a perfect patch of open soil. She grabbed the chiffon rose and buried it. Then she placed her hands over the dirt. Derrick wasn't allowed to see what she had to do next.

She looked at him. "Can you grab some water for it?" she asked. He nodded and trotted out of sight. She worked quickly, pulling on all the energy she'd just regained to encourage the flower to root, to grow, to flourish. When he returned, she was almost as drained as when she'd started. He knelt next to her, cup of water in hand. She signaled to the spot in the dirt.

"Go ahead."

Gingerly, he poured the water over the soil, then looked at Eryna as if checking that he'd done it right. She smiled in reassurance.

"Give it a few days. They grow surprisingly quick," she said. He returned the smile, his lip almost imperceptibly quivering. He grabbed her hand and gave it a squeeze.

"Thank you," he whispered. She squeezed his hand in return.

"Of course," she said. Then a ray of dappled sunlight hit her eyes and reminded her of a fantasy from another lifetime. Eryna bit her lip, hesitant. "Would you...would you maybe want to watch the sunrise up here with me sometime?" she asked.

Derrick's smile fell. His brow folded. Eryna bit her lip again, worried she'd asked something too strange. Had she just given herself away? Was he not interested in spending time with her?

"Oh. I don't think we can..."

"Sorry, I know that was a funny question." Eryna anxiously cut in. "Jenin might kill us if she—"

Derrick squeezed her hand and laughed.

"Oh, no, I didn't mean...it's just that this terrace is western facing. We could watch the *sunset* from here. It's very nice, actually. But if it's the sunrise you want, we'll have to watch that from the eastern terrace. Because, yes, I would love to watch the sunrise with you. Even if Jenin might kill us."

Eryna released a breath, and when she looked at Derrick again, he was staring at her intently. Gently, he hooked a finger under her chin, tilted her face up, and leaned in.

"What are you two losers doing?" A voice called from behind them. They turned to find a rare, barefoot Jenin.

"We're replanting mom's roses. Eryna needs to take it easy for a few days," Derrick said, scooting a few inches away. Jaw clenched, Jenin crossed her arms tight. Her eyes narrowed on Eryna, and Eryna knew she'd get an earful later.

"And you thought gardening was the activity to help her 'take it easy?'" Jenin asked, raising a skeptical brow at her brother.

"Got anything else in mind?" he asked.

Jenin pursed her lips and shifted her weight. "There are a few movies I've been wanting to watch. You probably wouldn't like them, though." She shrugged, and while her face was schooled into a cool, passive expression, the shake of her leg and the tapping of her fingers against her arms made Eryna think she might be more excited than she let on. Eryna had no idea what a movie was, having only heard about it in passing, and she was more than intrigued to learn.

Derrick smiled, looked between his sister and Eryna.

"Movie marathon it is, then," he said, helping Eryna to her feet. "I'll make some popcorn."

Jenin straightened.

"Absolutely not. You put too much salt on it."

"What's popcorn without salt?"

"Popcorn that doesn't make me bloat, that's what," Jenin argued. Derrick slung his arm over her.

"Fine, you can make the popcorn, then," he said. Then he paused, looked at her, and grinned. "If you can beat me to the machine."

Derrick broke into a sprint, Jenin following shortly behind, shouting curses in his direction. She looked back at Eryna and threw her arms out wide.

"You gonna help me beat him up or what?" Jenin asked, and Eryna chuckled. As she followed the Ashford siblings through the halls, for the briefest heartbeat, she felt like she belonged here.

She felt like she was home.

Chapter Twenty-Five

It'd been a week and Brody still hadn't called Eryna back. He hadn't even replied to her text.

Eryna sat on the edge of Jenin's bed watching her tear apart her room in search of something, though Eryna couldn't remember what. All her attention was focused on not looking at her phone.

Her first few days with the phone, it was reasonable to think Brody was too busy to call. Jenin had said his father needed him and he had mentioned needing to work. Of course, he wouldn't be available at all hours of the day.

So, she enjoyed her time watching movies with Derrick and Jenin, moving pictures that lifted the veil of what was possible in this world. It was like the stories the Dryads told around the bonfires, only acted out with people and settings and music and nothing short of manufactured magic.

"People make money doing this as their 'job'?" Eryna had asked Jenin when Derrick went to the bathroom.

"Oh yeah. Lots of money. I actually dated him briefly." Jenin pointed at the young man on screen who played the main love interest. "An absolute asshole, but so hot. Great kisser, too. Except he had this weird kink where…" Eryna had stopped listening to check her phone to see if Brody had called.

He hadn't.

Saturday came around and Eryna nearly ran to breakfast, assuming he'd be there. After all, he said he never missed a Saturday breakfast with the Ashfords.

Apparently, this was the first.

The next few days, she woke with a start and immediately reached for the phone beside her. Surely, Brody had found a spare moment to reply. Maybe he'd called while she was asleep, and she'd missed it.

But the phone was blank each time.

Eryna was still far too depleted to go in search of the Hearts, so she leaned into the days spent sleeping past sunrise, lounging around the penthouse in comfortable clothes, watching more movies and spending time in the garden with the wisteria and chiffon roses, which had sprouted two buds.

As she went to bed last night, she opened her text to Brody and three small dots appeared at the bottom of the screen. That was new. Her heart raced and she clutched the phone tight.

The dots disappeared. And nothing happened. She fell asleep with the phone in her hand.

However, she woke today resolved to remove Brody from her plans. As convenient as it was to use him to find the Hearts and then crush his soul afterward, he proved to be far more of a distraction. Eryna could still get into the manor with the Blackwell key to search on her own, and now that she was more replenished, it didn't seem so daunting a task. But even with her physical health on the mend, something heavy sat on her chest.

As Jenin scoured the room, she was deep in describing her "celestial" outfit to match the second Hunt's theme, which had just been announced for tonight. Eryna heard nothing else, her eyes on the phone.

"Ah hah! I found it!" Jenin exclaimed, pulling a sheer, sparkling black material out of a drawer. She threw it around her shoulders. "I knew I had it somewhere. What do you think?"

Jenin twirled, and Eryna watched as the crystals twinkled like a million stars against the night sky. It was breathtaking.

"It's nice," Eryna said apathetically. Her eyes slid to her phone. Jenin slammed her hand down over it.

"Stop it," she said firmly. "You've been glued to that thing for a week and I'm ready to confiscate it. I wouldn't have given it to you if I'd known you'd be like this."

Eryna sighed and fell back on the bed, covering her face with a pillow.

"Why do I feel this way?"

Jenin ripped away the pillow and pulled Eryna upright.

"Because a stupid boy set expectations he couldn't meet. They never can. They'll disappoint you every time, I promise."

Just then, Jenin's phone lit up.

They both looked at her screen.

Jenin's hand was lightning-quick, but not quick enough to hide Brody's name. Hot humiliation crawled up Eryna's neck. She was a fool. She was an outright fool, and she knew in that moment he had her right where he wanted her. She'd been so busy hoping he'd buy into her games she'd almost forgotten about his. And he was winning.

Jenin nudged Eryna.

"Enough of this," she said. "No more pouting. Screw Brody, he isn't special. You don't need him."

Eryna tried to believe Jenin, but she reminded herself that Jenin needed Brody's plan to work, too. She needed the third Heart to save her father. But then why was she being nice to Eryna?

Jenin disappeared for a moment, and when she returned, she held up an almost sheer shimmering dress that dripped in low hanging crystals. She looked at Eryna.

"Boring people will wear silver or something tacky with stars on it tonight. Only those worth noticing know to wear something that really shines. The best revenge is to look good, and you're going to look really, *really* good."

The smile that carved itself into Jenin's face was sharp, cunning, and one that Eryna was certain she used only for plotting revenge. It was a look Eryna would have been terrified to be on the other side of.

But since it was for her, she smiled back.

Chapter Twenty-Six

Jenin and Eryna arrived alone, Derrick having gone to Blackwell Manor earlier that day. With every step, the snug dress glistened, the crystals like a miniature meteor shower clinging to her body. The long, sparkling sleeves hung as low as her waist, and the purse Jenin let her borrow gleamed.

As they entered the Manor, Eryna swore humans had evolved owl necks, because when heads turned her way, they stayed there until the last possible second. Everyone looked at her, and she couldn't deny that it made her walk a little taller, hold her voluminous head of hair a little higher. She even smiled at a few people, and they smiled back like it was an honor to be seen.

Before tonight, standing out would have felt like a death sentence. Right now, she wanted everyone to see how good she looked. Maybe then word would spread to Brody faster.

"What did I tell you?" Jenin said, leaning into Eryna. Eryna smiled but replied, "I think they're looking at you."

Jenin did look incredible. Her billowing black ballgown inlaid with thousands of small crystal constellations sparkled like the night sky in the darkest corner of the Thornewood, the shimmering cape flowing behind her like smoke. Jenin adjusted the high slit of the dress so that more of her leg showed, and nudged Eryna.

"Stop kissing my ass. They're looking at you."

They grabbed some sparkling wine, and as a group of women enviously eyed Eryna, she heard one murmur, "Clearly, the Hunt Hangover hasn't gotten to *her* yet."

Eryna turned to Jenin.

"What's the Hunt Hangover?" she asked. Jenin laughed.

"Some people think the Hunt takes too much out of everyone; that all the drinking and partying takes its toll. It's a normal hangover. People just gave it a name to be dramatic."

Eryna laughed lightly and gazed around. Now that she was looking, she noticed that some people indeed seemed like they hadn't slept in a week.

Her eyes snagged on Brody deep in conversation near the stairs. His black shirt was like liquid silk, open down to his stomach, showcasing his bare chest. Atop his head was a circlet of stars that twinkled like true diamonds; a celestial crown fit for the prince of Aponyx.

He glanced at her.

Their eyes met.

She looked away.

"Ugh, just you two? Where's your brother? I bet he looks delicious," Sierra said, waltzing up in a thin, floor length silver dress frosted in shimmering white stars.

"Sierra, not tonight, please." Jenin sighed. "I don't have the patience, and you look incredibly dull standing next to us, so it's in your best interest to leave us alone."

"Okay, rude," Sierra scoffed. "I was about to invite you to my party tonight, though if it weren't for Heston, I wouldn't bother. He wants to see you. I can't imagine why after that dinner."

Jenin stiffened, and if her glass hadn't been full, Eryna was certain it would've shattered in her fist. Sierra smirked and opened her mouth to say more but was interrupted by her mother.

"Hello, girls," Parvati said, a vision in white with an elaborate gold piece of metal work starting at her neck and ending at her midsection. She glowed like the full moon in August. Eryna felt suddenly eclipsed.

"Hello, Mrs. Lundal," Jenin greeted. Parvati looked Jenin and Eryna up and down.

"Don't you both look lovely. What a spectacular dress, Miss Thorne."

"Thank you," Eryna replied. "Jenin was kind enough to let me borrow it."

Parvati looked at Jenin and studied her intently.

"Yes, that was very kind," she said, as if pondering the true kindness of the gesture. Then she glanced between Jenin and her daughter. "Ladies, if you wouldn't mind, I'd love to speak with Miss Thorne for a minute. Alone."

Eryna looked at Jenin, who looked back at her with wide eyes.

"Is there a problem?" Parvati asked.

"None at all," Jenin replied, shuttering her expression. She grabbed Sierra by the wrist and threw a final glance at Eryna. "We'll be by the stairs when you're done."

Please don't leave me, Eryna wanted to shout, but her voice caught in her throat and Jenin was already gone. A tray passed and Parvati picked up a glass.

"Remind me where you're from," Parvati requested. Without Jenin there for support, Eryna suddenly felt like a mouse cornered by a snow-white leopard, bracing for the fatal chomp. Except that death would be quicker than this.

"Meedra, the…the northern peninsula in Noridas," Eryna stammered.

Gaia, get it together, she cursed herself. She needed to be confident if Parvati were to believe her.

"Yes, Meedra," Parvati drawled, expression skeptical. "A small town whose people never leave the bounds of the peninsula. So then what brings you here, to a place where the high society of the Mainland comes to indulge in sin? Not very Meedran of you, if you ask me." She punctuated the end of her sentence with a graceful sip.

Eryna nearly choked. She drank to occupy her mouth while she gathered herself. All she could do was stick to her story and pray

"I met Brody while he was…traveling, and…"

"Save your breath, girl. It's a good lie. But you'll have to do better than that with me," Parvati murmured.

Eryna froze.

She had no clue what to do, what to say. Had Parvati sniffed her out? Was it all over now?

She scanned the foyer for the closest exit, but it was impossible to fight through this crowd. Even if she left the Hunt, what would she do? Go back to The Spire? Back to Euryalea without the Hearts?

The charade was up. It was over. The Hearts, Euryalea, the Dryads, everything was over. She was going to die, and all hopes of reviving the Dryad race would die with her.

Her shock must have bled through her expression because Parvati rolled her eyes. "Don't look at me like that, little flower. Like I said, it's a *good* lie."

"How…how…" Eryna started, but words slipped hopelessly from her grasp each time. Parvati sighed.

"Your secret's safe. For now. The women here won't speak to you because you're more beautiful and secure than they are, and they hate anything beautiful they can't buy or rip to shreds. And these men…" She resentfully eyed the first man who passed. "They're not even listening to what you say. They'll believe whatever words come out of that pretty mouth because all they're thinking while you speak is that yours is a face they've never seen, a body they've never touched, and ears that haven't bled from hearing the same unremarkable stories of their mediocre achievements." Parvati stroked her finger down Eryna's sparkling shoulder and watched the crystals sway. "You're fresh meat. And if you're smart—which, I believe you are—then you'll use that to get what you want."

Despite her racing heart, Eryna kept her eyes on Parvati.

"Who says I want anything at all?" she asked, mustering every ounce of confidence she could to look Parvati in her cold, dark eyes. Parvati laughed a full, elegant laugh, and smiled like Eryna had said the funniest joke she'd ever heard.

"Everyone here wants something, little flower. Why else would we be here, hoping that whatever magical key we find, what magical door we open might hold whatever it is we've been looking for to fill that deep void inside us all?"

Eryna's brow folded.

"What is it that *you* want, then? Why tell me these things?" she asked. Parvati sighed again, as if her point was beneath Eryna's nose, and she still couldn't see it.

Then something across the room caught Parvati's attention. Eryna followed her gaze to Damian and Mr. Blackwell talking, the two of them laughing like old friends. Parvati leaned into Eryna.

"Because Miss Thorne. Evil men aren't born men."

Parvati lightly pinched Eryna's chin and turned her gaze from Damian and Mr. Blackwell, toward Brody and Derrick on the other side of the room. The two of them laughed at something Brody said, perfect mirror images of their fathers. Eryna's chest tightened.

"They're born boys," Parvati continued. "And it's so much easier to change the ambitions of the boy than to kill the ambitions of the man." Parvati released Eryna's face. "As for what I want? That's none of your damn business."

Eryna's eyes were still on the boys. Derrick saw her, smiled, and waved her over. Brody barely even looked at her. Parvati cleared her throat.

"I think you're being beckoned, little flower."

Eryna turned to look at Parvati, but she was gone.

As Eryna walked toward the boys and Jenin and Sierra, she dwelled on Parvati's words.

It's so much easier to change the ambitions of the boy than to kill the ambitions of the man. Was that what she'd said? And what did it even mean?

That, even though Mr. Blackwell was in too deep, there was still time for Brody to change course, and Eryna could make that happen? If that was it, why? What was in it for her? And why Eryna?

"You look concerned," Derrick said by way of greeting, warily eyeing her. Eryna's reply stuck in her throat as he fully came into view. He was the perfect opposite of Brody, his white silken shirt rippling around his bare torso like soft moonlight, a golden halo of rays sitting atop his head. Where Brody was the dark, mysterious night, Derrick was pure sunshine.

"Don't worry about it," Eryna said, waving him off.

"Hey," Brody said, nudging her arm. "Haven't seen you in a while."

She looked at him, straight faced. "Yup," was all she said. Then she glanced at Jenin, who gave her an approving wink.

"What'd my mom want?" Sierra questioned. There was only one shred of that conversation she could freely share with the group.

"She asked about Meedra," she said, and by the confused look on everyone's faces, she wished she'd said something else.

"She asked about Meedra? Why the Hades would she care about such a shitty little town?" Sierra recoiled, the space between her perfect brows folded in disgust.

"Don't be rude, Sierra, that's Eryna's home," Derrick scolded.

"Whatever. I'm over it, no one cares," Sierra exclaimed loudly. Eryna blew out a breath, glad to no longer be the center of attention, and relaxed as Jenin pulled her across the circle and linked their arms together. "Back to me," Sierra continued. "Tonight's party is going to be so much bigger and better than the last one. Heston even got Masten Matrix to come play a live set. He's not going on until two in the morning and is playing until sunrise. It's going to be *AMAZING!*" Sierra all but shrieked the last word and everyone cringed in unison.

"Stop screaming, Sierra, you're so loud," Brody said, rolling his eyes. Sierra glowered at him, and something in her demeanor shifted. She sauntered up to Brody, put her hand on his cheek and brushed his lips with her thumb.

"That's the opposite of what you said every night this week." Then she walked away, a smile on her face that said she knew exactly which pot she'd just stirred.

So that's why Brody hasn't replied, Eryna seethed. An aching pain gripped her chest, but she fought every ounce of emotion that tried to burst through. She clutched Jenin tight.

Jenin ground her jaw and looked Brody dead on. Eryna had never seen such fury behind a gaze.

"You didn't," Jenin accused. "Tell me you *didn't.*"

Brody looked at Eryna. He opened his mouth, shut it, opened it again. He looked like a dying, gaping fish out of water.

He couldn't say it.

He didn't have to.

"Unbelievable," Jenin sneered.

"Yikes, dude, that was certainly a choice," Derrick said, clapping his friend on the shoulder. Brody shook him off and glared.

"Shut up, man, I'm not the only one here who's done it."

Derrick shrugged. His gaze floated to Eryna.

"That was before I knew better," he said, his lips tilting into a sideways smile.

Brody swallowed hard, the knot in his throat bobbing. He looked at Eryna with pleading eyes.

"Eryna, I—" he started, but then a loud siren echoed through the room. "Shit," he cursed.

The crowd stirred. The energy of the room rose sharply. Voices chittered around them.

"It's time!"

"Everyone have their keys?"

"Bet you I'll find the prize in the first ten minutes."

Eryna glanced at Brody again. He mouthed *can we talk?*

In that moment, all she saw was that boy in the trap trying to play her for her mother's Heart; she saw her sisters dying in front of her, the Thornewood ablaze.

In that moment, Eryna decided she'd had enough of the pity pond she'd been wallowing in. She was done letting Brody win, and if Parvati was suggesting she find a way to get him to divert from his father's path, then find a way, she will.

Jealousy was a poisonous emotion, one that had always made Eryna weak and desperate when she experienced it. She bet her life it did the same to Brody.

Eryna turned to Derrick, opened her purse, and flashed him her keys. "You ready, assistant?" she asked. A smile lit up his face, his dimples pushing deep into his cheeks.

Brody looked between the two of them.

"Wait, Eryna, can we talk?" Brody asked, desperately. Her and Derrick both ignored him, their eyes locked on each other.

"Couldn't be more ready," Derrick replied, just as the siren died and a loud *boom* cracked through the space. Then she took his hand and ran. The sound of Brody shouting after them faded into the distance.

Chapter Twenty-Seven

If Eryna thought the first Hunt was wild, then tonight was chaos given life.

Her and Derrick turned down the closest corridor on fast feet, but the space was already jammed with participants. Derrick cussed, throwing a quick look back at Eryna.

"Don't let go, okay? I don't want to lose you in the crowd," he shouted over the yells and the chatter, squeezing her hand. She nodded and kept her strides slow enough to just barely trail him.

He wasn't at risk of losing her in the crowd, but he didn't need to know that. If she led, she'd nimbly maneuver them through the mob in no time, even in her heels and tight dress. But there was no need to call attention to her paranormal agility and speed, and if she were being honest, she liked letting him completely command the situation.

There was no point in giving Brody even a moment of her thoughts. It was just her and Derrick tonight, and that's all she would focus on.

The world seemed stuck in slow motion like a movie. They dodged and weaved around people who moved too slow, periodically checking in with each other through a hand squeeze or a glance.

Individuals pummeled and leapt over one another to get ahead of the ever-growing crowd. A man and woman snaked past Eryna and Derrick and paused right in front of them, pressing against the wall to kiss passionately. Derrick looked back at Eryna, brows high, and chuckled through tight lips.

Then he stopped and pulled her close to his chest.

"You alright?" he asked into the side of her head. Her eyes tracked a bead of sweat that streamed down his neck until it disappeared below his abdomen.

"Yeah," she replied. She chewed her lip to satiate her desire to reach up and catch another bead of sweat. It was suddenly so hot in this hall, and Eryna wasn't positive it was from the hundreds of people in it.

"Let's get somewhere we can breathe," she suggested. He agreed, and they set off. At one point they got jammed up behind an elderly couple. They hugged the wall to slip past, and as they reached an open doorway, a body barreled into them, knocking them over.

"Watch it!" Derrick shouted.

"Hey, I wasn't finished!" The man yelled at another man who'd just pushed him out of the way of a door. He was rather average looking, though something about his large watch and several jeweled rings made Eryna think he might be very wealthy.

"You had your turn," the other man argued. He was much larger than the first, all muscles and arrogance.

"Find another! You have a whole mansion to choose from," the first man sneered.

"Baron don't," a petite woman begged, pulling on the large man's arm. He ripped out of her grasp and tackled the rich man to the ground. The sound of the brawl entangled with the shrill shrieks of the woman. "Stop it, both of you! That's enough!" she begged, trying to pull the men off each other. She was suddenly thrown back, and her elbow connected with Eryna's nose with a loud *crunch*.

"What the Hades!" Eryna cried, throwing her hand to her face.

Immediate tears welled in her eyes, pain split her face in half, and a trickle of something warm dripped from her nostrils.

She pulled her fingers away and saw blood. Lots of blood. It was broken beyond a doubt, something she could discretely heal so long as Derrick didn't see the true damage.

He turned and scanned her face.

"What happened? Are you hurt? Let me see it," he fussed, her face between his palms. "I have half a mind to go back there and throw them out."

She kept a hand over her nose and shook her head adamantly.

"It's fine. Just startled, that's all," she assured him. "Let's keep moving. We're almost through it."

She nodded toward a bend in the hall with fewer people. He narrowed his eyes, honing in on the hand covering her nose. After a moment, he nodded, and they kept moving.

Eryna closed her eyes, took a deep breath, and trusted her feet and Derrick to keep her steady. Her nerves curled around the broken bone and fused it back into place, though she left some mild swelling so as not to completely out herself. Then she wiped off the blood.

A cheer sounded up ahead, someone's key having found its match. When they drew closer, Eryna caught a glimpse of two people attached at the lips, slipping behind the door into a darkened room. Jenin once mentioned the Hunt wasn't really about the prize. Eryna was starting to believe that was true.

Her and Derrick stopped in front of a cherrywood door somewhere deep in the west wing of the Manor. It was far quieter and emptier here.

Derrick examined her face.

"Hm," he remarked. "I could've sworn it sounded like she broke your nose."

Eryna smiled and shook her head.

"Just a little bruised and bloodied, that's all."

"You're right about the bloodied part," he chuckled, "I suppose you haven't really participated in the Hunt if you haven't shed blood at least once."

He stroked his thumb across the soft skin below her nose, rubbing the last bit of dried blood off her face. He lingered there a moment, his thumb tracing the bow of her lip.

"How do I look?" she asked. He traced her lip again, his finger leaving a tiny trail of tingles like stardust in its wake. It spread rapidly across her whole body.

"Beautiful. Always."

His gaze fell on her lips.

Her gaze fell on his.

She took a shallow breath, closed her eyes, and leaned in.

Derrick retreated a step, cleared his throat, and turned toward the door in front of them.

"Should we start here?" he asked.

Eryna sighed, a heaviness weighing down her chest. This was why they were here, after all, she reminded herself. This was why he'd been excited to join her. Keys and doors.

"Sure," she replied, attempting to smile. She scanned the door in front of them and felt no vibration in her purse.

"Not a match," she said decisively, then moved on.

Derrick grabbed her arm and dragged her back to the door.

"What do you mean 'not a match?' You didn't even try." He pointed to the purse. She shrugged.

"I know, because it's not a match." She held the purse out to him. "Try it if you want."

He eyed her skeptically, then took the keys out and meticulously assessed each one against the lock. He handed the purse back and stared at her.

"How did you know that?" he asked. She tilted her head, confused.

"What do you mean?"

"I mean how did you know there was no match without even trying?"

She narrowed her gaze, even more confused.

"Because there was no buzzing?" she said, though it came out as a question. Curiosity suddenly rimmed the edges of his eyes.

"What buzzing?"

Eryna gnawed the inside of her cheek, wondering if she'd said the wrong thing.

"Both times I found a match the key vibrated near the door," she replied. Derrick's mouth fell open, then clamped shut.

"I've never heard of that being a thing," he said. Panic constricted Eryna's chest like a boa.

Gaia, she cursed. Could she only feel the keys because she wasn't human? Was there something in the keys only magical beings could feel?

"So, you're telling me that you can *feel* when a key matches a door?" he prodded, staring at her like she was written in a language he'd never seen but was trying his hardest to read.

She hesitantly nodded, ready to accuse her of being the monster he was convinced all Dryads were, or possibly something worse, whatever that might be.

But instead, he smiled. Wide. "So, we could fight our way through all this chaos and not have to stop at a single door until we find a match?" Eryna nodded again. Derrick's smile melted into a perfect smirk that pressed a dimple into his right cheek. His mossy eyes turned wildly giddy, crinkling at the edges. "Then what are we just standing here for?" he asked, and before Eryna could catch her breath, they were fighting their way through the crowds again.

They passed ten doors. Twenty. Turned down three more halls.

"Anything?" he called back to her.

"Nothing," she replied.

Four more couples slipped behind doors. Five more fights broke out.

"Still nothing?" he asked again.

"Nope."

One man dropped his keys, six of them spilling onto the ground. The entire hall erupted into screams and shouts and fighting over the keys.

"Let's not go that way," Derrick said. Instead, they went straight and rounded a corner to a dead end with only a single door that led outside. Derrick cussed.

"We'll have to turn around," he said. But something faint vibrated against Eryna's side, calling her attention. She stepped closer to the door. Her purse rattled like a bee was trapped inside. She would've thought it was her phone if Jenin hadn't made her leave it back at The Spire.

"Feel something?" Derrick asked excitedly.

"I do," she said, pulling him through the door into the fresh air.

The cool, crisp night sent a chill through her as it played on the dew at the dip of her chest. She inhaled deeply, luxuriating in the way it filled her lungs. She glanced at Derrick and caught him staring at her, a sheepish grin on his face.

"What?" she asked.

Hands in his pockets, he knocked his shoulder into hers and said, "Nothin'. Just glad you asked me to join you. Shall we?"

He signaled toward the structure in front of them. There, sat a massive greenhouse with the tips of tall pines sticking out the top. She reached into her purse and fished for the buzzing key. She pulled out the green one Derrick had found in the planter.

Of course, she thought, and smiled. She held it out to him.

"You sure?" he asked, his voice hesitant and thrilled and teeming with wonder.

"You found it. Technically, it's your key," Eryna replied, placing it in his palm. He startled.

"Oh wow. It does vibrate," he remarked, smiling as he studied the key. Then he walked toward the greenhouse. When the lock gave, Derrick whispered, "it worked." Eryna smiled to herself.

Then he swayed on his feet, and she steadied him.

"You okay?" she asked. He nodded and straightened.

"Yeah, just got a little lightheaded and...woah."

Derrick paused in the doorway, gaping. Eryna slipped in behind him and let out a sharp gasp. Pressure built behind her eyes and her chest swelled so hard, she had to rub it with her palm to make sure it wouldn't erupt.

It wasn't just a greenhouse.

It was a very small forest.

Bark and tree foliage lined the floor, and large pines stood high and straight through the half-opened glass ceiling. Bushes rattled as critters skittered about, and Eryna inhaled deeply, absorbing the scent of fresh air and decaying wood.

The scent of home.

She took off her shoes, starved of the feel of earth beneath her feet. The soil greeted her skin with glee, and she felt word of her presence spread from the dirt to the flowers, the bushes to the trees. She looked at Derrick to gauge his reaction, his expression a war of intrigue and discomfort.

"I don't think the prize is in this room," he said, turning to leave. "Let's find another."

"No!" she shouted, grabbing his arm. He looked at her, confused. "We don't have forests in Meedra. I've always wanted to see one. Can't we stay a little longer?" She wasn't ready to leave. Not yet.

Hesitantly, he scanned the room. She was certain he thought of the Dryads and of Tyler. But she couldn't leave this room. She wouldn't.

"This isn't really a forest. It's just a small replica of one," he said.

"What difference does it make if I've never seen one?" she insisted. "Please?"

As if on cue, nightbirds high in the trees began an evening lullaby, a sweet, slow, lilting tune Eryna had always loved on nights when her mind wouldn't settle. She took Derrick by the hand.

"Come on," she said. Silently, he let her pull him deeper into the greenhouse.

The crickets and the frogs added a rhythmic flow that Eryna longed to sway with. As her and Derrick stepped into a small clearing, the air lit up with a thousand fireflies like tiny stars suspended in mid-air.

"I've never seen anything like this," Derrick breathed. With the way he was smiling, and the way her feet couldn't stop moving to the room's rhythm, Eryna couldn't take it any longer. She needed to dance. It'd been far too long since she'd danced. She wrapped her arms around Derrick's waist and looked up at him.

"Dance with me?" she asked.

He eyed her for a moment, then his hands slid behind her lower back. He brought her tight to his body.

"Thought you'd never ask," he replied. She couldn't help the smile that broke free of her lips, so wide it made her cheeks sore. Slowly, they swayed to the song of the night forest, moving left, then right as they molded into each other with each passing breath.

For a second, Eryna forgot the dull ache in her chest put there by Brody. For a second, she forgot her home was gone, that her sisters were gone. For a second, she was back in the Thornewood.

She closed her eyes and laid her head on Derrick's chest. His heart stuttered under her ear, its beat like a Dryad drum hammering against her cheek.

"We should just stay here forever," she whispered, unaware she'd spoken the thought aloud until he chuckled, and the warm sound of it reverberated through her body. Eryna swiftly lifted her head and cursed herself for getting lost in the moment.

"I could be tempted," Derrick replied, settling his cheek against her temple.

She relaxed and leaned into him. And maybe it was the music; maybe it was the fireflies, or that ever since they'd met, she'd felt like being with Derrick was effortless, but she finally stopped fighting the urge that'd been bubbling beneath the surface for the last week. Eryna leaned forward and pressed a feather-soft kiss to the base of his throat.

He inhaled sharply through his nose, pulled his head back and looked at her, frozen. She mirrored him. Had she just done something horribly wrong? Maybe he wasn't experiencing this moment the same way she was, and she'd crossed a line. Had she so seriously misread him?

He scanned her face and chewed his bottom lip thoughtfully.

"Look, I know you're Brody's, even though he messed up—"

"I'm not Brody's," Eryna quickly cut him off. Is that what this was about? Brody?

He tilted his head.

"You're not? But you came to Aponyx for him. And I saw you two in the theater last week. I thought..." he trailed off, eyeing Eryna, as if the answer could be found in her face.

"First of all, I'm not an object to be owned. But I'm not Brody's," she reiterated, and she meant it. Like Jenin had said, screw Brody. He clearly didn't care about her, and they were only using each other to get what they wanted. "He said it himself. It's complicated."

"Oh." Derrick took a stuttering breath and adjusted his balmy hand in hers. "Well, I don't want to complicate things more. He is my friend, after all, and I know he messed up being with Sierra, which, I have too, but that was before. And that's not the point, I—"

Eryna placed a finger on his mouth. She raised up on her toes and hovered her lips in front of his.

"Derrick, stop talking and kiss me," she whispered, as if the words were a secret key that could unlock him like one of the Blackwell doors.

"Absolutely," he replied, his lips parting around hers without another wasted second.

Unsure what to do next, Eryna relaxed and let him lead. His mouth was soft and steady as he guided her through the motions, his pace patient and intoxicatingly slow. His hands rose to her cheeks and gently brought her face closer, her lips deeper into his.

Electricity sparked through Eryna's veins, and after a moment, she no longer needed his guidance. She finally understood what her sisters had meant. This wasn't teachable.

It was intuitive. It was miraculous. It was divine.

She followed the wills of her body and ran her fingers through his hair. She ventured to swipe her tongue across his lower lip, and a quiet, involuntary sound escaped his throat. His kiss turned from soft and smooth to heated and starved, his fingers sinking deep into her hips as they stumbled around until she was pinned against a tree. His lips traveled up her jaw where he nipped at the sensitive skin just below her ear. Her breath stuttered, and the muscles of her core tightened.

She wanted more. So much more.

She tugged at his shirt, trying to rip it over his head, and he laughed.

"Hey, this was expensive," he jokingly scolded as he unbuttoned it. Once the last button gave, Eryna dragged her fingers across his bare shoulders and pushed the shirt off his arms onto the ground. She continued down the mountains and valleys of his muscles, and when she reached his hands, she intertwined her fingers with his.

He leaned in and softly traced her lips with his own.

"Where have you been hiding all my life?" he asked, though it felt like something he didn't mean to say aloud. Regardless, she couldn't answer, for the truth would utterly destroy everything. Instead, she leaned into him.

Like winter slowly gives way to spring, her lips slowly gave way under his, the kiss gentle, mesmerizing, filling every inch of her with him until he was all that existed in her universe.

Then sharp, shattering glass interrupted them.

"What was that?" Eryna asked. Derrick shook his head.

"A bird, maybe?" he suggested, picking up his shirt and putting it back on. Eryna was about to protest, but then the shouting started.

"If you weren't so distracted by that girl, we might have the third Heart by now. We could use your help in there," Mr. Blackwell said. Derrick and Eryna moved toward the entrance of the greenhouse. The door was still closed, a single panel having presumably been shattered by a rock that lie nearby bits of glass.

"I'd hardly call Sierra a distraction," Brody said, his silhouetted form appearing.

"You know Sierra is not who I'm referring to. It's that girl you supposedly picked up during your university tour. When did you go to Meedra? That wasn't on your itinerary," Mr. Blackwell urged. Brody stiffened.

"You leave her out of this."

"See, that's exactly what I'm talking about. Your mind isn't in it anymore. How am I supposed to trust Blackwell Technologies in your hands when I'm gone?"

Brody scoffed.

"Like that will ever happen."

"It *is* going to happen, son. I'm dying. Jerry is dying. Damian is *dying*." Eryna looked at Derrick, his expression unreadable. She reached down and squeezed his hand. He didn't return it.

"The two Hearts we have are fading. We'll all be gone sooner than later if we don't find the third. I need you to prove you care about this family's future."

So that's what they wanted them for, Eryna thought.

Life. Youth. Power.

Everything the Dryads were freely gifted by the Gods in

exchange for a peaceful existence and caring for the land.

Then the humans came and took it from them.

Furious heat blazed across Eryna. Her fists clenched so hard, it felt as though her knuckles might burst through her skin. She needed to get those Hearts back home and get them to safety.

Derrick startled at her side and frantically searched his pockets until he pulled out his phone. He looked at the screen, cussed, then held a finger up to Eryna.

One second, he mouthed, and stepped out of earshot.

Brody and his father continued.

"Don't question my loyalty to this family. You know our legacy means everything to me," Brody challenged.

"Then I need you to step up. Do what you have to do. Send her back to Meedra or wherever she's really from," Mr. Blackwell said. So, he really didn't know what she was, then.

"No," Brody spat, then went silent, like he hadn't meant to react so strongly. He took a breath. "Being with that girl *is* stepping up, father."

Panic poisoned Eryna's breath. Her head went light.

Was he about to tell him what she was?

Even worse, if Derrick overheard whatever was about to come out of Brody's mouth, it would destroy everything.

A light tap on her shoulder made her almost leap out of her skin.

"That was Jenin," Derrick whispered. "We have to go. There's a back door over here."

Thank Gaia. Eryna blew out a thick breath and followed Derrick to the far corner of the greenhouse and out onto the grassy lawn. Her secret was safe from him for now.

"What'd Jenin want?" Eryna asked, taking Derrick's hand as they strolled along the grass toward the far end of the Manor. He sighed.

"Sierra's party started early. Something happened with Heston, but I couldn't get much out of her. She was mumbling about locking herself in a room or something. She's about half-bagged on wine already, so it's hard to say."

"Oh no," Eryna remarked through a grimace. While Derrick's tone was annoyed, Eryna picked up on the clear worry.

"Yeah." Derrick nodded as he folded Eryna into his arms and planted a warm kiss on her forehead. She melted into his comforting touch. "Looks like we need to make a pitstop on our way home. I just hope we don't have to carry her out this time."

Eryna laughed into his chest, and it jiggled beneath her head as they chuckled together. But as they made their way down the street toward the Lundal's, Eryna couldn't help but worry what they were walking into.

Chapter Twenty-Eight

Eryna and Derrick stepped through the doorway of the Lundal's home, and the first thing that greeted them was a thick, billowing cloud of strong smoke with a hint of pine to it. She knew this smell. It came from a leaf her and her sisters smoked sometimes when they wanted to relax.

The place was lit only by electric blue and purple lights that strobed in time with loud music. In the dim atmosphere, hundreds of young partygoers melted into a single silhouette, like a dark sea that rocked and roiled.

The house was a fraction of the size of Blackwell Manor, but even in the dark, it was large enough Eryna knew they wouldn't find Jenin quickly, especially since she'd stopped answering her phone.

Derrick pulled Eryna close and spoke directly in her ear.

"As much as I'd love to avoid Sierra, we need to find her. She'll know where Jenin went," he said. Eryna scanned the room, trying to make sense of what she could see. It was nothing but adolescents sipping from glass bottles and hanging off each other as they danced with red cups in their hands. Smoke jammed up the room, catching the colored lights. It was rowdier than even the most raucous of Dryad bonfire nights.

And the humans had the audacity to call Dryads the savage ones.

"How will we find her in this?" Eryna shouted, trying to speak over the music, not realizing Derrick's ear was right next to her. He jerked away, wincing as he tugged on his earlobe. She cupped his head and gave it a gentle squeeze.

"I'm sorry!" she apologized.

He laughed and planted several quick kisses on her lips, punctuating his acceptance of her apology with a single slow, heart-clenching kiss that made her whole body burn.

"Sierra always needs to be in the middle of the action," he said. "I think I know where she is."

Derrick grabbed her hand and the two of them dove headfirst into the sea of people, slowly snaking their way through. They entered a large, crowded room where a man stood behind some sort of electronic instrument, pressing and tweaking buttons. Sierra was next to him, casting him glances as she danced wildly, all but knocking him over. It reminded Eryna of a very strange bird trying to attract a mate.

Eryna and Derrick looked at each other and rolled their eyes. He grabbed a small, beaded bracelet from a nearby table, stretched it out with two fingers like a slingshot, and launched it at Sierra. It hit her square in the forehead.

She froze.

"Who the fuck did that!" she shouted, searching the room with fire in her eyes, sour disgust wilting her lips.

Eryna unraveled into uncontrollable laughter, lungs stuttering as she gasped for air. Her eyes blurred and welled with tears. Derrick collapsed onto her shoulder in his own fit of giggles, and it took several sighs and extra chuckles to pull themselves together. Sierra flashed them her middle finger as she spotted them, then stepped down from her stage, meeting them at the side of the dancing crowd.

"You could've blinded me, you know!" she yelled over the music.

"Lucky for you I have good aim. We're looking for my sister," Derrick replied. Sierra rolled her eyes and made a sound of disgust. Eryna couldn't help but glare.

"She's really done it now," Sierra said.

"What do you mean?"

"I mean good luck to your father trying to keep that deal he has with the Perrys. I doubt Heston will marry her now."

Marry?

Heston and Jenin are supposed to get married? Since when? From how Jenin acted, Eryna was certain she hated him.

"Just tell us where she is, Sierra," Derrick urged impatiently. Sierra sighed and silently pointed toward a spiral staircase.

"Let's go," Derrick said, taking Eryna's hand. They bounded up the staircase as quickly as they could. The only problem was that there were about thirty rooms up there.

"You go left, I'll go right?" Eryna suggested, scanning the long hall. Derrick nodded.

"Meet back here in ten," he said. Then he gave her a parting kiss.

The first five doors Eryna tried were locked, and on the sixth door, she opened it and immediately shut it, seeing two bare bodies and crumpled sheets. She should probably give a warning knock going forward.

On the tenth door, she knocked, and even through the loud atmosphere, Eryna heard a sharp, "Get lost!"

Jenin.

Eryna jiggled the handle. It was locked. She knocked again.

"I said get lost!"

"Jenin, it's me. It's Eryna," she said. She wasn't sure that would make Jenin open the door. If anything, it might be why she *doesn't* open the door.

But it opened an inch.

A hand shot out and pulled Eryna through the small crack.

She caught sight of Jenin's puffy eyes and red nose, like she'd been crying for at least an hour.

"Jenin," she started, but Jenin held up a palm.

"Don't," she said, striding to a bed and sitting on the edge. She held up her phone, flashing the dark screen. "Couldn't find a charger."

"That's okay. We still found you," Eryna said. She was about to tell Jenin they should go, that Derrick was waiting, but something about the curl of Jenin's shoulders, the heaviness in her chest made it clear that she wasn't ready to leave yet.

"What happened?" Eryna asked instead.

Jenin scoffed and rolled her eyes.

"Nothing that wouldn't have happened at some point," she said, looking vaguely off to the left. Eryna had no idea what Jenin meant, and her expression must have said as much. Jenin sighed. "Heston cornered me on the dance floor. He wouldn't back off, so I spilled another drink on him."

Eryna shrugged. "That doesn't seem so bad."

Jenin winced.

"It didn't work this time. So..."

Jenin held up her right hand, her light pink fingernails tipped in a rust color.

"Gaia," Eryna breathed, mostly surprised but also impressed.

"Yeah. My contribution to that pretty face of his." Jenin grimaced and shook her head at a thought that seemed to weigh on her mind.

Eryna knew Derrick was probably waiting for them by the stairs but having Jenin in this private moment presented a rare opportunity for Eryna to ask a question she'd been pondering the answer to.

"Is...is Heston why you don't like men?" Eryna asked, stepping closer to Jenin. Jenin snorted and rolled her eyes. Her favorite response to everything.

"I've never really liked men."

"Are they all so bad, though? I mean, your brother—"

"No, Eryna. Gods," Jenin cut her off, huffing a short,

contemptuous laugh, but her eyes were cold and honest. "I mean I've never really *liked* men."

Eryna waited for Jenin to say more.

Then she realized there was no more.

"Oh," Eryna said, and looked down, feeling suddenly stupid for not immediately catching on. Then she asked, "What about that actor you dated?"

Jenin pursed her lips and glanced at her feet.

"He needed some arm candy to be more 'appealing' as a celebrity. Heartthrobs land more leading roles. And I suppose I just needed a distraction."

Eryna wasn't sure when she'd sat next to Jenin.

"Many of my sisters had female human lovers back in the day," Eryna said. "It didn't sound like something they had to hide. Is that not the case for you?"

Jenin folded her hands in her lap and stared at them, repeatedly rubbing at a spot of dried blood on a nail.

"It's fine for most people to be public about their preferences. But when your father sells you to Mainland royalty like fucking cattle, it's...frowned upon." Jenin turned her attention from the dried blood to a particularly tenacious hangnail. "Earlier this summer, Heston and his father came to visit to discuss the 'arrangement,'" she emphasized the last word with her fingers. "Our fathers left us alone so they could talk business, but I knew they were forcing us to get to know each other."

Eryna swallowed around a dry lump that had formed in her throat. Her heart raced in her chest. Without knowing anything, she already knew Heston deserved whatever scar his face would bear from Jenin's nails.

"He put a move on me," Jenin continued, her breath shortening. "I told him to leave me alone. That I wasn't interested. That I would *never* be interested, because he wasn't my type..." Eryna caught a small tremble in Jenin's hand. Without hesitation, she grabbed it, folding it in her own.

Jenin looked at their joined hands. "…but Heston is a duke. And dukes aren't used to hearing the word 'no.'"

Eryna's heart clenched. Jenin finally looked up and tears spilled from her red eyes. Before she could say more, Eryna did the only thing she could do; the one thing she knew spanned languages and races and beings of all kinds: she hugged her. Tight.

Eryna wrapped both arms around Jenin and pulled her to her chest. Jenin folded into her without resistance, her petite frame shaking in Eryna's arms.

"He s-said the only reason I like women is because I've never b-been with a 'real man' before," she stuttered through broken sobs. "As if he's some shining beacon of that ideal," Jenin scoffed.

Eryna hugged Jenin tighter, a sob of her own escaping her. Jenin continued, "I screamed. I cried for help. My father didn't come. He-he was in the next room, and h-he didn't come. Why didn't he come? Why didn't he come?"

"I'm so sorry," Eryna whispered repeatedly as she stroked Jenin's hair. "I'm so sorry."

Eryna's heart shattered for Jenin. Her eyes burned with hot, furious tears as she cried for her, with her, in solidarity.

This wasn't about Eryna, but her and Jenin's common ground was now clearer than ever. While Eryna's body hadn't been assaulted back in the Thornewood, her mother's had; her entire realm's had. Both girls had something deeply personal and sacred stolen from them by the same group of people.

After several minutes and several deep, shuttering breaths, Jenin relaxed in Eryna's arms and laid her head on Eryna's shoulder. A sudden pit weighed Eryna's stomach down as she thought about the other person who also lived in The Spire.

"Does Derrick know?" Eryna asked. Jenin sniffled and shook her head.

"No," she replied. "You're the only one who does. He was with

Brody and Tyler that night."

Eryna chewed the inside of her lip and thought of how worried Derrick was about his sister, how he'd spent his summer trying to understand her.

"He might like to know, if you're comfortable telling him," she said, keeping her words as vague as possible. She didn't need to be warned to stay away from Derrick again, especially now that it was never going to happen. A crease appeared between Jenin's brows.

"I've wanted to tell him all summer, but I just..." Jenin took a shallow breath, followed closely by a second deeper one. "...I'm afraid he'll look at me differently. And he's so sensitive. He wears his emotions on his chest. Ever since our mom died, that's the one thing I've tried to protect. He loves so fiercely. It's so rare. And if I tell him what happened...I think it might break him."

Jenin's gaze met Eryna's, and her eyes were the most open, most vulnerable she'd ever seen them. In that moment, Eryna finally realized why Jenin had so adamantly warned Eryna away from Derrick.

It wasn't because Jenin thought he might kill Eryna if he knew she was a Dryad. It wasn't to protect Eryna at all.

It was to protect Derrick.

Just then, the door opened, and he stepped through. He paused at the threshold, taking in the sight of both girls with tears in their eyes.

"Everything okay? I waited for you at the top of the stairs, and when you didn't come..." he looked at Jenin, brows tilted down, and Eryna swore she could see his heart actively breaking in his chest.

This sweet boy and his sweet, sweet heart.

Jenin nodded, then stood and brushed out her dress. She straightened her shoulders, grabbed her purse, and snapped her usual mask of indifference and mild disgust over her features, destroying all evidence of vulnerability.

"Fine. Let's go," she demanded as she joined her brother at the door. Eryna followed.

Derrick and Eryna lingered a few feet back as they made their way through the Lundal's home. He leaned into her.

"What happened?" he asked. Eryna contemplated what to say, how she could paraphrase the conversation, but then decided it was none of her business to say anything at all.

"You'll have to ask her," she said, and to her surprise, that was answer enough for him.

A sudden arm hooked around Derrick's neck and yanked him away. Eryna turned to see a very drunk Heston hanging off Derrick like they were old friends, four perfect slashes across his left cheek. Eryna set off toward them, but Jenin pulled her back and held her in place.

"Heeeyyy, little brother!" Heston slurred.

"Get off me, man, I'm not your brother," Derrick said, trying to shrug him off but Heston squeezed tighter.

"Well, you will be. That is, if your prude of a sister decides she's done being an absolute slag."

Jenin's arm tightened around Eryna, and Derrick lunged at Heston but couldn't get a good enough angle to hit him. Eryna was ready to jump in when she was needed. She could kill him in seconds. Happily.

"Derrick, don't," Jenin urged, and Derrick stopped. Heston cackled.

"Aww, wittle baby bwother needs to wisten to his big sister, huh?"

Jenin waltzed up to Heston and crossed her arms.

"Were my claws not enough for you?" she asked. His expression turned lazy and drunk as he waggled his brows at her.

"You know I like a little pain, Neens." He winked.

Jenin smiled that terrifying, sharp smile.

"Really? Then you'll love this."

Jenin wound up and punched Heston in the groin. Observers within a thirty-person radius audibly groaned and gasped. Derrick ducked out of Heston's arm and met Eryna where she stood. He high-fived Jenin as she rejoined the two of them.

"Thanks, sis," he said. But Eryna wasn't so easily satisfied. She looked at Heston, let her face melt into the most unsettling smile she could muster, and feinted at him. He gasped and coward against a bystander, and the room dissolved into laughter.

Then Derrick draped one arm around her, the other around Jenin, and the three of them left the party without another glance back.

Chapter Twenty-Nine

Eryna, Derrick, and Jenin spent the ride to The Spire reminiscing on Heston's face as he doubled over in pain from Jenin's groin punch, and how he coward from Eryna like a rat. But the elevator ride was peacefully silent with exhaustion. Derrick pulled Eryna into his arms. Jenin eyed them but said nothing.

"I'll walk you to your room," Derrick offered Eryna as they entered the foyer.

"Actually, D," Jenin said, calling his attention. "Can we, uhm… talk?"

He hesitated, looking at his sister with a million questions. He looked back at Eryna.

Even if Jenin shared only a little of her story with Derrick, Eryna was glad. Jenin needed the emotional support, especially if Eryna was the only one who knew, because she would be gone soon, anyway.

Gone soon, she thought, and suddenly the idea of leaving was strangely uncomfortable. She tucked the thought away for later.

"You should go," she encouraged.

Derrick gently wrapped his arms around her and kissed her, then whispered into her lips, "We'll pick up where we left off later."

"Gods, why did I even bother?" Jenin gagged. "I should've known neither of you would listen to me."

Eryna and Derrick chuckled, and he kissed her one more time before following his sister down the hall. Before they turned the corner, Jenin looked back at Eryna and gave her a warm, grateful smile, however small it was. Eryna returned it, hoping it gave Jenin a boost of confidence.

Once in her room, Eryna waltzed to her phone on the nightstand and glanced at the screen. There were twelve missed calls and at least ten texts from Brody. There was even one voicemail.

So now *he can reply?* she thought, and without reading a single one, she washed herself up for the night and took her next tonic. She dressed in night clothes she thought Derrick might like, then fell on the bed and waited.

And waited.

Her lids grew heavy, her mind slowed, and her bed started to feel far too comfortable for her to be awake. Eryna knew the conversation between Jenin and Derrick would take time, and she didn't want to detract from the moment, but her impatience pecked at her, so she sent Derrick a quick text:

> Getting tired, heading to bed for the night. Will see you in the morning.

After rereading it, she decided to add a smiling face at the end, so it sounded nicer. Eryna could wait until tomorrow just fine. Jenin needed her brother tonight.

Just as Eryna teetered off the edge of sleep, a knock woke her.

Heart first, she leapt out of bed. She threw the door open, grinning so hard she thought her face might split in half.

"How'd it go? I wondered when you would—"

Eryna froze. Her face fell.

There, leaning against the doorway was a very wet, very miserable looking Brody.

"Not who you were expecting?" he asked. A quick smile rose and fell on his lips in the same breath. Eryna's heart tumbled into her stomach. She hated her body for reacting.

He stared at her, biting his lip like he was holding something back.

It was all she could do not to slam the door in his face. The only sound that could be heard was the steady *drip, drip, drip* of water off Brody's clothes. He inhaled deeply, opening his mouth to speak.

But Eryna spoke first.

"You asked me to call you," she said. He glanced at his feet, barely shielding a wince.

"I know," he replied. His gaze didn't leave the ground.

"I called you," she challenged.

He rubbed the back of his neck. His jaw clenched. His voice dropped to a near whisper.

"I know."

Silence settled between them like deep snow in winter, thick and layered. Brody tried to speak several times, unable to meet Eryna's gaze. If she didn't know it were an act, she might think he was genuinely ashamed of himself for the last week. But that was not the case, and he was an impeccable actor.

"Why are you wet?" she asked, unable to stand the silence any longer. He finally looked up. Their eyes met, and Eryna tried to block out the pulsing heat beneath her skin.

"Sierra pushed me in the pool," Brody replied, laughing a little. Then he glanced around the empty hall behind him. "Can I come in?"

Right then, she should have shut the door. She should have told him to leave; that she had no interest in what he had to say.

Instead, Eryna opened her door wider. She told herself it was because she needed those Hearts, and he was still her best chance of getting them. She repeated it several times before she believed it.

Hands deep in his pockets, he slid past her into the room and looked around.

"They gave you a nice room. I'm glad. Have you been comfortable here?" he asked, his finger grazing a flourishing fern that Eryna had coaxed into sprouting several new delicate fiddleheads.

"Comfortable enough," she replied, leaning against the door as she shut it. Brody nodded, his eyes still wandering about the room, falling on tonight's dress, now a glistening puddle on the floor.

"And Jenin and Derrick? How's it been with them?"

They treat me better than you, she wanted to say. She wanted to tell him about how they hadn't just made her feel comfortable, but welcome. They hadn't just fed her and housed her, they'd taught her about their world and introduced her to things like movies, popcorn, candy, pop music, even though Derrick didn't know it was all new to her. She wanted Brody to feel like an inadequate host. She wanted to unleash all her anger and frustration at him for vanishing.

But that wouldn't get her what she needed.

"Clearly you want to say something, Brody, or you wouldn't be here, so just say it," Eryna said, done with the forced chatter. They'd been beyond small talk since the moment she first spared his life. Hands back in his pockets, he sighed.

"Did you read any of my texts?" he asked. Eryna lifted a brow at him and pushed her lips into a flat line.

Of course not, she tried to make her eyes say. He read her perfectly.

"That's fair, I guess," he said. "I wanted to tell you that I'm sorry."

Eryna waited for him to say more, but he just looked at her expectantly. She tilted her head.

"That's it? You're 'sorry?'" Eryna nearly snorted in disbelief. This was what he'd come all the way to The Spire for?

He shrugged.

"Well, yeah, I mean, what else is there to say?"

"There's plenty else to say!" Eryna's voice rose, surprising them both. She took a breath to reset and tried to make herself seem smaller, quieter; more sad, less angry. They were in *her* game now, not his. He needed to think she was innocent. He needed to believe she was a fool.

"Was it something I said? Or did?" she asked, trying to channel the energy of an injured animal. "Just tell me what I did wrong. I can try and change. I can be different..."

"No, Eryna, it wasn't you." Brody crossed the room in three strides. He gently grabbed her arms and ducked his head, catching her eye line. "It was nothing you said or did. It wasn't you at all. You've been nothing but perfect, I promise."

"Then what happened? I thought that we..." her voice trailed off, and she let his imagination fill in whatever it was he wanted to hear. He took the bait, trailing a finger up her bare shoulder, playing with the thin strap of her shirt. Involuntary chills rippled across her skin.

"I—" he paused, scanning her face, leaning in an inch. "I got scared."

Her brows folded.

"Scared of what? Of me? Because of what I am?"

"No, not that. I scared myself," he said. "When you fainted in the theater, I panicked. I was so worried I'd lost you somehow—or would lose you if you didn't get help—and I hadn't felt like that since...well since my mom. But once I knew you were okay I just...I couldn't deal, I guess. I fell back on a bad habit. I've never been in this situation before. I've never felt like this about anyone."

Gaia, he's really laying it on thick, Eryna internally rolled her eyes. *He even brought his mom into this.* But she kept her exterior soft, fragile. Eyes wide as a doe's, she tilted her face closer to his.

"Like what?" she whispered. He leaned closer, his wet shirt soaking the front of her tank top. His hand trailed up her neck and cradled her jaw. Eryna's stomach roiled as thoughts of Derrick pushed their way to her heart, but she picked them up and shoved them somewhere they couldn't reach her. She couldn't have him on her mind right now. As unclean as it made her feel playing into Brody like this, as much as she wished he were Derrick instead, she had to focus. Her whole world depended on it.

"Like I can't breathe without you," Brody replied, their lips touching. She pulled back at the last second and looked up at him.

"Is that what you said to Sierra?" she asked. Brody's eyes sparkled with laughter, and he smiled, the wolf peeking through the façade.

"The exact opposite, actually. Why do you think she pushed me in the pool?" He stroked her cheek and leaned in again.

This time, she let him.

His kiss was tentative and soft, like he was asking for permission before going any further. It was unexpectedly gentle, making her head go light and body warm. Her lungs stopped, and she had to remind herself what it felt like to breath.

"I don't know how to be around you, Eryna," he whispered between slow kisses. "You're all I ever think about."

At that, something in her bloomed like a lotus, opening up to him. She let his lips explore more, his tongue find hers. Her fingers climbed his damp neck and pulled him closer. She barely had time to gasp between needing to breath and needing to feel his lips on hers again. Before she knew it, he was on top of her on the bed, his curious hand exploring the expanse of her stomach beneath her shirt and climbing higher.

Then a door slammed on the floor above them. They paused and looked up.

"Father!" Derrick shouted, loud enough to be heard throughout the entire penthouse. His heavy, furious steps reverberated through the ceiling.

"Derrick, no, don't!" Jenin's muffled plea followed him.

"Oh no," Eryna breathed.

"What? What's going on?" Brody asked. Eryna didn't answer.

She scrambled out from beneath his body and ran for the door. Whatever was about to happen wouldn't be good, and for whatever reason, Eryna felt compelled to be there.

"Eryna wait!" Brody called after her and she paused to look at him. He pointed at her. "Your shirt."

She looked down and realized her shirt was now completely see through.

"Oh," she said as she crossed her arms over her chest. Brody grabbed a sweatshirt off the floor and tossed it at her. She threw it on and the two of them bolted toward the second floor. The shouts escalated.

"You monster! She's your daughter!" Derrick screamed.

"Derrick, please!" Jenin begged.

"Shut up and calm down, son. Listen to your sister," Damian urged.

Brody tugged on Eryna's hand as they followed the voices.

"Eryna tell me what the Hades is going on."

"Later," she replied, waving him off. They crossed through the foyer toward the other wing of the penthouse where Damian's office was.

"You let him hurt her. You let him violate her and you were *right there*. How could you?" Derrick shouted. "*How could you!*"

They turned the corner and saw the three Ashfords standing in Damian's office, Damian's back to the entrance. Eryna tried to go in, but Brody held her back. She knew this wasn't her business, this wasn't her family, but she couldn't just stand by.

"You honestly believe what your sister is saying?" Damian asked, laughing. "For all we know, she gave herself to him and turned this all around to make herself look better. That seems a more likely story."

Damian really was a monster, Eryna fumed, bile burning her throat. She stepped forward to do something, anything, but it all happened so fast.

Jenin slapped Damian across the face.

He slapped her in return, her face immediately welling with a large handprint.

Derrick tackled him to the ground, landing several punches, but Damian was quick. He landed a single punch across Derrick's face and knocked him out.

"Enough!" Eryna exclaimed, more to herself than anything.

She grabbed the heaviest thing she could find, a white marble bust of some important man.

"No, don't!" Brody called after her.

She brought it down over Damian's head.

He fell to the floor.

The room went silent.

Brody, Jenin, and Eryna stared at the two Ashford men on the ground.

What have I done? Eryna worried, but as Damian's chest rose and fell, relaxed an inch. She hadn't killed him.

"Brody," Jenin said. "Brody get her out of here."

Eryna looked up at Jenin.

"Wait, no," Eryna protested. She couldn't leave. She didn't want to be away from Jenin and Derrick. Jenin took the bust from her hands and set it aside. She grabbed Eryna's shoulders.

"You need to leave before he wakes up, or he'll kill you. I mean it. He will *kill* you."

"I can't, I won't, I can't," Eryna tried to form a coherent sentence, but nothing came out as the realization of what she'd just done settled. She'd attacked Damian Ashford. She couldn't stay there. Not anymore. Jenin said something else, but Eryna didn't hear it.

"I can heal him," she offered. "He'll never know. Let me heal him and I can stay."

Damian stirred on the floor.

"There's no time. Get her out now, Brody. Now!"

Eryna tried to move, but she was glued to the spot like being stuck in a bog. Her eyes were trained on Damian. A warm hand wrapped around hers. Brody's calm voice said, "Come on. We need to go."

Before Eryna could react, Brody was pulling her through the penthouse and out the door.

The elevator lasted for a blink.

The car ride lasted for a breath.

And suddenly, she was walking into Blackwell Manor—the only place she had left to go.

Chapter Thirty

The marble tile was ice against Eryna's bare feet, so much colder than the mahogany floors and carpeted halls of the Ashford's penthouse. The high ceiling made the space around her heavy and suffocating, as if the weight of so much empty air could crush her like a snail underfoot. The only bit of warmth tethering Eryna to reality was Brody's hand in hers.

"Wait here one second," he said. Then he stepped away and left her frigid and shivering as he spoke to a nearby staff member. Eryna crossed her arms to hold tight to whatever heat she had left as the room flurried around her.

The Hunt had only just ended.

Handfuls of left behind garments were being hauled away, spilled drinks and smashed food cleaned off the floor. More than once, a staff member almost knocked her over, like they hadn't even seen her there. She might as well have been one of the candelabras on the staircase, the one near the center landing with its flower circlet and precariously placed leaves that covered only the most intimate of parts, a human's depiction of a Dryad.

Warmth once again embraced her as Brody wrapped an arm around her. He nodded toward the stairs.

"Let's get you to a room," he said. She nodded but remained silent as they made their way to a door somewhere on the second floor. Or maybe it was the fourth. Eryna wasn't paying attention.

All she could see was the red handprint on Jenin's cheek, Derrick's unconscious body on the floor. All she could taste was burning hot rage, the fire in her lungs. All she could feel was the heavy marble bust in her hands, how solid it felt when it connected with Damian's head.

"Since the rooms automatically lock during the Hunt, you'll need a key," Brody said as he pulled a slender gold key from his pocket. A small black bead was fastened around its neck, and on its head was a bluebird carrying a branch of berries.

"Pretty," Eryna remarked, not realizing she'd said the thought aloud. Brody smiled slightly, though the downturn of his eyes made him look sad. He nodded.

"It's the only room I won't let them use for my father's guests. It's a little messy. Someone's coming in a few minutes to clean it and change the sheets and stuff, but I figured…"

His voice trailed off and he shrugged as he held the key out to Eryna. She opened the door.

Where all of Blackwell Manor was dark wood and wrought iron and black and white marble, this room had a certain feather-lightness to it, though a little dusty and stale, like it hadn't been touched in years.

Three tall, arched windows were set deep in white, intricately molded walls. One side of the room held a large upholstered bed and nightstands. The other held a wide-mouthed fireplace and a chaise, capped by two large bookshelves with all manner of books crammed in every which way. But what brought the room to life the most were the pictures.

Eryna's eyes fell on a one on the mantel: a young woman holding a young child, a little boy with dark curls and dark eyes. They looked at each other as if no one else existed, the woman's smile as bright as the morning sun.

Eryna recognized her immediately.

"Your mother," she said, looking back at Brody. He tilted his head as he distantly eyed the picture and nodded.

"Was this her room?" Eryna asked, scanning the space through more informed eyes. Brody nodded again. Now she understood why it looked so untouched. Because it was.

Eryna studied the key in her hand.

"I can't stay here," she said, holding it out to him. "I don't want to impose. Put me in a different room. I don't mind how small it is. I sleep in a hole in a tree, for Gaia's sake."

Eryna chuckled, but Brody closed her fist around the key and gently pressed it to her chest. His eyes burrowed deep into hers, wide and earnest.

"No, please. I want you to."

"Brody—"

"Please. It hasn't seen life since she died, and I can't think of anyone else she'd be more happy to see use it." Brody reached up, traced the length of her cheekbone with his thumb, and smiled. "She would've really liked you," he said, and leaned in for one slow, lingering kiss that threatened to pull Eryna off the ground as she stretched high on her toes.

This isn't real, it isn't real, it isn't real, she had to repeat, reminding herself of the one thing she was sure of. And even though her heart ached for Derrick, when Brody pulled away, she couldn't help but hold her breath a second longer in hopes he'd come back for more.

"I have to get a few things in order, and we'll need to get you more tonic. Also, Damian might not have known it was you who knocked him out, but just in case, we need to make a plan of keeping him away from you. I'm thinking we should scour the Manor and find every door your keys may unlock. That way, if he comes around, you have a few places to hide where he can't get to you."

Eryna's stomach clenched, and she nodded in agreement. Brody was right. While Damian might not have seen her, chances were high he suspected it was her. Who else could it have been? She needed to stay far away from him.

As soon as Brody slipped through the open door, a young woman popped her head in.

"Miss Thorne?" she asked. Eryna nodded. The woman entered, carrying a box in one hand and a wheeled case in the other. "These were sent over from Miss Ashford. There are a few more coming, but the driver noted this was the most important."

The woman held out the box, and Eryna took it. Inside was her cell phone, her purse of keys, and her stash of beauty tonic. Eryna grabbed her phone and saw a text from Jenin waiting for her.

> Sent the essentials with the driver. I won't let Brody's personal shopper undo all the hard work I put into your wardrobe. And as much as I hate the stupid Hunt, I know you like it, so I figured you'd want your keys. You might not hear from us for a bit, but Derrick and I are okay.

Eryna released a breath she'd been holding since leaving The Spire. She couldn't care less about the clothes. She was a little disappointed there was nothing from Derrick but knowing him and Jenin were okay was all that mattered. There was no point in denying that she cared about them now, and if she were being honest, it felt nice to care about people who were still alive. It was a lot less lonely.

"Miss Thorne, may we start cleaning the room?" Another woman poked her head into the room. Eryna tried to ignore the uncomfortable sensation that curled in her stomach, still not used to the idea of people waiting on her.

"Sure, go ahead," she replied as she grabbed her phone and purse out of the box. Eryna couldn't stand the thought of staying in there while they cleaned. It felt haughty and arrogant, and she would only get in the way. She might as well wander while she waited.

This was, after all, what Eryna had wanted from the beginning. To be alone in Blackwell Manor, the whole place at her fingertips.

It just wasn't how she wanted it.

Chapter Thirty-One

A light buzz at Eryna's side pulled her into the present.

How long had she been wandering? Where even was she?

Her feet ached enough to guess she'd walked the Manor for at least an hour, but she'd been so lost in thought, it felt as though it'd been half that time.

She scanned the hall around her and found nothing but one large painting of a nondescript ship on a swelling ocean wave.

Eryna stepped closer to the painting, and her purse violently buzzed. She pulled out the marble key and searched the frame of the painting, finding a small keyhole on its outer edge.

It clicked into place. The painting slid to the side. Eryna fought the wave of lightheadedness that washed over her, the slight pain in her chest, and when she saw what was behind the painting, she gasped.

In front of her was a large, bright room filled with all manner of art and artifacts. No wonder there were no other doors in the hall. The gallery spanned the entire length of it.

Eryna strolled past paintings of peacetimes and paintings of war, and statues of leaders she didn't know the names of. She passed by perfectly preserved artifacts displayed behind thick glass. Some were clothes and accessories that belonged to famous humans, others were ancient weapons once used by the humans in the Titan wars.

Then a sign above an open archway caught her eye.

"Nymphs," Eryna read aloud.

Her heart raced like a wild horse in her chest. Her throat went dry, and she almost choked on her own air. She couldn't get through the arch fast enough.

The first piece to greet her was a painting of the Polaris Mother Mountain, the northern mother of Thessalia, the realm of the Oread mountain nymphs.

Eryna traced the shape of the mountain with her eyes, climbing up its soft base before shooting up its sharp, edged summit. It was the pinnacle of the Polaris Range, the largest of the three ranges in Thessalia just as the Sylvanwood had been the largest of the three woods of Euryalea. Eryna had always liked the few Oreads she'd met, though they were often cold and taciturn and hard to read, just like their mother mountains and the rest of their mountainous realm.

Eryna moved deeper into the gallery. She passed a thick glass case that held two small, steel spheres, claiming to be Thessalian artifacts. Her sisters had told her stories about them. Ancient nymphs had manipulated steel into magical contraptions that trapped the spirits of the Titans after the war, ensuring they never rose to power again. A chill fell over Eryna, and she hurried off to a different section, worried that if she looked at the spheres too long, the Titans might burst through their shells.

She stopped at a large stone carving of a woman on her knees, embracing a laurel tree. Her face was carved in eternal agony, and everlasting tears stained her cheeks as she wept into the bark of the laurel.

Eryna didn't have to read the description to know who it was.

Ardian.

Except, they'd gotten her face all wrong, giving her round eyes and thinner lips like a human. Eryna had met her once and she was beautiful, albeit a wilting thing. Her tilted almond eyes were forever glassy, her full lips always downturned. Eryna had been scared to hug her, worried she'd crush her if she gave her more than a light embrace.

The humans were utterly obsessed with her tragic story, claiming it was one of true love; a story where, even in the face of tragedy, the Gods showed pity. They gifted Ardian's dying human love a long enough life as a tree that they could finally "live" together, for even in his best human health, she would've outlived him by hundreds of years.

The Dryads rolled their eyes at that take. There was nothing beautiful about Ardian's tragedy. She lived in constant pain for six hundred years. Her sisters said the true reason humans loved it was because it immortalized the human man Ardian had fallen in love with. Little did they realize they killed him, too, when they killed the Fiddlewood.

Eryna sighed, stood, and nearly leapt from her skin as she saw a small, round woman with brown hair seated on a bench nearby, observing a painting. The woman hadn't noticed Eryna yet, so she contemplated leaving. She was exhausted anyway, her limbs achy and weak. She stifled a cough that threatened to erupt from her chest and started to walk away.

But then Eryna saw the painting the woman was looking at: Women dancing around bonfires, flower circlets atop their heads, and at the center of it all was the Thornewood Mother Oak.

The blood rushed from Eryna's face, and she inhaled sharply through her nose. The woman turned around. It was Brenna.

"Oh! Hello, dear. I didn't realize anyone else was here," she said cheerfully. She patted the bench next to her. "Come sit."

Eryna didn't want to be rude, and it was too late to turn away now. She moved her heavy legs forward and joined Brenna on the bench, stifling another cough. Brenna leaned toward Eryna.

"So, you're the lucky one who found the gallery key. I'm surprised they let this room participate this year. They never do. But it's my favorite," she said, her smile gleefully wide. Eryna gave her a small nod and pulled out the marble key. Brenna patted Eryna's leg.

"Good. I'm glad it's you."

"But how did you get in?" Eryna asked. Brenna flashed a simple silver key with a small black bead around its neck.

"Oh, us staff have our own special keys. The Blackwells couldn't very well lock us out when they need us to keep the rooms clean and stocked." Brenna sighed and leaned back on her hands, gazing at the painting in front of her. Eryna glanced at it but looked away, too scared to look too closely with Brenna at her side.

"I know we're meant to dislike the Dryads, but there's just something about this one. They seem so happy. So full of life and so…peaceful. No matter how often I come in here, I find myself on this bench every time."

Eryna pretended to look at the painting, but kept her eyes just off to the left, studying its intricate gold frame. Brenna took Eryna's hand. Eryna looked at her, wide-eyed.

"Our boy really cares for you, you know," she said, her eyes watering at the edges. "It's hard for him to care. He doesn't have many people in his life that care for him back, besides the staff."

Eryna snorted and rolled her eyes as she recalled the feral screams and fainting girls on the first night of the Hunt.

"I find that hard to believe. From what I hear, there are plenty of girls to keep him company," Eryna said, surprised at the jealousy in her tone. She bit her lip. Brenna scoffed.

"Oh, all they care about is money and fame. He's a box for them to check, a popularity marker. And all they are for him are bandages and placeholders. He doesn't care for them, and they certainly don't care for him. Not the way we all do," Brenna said.

Eryna swallowed hard around a lump in her throat. Brenna was kind, and she clearly loved Brody. Guilt rubbed at Eryna for the fact that she was using Brody just like everyone else.

"And you believe I'm different?" Eryna asked. Brenna lovingly patted the top of her hand and met her gaze, her eyes bursting with hope.

"I know you are, love. He wouldn't let just anybody stay in his mother's room, and he's certainly never brought a girl to the kitchen for fresh cookies." Brenna stood to walk away, but then Eryna realized she might know how to get back to her room.

"Wait, Brenna, how to I get back to—"

"Fourth floor, third corridor in the east wing," Brenna replied with a wink. Then she paused, her eyes going somewhat distant. "Her name was Marisa. She was a very lovely lady. We loved her very much. Our boy has much more of her in him than his father, though he won't admit it. He's always looked up to Alexander."

Alexander. So that was Mr. Blackwell's name.

"Also, dear," Brenna continued. "Don't judge the boy on the men he's surrounded by. Not everyone deserves to answer for the sins of their fathers."

Eryna stared at Brenna blankly, her words striking a familiar chord that Parvati had plucked earlier, only this time it played a different tune. One much less ferocious.

Before Eryna could reply, Brenna was gone.

Finally alone, Eryna stood and examined the painting in front of her. It had to have been shortly before the war began, because all her sisters were there.

Eryna's heart cracked in her chest, then splintered into a thousand pieces.

Althea, Mori, Illana, Maya, even a young Oihane and Dera hand-in-hand dancing around the bonfire. A century or two later, Eryna would be the third link in that chain.

She could taste the berry wine sliding down her throat and warming her stomach, feel the heat of the bonfire on her skin, the earth beneath her feet, the laughter and music in the air, and the way her body swayed and twirled to it all.

She stared at the painting until she no longer could, her sisters blurring as her eyes filled with hot tears. She blinked them away and glanced at the description to see who the artist was, for this person had to have been right there in the middle of it all to depict it so perfectly.

Martin Blackwell, the placard read.

Eryna's eyes widened.

The very man who captured such raw beauty was the one who destroyed them all.

Eryna's fists clenched. Her teeth ground. Her pulse beat furiously in her veins.

This painting was all she needed to remind herself of why she was here and not seeking refuge in another nymph realm. It was enough to remember who she was and what she was trying to save. For as much as Eryna believed she'd held onto herself coming into the human world, she knew deep down that she'd gotten lost, pulled in by what it was to be human.

But she was not human.

She was not Eryna Thorne.

She was Eryna of the Thornewood, the Dryad who would destroy the Blackwell legacy.

And after what both Parvati and Brenna had said, a small seedling of an idea sprouted in Eryna, one she hadn't realized was an option until now.

Eryna might not need to touch the legacy at all to destroy it, for it wouldn't be her hands that did the wrecking.

It would be Brody's.

Chapter Thirty-Two

It took nearly half an hour for Eryna to find her room, and with heavy limbs and a heavy heart that ached for Jenin and Derrick and The Spire, she crawled into the freshly made, unfamiliar bed and slipped beneath the veil of the dreaming world.

It lasted for what seemed like seconds.

A small *crack* woke her. She sat up and scanned the dark room. It was so quiet, she could hear a mouse's whisker twitch, but nothing that might could the source of the noise. Another *crack* sounded, like something small and solid hitting glass. Eryna looked toward the windows.

Crack. Crack. Crack.

What on earth…? Eryna wondered.

Hesitantly, she walked to the windows and gazed out.

Four stories down, Derrick smiled up at her and waved, a handful of gravel in his fist.

Eryna beamed. Her heart surged against her breastbone.

She made it to the first floor in under a minute.

She was out the back door in two.

She threw her arms around his neck, and he buried his face in her shoulder, his warmth seeping through her thin night clothes.

"I had to see you," he said into her skin. "I had to know you were safe."

She squeezed him tight, and he flinched.

"Are you okay? How bad is it?" She fussed as she pulled back to scan his face.

"Eryna, don't—"

Before he could turn away, she saw the beginnings of a large purple and blue bruise ringing his left eye and cheekbone. It would look worse tomorrow, and even worse the next day. It might not fully heal for two or three weeks, maybe a month.

Unless I heal him, Eryna thought. But she knew she couldn't. She shoved off the desperate urge to reach up and take his pain and swelling away. It was far too risky. He'd have too many questions.

"That bastard," she breathed.

"It's not as bad as it looks," Derrick said, trying to smile through the obvious pain.

"You don't have to act like you're okay, you know. Not with me," Eryna said, running her finger along the edges of the bruise. It wouldn't take much to simply dull the pain, shorten his healing time…

No. She couldn't. Eryna slipped her hand back around his waist, rose up on her toes, and kissed him. Her lips moved fast, hungry, ready to pick up where they left off in the greenhouse.

"Eryna, wait," Derrick interrupted. Eryna's brow folded.

"What's wrong?"

Derrick shook his head.

"Nothing, I just…"

But Eryna could tell from the set of his jaw, the distance in his eyes as he stared distantly at the Manor, it wasn't nothing.

"Derrick, what is it?" she insisted. She took his head in her hands and pulled his gaze to hers. He sighed, his breath tickling her face.

"It was almost impossible for me to slip away. My dad will

224

probably have Jenin and I on lock down for a while, and I don't know when I'll be able to see you again, or even talk to you, and..." his eyes shifted toward the Manor once more, toward a far corner where a light illuminated a window. He looked back at her with pain in his eyes, and not from the bruise growing darker by the second. He shrugged.

"I just won't be around much, if at all, and with the two of you here...together...with me out of the picture, I'd understand if—"

"Derrick," Eryna interjected. She brought his face close and gave him a feather-light kiss. "I like you a lot. *You.* Okay?"

He eyed her skeptically, but a slight smile found its way to his face, and he nodded, pressing into her kiss again. After a few seconds, he broke away.

"Oh no," he groaned dramatically, his head falling into his hand.

"What?" Eryna tightened, worried she'd done something wrong.

"We never got to watch the sunrise!" he lamented. Amidst the chaos of the night, Eryna hadn't realized her unfulfilled fantasy had now fallen out of reach. Her chest caved a little, but she shielded her sadness. Derrick and Jenin were okay. That was all that mattered. Eryna shook her head.

"Maybe we can catch it when all this has blown over," she said, but the moment the words left her lips, they felt hollow. Soon Eryna would be gone, back to the Thornewood, and she was never coming back to Aponyx.

Derrick suddenly tensed and he fumbled around in his pocket, fishing out his phone.

Dad, the screen read. Derrick looked at her and frowned.

"I have to go. Stay safe, okay? I'll miss you."

Eryna nodded, knowing she should let him go, but her arms involuntarily tightened around him.

"I'll miss you too," she whispered.

He smiled down at her, brought his hands to her face and said his goodbyes with his lips against hers.

And then he was gone, her lips frozen mid-kiss, her arms and chest suddenly cold. She opened her eyes to find him trotting away across the lawn, and just before he was out of sight, he looked at her, brought the tips of his fingers to his mouth, then touched his heart.

Eryna did the same, and even from far away, she saw a flash of white teeth and dimples, and carried the image to bed with her, hoping that even if she didn't see him for a while, maybe that smile would find her in her dreams.

Chapter Thirty-Three

When Derrick had said Eryna might not see him for a while, she didn't realize he truly meant it.

One week passed.

Then two.

She didn't see or hear from Jenin either. Eryna's heart ached every time she texted her friend and a red message flashed across the screen.

Error, it read, *Unable to send message.*

She tried calling them, too, but some strange voice repeated that the "line has been disconnected."

So, Eryna busied herself searching for doors and Hearts, though the fruitless search was starting to take a toll on her. Her skin had developed a dull and tired hue, and the circles beneath her eyes darkened with each passing day. Not even the beauty tonic could remove the visible exhaustion, and no amount of food or time in nature seemed to restore her energy.

Eryna groaned and sagged against a wall somewhere on the fifth floor, irritation pricking at her like a woodpecker on a rotting pine. While she hadn't expected the Hearts to be sitting on a silver platter, not having a single lead after two weeks was more infuriating than when Oihane would steal Eryna's favorite comb.

Eryna's heart cracked at the thought of something that was once so frustrating now being something she missed desperately. She fought the burn in her eyes as tears begged to burst forth. She missed her sisters and her home so much, and it was starting to feel like she'd never get back to Euryalea.

And, on top of it all, her plan to use Brody to find the Hearts was proving more difficult than anticipated. He was surprisingly inaccessible. She barely got a moment alone with him as he was bogged down with whatever work he did for Blackwell Tech and preparations for the third and final Hunt, which they'd postponed for undisclosed reasons. Though, if the chatter around the Manor was to be believed, it was because Alexander wasn't in his best health.

Eryna did believe it. In the two weeks she'd been at Blackwell Manor, she hadn't seen Alexander once.

"You okay?" Eryna asked Brody a week earlier as they walked the Manor gardens during a rare afternoon alone. She'd started to notice the wear on his face, the worry in his eyes, the deep crease between his brows. Brody sighed, repeatedly tracing the "B" ring on his pinky.

"It's just hard watching him get so weak," he said.

"I'm sorry," was all she could think to say. But she didn't feel sorry for Alexander in the slightest. Then a small wave of sympathy for Brody crashed over her, and as he silently stared at the ground, Eryna felt compelled to say more. "I know your father means a lot to you."

Brody nodded and took her hand, intertwining their fingers as they walked along an immaculately trimmed stretch of boxwood hedges. "He does. I'm proud to be his son and a Blackwell. I just worry I won't know what to do when he's gone. I don't think I'm ready for the responsibility."

Eryna stopped. She looked at Brody and pursed her lips.

"I don't think anyone is ever ready," she said, surprised at the words coming out of her mouth, as if Dera had found a way through her from beyond the veil. "When it's time, you have to choose to be ready, or let the opportunity to be something greater pass you by."

Brody froze. After a moment, a smile stretched across his cheeks. He tugged Eryna closer until their chests touched.

"You," he said, touching his forehead to hers. "Are very smart. Has anyone ever told you that?"

"A hundred years of life will do that to you," she replied. Brody's chuckle rattled her teeth as he closed the gap between them. Every nerve in her body sparked as his lips enveloped hers, and she leaned into his kiss, letting him steal her breath away.

Kissing Brody was captivating, exhilarating, and a little dangerous, like dancing with a wolf pack on a night they hadn't had a full meal. She liked it. A lot. But sometimes she couldn't tell if she liked kissing Brody, or if kissing Brody made her forget how much she longed for Derrick.

Eryna's stomach grumbled, bringing her mind back to the fifth-floor corridor she was standing in, and she realized she hadn't eaten all day, her appetite having slowly decreased since being at the Manor. She sighed, pushed off the wall, and started toward the kitchens to see if Brenna had anything she could snack on before dinner preparations began.

Eryna tried texting Derrick while she walked.

Unable to send message, the screen flashed as usual.

Worry flared through her chest, bringing with it a sickening ache at her lack of contact with him and his sister. She'd heard from a staff member that they were doing okay, but Eryna wouldn't believe it until she saw them in person. She tried her best to swallow her worry and remind herself that the distance was probably for the best. Cutting ties would be easier when she left if the threads were already frayed.

"Ah, our young guest!" A deep voice declared from down the hall. She looked up and halted in her tracks.

Alexander smiled at her, all teeth, a wolf dressed in a nice white collared shirt and fitted black pants. While he looked somewhat gaunt and frail, he was still handsome. Eryna quickly remembered herself and returned the smile, shoving her phone in her pocket. Alexander braced his hands behind his back and met her where she stood.

"I've been meaning to find you. I haven't given you a proper welcome to Blackwell Manor, but as I'm sure you've heard, I've been a bit put out," he said, chuckling as he signaled to his fatigued face. "Sorry to hear it didn't work out for you at the Ashford's. Damian can be…" He sucked his teeth thoughtfully. "Abrasive. But we're happy to have you. I know the staff is excited at the female presence. I've even seen some pink decor around the place. I haven't seen pink here in ages."

Alexander laughed, the sound loud and playful. Eryna tried her best to reciprocate, but it felt as though he was trying to laugh over her, not with her.

"My apologies, then," she said. "I'll be sure to tell them pink isn't my color."

Alexander laughed harder, louder, head tilted back and mouth wide. Eryna tried not to roll her eyes. What she'd said wasn't that funny.

"Don't apologize. It's nice to see, though you're right, you don't seem like a pink girl." He narrowed his eyes and studied her. Eryna simply smiled her most placid smile and tried not to squirm. Prickles crawled across her skin as he bit his lip and smiled again, the expression hungry, calculating.

"No, you're not a pink girl at all. You're green. Like fresh grass. Or a very beautiful tree."

Eryna's breath died on her lips.

She swore a knowing gleam sparked in his eyes.

He cleared his throat and straightened.

"Welcome to Blackwell Manor, Miss Thorne."

He nearly brushed against Eryna as he walked past her, down the hall and around the corner. Nausea churned her stomach, unsure if

Alexander's observation was simply astute, or very pointed. Whatever the reason for his comment, Eryna suddenly realized she'd gotten far too comfortable in the human world.

She'd leaned into a perceived sense of safety, but she wasn't safe in the least. Not around Alexander or Damian or Brody or Jenin or Derrick or anybody. She needed to watch her back. She may care for a handful of humans now, but that didn't mean she could trust them. She shook her head and started toward the kitchen again, though her meager appetite was long gone.

Then echoed whispers caught her attention.

She recognized the voices immediately—Parvati and her husband, Jerry.

Eryna panicked, praying to Gaia not to get caught in another conversation with Parvati. It was too late to flee, so she scanned the space around her. A set of heavy drapes caught her attention, and she quickly dashed behind them. She held her breath as footsteps approached.

"Well, that was embarrassing, Jerry," Parvati scolded her husband. "Next time you speak, at least act like you're the brains behind our operations."

"How am I supposed to know how those things work? You're the expert on this nymph technology."

Eryna stifled a gasp.

Nymph technology?

What kind of technology could they possibly have gotten ahold of and what was it for? And why was Parvati the expert? The more Eryna thought about it, the more she realized she knew exactly what the technology was for.

The Hearts.

But what technology did they need and why?

Eryna listened harder.

"I'm only an expert because I've studied it, which is what you *should* have been doing instead of fooling around with your secretary,"

Parvati said. Eryna involuntarily snorted into her hand, then held her breath, worried they'd heard her. After a brief pause, they continued, their voices quieting as they walked down the hall.

"How did you know about—"

"Oh, please. I'm neither stupid nor blind. You know me better than that. We entered this marriage under the assumption that it was a business partnership, but I've been carrying all the weight, as of late. So, carry your weight, Jerry, or you're done taking the credit." Parvati sighed, clearly exasperated. "All I ask is that you're more discreet for our daughter's sake. If she finds out..." Parvati's voice trailed off as they walked out of earshot.

Eryna waited a full minute before unraveling herself from the drape to be sure she was alone. Threads of questions knotted tightly in her mind. She was unsure where one started and another began, slowly picking at the strings until one gave a little.

What was this technology and why was it needed for the Hearts?

As far as Eryna knew, the Hearts didn't need assistance. They simply existed. And how had Parvati come to know so much about nymph technology that she was advising Blackwell Tech's lead scientist on the matter?

Eryna paused in her tracks.

The harder she tugged on that last thought, the more the thread loosened.

"At least act like you're the brains behind our operations," Parvati had said. *"So, carry your weight, Jerry, or you're done taking the credit."*

Parvati wasn't advising at all. She *was* the lead scientist and using her husband as a prop.

Her last conversation with Parvati grew another layer; all her talk about the ambitions of boys and men.

Was that why Parvati had married Jerry? To use his ambitions to feed her own?

Eryna needed to know more. Maybe she could ask Brody what

he knew about Parvati, where she was from, how involved she was in Blackwell Technologies.

"Oh, Gaia," Eryna exclaimed as she stumbled into the corner of a wall.

She'd been so lost in her tangled threads, she hadn't realized she'd been aimlessly walking until she looked around and suddenly had no idea where she was. She'd never seen this part of Blackwell Manor before, and she thought she'd seen it all by now.

Tucked into a small nook of a hall, three bay windows looked out onto the sprawling Manor gardens. Each window held a heavily cushioned bench, and the walls were saturated with framed images. Some of them were old and yellowed with age, some sharp and colorful as if taken yesterday. Some were portraits of people stoically smiling, others held multiple people with arms lovingly wrapped around each other or chatting over drinks or gleefully chasing after children.

The harder Eryna looked, the more she realized they were all women.

Every single image.

Her eyes landed on the clearest picture. It was of three women: Parvati, Marisa, and a beautiful, slender woman with moss-colored eyes and dark blonde hair, a light pink chiffon rose tucked behind one ear.

Derrick and Jenin's mother.

"I didn't think anyone besides the Blackwells knew about this spot," a cold but soft voice said.

Eryna flinched, throwing her gaze to a window down the way. There, Parvati sat on the bench, the back of her head leaned against the wall, her legs tucked up under her arms.

It was the smallest Eryna had ever seen her look.

"Sorry, I didn't mean to intrude," Eryna apologized, turning to leave. Even though Eryna was bursting to know more about Parvati, she knew better than to ask. Parvati wasn't the most forthcoming person. Whatever Eryna wanted to learn, she'd have to learn on her own.

"I hear you're staying in Marisa's room," Parvati said, the words quiet, yet barbed. An accusation.

Eryna swallowed and looked back at the image of the three women. It wasn't hard for her to guess they were great friends, and Eryna staying in Marisa's room probably offended Parvati.

"I told Brody to put me in a different room, but he insisted."

"Of course he did," Parvati scoffed, and Eryna swore she saw her swipe away a tear. "Well, you certainly took my advice seriously."

"Was I not supposed to?" Eryna snapped, the words quick and ready.

Parvati looked at her, eyes rippling with her usual disgust. But there was an undercurrent of immense hurt and something else Eryna couldn't quite put her finger on. Grief? Nostalgia?

Eryna fought every instinct to break from Parvati's gaze, and the longer she looked at her, the sorrier she felt. This woman was magnetic, intense, condescending, a force as strong as the ripping winds of a hurricane. But in this moment, in this light, she was so fragile; like the flutter of a butterfly wing could tear her in two.

If there ever was a time to ask Parvati about herself, now might be that time. Eryna opened her mouth, to say what, she wasn't sure, but before she could speak, Parvati joined her at the wall of women.

She nodded at the picture of herself, Marisa, and Jenin and Derrick's mother.

"Genevieve. Her name was Genevieve," she said.

"Jenin and Genevieve. Jen and Gen?" Eryna chuckled a little. Parvati simply nodded.

"She'd always wanted a daughter. She was beside herself when Jenin came. They were very close. Since she died, all I've thought about is how defenseless Jenin has been navigating this male-driven world without her mother, especially considering who her father is. Jenin was fifteen when Gen died. The most formative years for a girl."

"Then why didn't you help her?" Eryna jabbed, unable to help herself. Jenin had been left more defenseless than Parvati could know. Eryna's blood boiled just thinking about it, and she had to take several slow breaths to pull herself from the ledge. Parvati glanced at the ground.

"I admit, I should have. But I had more pressing concerns when Marisa and Genevieve died and had my own daughter to think of."

Eryna tried not to roll her eyes at the mention of Sierra, but the way Parvati grouped Marisa and Genevieve's deaths caught her attention.

"They died at the same time?"

The shift in Parvati was almost imperceptible, but Eryna caught it. Parvati's muscles tensed and her breath shortened, like she'd just been caught in a lie, or a truth she wasn't supposed to disclose. Less than a second later, she shielded it perfectly with a relaxed posture and slow inhales.

"About a year apart. They were both sick."

Eryna looked back at the photographs of the women, scanning each of their faces. They all looked in perfect health, especially Marisa and Genevieve. She side-eyed Parvati.

"And there was nothing Blackwell Technologies could've done?" she asked, testing for a soft spot in Parvati's resolve. This time the shift wasn't so subtle. Parvati straightened and turned cold, immediately shutting off.

Gaia, Eryna cursed. She knew Parvati would be tough to crack. Even in this moment of vulnerability, she wasn't giving.

"Not for what they were sick with," Parvati said. She scanned the wall again and clucked her tongue. "It really is such a pity."

"What is?"

Parvati nodded at the photographs.

"These women. Their fates."

Eryna screwed her eyes and examined one of the women with long wavy brown hair and sapphire blue eyes, her wide smile softened by rosy lips and cheeks.

"Who are they?" she asked. Parvati bit her cheek and studied

Marisa and Genevieve again. She exhaled sharply.

"Trapped birds, all of them. Every woman who has ever loved or been loved by a Blackwell. Or an Ashford, in Gen's case."

Bumps raised across Eryna's skin, and she blamed it on a draft that had suddenly curled through the nook. Slowly, she pointed to Parvati in the picture, sandwiched between the two women.

"What about you? You're on this wall, too," she said. Parvati snorted, turned to Eryna, and smiled a smile so sharp and cold, a chill shot down Eryna's back. It was most certainly not a draft this time.

"I can't be trapped, little flower. I'm not a bird. I'm a mountain."

Parvati walked away, but before leaving the nook, she stopped and looked Eryna directly in the eye.

"Flowers aren't good at staying trapped, either. Don't let them trap you," she said, and disappeared. For the next three nights, Eryna replayed the exchange in her mind before she fell asleep. There was something there, hidden in Parvati's words that Eryna was certain she was meant to find. But it was buried too deep. She hoped that the more she revisited the moment, the closer it would rise to the surface so Eryna could finally pluck it out.

It never did.

Chapter Thirty-Four

The quick patter of feet and excited voices woke Eryna from a deep sleep. She poked her head out of her room to see what all the fuss was about. Music and loud voices echoed through the halls, every staff member doubling their usual speed as they flitted about the Manor doing their morning chores.

"It's today! The last Hunt is today!" A young staff member squealed to her friend as they scurried past, arms stacked high with linens and decor.

"I wonder who has the prize key," her friend replied as Eryna's eyes followed them down the corridor.

"Maybe the young Ashford boy will come. He hasn't been around in ages. I miss his handsome face," the girls giggled and strode out of earshot, unaware of the hurt that now burst through Eryna. She stepped back into her room and shut the door against the chaos of the Manor.

It'd been almost three weeks since she'd seen or heard from Derrick or Jenin, and she hated how distant their memories and faces felt. But maybe Damian would let them out of the penthouse tonight. Maybe she'd finally get to see them. Derrick would probably look deliciously handsome, his black eye faded to light yellow and green, and Jenin would probably wear something outrageously loud and magnificent.

Jenin, Eryna's heart clenched. Getting ready for the Hunt wouldn't be the same without her. Eryna had no idea where to start. She didn't even know the theme. Eryna went to pop her head into the hall to ask someone, when she opened her door to a young staff member already standing there hidden behind full arms.

"Miss Thorne?" the girl asked.

"Yes?" Eryna replied, slightly confused.

"This is from Miss Ashford," she said, handing Eryna a glossy red box with a brand name embossed across the top.

Eryna's heart pounded in her chest, tears welled in her eyes. Even separated by three weeks, a city, and centuries of bad blood between their kind, Jenin had found her own way of saying, "I miss you, too, demon."

Eryna wasted no time ripping the box open. From the way the young woman excitedly eyed it and lingered in the doorway, Eryna could tell it must be some fancy brand.

A note sat on top of fine white paper covering something large and soft.

Thought I forgot about you? Never. Saw this and thought it suited a sharp-eyed, clever little demon like you.

-J

She set the note aside and tore the paper down the middle, revealing a mass of fiery orange, dark rust, and white tulle. She pulled it from the box and laid it on the bed to examine it. The top was a tight fitted bodice shaped like a heart and covered in bright orange tulle. The soft material seamlessly melted into the rust color through the midsection and down to a small stretch of white at the bottom hem.

Instead of sleeves, a sheer orange cape started just below the shoulder line, adorned with small orange crystals that gave the dress the slightest hint of sparkle. It was breathtaking. But Eryna couldn't figure out what the theme was.

She searched the box and found a small object bundled in more white paper. When she ripped it open, she found herself staring at a soft mask with triangular ears, a small black nose, and long, wispy whiskers.

"Is tonight animal themed?" Eryna asked the girl who was still haunting her doorway. She nodded and smiled vibrantly.

"'Animals of the Wild,' yes! That's a beautiful costume for tonight. Miss Ashford has always had great taste," she remarked. Eryna smiled, staring at the mask.

Sharp-eyed and clever.

Along with great taste, Jenin had a biting sense of humor, too. Oh, Gaia, how Eryna missed it.

"Wait," Eryna called out just as the girl turned to leave. She immediately stopped.

"Did you need something else?" she asked, beaming at her. Eryna smiled.

"Yes, actually. Would you mind helping me get ready?"

Eryna twirled in the full-length mirror, admiring the dress as it floated on the air like a cloud. Unlike her first two dresses which restricted her movements, this one was light, fluid, and made it look like she levitated everywhere she went. The young woman—Taryn—helped form her hair into soft waves, and gave Eryna's face a fresh, natural look.

"The mask covers a lot of your face, and you already have such beautiful eyes. You don't need much," Taryn had remarked as she delicately painted Eryna's lashes. She wasn't Jenin, but she was kind and helpful enough.

Just as guests started arriving, Eryna took a fresh dose of tonic and stepped out of her room. She silently counted the keys in her hidden pockets to make sure she had each one just in case. With the Ashford's potentially attending tonight, these keys were no longer a game; they were safety, little havens where Damian couldn't reach her.

"Good Gods, Thorne," a voice sounded from behind her, followed by a long, approving whistle and a soft hand on her back.

Brody.

Heat climbed her neck and she smiled to herself. Eryna turned toward him but was almost knocked in the face by a set of large ram's horns protruding from his head. Eryna gasped.

"Wow you look—"

"Handsome? Strong? Masculine?" Brody said, lifting a brow, cracking a smile that made her knees weak.

"Yes," Eryna agreed with all the ways he'd just described himself. "But also..." She couldn't find the words for how he looked. His short hair was intentionally tousled, the heavy horns curled at the sides of his head, and his thick wool vest opened to his bare chest. But the more Eryna looked at him, the more she realized it wasn't his outfit that she couldn't describe.

It was his face.

He looked softer, less hungry and mischievous. His eyes shone with a sweetness she wasn't sure was there before. It caught her completely off guard. She cupped his face.

"Lovely. You look lovely," she said. Brody's expression dramatically soured.

"Lovely?"

"Yes."

"But I was going for manly! Rugged! Battle hardened!" Brody exclaimed. Eryna snorted and side-eyed him.

"Battle hardened in a wool vest?" she asked. Brody pursed his lips and narrowed his eyes.

"Fair. But what about the horns? They're cool, right?" Brody pointed to his head. Eryna traced the perfect curl of a horn. They were real, fixed to his head by a hidden band. Eryna briefly wondered what poor ram had to die for him to have those horns.

"Very 'cool.' Very rugged," she said as Brody stepped closer. He ran a finger along the edge of her jaw, then hooked it under her chin. As he lifted her face, he touched his lips to hers and held them there for a breath before kissing her slowly, gently, like they had all the time in the world to stay in this moment.

"I hate that we haven't had more time together," he said between kisses.

"Me too," Eryna breathlessly replied. With what little time they did have, Eryna had to throw all her effort into each interaction, but she worried it still wasn't enough for him to have fostered genuine feelings for her. But something about the way he was touching her now, cradling her in his arms like she could slip from his grasp at any moment, gave her the slightest bit of hope.

"We really have to go," he said into her lips. "I am the host, after all. The people must miss me." He laughed.

"They can miss you a little longer," Eryna replied, as she kissed him deeper, harder. He broke away, panting, smiling.

"We really should go. It's time to make our entrance." He reached down and grabbed her hand and tugged her toward the main staircase, but Eryna dug her heels in.

"We? *Our* entrance?" she asked. Brody looked at her, genuinely confused.

"Of course. You are my guest, after all. It'd only make sense if you were my date, too." He shrugged. Her throat tightened. Eryna didn't mind the thought of Aponyx society seeing her on Brody's arm. It was the thought of Derrick seeing them that bothered her.

"Are you sure you're ready for that? I don't mind taking the back stairs. I mean, you're the host. It's your night. Girls won't be fawning at your feet when they think you're off the table," Eryna offered. Brody smiled, tucked her in his arms and kissed the top of her head, the tip of her mask covered nose, and brushed his full lips against hers.

"I *am* off the table," he whispered, his words so sweet, she could almost taste the truth in them, if there was any.

Her pulse spiked, her breath shortened, and as he kissed her again, she got the feeling that her plan might have actually worked. Maybe she was winning her game, after all. But he could still be playing his game, too.

His lips were gone, and before Eryna could object, she was standing at the top of the landing staring down at the bustling crowd, her hand in Brody's. She didn't spot Derrick but panic still choked her. He'd been so worried about this very thing on the last night she'd seen him.

"No, wait, Brody, really I—" she tried protesting, but it was too late.

"Ladies, gentlemen, our dearest friends," Brody greeted the attendees, his voice low, loud, and deep in his chest. "Welcome to the final night of the tenth annual Blackwell Hunt. If the rumors are to be believed, one of you actually has the prize key this year."

Several gasps and squeals sounded around the room, and Eryna couldn't help wondering whether she had the key, even though she'd nearly searched the place top to bottom. Brody continued.

"The Hunt will begin in thirty minutes, so drink up, be merry, and may luck be on your side tonight."

The room raised their glasses to their host and saluted him. Brody and Eryna started down the stairs. The room returned to their previous conversations, though at a much more hushed tone. The loudest sounds Eryna could hear were the soft cries of several young women, and the distant melody of the live orchestra. Eryna faltered on a step, but Brody caught her before anyone noticed.

"I've got you," he assured her. She regained her balance and smiled at him.

"Thanks," she said.

"Always," he muttered in her ear, paired with a light kiss to her neck, and Gaia if it didn't set her heart racing. More soft cries sounded around the room.

Eryna glanced at the crowd, searching for Derrick, and sighed with relief when she didn't see him, thought she did spot Sierra near the base of the stairs, seething. She was dressed in a tight, sparkling floor-length dress with a large furry boa draped around her shoulders. Pert triangular ears sat atop her head and a thin collar and bell hugged her neck. Eryna chuckled to herself. Domesticated cats weren't exactly wild animals, but the costume perfectly suited Sierra.

"So does someone actually have the prize key?" Eryna quietly asked Brody. He smirked and gave her a sideways glance.

"Possibly," he replied. Unsatisfied with that answer, Eryna narrowed her eyes at him.

"Is there even a prize?" she asked. If there wasn't, then what was the true purpose of the Hunt? Brody's arm slightly stiffened beneath hers, but his charming, playful expression remained.

"Maybe, maybe not. But it gets the people excited, doesn't it?" He looked at her and winked. Before she could press him for more, they dove into the crowd of attendees.

"Brody," a voice called from a ways away. They both looked toward the source and saw Alexander waving him over. Brody grabbed two glasses of sparkling wine off a passing tray and held one out to Eryna. She took it.

"You gonna be okay if I step away for a minute?" he asked. She nodded and smiled. He kissed the side of her head and murmured, "Stay in the crowd, stay around people. Damian hates making a scene, so even if he's here and he sees you, he won't do anything while others are around. I won't be long."

Then he was gone, and Eryna was alone in the middle of the packed entryway, sipping her drink. She slyly scanned the crowd, trying hard to make it look casual and observant and not so obvious that she was uncomfortable standing alone. As she looked for any familiar face she could cling to, she noticed something strange about those around her.

While the attendees donned their finest ensembles and seemed in the best of spirits, many of them looked a little paler, a little gaunter than the previous two Hunt nights. Arms were thinner, smile lines and wrinkles around the eyes were deeper. It wasn't everyone, though. Eryna studied them harder and realized that the only people who looked sickly were the ones with purses.

The participants.

She caught sight of herself in a passing reflection, and while she knew she looked and felt more exhausted than when she'd first come to Aponyx, she hadn't noticed just how severe the difference was. She hardly recognized herself. Eryna scanned the room again, noticing more and more participants that looked ill and faded, when a tall, fair man halfway across the room caught her eye.

He was in a gray suit, eyes blue as the Marinthian Ocean.

Eryna froze.

Damian.

He smiled wide, sharp as a shark's teeth; the weight of his stare could crush her in its jaws. He started toward her.

Eryna set her drink down on the first surface she could find and shoved her hands in her pockets, touching each key.

The art gallery was too far away, and the theater was blocked by hundreds of attendees milling about, waiting for the Hunt to begin.

The greenhouse, then, she decided, and as she sped toward the back of the Manor, she didn't dare look back to see if he was following her. If the heat on the back of her neck and the quick footsteps behind her were any indication, he was. And she couldn't let him catch her.

If he did, it would undoubtedly be the end of everything. Including her life.

Chapter Thirty-Five

The *crack* that signaled the start of the Hunt echoed through the Manor, and a rush of attendees swarmed the halls, completely drowning Eryna.

She turned left, then right, then left, trying to lose Damian's tail, but he kept pace. As she turned a corner, she pushed herself harder and shoved through participants as fast as her weak body could move. After a moment she checked over her shoulder and no longer saw Damian.

Thank you, Gaia, Eryna breathed. Still, that didn't mean he'd stopped following her. While she knew Damian being there meant Derrick and Jenin might also be, it was still a good idea to hide in the greenhouse until the danger passed, no matter how badly she wanted to see them. She texted Brody to let him know her plan, then headed toward the greenhouse.

Just like the last Hunt, shouts of excitement broke out each time a person found a door that matched their key. Eryna watched it happen over and over again.

Someone would try each of their keys in a lock, and one of two things would happen: immediate disappointment followed by a mad rush to the next door, or the lock would *click*, the person would cheer, then rush through the threshold to presumably scour the room for the supposed prize.

But now that she was alone and no longer focused on her own keys, Eryna noticed something she hadn't noticed before: Each time someone opened a door, they would pause and shake their head, or sway on their feet, or say they "need a moment." Eryna recalled the pain that struck her chest and the lightness in her head when she'd first opened the theater and the art gallery, and the way Derrick swayed as he opened the greenhouse. It also happened every time she'd visited those rooms since, and Eryna realized she knew well what the other participants were experiencing. She simply thought it was specific to her.

She watched a disappointed person come out of a room and noticed as the wrinkles around his eyes seemed deeper than a minute prior, the sag of his cheeks heavier.

Lightning struck Eryna so deep, she felt it on her bones.

She pulled out her keys and examined them. One in particular caught her eye, the one that matched the only room that didn't make her sick when she opened it. She studied the key to Marisa's room. Her gaze stopped on the black bead clasped around its neck. She thought back to the only other times she'd seen something similar: the Blackwell key, and Brenna's key.

The keys, Eryna gasped.

There was something about the keys that was weakening the participants. Disgust rooted deep in Eryna's stomach. The Blackwells were up to something, and they were using the Hunt to do it.

But what? And why?

Eryna changed course toward Marisa's room, and as she turned the corner, a mass of light pink feathers caught her off guard. She was almost knocked over as two arms flung around her neck and crushed her into a petite chest. The scent of jasmine and sandalwood surrounded her, and she knew exactly who it was without needing to see a face.

"Jenin!" Eryna cried and wrapped desperate arms around her friend as pressure built behind her eyes. The tight ache that'd been buried in her heart eased as Jenin silently squeezed her harder. Eryna laughed.

"I've missed you, too," she said. Jenin took a couple steps back and swiped a finger beneath her mossy eyes. Eryna eyed her dress. It was a simple cut on top, straight across the chest, but the front of the skirt started at her thighs and gradually lengthened until it touched the floor. The bodice was studded in silver crystals, and heaps of light pink feathers covered the entire ensemble. She was a sparkling, perfectly preened flamingo.

"You look incredible," Eryna said.

Jenin sighed.

"I know." She grabbed Eryna's hand and twirled her in a circle. "And you make the perfect fox. I knew I chose right." Jenin softly smiled, but the expression faded quickly. "He disconnected our phones. We were being monitored every second, still are. Honestly, I'm surprised he let us come tonight. But I think…"

Jenin's eyes skimmed the hall, then she grabbed Eryna's hand and dragged her through the crowd.

"Jenin, where are we going?" Eryna asked.

"One second," she replied.

They crossed through the main entryway, and as they did, Eryna's eyes landed on a tall boy with fair hair and moss-colored eyes, one of which was still ringed in a bruise. He donned a fur vest over a bare chest—the pelt of a lynx—and held a bursting bouquet of light pink chiffon roses.

Derrick, Eryna smiled, so elated, her heart nearly sprouted wings and flew away. He smiled back at her, his face lighting up like the sun after a long, dark winter. He waved and mouthed *hi*, but before she could reply, she was pulled out of sight.

Jenin took her to a far, empty hall. She looked at Eryna for a long moment and swallowed.

"What is it?" Eryna asked, unsure what to make of Jenin's unusual behavior. Jenin dropped her voice into a quiet murmur.

"I think my father knows."

Eryna raised a brow.

"That I'm the one who attacked him?"

Jenin shook her head.

"No. That too, but no. I think he knows what you are. I overheard him in his study trying to convince Alexander you weren't human, and that you were up to no good. He didn't say 'Dryad,' but he implied as much."

Eryna's blood curdled. A dry lump formed in her throat, her mouth turned to sand, her tongue leaden. Was it Brody? Did he let it slip? Or was Eryna more obvious than she thought?

"H...how would he know that?" Eryna stammered, her vision tunneling, her head going light, pulse pounding in her ears. She braced a hand on the wall to remain upright.

"I don't know, but I'm getting you out of Aponyx. Tonight."

"No!" Eryna nearly shouted. Jenin looked at her, startled. Eryna lowered her voice. "I can't go. Not yet. I..." Eryna paused, unsure if what she was about to say was the dumbest thing she'd done yet. No matter how much she'd grown to care for Jenin, she still wasn't sure she could trust her. Eryna studied her friend a moment longer, determining that the worry in her eyes was genuine, and decided to throw all caution to the wind. She inhaled deeply. "I need the Hearts first."

"What?" Jenin's eyes went wide. Eryna bit her lip.

"I need the two Hearts," she repeated. "I can't leave without them."

"Screw the Hearts, Eryna, this is your *life*. Euryalea is gone, but you're still here. You're still alive. You may be the last of your kind, but you can make a life somewhere else. Just let me help you."

Eryna vehemently shook her head.

"No, Jenin. I'm not leaving without the Hearts. If I have them, I can save Euryalea. I don't have to be the last Dryad."

"What?" A nearby voice croaked. The two girls turned to find

Derrick standing only a few feet away.

No! Eryna screamed inside.

Not here. Not now. Not this way.

"Derrick," Jenin started, but he held up a firm hand. He leveled a glare at Eryna that felt like a thousand daggers piercing her skin, ready to flay her to death. He pointed a finger at her.

"Repeat what you just said," he demanded.

"I…Derrick, I…" Eryna fumbled for words. He stepped closer, angrier. Jenin slid between them and placed both hands on her brother's chest.

"Enough. We'll talk about this later."

He turned his glare on his sister.

"You knew? You knew about this?"

Jenin nudged him another foot back.

"Yes, but we can't talk about it here. Not now."

"Why not? I think now is a perfectly good time to talk about how we'd been housing a *murderer*." He spat the accusation, shattering Eryna's heart into a million tiny pieces. She would've told him eventually, in a way where it might not have been such a shock. But him finding out like this was the worst possible case, and she couldn't fault him for being angry. Still, it hurt like Hades. Eryna clutched her chest. Tears pushed their way to her eyes, and it wasn't until something solid touched her back that she realized she'd backed herself into the corner like a frightened animal.

Just over Derrick's shoulder she saw Brody approach. He was at Derrick's side in seconds.

"Not here, man. Let's take a walk and I'll fill you in on everything," he said in a hushed tone. Derrick shook out of his grip and looked at him, eyes wide. A deep crease formed between his brows.

"Don't tell me you knew, too. Don't tell me you've all been keeping this from me for weeks!" Derrick's voice shook, and Eryna swore a single tear streamed down his cheek. Brody raised his hands in surrender.

"This is my fault, not Eryna's. I'm the reason she's here in the first place. I'm sorry we didn't tell you before. Just come with me and I can tell you everything."

"You're right. It *is* your fault. If you hadn't made Tyler go into the Thornewood, none of this would've happened. He would still be here, and *she* would be back in that wasteland where she belongs!" Derrick looked back at Eryna, pure fury in his expression, and it destroyed whatever parts of her heart were left to salvage. "I want her to tell me why those savages killed our uncles and cousins and grandfathers. I bet she killed Tyler. I want her to admit it."

"Don't make me throw you out, D," Brody warned.

"I didn't kill him, I swear, Derrick, please," Eryna said through a sob.

"Don't say my name!" he shouted, and several curious onlookers poked their heads into the corridor. "I can't believe—" He stopped to take a shuddering inhale and pinched the bridge of his nose. "I can't believe I..." his shoulders curled, his head hung low, and a single sob sounded from him. He looked at the flowers in his hand, looked at Eryna with tear-filled eyes, then tossed the flowers at her feet. The petals exploded like confetti.

"Let's go this way," Brody said, gently guiding Derrick away. Jenin started to follow, but at the last second, she ran back to Eryna and hugged her tight.

"I'm so sorry," she whispered. "I...I'm so sorry."

Eryna sobbed into her shoulder. Jenin pulled her closer.

"Keep your phone on," she said. "I meant it when I said I wanted to get you out. I'll make sure Brody keeps you safe until I can come up with a plan."

Then Jenin was gone, leaving Eryna paralyzed in the corner of the hall, dozens of curious eyes on her. Unable to take their stares any longer, she slipped down another corridor and started running toward a hidden staircase she'd found a week prior.

Just as she reached it, a palm clamped over her mouth and rough hands dug into her arms. She tried to scream, but her voice was muffled by skin.

"You're not getting away this time, you savage." Damian's poisonous voice was in her ear, coated in something that smelled harder than wine. Eryna thrashed and flailed, but her weakened limbs made her unable to fight. He slammed her back against the wall, and her head hit it so hard, her vision faltered. He brought his face within an inch of hers.

"I don't know how you survived or how you made it into our city, but you're not making it out alive," he hissed, his sharp blue eyes piercing into her. She clenched her jaw.

"Go ahead. Kill me. Then you'll never find what you're looking for," she bit. Maybe it was the splintering pain in her chest that gave way to such recklessness, but Eryna suddenly felt like it was no use hiding what she was anymore.

"You know where it is, then?" Damian asked, pressing her harder into the wall. "Tell me."

Eryna laughed in his face.

"Why should I? You have plenty of power. Why take mine?"

Damian glared at her for a moment, and quicker than lightning, he flipped her around and pinned her chest to the wall. He grabbed her hair and pulled her head back. He placed his lips on the shell of her ear.

"I know plenty of ways to make you speak," he whispered, hiking the side of her dress up and running a hand down her thigh. Eryna trembled, fighting against the panic that choked her. Damian's grip tightened. She struggled against him, scraping at his hands with her sharp nails. He hissed, his grip loosening, and she used his brief pause to slam the back of her head into his nose. It crunched, and he wailed, but he was still stronger than her, and recovered quickly. He shoved her against the wall once more. "You know what? Making you speak isn't enough. I'm going to make you scream. I like screaming."

"Just like how your daughter screamed?" Eryna said through

gritted teeth. Damian's grip on her thigh turned violent.

"Why you little whor—"

"Damian Ashford. Let go of Miss Thorne this instant, so help me Gods," a cold, sharp voice said, and from the corner of her eye, Eryna could see Parvati standing tall and steady only a few feet away. Damian still hadn't let her go. Parvati stepped closer. "Let the girl go. Now."

Two heartbeats passed, and Damian retreated. Eryna remained pinned against the wall, unable to pry herself away. Without missing a beat, Parvati closed in on Eryna and enveloped her in a surprisingly kind touch.

"Leave right now, Ashford, and don't you dare touch her again or I will mutilate you in your sleep beyond recognition, do you hear me?" Parvati asked, her voice sharp as a knife against Damian's throat. When he didn't respond, she stepped closer, the perfect picture of a mountain lion in her Hunt outfit. "You know what I'm capable of. Don't you dare push me, *Orion Astor Ford.*"

Whatever Parvati had said put the fear of the Gods in Damian, for he blanched and turned on his heel, disappearing within seconds.

Parvati scanned Eryna.

"Are you okay? Did he hurt you?" she asked. Eryna had never seen her so soft, so worried. She tried to think around the pounding in her head and blinked to clear her foggy mind.

"A little, but I'll be fine," she said. Parvati narrowed her eyes, scrutinizing her face.

"Are you sure?" she asked hesitantly. Eryna nodded, but the trembling in her hands said otherwise. Her heart rate hadn't yet slowed. She could still smell the hard alcohol on Damian's breath, hear his ugly words in her ear, feel his angry hands on her thigh. Parvati gently squeezed Eryna's arms.

"I can stay with you as long as you like," she said, but Eryna shook her head.

"I'll be okay," Eryna assured. Parvati looked Eryna over one final time, nodded, and stepped back. Just before she walked away, Eryna added, "Thank you, Parvati. I don't know what might've happened if—"

"It was nothing," Parvati cut her off. "A grown man has no business putting his hands on a young girl—any woman—like that. But stay vigilant. You have something they need, little flower, and they'll do anything to get it."

Eryna had never been more certain that Parvati knew what she was. Before she could ask more, Parvati was gone, replaced moments later by Brody rushing toward her.

"What happened? Parvati saw me looking for you and said Damian attacked you," he fussed. She waved him off.

"I'm fine, really. She found us before anything happened."

"I'm going to kill him. I swear, I'll kill him."

"Brody, please. I just want to go back to my room and forget about it. I'm not really in the mood for the Hunt anymore," she said, her hands still trembling violently. Brody looked down, cupped his hands around hers, and nodded.

"Okay. We can do that. I don't like the idea of you being in your room, though. He might come looking for you there. I know somewhere we can go where no one will find us."

Eryna paused at his use of the word "us." Her brow folded.

"But you're the host. What about the party? It's the last night, and…" Brody rolled his eyes and smiled. A slight warmth stirred in Eryna's chest, and it slowed her racing pulse.

"I did my part. They'll never miss me. Come on," Brody said, taking Eryna under his arm.

As they walked, Eryna couldn't stop seeing the fire in Derrick's eyes, the way he looked at her with such disgust. It was like he didn't even know her. Like he regretted every second he'd spent with her.

It's fine, Eryna tried to tell herself, focusing on logic over the debilitating pain in her heart. *It's better this way.*

Soon she'll be gone and back to the Thornewood, and they'd

never see each other again. But "soon" didn't feel soon enough.

Tomorrow, then, she decided.

Tonight, she would rest. But tomorrow, it was over. Tomorrow, she would find those Hearts even if she had to tear this manor down brick-by-brick; even if it would be the death of her. Then, like a fox, she'd slip away quickly and quietly before Damian or Derrick or anyone could catch her.

Tomorrow, she was going home.

Chapter Thirty-Six

Eryna and Brody walked in silence through the Manor, though Eryna hardly paid attention to where they were headed. The heat of Damian's breath was still on her neck, the anger in his touch still on her skin.

She thought back to something Dera had once said:

While I'd never, ever wish for you to have felt the violent hands of greedy human men...I wish you knew the brokenness that followed.

Damian's violent hands had only just begun, and Eryna was still shaken. She couldn't imagine if Parvati never saw them, never stopped him.

Her heart ached at the realization that Jenin *did* know that brokenness. Eryna couldn't believe the strength Jenin had to continue living like normal after what had happened; the pain she must have held in, the pain she must still be in. She was going to hug Jenin the tightest she ever had the next time she saw her—if she ever saw her again.

Eryna and Brody stopped in front of a large chestnut bookshelf filled with tomes. He dragged his finger across the spines then paused on a large book bound in navy blue material. He tugged on it and the shelf slid aside, giving way to a large room with a high vaulted ceiling. Inside was a dark leather couch situated in front of a large television, a set of pewter stairs that led to a lofted bedroom, and toward the back was a small kitchen area and a bathroom.

Brody smiled and tugged her hand.

"Come on," he said. He rummaged through some drawers and pulled out a long-sleeved shirt and loose cotton pants. He handed them to Eryna and nodded toward the bathroom.

"I'll be out here when you're ready."

Eryna thanked him and made her way to the bathroom. She had no intention of showering, but the thought of scalding hot water on her skin sounded far too inviting. She drenched her face, her hair, her back for what felt like an eternity. She leaned her head against the white tile and glanced at her thigh, the beginnings of a bruise where Damian's hand had been. She breathed deep and willed the water to peel his touch from her skin. She might be weak, but she could still feel lingering bits of her power. The bruise was gone in a few minutes and her headache dulled to a slight throb.

She stepped out feeling cleaner than before in more ways than her skin. She threw on the clothes and inhaled deeply. They smelled like clean cotton and forest pine and a hint of amber. Fresh, warm, and just a little sweet. She pressed the sleeves to her nose and inhaled again, taking Brody's smell into her lungs, imprinting it on her skin, wearing it like a safety blanket. As she stepped out of the bathroom, the smell of toasted bread and melting cheese instantly made her mouth water.

Brody—who'd changed into similar clothes—worked diligently at the stove. Eryna leaned her elbows on the counter and watched him, the focus in his eyes, the grace in his movements. He glanced over his shoulder and smiled.

"Not sure if you're hungry, but I made a couple grilled cheeses," he said as he slid two sandwiches onto plates and cut them in half. He nodded toward the couch. "Want to watch a movie?"

She nodded. Getting lost in a movie sounded perfect.

She followed him to the couch where a tray of snacks awaited:

popcorn, candy, crackers, slices of cheese and cured meats, and various drinks. Brody saw her eyeing the tray and nervously chuckled. "I might've gone a little overboard."

Eryna smiled, sat on the couch, and curled up underneath a heavy blanket.

"It's perfect. Thank you."

He handed her a plate, and she took a bite of the sandwich. The bread was immaculately toasted in butter and filled with three different warm and gooey cheeses.

"Oh, my Gaia," she said through a mouthful and took a second bite. And a third. And a fourth. She caught Brody looking at her, his smile wide and humored.

"I'm glad you like it. It's one of the few things I've perfected. When I was younger, I would wake Brenna in the middle of the night for a grilled cheese, so she figured I might as well learn how to make them myself." Brody laughed, and Eryna laughed with him, imaging a rather grouchy and exhausted Brenna getting up in the middle of the night to make young Brody a snack.

Eryna took another bite and leaned her head against the couch as Brody suggested movies for them to watch. He lingered on one he claimed to have seen a million times about a war between vampires and werewolves over a young woman. It sounded silly, but he seemed to secretly really want to watch it, so Eryna acted like it was the only movie that sounded appealing. As it started, her mind drifted, and she couldn't stop thinking about something Derrick had said.

"Why did you make Tyler go into the Thornewood?" she asked.

Brody paused mid-bite. He set down his plate, dusted off his fingers, and leaned into the couch. He looked at Eryna.

"Before I say anything, just know I'm not proud of this," he said. He pursed his lips and sighed. "The night Tyler went into the Thornewood, we'd all had a little too much to drink. I bet him that he wouldn't spend an hour in the Thornewood, and...well, Tyler wasn't exactly the type to back away from a bet."

Eryna closed her eyes against the nausea churning her stomach. She was once again at Tyler's execution, watching as the life left his Forget-Me-Not eyes. Eryna knew it in her pith that day he hadn't been there for the Hearts. She bit her lip and looked at Brody.

"You came after him," she realized aloud. Brody nodded.

"After he'd been missing for two hours, we worried. After five, we panicked. By twelve hours, we'd assumed the worst, and the family rallied the troops to rescue him. After a day, you answered his phone, and confirmed our fears. The family wanted to recover his body, but I felt— still feel—responsible, so I snuck out to find him first. That's when I fell into that trap, and..." he trailed off and solemnly looked at Eryna. She knew the rest.

And suddenly, she felt guilty for assuming Brody had planned the entire thing to wipe out the Dryads. For thinking he'd acted as bait. All he'd tried to do was save his friend, and there was nothing dishonorable in that. It was brave, even. Eryna touched his hand.

"I think you're more ready to take on the Blackwell Legacy than you realize," she said. Brody smiled at her, then his gaze fell to his lap.

"I only wish my mom was here. She always knew what to do."

Eryna picked up his hand and traced the "B" ring on his pinky finger as she watched Brody's eyes go distant.

"Everyone talks about how much they loved her. She seemed wonderful," she said, hoping it might perk him up.

"She was amazing. She had this room built for me a year before she passed, said she wanted me to have a space that was only mine. My father doesn't even know about it." Eyes rimmed with tears, he gazed around the room. He blinked them away, leaned deeper into the couch and scooted closer to Eryna, his hand still in hers.

"Parvati said she got sick?"

Brody nodded.

"Very. Gen, too. They couldn't figure out what was wrong with them, but whatever it was, it took them quickly. I like to think they weren't in pain, but…" Brody's voice trailed off. Eryna waited a couple breaths.

"You don't have to talk about it," she said, memorizing the ridges of his ring against her skin.

"No, it's okay. I don't get to talk about her much. My father doesn't like talking about her. They weren't exactly the picture of a happy marriage, but I think she meant a great deal to him."

Eryna studied Brody for a moment, and in this light, he was simply a boy who had lost his mother and was about to lose his father. For the first time, she saw his desire for the third Heart not as a sinister thing, but as a last resort; it was a way to save the only parent he had left.

Pity must have bled through her expression because he gave her hand a light squeeze.

"Don't worry about me. I'll be okay," he said. Then his sad eyes turned soft. "Come here." He pulled Eryna onto his chest and leaned back. Her head rested just over his heart.

Thump thump. Thump thump. Thump thump.

It beat out a steady rhythm, like a soothing lullaby she could listen to forever. It was so familiar it almost felt like her own. She nuzzled her head further into his chest, trying to get as close as possible to it, like if she could touch his heart, see it, it would greet her with the open arms of an old friend. It kicked up several beats, and Eryna smiled to herself. But then she wondered just how special she really was, how often he found himself in this situation. She looked up at him and narrowed her eyes. He looked down at her and lifted a brow.

"Yes?" he drawled.

"Is this how you get all your human girls, then? You bring them here, ply them with grilled cheese and movies about vampires and they immediately swoon?" Eryna chuckled, but to her surprise, Brody didn't. His face fell, filling with a seriousness Eryna had never seen. He sat up and looked at her, his gaze clear and bright.

"I like you, Eryna. A lot. I wasn't lying when I said you're all I think about. I…" Brody paused, the knot in his throat bobbing. Eryna waited intently, her breath suddenly short. "I know I haven't made that very clear, and I understand if you don't believe me. But I want you, and I want to be with you for as long as you'll have me."

He brushed a damp lock of hair from her cheek and settled his hand beneath her jaw. Slowly, he pulled her face to his and paused an inch away, as if waiting for her reply. She leaned in and took his lips between hers, and even though they'd kissed so many times before, it was as if this kiss was their first.

It was impossibly slow and delicate, like brushing against the soft petals of a tulip. They lingered there for a breath. Two breaths. Three breaths. A shiver ran down her spine, and from the way his grip tightened, she was certain one ran down his, too. In that moment, she decided that if he really felt how he claimed he did, then it was time to finish this. She was ready to find those Hearts and get home. No more games between them.

"Brody," Eryna said, pulling back. He looked at her curiously. She took a deep breath. "I need you to help me steal back the two Hearts your family has."

Brody blinked. He blinked again.

"What?"

"I need you to help me steal the Hearts. I need to get them back to Euryalea. I can save my home. I know I can."

"But…my father…he needs them to…" Brody stammered.

"I know. I know they're keeping him alive. I also know that he's been using the Hunt to take energy from the participants or something, so clearly the they don't work anymore. I fear they may die forever if they aren't returned home, and you're the only one who can help me do that."

Brody silently stared at her, his expression cycling through confusion, understanding, confusion again. Eryna grabbed his hand and held it tight. She looked him in the eye.

"You are *not* your father, Brody. You don't need to take what isn't yours to feel powerful. That isn't who you are. Not in here," she said, placing her hand on his chest. He glanced down at it. "If you really feel for me the way you say you do, then I need your help. We will find another way to save your father. I promise. But the Hearts are not the answer."

Brody bit his lip, then thoughtfully rubbed his jaw. "I don't even know where they are. My father doesn't tell me those kinds of things." Eryna deflated, hope dying in her chest. She was so certain he knew where the Hearts were. Then Brody tilted her face to his. "But I may have an idea. Of course, I'll help you."

"Really?" she asked, not believing that those words truly came out of his mouth. But Brody nodded. She squealed an excited "thank you," and as she threw her arms around his neck, she caught sight of her hand.

It was white, and her textured skin had returned.

Eryna gasped. Brody followed her gaze, and Eryna cradled her hand to her chest to hide it.

"I took a fresh dose of tonic before the Hunt. It should've lasted until at least tomorrow afternoon."

Brody grabbed her hand and examined it.

"Maybe you've built up a tolerance," he suggested, shrugging. Eryna pulled her hand back and stood.

"I need to get to my room. I need to take another dose."

Brody pulled her into his lap.

"Don't. I'll get you a tonic before leaving this room tomorrow, but not tonight." He brought her hand to his face and kissed her palm. He skimmed his thumb over the soft, raised texturing on her skin. "I don't want to be with Eryna Thorne tonight. I want to be with Eryna of the Thornewood."

Eryna inhaled sharply. Her chest swelled. It was the first time she'd heard her name—her *real* name—since leaving Euryalea, and it sounded so solid, so perfect coming from Brody. She may still have feelings for Derrick, but Brody was the one who accepted her for what she was. Brody didn't hate her.

Eryna reached up and ran her textured finger down the center of his forehead, his nose, his lips. He closed his eyes against the sensation and smiled. Then she leaned in and kissed him.

They kept it slow, savoring each other's movements until she gently nipped Brody's lower lip and he involuntarily moaned. He turned ravenous, quickening his pace, and crushing his lips into hers, exploring every inch of teeth and tongue and sensitive skin. She ran her hands up his neck, and he pressed himself hard into her hips. Hands found hair, fingers interlaced, lips skimmed jaws and necks and shoulders.

She pulled him upright and sat astride him, grabbing the bottom of his shirt and ripping it over his head. He slid his hands under her shirt and tugged it off, barely breaking their connected lips, the two of them now skin-to-skin. Their breaths were rapid and fevered, Brody's eyes wild, a mirror reflecting the intense burn inside Eryna.

"I want you so badly," Brody gasped, dipping his head into her neck and down her chest where he trailed small nips and kisses. Her entire body prickled with a thousand little bumps and her core emulsified.

"I want you too. But I…I've never…" Eryna trailed off as Brody lightly tugged on her earlobe with his teeth and a soft groan escaped her throat. He smiled up at her, ran his thumb across her cheek, and pressed a long, full kiss into her lips. When he pulled back, he took all the breath from her lungs with him.

"We don't need to rush. I'm not going anywhere," he said. He touched the tip of his nose to hers and whispered, "I'm all yours, Eryna of the Thornewood."

She stared down into his dark eyes. The air in the room turned heavy and charged. A thousand thoughts crossed her mind in a split second, over half of which had to do with Derrick, but she quickly banished them to the deepest, darkest recess she could find. There was no room for thoughts of him in this moment. There was no space for heartache.

Only pure wanting.

Eryna laced her fingers behind Brody's neck and settled her lips against his. "Touch me, Brody."

He swallowed hard and his mouth crashed into hers a second later, hungry and exhilarated. His fingers found the waistband of her pants and skimmed the skin around her hips with several teasing strokes until he slid his hand down the side of her thigh.

She withdrew at the touch as the memory of Damian's hand resurfaced. Brody froze.

"Should I stop?" he asked. But Eryna wanted nothing more than a welcome, caring touch to replace the memory of a greedy, hateful one. She shook her head.

"Please don't."

She leaned in to keep kissing him, but Brody pulled back an inch and smirked. He shook his head. "I want to watch this," he said, and before Eryna could ask what it was he wanted to watch, his hand slid in toward the apex of her thigh and found the small, tight bundle of nerves at her center. Her breath hitched. "Oh," she breathed, her fingers clamping down on his shoulders.

His thumb worked her in slow circles and her eyes rolled back as her entire body tightened, her nipples peaking against his warm chest. It wasn't like she'd never experienced this sensation. It was only natural for a Dryad to explore herself occasionally. But enjoying such intimacy in the hands of another was entirely different. Her sisters had described such things from before the war, but nothing could've prepared her for experiencing it firsthand.

"Tell me what you want," Brody urged, his circles growing harder, faster. She felt him bulge beneath her through his pants and had to bite her tongue to keep from asking for more than she was ready for. Still, she wanted more than just this.

"More," she whimpered, and he obediently slid two fingers inside her, the heel of his hand replacing his thumb. She gasped at the sensation, the pressure as he pumped in and out of her, his fingertips finding that intensely sensitive spot deep inside that she'd only managed to get to a few times on her own. His free hand found her neck and tilted her head to the side, creating a blank canvas for his lips to freely paint.

"Like that?" he murmured into her skin, and the heat of his breath made her core tense. She ground her hips, his palm winding her up tighter and tighter with each stroke. He curved his fingers inside her and firmly pressed against that sensitive spot, and she just about erupted.

"Fuck, Brody, *more*," she moaned, her fingers clutching his hair tight. She barely had a hold on her sanity when he pulled her head back, captured her breast in his mouth, and gently sucked while he flicked his tongue over her nipple. Her back arched, her muscles going taught as she lost all sense of control. She was nothing but clay in his hands.

"Come for me, Eryna," he encouraged, and it tipped her over the edge, like plummeting down the rapids of the highest waterfall, freefalling into unknown waters.

"Oh, Gaia." She gasped and panted as she came undone. He captured her gaze and held her through each tremor as she repeatedly tightened and relaxed around his fingers. He kissed her as the last few trembles rocked her body, an indulgently lazy, almost deliriously slow kiss until she went slack in his arms. She rested her sweat-beaded forehead against his and simply breathed as she gathered herself.

"That," Brody said as he kissed her nose, "Was fucking fantastic to watch."

Eryna burst into exasperated laughter and pulled him down on the couch with her, kissing him again and again as that strange movie played in the background, and they didn't watch a single second.

Chapter Thirty-Seven

Eryna startled awake, her eyes opening to the darkened room, save for the light from the television.

Cheek pressed against Brody's chest, Eryna lifted her head and gazed at him for a moment. He was good looking when awake, but somehow even more so asleep. She considered staying like that and attempting to fall back into a dream so they could wake in the morning together, but her mind was too alert and restless. An aching guilt over being intimate with Brody instead of Derrick pricked at her, even though she'd thoroughly enjoyed it. She needed to collect herself. She needed to wander until that guilt fled her system. Derrick hated her now, she reminded herself, not only because she'd lied, but because of what she was, what she was born as. He didn't hate her actions. He hated *her*. And that, above everything else, was the most painful part of it all.

She gently brushed Brody's hair back, softly kissed him, threw her shirt on, and left. The Manor was dark, silent, and spotless, which meant the Hunt had ended some time ago. It had to be four or five in the morning, though the black cloud cover and torrential downpour slapping against the windows made it hard to tell.

Eryna studied it for a moment.

It was an unseasonable summer storm, rare, though not unusual.

She walked through the Manor in no particular direction and closed her eyes for a moment, listening to the rain. She recalled how it felt to dance in these summer storms; they always brought out a rambunctious energy in the Dryads. But Eryna also found them serene, meditative, cleansing. It was the only time besides execution days where she could find a rare moment of peace. At the thought of home, Eryna's eyes suddenly shot open, and she looked down at her arms.

They were white. She felt around her neck, her face. All her texture had returned. She'd completely forgotten the tonic had worn off, and she was walking around Blackwell Manor as her true self.

As a Dryad.

I need to get back to my room, she urged herself, but her body didn't seem to feel the same urgency. She looked around to orient herself and realized she was standing at the wall of women.

"How'd I get here?" she wondered aloud. This nook was on the opposite side of the Manor as Brody's loft.

She turned and gazed out at the garden, though it was barely visible through the rain. Eryna placed her hand on the glass, like if she could just press hard enough, it would give way beneath her touch. She could escape into the storm like a trapped animal fleeing its cage.

No, not a trapped animal.

A trapped flower.

Parvati's words suddenly rang in her ears.

Don't let them trap you.

But Eryna wasn't in danger of that.

It's not like she was being held there against her will. The only reason she was still there was because she needed those Hearts. Once she got them, she could go. She *would* go. In fact, she'd already decided was leaving today.

Wasn't she?

Eryna wanted nothing more than to be home, than to restore her realm and help revive the Dryad race. But the longer she'd been in the human world, the easier it'd been to forget the real reason she was here, and the more never seeing Brody or Jenin or Derrick—despite how much he hated her now—stung like a fresh wound.

Had Eryna trapped herself without realizing it?

"Ah, Miss Thorne," Alexander's voice said, making Eryna jump. He stood near the wall of women, drenched in shadow. Had he been watching her?

The realization that he was seeing her as a Dryad hit too late. She couldn't hide now.

"What are you doing up this late?" he asked, stepping closer. He eyed her, his gaze burrowing holes in her birch skin. He seemed so much larger, so much more formidable in this darkness, and so much younger and healthier than he had only a few days ago. He must've gotten what he needed from the Hunt.

Eryna stepped back and swallowed.

"Couldn't sleep," she said. She hated how weak her voice sounded in her ears. Alexander chuckled, the sound musical but somehow off-key.

"Neither could I," he said, shrugging.

Then he cocked his head to the side, his handsome face catching the dim light from the window just enough to highlight the sharp planes of his cheek, his dark eyes. He took another step forward.

"I've actually been looking for you."

"Oh? What for?" Eryna took another step back. Her legs bumped into a bench, pinning her in place. Alexander glanced down. He smiled, the expression absolutely feral.

"You're going to help us with a little experiment for Blackwell Technologies."

"Am I? I'd love to. Let's talk about it tomorrow. Good night," Eryna stammered, attempting to sidestep Alexander, but he stopped her.

"Actually," he hissed sharply through his teeth, "It can't wait.

You see, Brody can't know. It's best he thinks you simply ran off. I'd wondered why he'd grown so attached to you, but now..." Alexander reached up and ran a thumb across Eryna's cheek, an action his son did only hours ago, except Brody's touch was filled with adoration. Alexander's was dissecting and cold. "Now I understand. I loved one of your sisters once. My son won't repeat that mistake."

Eryna jerked out of his grasp. His hand fell to his side, and he took a small step back.

"How could you have..." her voice trailed off. She narrowed her gaze and studied him carefully. So carefully. And suddenly, realization hit her.

"You're Martin Blackwell, aren't you?"

Martin smirked at her and bowed.

"In the flesh."

Eryna glared at him, fighting every drop of rage that cracked through her bones. He wasn't just an ancestor of the monster who killed more than half her kind.

He was the monster itself.

"If you loved one of my sisters, you wouldn't have killed her people," Eryna challenged.

Martin clucked his tongue and shook his head and finger.

"Ah, see, that was never my intention. When I learned how your Hearts could give life and sustain it, could heal sicknesses and wounds, I only meant to borrow one to study, to see if I could synthesize its properties. I never thought the Sylvanwood Sisters would die after the Heart had been gone long enough."

Eryna's chest constricted as he said her cousin-realm's name. It felt wrong, perverted coming from him.

"And the Fiddlewood, then? You just *needed* to study a second Heart? The decimation of one clan wasn't enough?"

Martin fell silent for a second, his eyes drifting some vague direction out the window.

"Tasting that power...it might not feel like anything to you, but that's because it was made for your kind. To a non-Dryad, it's intoxicating. We needed more, and the Fiddlewood Sisters underestimated our determination." Martin glanced at her and smiled. "I wasn't completely ignorant of your activities here, you know. I caught you wandering about the place, looking for the other Hearts. I hate to say it, but you were so very close, several times in fact. I used to store them in a vault, but it blocked their powers and I learned I needed to keep them closer. Hidden in plain sight if you will."

Eryna's mind raced, scanning her memories repeatedly for when she could have possibly been close to finding them. The theater? The greenhouse? The art gallery? Or was it not one of her rooms at all? She looked at Martin with wide eyes.

"Where?" she asked, unable to keep the question to herself. Martin shoved his hands in his pockets and laughed deeply.

"I may have been born at night, Miss Thorne, but I wasn't born last night. I wasn't even born in the last several centuries. If you must ask where the Hearts are, you'll never know." Martin sighed.

Eryna stepped forward, courage suddenly finding her.

"So, what is it you need from me, then? Help finding the third Heart? I hate to disappoint, but I don't know where it is."

Martin cocked his head to the side.

"Baby steps, Miss Thorne. Or should I say, *Thornewood?* We don't need the third Heart just yet. We're going to try something else first."

"We?" Eryna questioned.

Martin's eyes slid over Eryna's shoulder, and just before she could follow his gaze, a damp rag soaked in something sickly sweet was thrown over her nose. Hot breath coated her neck as angry lips touched her ears.

"Miss me?" Damian murmured, and Eryna kicked and fought and screamed, but her voice never left her lips, and her muscles gave out in seconds. Darkness took hold of her vision, and her last thought was that she should have left with Jenin when she'd asked, because Eryna was never going to find the Hearts now.

Maybe she never stood a chance to begin with.

Chapter Thirty-Eight

Beep. Beep. Beep.

Rhythmic chirping like a far too loud morning bird woke Eryna. The surface on which she lay was rigid and cold.

Where am I? she tried asking, but her lips wouldn't move.

They *couldn't* move.

Panicking, she tried to open her eyes, but it was as if her lids were sewn shut. She focused all her concentration on simply moving her pinky finger. It wouldn't even twitch.

Fear crested in her chest. The rhythmic chirping intensified, matching the rapid beats of her pulse.

"What's happening? Why's her heart rate spiking?" Martin asked. "Is she awake?"

Yes, I'm awake, you lunatic! Eryna screamed, but the words stayed within the prison of her mind. Someone snapped their fingers in her left ear, then her right. They lifted one of her lids and flashed a light in her eye. Her vision was blurry, but she could see Damian's vague outline. Eryna wanted to vomit. She wanted to set fire to her veins and explode in front of them all, taking them down in a furious, fiery death.

Her lid shut.

"Her body's not responsive. She's still unconscious. Must be a reaction to the drugs or something," Damian said dismissively. "You sure it'll work this time?" he asked someone in the room, his voice skeptical and annoyed.

"Yes," the person responded. Jerry Lundal.

It seems Eryna wasn't helping Blackwell Technologies with an experiment. She *was* the experiment.

"Good. We can't afford to have a repeat of what happened with Gen and Marisa," Damian said.

"Or any of the other wives," Martin scoffed. The wall of women flooded Eryna's mind, and Parvati's words about their terrible fates bounced off the echo chamber of her skull. The other women had been their former wives, and there was at least a dozen.

"If Miss Thorne is what you say she is, it should work this time," Jerry replied. "The human bodies couldn't handle the Hearts. Gen and Marisa lasted the longest because of the protective casings we created, but even then, it was too much. But since the Hearts are her peoples' life source, I can only imagine putting one in her would be like screwing a lightbulb in a socket."

Eryna let out an imaginary scream that nearly burst her eardrums. She heard nothing beyond it.

They were going to put one of the Hearts *inside* her. It would be a blessing to be home to one of the Dryad Hearts, except she knew that once it was in her, she would be a trapped flower forever. They'd never let her leave. She'd be a permanent fixture in this mansion. They might as well nail her to the staircase and stick a candelabra in her hand like the nymph statues.

But why did they need to put it inside her in the first place?

"Parvati should be here for this," Martin remarked.

"Screw Parvati," Damian spat. "Her solutions are taking too long and we're out of time. We only have one year left with the energy from the Hunt. This is the best chance we've got. If this works, we'll need to make a run back to the Thornewood for another one of *these*." Damian poked Eryna's arm, his touch like a hot coal against her skin. "Maybe we grab your favorite, Blackwell? What was her name? Dena?"

"Dera," he said through gritted teeth. "And you can't have her. You know that."

DERA! Eryna tried to shout, the rhythmic chirping mounting quicker and quicker. The room around her stirred, but she hardly paid attention.

Dera was alive. *Alive.*

Somehow, some way, some of her sisters had survived, and Eryna was no longer alone. She had never been alone.

A sob erupted through Eryna's lips.

"She's awake," Damian breathed. "More anesthesia. Now, Jerry!"

"That's not possible. She's on near lethal levels, any more and—"

"I don't care. More," Damian commanded. There was a moment of silence, then a shuffling of feet and clanging of metal. A warmth coursed through Eryna's veins; a dreariness settled in her mind.

No, no, no. Stay awake, stay awake, Eryna silently pleaded with her body. Her lungs sputtered and coughed; her head felt like it was made of solid stone. The chirping slowed.

Beep...

Beep...

Beep...

She heard mumbles and movement and caught a few of Damian's words as he passed by her head.

"I'll go get the Hearts, it's time—"

There was a loud bang, almost like an explosion, followed by several shouts. The inside of her elbow stung slightly, and the warmth rushing through her veins disappeared. The chirping stopped. Her senses sharpened. Whatever was in her system was leaving fast, thanks to her

Dryad body.

The flat surface she was on moved.

Someone stroked her hair.

"We've got you," Jenin said, her voice shaking.

Eryna's eyes opened to a petite figure with dark blonde hair hovering over her as the rest of the world moved around them.

"What's happening?" Eryna rasped, the words like sandpaper against her larynx.

"We're getting you home," Jenin replied. "I'm sorry we didn't come earlier."

"We?" Eryna whispered.

"Brody's waiting in the car and…" Jenin's voice trailed off as her eyes slid to her left. Eryna's gaze followed. Next to her was Derrick, his expression serious and dark. Her throat tightened; her eyes burned with hot tears. She tried not to give into her guilt for what she'd done with Brody the night before, but in that moment, nothing else mattered.

Derrick had come for her. He hated her and he'd still come for her.

Silently, she wrapped her hand around his. He quickly pulled it away, a pained look on his face as if Eryna touching him was the last thing he wanted. Humiliation squirmed through her like a living thing, but before it could take root, he slid his other hand into hers and laced their fingers together.

"We're getting you out of here," he murmured, his words warming her. She nodded and relaxed, letting them execute whatever plan it was they'd come up with. They passed a painting of the night sky and it reminded her of the one outside her room in The Spire.

Eryna laughed to herself thinking about those first days, the first time she met Derrick, and that small, barely decorated room that held her like a prisoner. Only now when she thought of it, a small pang of nostalgia welled up in her. She wondered if that horrendous steel sculpture Jenin clubbed her with still had blood on it. It made her think of the art gallery, the similar looking artifacts encased in glass in the nymph section.

Artifacts created with nymph technology intended to trap magical objects.

Eryna sat bolt upright.

Jenin and Derrick slowed but didn't stop. The shouts of Damian and Martin echoed some distance away.

"The Hearts," Eryna gasped, looking between the siblings. Jenin shook her head.

"We don't have time," she protested. Eryna grabbed Jenin's arm and looked her straight in the eye.

"Then make time," Eryna urged. "I know where they are."

Jenin looked at Derrick, who pressed his lips tight, deliberating. He glanced at his watch, then quickly shoved his hand in his pocket and nodded.

"We have ten minutes."

Chapter Thirty-Nine

They were already on borrowed time when they got to the main floor. They'd been on an underground level of the Manor Eryna had no idea existed, and it had taken them far too long to emerge.

Still groggy and barely recovered from the sedation, Eryna's pulse pounded furiously as they stopped at the base of a side staircase and she slid off her contraption.

"Wait here," she said to Derrick and Jenin.

"You're crazy if you think you're going alone," Jenin protested.

"I'm faster alone," Eryna said, then ran as hard as she could up the stairs so neither of them stood a chance of catching up.

Halfway to the gallery, a distant clamor echoed from the far side of the Manor.

Martin and Damian must have made it to the first floor.

Eryna ran faster. Her lungs burned as she sprinted down the doorless hall and stopped in front of the painting of the ship. But she didn't have the key. She'd left it in Brody's loft along with the rest of them, and there was no time to double back now.

Eryna's eyes caught on a crack of light coming from behind the painting. Her stomach dropped five stories through the floor.

It was open, which meant someone was already inside.

Eryna slipped in on light feet, the room silent and still. It only made her more skittish. She craned her head in all directions and glanced around each corner. She held her breath as she entered the nymph section. Was someone lying in wait with another syrupy soaked rag?

Eryna froze.

A small, round woman with brown hair sat on the bench in front of the Dryad painting.

Brenna.

She looked at Eryna.

"I wondered when you'd be back," she said, her smile wide, kind.

Eryna wasn't sure she could trust it, and there was no time to stop and chat. Her eyes landed on the glass case that held the small steel spheres. The Hearts.

Brenna followed her gaze. She stood and walked toward Eryna.

Eryna retreated several steps. Brenna may have been kind to her, but she was still a loyal member of Martin's staff.

Silently, Brenna grabbed one of Eryna's hands and placed a small but heavy rolling pin in it. Eryna eyed the object, entirely confused. Brenna smiled at her again, softly patted her on the cheek, then nodded toward the glass case.

"They've been stuck in the human world long enough," Brenna said.

A question formed between Eryna's brow as she looked at her and remembered what Brenna had once said.

I'm surprised they let this room participate this year. They never do.

Then she remembered seeing a small round woman with brown hair fleeing the hall of statues on the first night of the Hunt.

"It was you, wasn't it?" Eryna asked. "You slipped the gallery key into the game."

She touched Eryna's arm affectionately. "Into the game for *you*. My grandmother was a Naiad. I knew what you were the moment you walked into the Manor."

The more she looked at Brenna, the more she recognized the watery blue eyes of the Naiads. There was indeed nymph in her.

Eryna stepped toward the glass box, covered her eyes, and swung. The glass shattered. Eryna grabbed the two spheres and studied them in disbelief, their steel exteriors intricately carved with ancient symbols and runes. The Hearts were real, and they were in her hands. And after all these centuries, all the death and destruction and heartbreak and loss, they would finally be home in Euryalea.

Suddenly, the gallery went black. Then an ominous red light coated the room, and a loud siren blared.

Shouts sounded from the hall outside the gallery.

"You need to go. Now," Brenna urged, pulling Eryna toward a wall at the back of the gallery. She touched it and a panel opened, revealing a dark set of stairs. Eryna had no choice but to trust. She shoved the spheres into her pockets and hugged Brenna tight.

"Thank you, Brenna," she said.

"Be well, sweet girl," she replied.

A shout came from the front of the gallery, and Brenna shoved her toward the stairs.

"I'll hold them as long as I can," she said, and shoved again.

Without another look back, Eryna descended the stairs two at a time.

Three.

Four.

Her knees ached, and when she heard a loud *boom* and a shrill scream, she tried as best she could to ignore the ripping ache in her soul and the guilt that blossomed in her stomach. She had to focus on getting down and out of the Manor.

Loud steps echoed in the staircase. Eryna was no longer alone.

She moved faster, now skipping over five stairs. Six.

"You can't run from us forever, demon!" Damian shouted. All

her rage, frustration, and fear crashed over her at the sound of his voice.

"Fuck you!" she shouted back. Several mocking chuckles replied, as if she were a kitten who thought she was a mountain lion.

Their steps pounded closer.

Panic nipped at her heels. She had to be close to the exit by now.

She almost cried as she spotted a door. She grabbed the handle and yanked on it.

It wouldn't budge.

"No!" Eryna cried.

"What's the matter, Miss Thorne? No way out?" Martin's voice rang out, only two flights up. Eryna banged on the door.

"Please, someone help!" she screamed, pulling on the handle again and again.

"No one's coming for you. You're ours now," Damian said.

They were one flight up.

A light buzz in Eryna's pocket caught her attention. She shoved her hand in and pulled out a small silver key with a black bead on it.

Brenna's key, Eryna gasped. She must have slipped it into Eryna's pocket.

There was no time left to think. She shoved the key in the lock and the handle turned. Eryna sprinted through the door to where Jenin and Derrick waited.

"Come on!" They shouted in unison, jumping up and down, waving her forward, urging her on. Derrick's gaze slid over Eryna's shoulder, and his expression turned panicky, his eyes wide.

"Eryna move!" he shouted, but a bite in her shoulder told her it was too late. She quickly glanced to see a small metal dart with a red feather protruding from her skin. She looked back at Jenin and Derrick, and the world immediately slowed.

Her vision tunneled. Her legs went limp. Her breathing lagged.

The last things she registered was a set of strong arms grabbing her and Derrick's voice whispering, "I've got you."

Chapter Forty

$\mathcal{S}$hadows and daylight blurred across Eryna's vision.

Her body jostled against cold leather and her head rested on a warm lap. She opened her eyes and looked up.

Jenin looked down at her through a mischievous smile.

"You have a good little demon nap?" she asked. Derrick turned around in the passenger seat and looked at her, relief filling his face.

"She's up?" Brody frantically asked from behind the wheel. He reached his hand back, feeling for her. "Are you okay? Did they hurt you?"

Jenin brushed him away.

"Gods, give her a moment, will you?"

Barely able to lift her head, Eryna glanced out the window. She couldn't tell where they were, but with how light it was outside, it had to be late morning.

"How long was I out?" she asked, yawning.

"A few hours. Dad got you pretty good with a horse tranquilizer," Jenin said. Eryna touched a tender spot on her back and winced. Then she frantically shoved her hand in her pocket, checking the two spheres still there, safe and sound. She blew out a breath.

Then Brody swerved, and a large shadow passed by. Eryna sat up so quick, it took her a few seconds to see straight.

Her heart slammed furiously against her ribcage.

They were driving through trees.

Dead trees.

Twisted and bare and angry and familiar and the best sight Eryna had ever seen. She rolled the window down, letting the rain soak her face.

"We're in the Sylvanwood," Eryna breathed, inhaling the familiar territory, unable to distinguish between her own tears and the raindrops on her cheeks.

"Almost to the Thornewood," Brody said. They drove the cut trails in silence for several minutes as Eryna watched the familiar surroundings pass by.

"Was it beautiful?" Jenin asked quietly, staring out the window. "Before, I mean." Eryna eyed the passing trees, imagining what they would look like once she restored the Heart of the Slyvanwood Mother Oak, full and green and bountiful. She nodded.

"I wasn't alive then. But if it was anything like the Thornewood, then it was the most beautiful thing you've ever seen."

Then the bare, dead trees turned to recently charred ones. Eryna breathed in the scent of fresh pine and decaying wood and ash—the scent of her home that refused to be destroyed.

They'd entered the Thornewood.

If what Damian had said was true and some of Eryna's sisters were still alive, chances were, they'd be even more hostile toward humans. And if she knew anything about her sisters, they'd probably been tracking the car since it entered Euryalea.

"Stop!" Eryna called. Brody slammed on the breaks nearly swerving them into a tree.

"What? What is it?" he asked.

"What's happening?" Derrick chimed in.

"According to your fathers, some of my sisters are still alive," she replied, staring warily out the window.

"What?" Jenin, Derrick, and Brody replied in unison. Clearly, they didn't know.

"I thought they burned the whole forest down?" Jenin asked. Eryna shook her head.

"Clearly not. Roll up the windows, lock the doors, and don't come out until I tell you," Eryna ordered. Brody unbuckled his seatbelt and made to open the door, but Eryna put her hand on his shoulder.

"I mean it. Stay here. You got lucky before. You won't get lucky again," she said. He offset his jaw and eyed her for a moment.

"This is her territory, man, I'm doing what she says," Derrick remarked.

"Yeah, no way am I going out there yet," Jenin added.

Brody hesitated a moment longer, then slumped back in his seat like a frustrated child. "Fine," he said. Eryna rolled her eyes. He of all humans knew firsthand what happened when humans entered the Thornewood.

Eryna shut the door, waited until she heard the light *click* of the locks, then walked several feet away from the car. Inhaling deeply, she let the Thornewood air fill her lungs, the heavy summer rain drench her skin.

The air tasted like petrichor and a thousand endless bonfire nights. Eryna studied the charred trees around her. She touched a thick cedar, and it leaned into her, crying out at her presence.

You're home, you're home, it whispered.

I'm home, I'm home, she replied. When she pulled away, the trunk was already a little less charred. But now was not the time to soothe her forest. She needed to know for sure if any of her sisters were alive. Eryna knelt and buried her hands deep in the mud, the soft liquid earth squelching between her fingers. She closed her eyes and let it speak its memories to her.

There was death. So much death.

A heaviness pulled at Eryna, the unbearable weight of the lost lives of over a hundred sisters. Pain and emptiness and fear rooted itself within her as she relived that horrifying day through the earth's eyes.

Then there was fire. So much fire.

It spread through the bushes and the trees, and such excruciating anger welled up inside Eryna that she screamed in fury. There was so much sadness, so much loss here, and not just her sisters. Unable to take it anymore, she was about to withdraw when a small light pushed its way through.

Life.

There was still life here.

Only a small portion of the Thornewood had burned, the forest able to snuff it out before it spread beyond a hundred acres. Eryna's tears of anger turned to tears of joy. And there were still animals, and still—

A sudden spike in energy caught Eryna's attention, and just as she opened her eyes, she ripped her hands from the earth and rolled away, narrowly escaping a spear flying right at her. Eryna looked back at the car and saw thirty Dryads headed toward it.

"No! Stop!" she screamed. But they didn't stop. It took a moment to realize she'd spoken the human language. She tried again.

"Leave them alone, they're my friends!" Eryna shouted in her native tongue. Making its round, full mouth movements after weeks of speaking the human language felt like stretching after a long day of sitting.

She called after her sisters again. They still didn't stop.

"Don't hurt them, they're here to help!"

A head turned her direction, and she locked eyes with wild green eyes and brown skin like that of the sweet birch tree.

And everything was suddenly right in the world.

"Dera," Eryna cried, running toward her.

Dera stared at her, confusion staining her enraged expression. The sister next to Dera followed her gaze. Her ash tree complexion blanched, and she clutched Dera for support.

Oihane.

"Oh, my Gaia," Oihane cried and broke into a run toward Eryna.

"Eryna!" Dera called out, the violence and confusion dissolving into surprise, relief. Oihane tackled Eryna to the ground and scanned her.

"You're alive? You're alive?" she asked repeatedly. But before Eryna could spout the obvious answer that, yes, clearly, she was alive, Dera collapsed onto the two of them and crushed Eryna tight to her chest.

"*Faémona*," she sobbed. "I thought we'd lost you forever."

"I thought I'd lost *you*," Eryna said, holding Dera tight, breathing in her orange blossom and honeysuckle scent, for once not resenting her nickname. She threw an arm around Oihane and pulled her in. "All of you."

More sisters piled on, pulling at Eryna, squeezing her in tight embraces. They scanned her face, asked about her clothes, where she'd been, how she got home. After a minute, Oihane elbowed Eryna. She nodded toward the car.

"Care to explain that?" she asked, ferociously eyeing the three passengers.

"I do. But first..." Eryna said, digging into her pockets. She pulled out the steel spheres. Her sisters' eyes went wide, and they let out a chorus of gasps. Eryna smiled. "I brought gifts."

Dera cupped her hands around Eryna's and studied the vessels with greedy, disbelieving eyes. She looked up at her, tears slipping through her lashes, pride inflating her chest.

Dera patted Eryna's hand and smiled.

"Well done, *faémona*. Tomorrow at dawn, we take the Hearts back to the other woods. But tonight..." Dera paused to throw a conspiratorial look at the rest of the sisters. "Tonight, we celebrate."

Chapter Forty-One

Only forty-five of Eryna's sisters had survived.

Only forty-five Dryads were left in all of Euryalea.

Forty-six, now that Eryna was back. It was a small, meager number compared to the two hundred who were alive before the attack, but it was a strong, precious number considering Eryna previously thought none had survived at all.

After they made it to the *Domecowé*, Eryna braced herself against the Mother Oak as Dera shared what had happened since she'd been gone. From the sounds of it, many of the lost sisters hadn't died during the attack. The majority passed from their wounds days later.

Eryna couldn't stave the guilt from curdling her blood. She could have saved every last one of her injured sisters. But then Dera mentioned that many uninjured sisters also fell sick and deteriorated quickly.

"Sick? With what?" Eryna asked. Dryads didn't get sick. But as Dera opened her mouth to answer, Maya called her away to begin the questionings of Derrick, Jenin, and Brody. Eryna's sisters promised no harm would come to them. Of course, Eryna wasn't allowed to be there.

"We'll finish this later," Dera promised Eryna. She scanned Eryna's face and read her impossible-to-hide worry. "Your friends will be fine, *faémona*. We need to make sure they're not a threat."

Eryna sighed and nodded, and when Dera disappeared into the thick forest, she went to help build bonfires for tonight's celebration. As the Dryads worked through their preparations, Eryna scanned each of her sisters' faces. They looked so tired, so strained, so frail. They were weaker than Eryna had ever seen a Dryad look, except maybe Ardian. It made her think of the humans during the Hunt, wan and gaunt.

But her sisters seemed in good spirits, and as she watched them work for a moment, her heart both burst with happiness for those who had survived and shattered with despair at those who had not.

Althea. Mori. Ilana.

Just three among more than a hundred and fifty sisters who would never again dance around a bonfire or indulge in berry wine; never feel the soft earth beneath their feet as they ran through their forested home. Eryna reached into her pocket and squeezed the spheres tight, promising on the souls of those sisters that such a loss wouldn't be in vain; that she would restore all three woods of Euryalea to their former glory. The lost sisters might not witness it, but she knew that wherever their souls met Gaia in the unending sky, they would feel Euryalea's life return.

Dera came back nearly an hour later, clearly satisfied with whatever answers she'd received, as Jenin, Derrick, and Brody followed shortly behind and were immediately put to work.

Eryna headed straight for Dera, curiosity nipping at her heels.

"How'd it go?" she asked. Dera shrugged.

"They passed. For now."

"Good." Eryna sighed and relaxed onto Dera's shoulder. "I missed you all so much."

"And we you. More than you'll ever know."

"You weren't happy to be rid of such a disappointment of a sister?" she asked facetiously, though she held her breath for the answer. Dera retracted and looked at Eryna as if she'd just claimed to have ten arms.

"Eryna of the Thornewood, don't you dare ask that again. You were never a disappointment. Never. You are the bright, shining spirit of our clan," she scolded, but folded Eryna into her arms. After a long, silent moment, Dera cleared her throat.

"You really trust them?" she asked, nodding toward the three humans who were helping build bonfires, or at least trying their best to.

Unsurprisingly, Derrick took to it like second nature, while Brody needed a correction here and there, and they put Jenin on wine duty after she refused to touch raw wood. But if there was ever a perfect job for Jenin, it was making sure everyone had plenty of wine. Eryna eyed her friends and smiled.

"With my life," she replied, and she meant it. But Dera simply pursed her lips. "You're still unsure," Eryna remarked, certain to keep her tone neutral.

"I'll always be unsure. Them, I might be inclined to consider trusting," Dera said, slyly signaling toward Jenin who was topping off Oihane's wine, and Derrick who was helping Maya stuff dry brush beneath tall pyramids of wood.

"But *him*..." Dera's eyes slid to Brody, who was smiling and making their sister Terra laugh. Eryna leveled a serious gaze at Dera.

"We can trust him."

"He's a Blackwell. You truly trust a Blackwell?"

"I trust *that* Blackwell."

Dera sighed deeply. It was a familiar sigh, one she only used when Eryna was being particularly vexing. Of all the reasons Eryna had missed her sister, that sigh was not one of them. Dera brushed a lock of Eryna's yellow hair behind her ear.

"Sometimes the way we feel about a person can overshadow whether or not they should be trusted, *faémona*," she said, smiling softly, sympathetically. Frustration nettled Eryna. She was wiser now and had experienced more life since Dera had last seen her. She wasn't just *little sister* anymore. She took a deep, calming breath, and opened her mouth to protest, but was interrupted.

"We're ready!" Oihane sang loudly as she and Jenin trotted up. "Sunset's in an hour and we'll be ready to light…" Oihane trailed off, her face falling as she took Eryna in, still dressed in Brody's shirt and pants. Oihane then looked at Jenin, who was in a pair of semi-relaxed jeans and a black t-shirt and frowned.

"No, these won't do," she said, grabbing Eryna's and Jenin's hands. Jenin looked at Eryna for translation.

"What's happening?" she whispered, somewhat panicked. As Oihane pulled them out of the main clearing and deeper into the half-charred woods, Eryna chuckled.

"This is payback for making me wear all those jeans," she said with a wink. Oihane threw a mischievous glance at Jenin and smiled.

"I hope you don't mind silk."

"This? This is what you wear *all the time?*" Jenin asked, running her hands across her short silk dress that burst with climbing ivy and fragrant jasmine and soft ferns and delicate lily of the valley. She smiled and touched the circlet of pale peonies and gypsophila atop her head. "If this is payback for jeans, then you clearly don't understand revenge. I'm a walking bouquet."

Eryna laughed, tying the two Hearts around her neck on a strong piece of hemp thread. She was adamant about holding onto the Hearts until they arrived at the Mother Oaks. It felt only right that she be the one to deliver them back to their homes.

She adjusted her dress and smiled, comforted by the familiar fit and scent. The silk was lined with fresh, flexible willow reeds woven with ranunculus and white poppies and light blue delphiniums. Her fingers skimmed her circlet of eucalyptus and mourning dove feathers and, of course, chiffon roses. She sighed, an ease filling her chest. This was home. This was where she belonged, not the human world.

Jenin touched Eryna's shoulder.

"You look beautiful," she said, tucking an errant poppy back into place. "My brother's going to lose his mind."

Eryna's heart constricted as she thought of Derrick. The last time he'd said more than a few words to her was at the Hunt. He'd been so enraged, so disgusted by her. Eryna swallowed and glanced down at her feet.

"I doubt it," she replied quietly. "I'm pretty sure he hates me."

Jenin ducked her head to catch Eryna's lowered gaze.

"Don't mistake fear for hatred. He doesn't hate you in the slightest. Under the right circumstances, I think him finding out would've gone differently. But it's not my place to put words in his mouth. He needs to explain himself to you on his own terms."

Eryna wasn't sure she believed Jenin, and Jenin must have seen it on her face. She lightly nudged Eryna.

"Don't give up on him, okay? I was just getting used to having you around. It was kind of like having a sister."

Warmth rippled through Eryna, and her gaze went soft. Tight pressure burned behind her eyes. She pulled Jenin into an embrace, careful not to crush their fresh flowers.

"*Osea yao faémo,*" she said. Jenin stiffened in her arms.

"Did you just put a spell on me or something?" Jenin laughed. Eryna laughed with her, then hugged her harder.

"It means 'you are my sister,'" Eryna said. She pulled back and placed her hand on Jenin's chest. "In here."

Jenin's mouth turned down and her eyes went wide, tears pooling at the rims. She threw herself onto Eryna and squeezed her hard.

"Osay yay feemo, too, or whatever. You know what I mean."

The girls chuckled, no longer caring if their flowers were crushed.

"This is all very touching," Oihane said, smirking at them as she lifted three cups and a fresh bottle of berry wine. "But we've got a celebration to start. Let's drink!" she exclaimed brightly. Jenin looked at Eryna then nodded toward Oihane.

"She might be my favorite sister of yours," she said. Eryna threaded her arm through Jenin's elbow as they walked.

"Why does that not surprise me?" Eryna remarked, laughing.

The three of them filled their cups and joined the Dryads around the bonfires, the forest now dim, the sun mere seconds from setting.

Brody and Derrick stood near Dera, dressed in nothing but pants and circlets of olive branches. Eryna's heart pounded as she eyed them, the curves of their muscles, the smoothness of their skins.

They saw her at the same time.

Derrick hesitated.

Brody didn't.

He walked toward her and stopped less than a foot away. He looked her up and down, grabbed her hand and twirled her in a circle.

"I remember you," he breathed, smiling his most perfect, most wolfish smile and Eryna's heart gave a *thud* so loud she worried he might've heard it. He cradled her face in his hands and kissed her softly, sweetly, raising each hair on her body.

Eryna heard Jenin make a quiet sound of disgust then take a long sip of her wine. As Brody pulled away from her lips, Eryna caught Derrick's stare just over his shoulder, a deep hollowness in his eyes. He looked away, suddenly finding one of the bonfire piles incredibly interesting.

"Eryna of the Thornewood," Dera called. Eryna looked to where her sister stood at the center bonfire holding a lit torch. She held it out and smiled. "Will you do the honors?"

Never in all her hundred years had Eryna been asked to light the center bonfire. It was an honor held only for clan leaders, elders, or those who'd achieved something truly great. And now here she was, returned to her clan with the two missing Hearts of Euryalea being asked to do just that. Pride was not a strong enough word for what burst through her.

Brody nudged her forward.

With shaky hands, Eryna grabbed the torch.

She took a deep breath and cleared her throat.

"The Hearts have returned, and the debt has been paid. No more blood shall be spilled, human or Dryad," she said. Then she raised the torch. Every sister followed, forty-seven torches held high in the air. They'd even given Jenin a torch.

"To a time of peace in Euryalea!" Eryna called.

"To a time of peace in Euryalea!" Her sisters chanted back, their voices echoing through the *Domecowé* and beyond.

Eryna held her torch to the center pile, and as it caught fire quickly, the primal urge to yelp and holler and scream with excitement at the top of her lungs took control. Her sisters followed, lighting the piles, and crowing with glee.

Drums kicked up, wine poured heavily, and dancing started immediately. Eryna scanned the scene in front of her, tattooing it into her soul, deciding it was the happiest she might ever be.

She was home.

She was back with her people, her sisters, and she was, above all else, a Dryad.

In that moment, Eryna swore to Gaia that she would never, ever forget that again.

Chapter Forty-Two

Two dozen bonfires blazed high and bright around the Mother Oak. Thick heat rose up in transparent waves and distorted the faces of Eryna's sisters and friends as she danced.

Every minute or two, she was intercepted by an embrace or soft kiss on the cheek and a loud praise. She would pause, accept, then keep dancing, unable to stop as the drums thrummed through her veins. Her legs and arms moved of their own accord; the dances written into their memory. She danced until her lungs burned for more air, her cheeks aflame with heat. Her feet ached desperately, having softened from weeks of wearing human shoes. As hard as it was for her to admit, she needed a break.

She spotted Jenin, Brody, Derrick, Oihane, and Dera passing around a bottle of wine and joined them. Oihane lit up as she saw Eryna, her arms drunkenly flinging wide before clasping around her.

"*Faémona*, our savior, come!" she squealed. She grabbed the wine out of Dera's hand and topped off Eryna's cup. "Young Blackwell here was just apologizing on behalf of his entire bloodline."

Eryna's brows rose as she looked at Brody. He blushed.

"I was just saying that I…I had no idea what would happen that day, and I never intended for harm to come to you all. I was…naive about what my father's intentions were and…well…I've been raised a certain way and it's hard to break free from that." Brody punctuated his stuttered apology with a long pull of wine from his cup. Oihane was quick to refill it.

Eryna's eyes slid to Dera to gauge her reaction. From the tight set of her jaw, the flat line of her lips and her narrowed gaze, it was clear she was still skeptical. However, she nodded and uttered her thanks.

Oihane set the wine on a stump.

"Yes, well, the least you can do is start making it up to us with a dance!" she sang as she reached across the circle and grabbed his hand. As she whisked him away, he looked back at Eryna with wide eyes and an expression that screamed, *help me.*

Laughing, Eryna shrugged and pointed to her cup of wine as if it required all her attention. The rest of the circle laughed, even Derrick, though he stood uncomfortably to the side, left hand shoved in his pocket as it had been all day. Dera eyed him.

"You can stop acting like you'll need to run at any moment, boy. I already said we wouldn't kill you." Dera smirked. Derrick bit his lip and nodded, unconvinced.

"Sorry. Habit," he replied. Dera's smirk grew, clearly enjoying how he squirmed around her. She turned to fill Jenin's cup, and as she poured, she glanced at Jenin's face.

Dera's eyes flared. She set the bottle down and took Jenin's chin between her fingers, tilting her head left and right.

"What're you doing?" Jenin asked. Dera silently examined her. Jenin looked at Eryna. "Is there no such thing as personal space around here?"

"There's something in you," Dera remarked. "Some magic."

"What?" Jenin, Derrick, and Eryna all said in unison, both Derrick and Eryna nearly spitting out their wine. They caught each other's gazes.

"You must be mistaken," Jenin said, pulling from Dera's grasp.

"I don't mistake such things. There is something in you."

"What, like a darkness?" Derrick snorted. "A black heart?"

"Or maybe a magical eye for judging people who wear the same outfit twice?" Eryna added.

"Or, like, the ability to walk into a store and walk out two seconds later and three thousand dollars lighter?" Derrick said through a wide smile. Him and Eryna fell into a fit of giggles. It felt good to laugh with him again. Eryna knew she missed it, but she didn't realize just how much. Jenin scowled at them.

"Screw you two, this isn't a gang up on Jenin party, so shut your traps or I'll shut them for you," she threatened. Derrick and Eryna went silent, biting down on their lips to stifle their laughter.

But then Derrick looked at Eryna.

And Eryna looked at Derrick.

They erupted into laughter again, tears welling in their eyes. Eryna's stomach cramped from laughing so hard, and it took several big, interrupted sighs to pull herself together.

"Actually, I see light," Dera said. "What was your mother?"

"Our mother?" Jenin asked, taken aback. Her and Derrick looked at each other, both thoroughly confused. Jenin narrowed her eyes at Dera. "Human, obviously?"

Dera simply smiled and sipped her wine.

"Curious," she remarked. Then her gaze floated between Eryna and Derrick, and before Jenin could protest, Dera grabbed her arm and said, "Come. Let's dance."

And Eryna and Derrick were suddenly alone.

There was no more buffer, no additional person to focus their attentions on or fill the empty silence. Eryna's pulse pounded at the pace of the racing drums, and she wanted to reach out, to tell him how much she'd missed him and wished they'd gotten more time.

But the words stuck to her tongue like sap.

They looked at each other.

They looked away.

They silently looked at each other again, and Eryna's stomach knocked into her heart. Derrick took a long sip of his wine. Eryna did the same, unsure what else to do.

"Did you kill him?" he asked quietly.

Eryna's head whipped toward him, taken aback by the abrupt question. She knew exactly who he meant, as Forget-Me-Not eyes stared back at her through a memory.

She shook her head.

"No," she replied. Derrick bit the inside of his cheek, nodded, and gazed down into his half-empty cup.

"I—" he started but stopped himself. Eryna held her breath, waiting, hoping he would find his words. He swallowed, licked his lips, then looked her right in the eye.

"I'm not going to apologize for how I acted. This...*hate*...has been engrained in me since birth, and it was a shock to find out what you are. I'm not sure if I can adjust to it."

Eryna's heart sank deep, deep into the ground beneath her soles, but she didn't want to cry in front of him, so she pursed her lips and nodded. "I understand," she replied, because how could she blame him? Just as she'd been raised to hate humans, he had been raised to hate Dryads.

Maybe Eryna had put too much hope in thinking they could overcome that. She hadn't realized she'd lost the battle with her tears until Derrick's thumb swiped across her cheek and he tilted her face to meet his.

"But I'll try," he said. "I've missed you too much not to." Then he smiled, and Eryna could barely keep her balance. She didn't feel like rejoining her sisters anymore. Not when she could stay like this the rest of the night, staring into Derrick's mossy eyes.

"Do you want to walk with me?" she asked. She had no idea

where she wanted to walk to. All she knew was that she wanted him all to herself for a moment, away from the eyes of her sisters and Jenin and Brody. To her surprise, he nodded.

"I do."

They slipped away from the ruckus toward the Hollow, and just before they lost sight of the crowd, Eryna looked back to see Brody completely distracted, Oihane leading him in a dance.

Her and Derrick walked a few inches apart in silence, the drums and the singing fading with distance. The song of the nightbirds started up, accompanied by their cricket companions. For a moment, they were back in the greenhouse, and Eryna could feel his warm lips on hers, his strong hands on her waist, pulling her close. Her breath caught on the memory.

She looked at him, nervously tinkering with the hearts around her neck. He looked at her, anxiously chewing his lip. Eryna stopped walking and reached up, grazing the bruise that still ringed his eye.

"Can I just...?" she started, but before she could finish the sentence, the last of his swelling was gone, the bruise faded to nothing. He felt around his eye and gaped at her a little.

"Well, that would've been helpful a few weeks ago," he laughed. Then he pulled his left hand from his pocket and held it up. "You couldn't possibly regrow body parts, could you?"

Eryna gasped as her eyes fell on his pinky finger, now half the size it used to be.

She grabbed his hand and frantically studied it. That's why he'd pulled it away so quickly before, why he'd kept it hidden.

"Oh, my Gaia, Derrick, what happened? Did your father do this?" Rage filled her heart, her body nearly shaking at the thought of Damian not only hitting him, but maiming him. But Derrick laughed a little and shook his head.

"You can put those daggers for eyes away. He didn't do this to me."

Eryna repeatedly ran her thumb over the tip of the shortened finger, the skin perfectly healed and smooth. The only way this could've been done was by magic. She looked at him, questioning. His brows tilted down, and his eyes turned soft as he scanned her face.

"When you went missing, Brody called us in a panic. He said he'd searched the entire Manor and you were nowhere. Then *I* panicked. We all did. I remembered something you'd said about crows and—"

"Derrick, you didn't," Eryna gasped. He shrugged.

"I went out to my mother's garden on a whim, and he was just sitting there in the wisteria, waiting, like he was expecting me. It was the tip of my pinky for where they were keeping you. Felt like a fair trade."

Eryna squeezed his hand tight to her chest as if she could protect it forever.

"You shouldn't have done it. I would've found a way out, or maybe Brody would've found me, or a member of the staff. I'm not worth losing body parts over."

Derrick pulled his hand out of her grasp and slipped it around her waist, pulling her so close. "Eryna, you are worth so much more than a single knuckle," he laughed. Then he fell silent, his eyes turning serious. "I know you spent a lot of time with Brody since you left The Spire, but I want you to know that I don't care whatever happened between you."

Eryna attempted to object, to make excuses, to say nothing happened, but she couldn't deny it. He saw them kiss only a few hours ago; surely, he knew they'd gone beyond that.

Derrick shook his head like he could tell exactly what she was thinking. "I mean it. I don't care. Because I know that in the end, I'm going to fight harder for you than he ever will. No matter what happens, I will never stop fighting to be yours until you tell me to, Eryna. Never."

She'd never seen such conviction in a person's eyes, never heard such faith in their own words.

"Even though I'm a Dryad?" she asked, flashing her stark white, textured hand.

Derrick squeezed her tight and leaned his face close to hers.

"You are the most beautiful thing I've ever seen, Eryna of the Thornewood."

Eryna lifted up on her toes, and when Derrick's lips parted around hers, it was like returning home all over again. His kiss was soft as a rose and sweet as fresh honey off the comb. Where being with Brody was wild and explosive and electric as a storm, being Derrick was like swimming in a soothing river on a mid-summer day. He was steady, he was effortless, and as his kiss deepened and the rhythm of their lips matched in perfect time, Eryna knew that this just felt right. Despite the last few weeks with Brody, the way they'd kissed and touched, there wasn't a question in her mind.

For her, it would always be Derrick.

A feral yelp shattered their perfect moment, calling their attention to where a gleeful Jenin stood watching them.

"You two are disgusting." She exaggeratedly gagged, but the berry wine had broken her mask, and she couldn't keep a smile from forcing its way to her cheeks. Derrick laughed, rolled his eyes, and rested his head against Eryna's.

"Thank you, Jenin, for your notable contribution to what *was* a very nice moment."

Jenin walked up to them and winked.

"Just doing my sisterly duty. Now come on. I want to dance until my flowers wilt and you're hogging my best friend."

Derrick raised his brows as they walked.

"Best friend, you say? But what if she's *my* best friend?"

Jenin scowled at him.

"That's not possible. *I'm* your best friend," she said.

"Wait, but what if I'm Eryna's best friend?"

"Wrong again. *I'm* Eryna's best friend."

"That's not fair, you can't be both our best friend and neither…"

Eryna stopped listening as the siblings dove into a petty

argument. She was too caught up in simply watching them and enjoying how happy she was to be caught in the middle. Eryna found a cup of wine on a stump and drained it, then grabbed both their hands.

"Enough you two. We're dancing!" she exclaimed, and then they were lost to the beat of the drums and the light of the bonfires for the rest of the night.

Chapter Forty-Three

Dirt kicked high into the air as Eryna sped through the forest on light feet. Her heart soared in her chest as she trampled through ferns and stopped just beneath her redwood. The fire hadn't spread here, its branches still strong and intact. Eryna sighed with relief.

She backed up several feet then launched at the lowest branch. Sharp bark bit into her palm, an uncomfortable but familiar feeling. Her limbs shook violently and sweat coated her body as she pushed harder, but it felt good to climb, to move her out-of-practice muscles.

The bonfires had died hours ago, everyone deciding to get a brief rest in before heading to the other Woods. But Eryna was far too restless. She needed to breathe the quiet forest air in solitude, and no one objected when she said as much.

Perched atop her redwood, Eryna counted the seconds until the sun peaked its crest over the eastern horizon. She looked to The Spire, its body aflame with sunlight like always.

It was once the most beautiful thing she'd ever seen. Now, Eryna wished it was truly on fire with Damian trapped inside.

Disgust roiled her stomach as she recalled his hands on her body, intent on violence. She shoved him out of her mind, reminding herself she would never see him again.

Eryna would also never get to see the sunrise from there, but she was oddly at peace with that. She plucked that fantasy from her heart and let it drift away on the morning breeze.

A rapid flutter of small wings caught her attention, and a tiny finch perched itself on a branch next to her. It wasn't just any finch. It was the finch from Genevieve's garden.

Eryna smiled.

"It seems you found me," she said, stroking its soft feathers. But as she did, intense panic screamed through her to get back to the Mother Oak immediately.

Chirp chirp chirp, the finch ordered, and Eryna knew she needed to hurry. She thanked the bird for his time and ordered him to rest as he must have flown all night to get there. Then she quickly descended the tree and sprinted back to the Mother Oak.

She held her breath as she entered the *Domecowé*. By how panicked the finch was, Eryna was prepared to enter upon a tragic scene, a massacre.

But all was well. Joyous, even.

The sisters sang a sweet song with the morning birds as they cleaned up the bonfires. Derrick, Jenin, and Brody helped Maya and Terra with breakfast. Brody looked up and saw her, his smile wide and eyes creased at the corners.

But anxiety must have been set deep in her expression because his smile fell. Concern settled between his brow, and he reached her in a few strides. His hands skimmed her shoulders, then her collar bone. His fingers gently stroked circles on the back of her neck. He scanned her face.

"Are you okay? Did something happen?" he asked worriedly. She took in the peaceful scene once more and wrote it off as a fluke. Maybe the finch had simply been excited and exhausted from its flight. Maybe it'd been anxious about leaving the city and being in a new place.

Brody gave her shoulders another gentle squeeze, and Eryna sighed.

"Yeah, I'm okay. I think I...I must have fallen asleep and had a bad dream, that's all," she lied, waving off the panic, though it wouldn't dissipate.

The subtle weight of the Hearts slipped from her neck, the spheres tinkering into the dirt like a tiny wind chime. The knot in the necklace must have come undone in her haste to get back to the Mother Oak.

"Oh, oops," Eryna remarked as her and Brody both bent to pick them up. They knocked heads, chuckling as they fumbled for the Hearts, Brody getting to them before her. They stood, still laughing, rubbing tender spots on their heads. Eryna held out her hand.

"Thanks for getting those," she said, smiling.

But Brody's laughter stopped. His fist remained tight around the Hearts. The panic that never fully died in Eryna came back in a flash flood.

"Brody, can I have them back, please?" she asked, her voice pitching half an octave higher.

Brody looked at Eryna, eyes clear, empty, cold. His jaw clenched. He swallowed.

"I'm afraid I can't do that."

Chapter Forty-Four

Eryna used to think it was only quiet in the Thornewood on execution days.

That was because she hadn't yet lived this moment.

Every Dryad paused what they were doing. The morning birds stopped singing. Even Jenin and Derrick froze.

Everyone and everything in all of Euryalea held a collective breath, waiting for Brody to give the Hearts back and fess up to making a very bad joke. Hand outstretched, Eryna stepped toward Brody, regarding him like a frightened animal about to bolt.

"Brody, please," she urged quietly. From the corner of her eye, she saw her sisters picking up any weapon within reach. Eryna held out a firm hand hoping it would hold them off. She could talk Brody down from this. She could help him see the mistake he was making.

"Brody, quit it," Jenin sternly called from where she stood, arms crossed.

"You're making a huge mistake, man, don't do this," Derrick added.

Brody's jaw went tight, but he ignored his friends.

"You know why I need these, Eryna. I can't lose my father," he murmured.

"Your father is a deceitful, disgusting little snake—" Dera started, but Eryna cut her off with a fiery gaze. She couldn't let them pounce on Brody yet. Not if she could get the Hearts back without blood being spilled.

"You know those aren't your father's to have. They can't keep him alive without the third Heart. Remember what we talked about," Eryna said calmly.

He looked at the spheres in his fist, his mind clearly turning. Eryna inched forward. If she could just get him to look her in the eye, he would change his mind. She was sure of it.

His mouth turning down ever so slightly.

"I know. That's why you're going to help us find it," he said.

"What?" she asked, confused.

Us? She looked at Jenin and Derrick, but they both shook their heads.

A sudden rumble echoed through the forest. Eryna recognized the sound immediately.

Cars.

She shoved her hand into the ground and asked the trees to show her what they saw.

Seven cars.

They were big, fast, and mowing down everything in their wake. Eryna caught glimpses of Martin and Damian through the windows, and her stomach turned to acid. They were coming for the Hearts, and they were coming for her, too.

"What have you done?" she spat at Brody.

"What did you see, *faémona?*" Oihane asked. But Eryna didn't have time to explain. Seven black cars barreled through the trees and halted at the edge of the *Domecowé*. Their doors flew open and men with large guns stepped out, pointing them at the Dryads, who had backed themselves against the Mother Oak.

Eryna took the opportunity to reach for Hearts, but Brody pulled out a gun of his own and pointed it at her chest. She froze.

He must have brought it with him. He'd prepared for this.

The thought burned deep as if he'd already shot her.

"Brody what are you doing!" Jenin screamed at the same time Derrick shouted, "That's it, I've had enough of your shit!"

"Derrick, don't!" Jenin called after her brother as he charged toward Brody. Brody lifted the gun just over Eryna's shoulder and pointed it at him.

"No one move. I won't hesitate," he said through gritted teeth. To anyone else the expression would look like rage, but all Eryna could see was sadness and fear.

She tilted her head and frowned.

"We're your friends, Brody. This isn't you," she said. He scowled at her.

"Friends who betrayed me," he bit. "I saw you two last night."

Eryna straightened.

"Is that what this is about? Me and Derrick?" she asked. He paused for a moment, then shook his head.

"No. This was always going to happen," he said, his words soft, like he'd faltered in his reserve. Then he hardened. "I just feel less guilty about it now. I've always been this, Eryna. I told you I was proud to be the Blackwell Legacy. I showed you what I was. It's not my fault you saw what you wanted to see in me."

Eryna studied Brody, confused how she could have read him so wrong the other night.

"You were right about him, Martin. Your son did good," Damian remarked as he stepped out of a car, a thick white bandage across his now crooked nose.

"I told you he'd come through," Martin replied as he moved from behind an open door. He looked at Brody and smiled. "This is the proudest you've ever made me, my boy." Brody smiled at his father, but the expression barely reached his cheeks.

Eryna's sisters growled and hissed and jeered at Martin as he looked their direction and smirked.

"Ladies. It's been, what, a couple centuries? It's good to see you all, though I'm sure you don't feel the same," he greeted. Eryna carefully watching him saunter up to her sisters, hands shoved deep in his pockets. He stopped a few feet from away and his eyes landed on one sister in particular.

Dera stepped forward, knife clutched tight in her fist. She met Martin where he stood, leaving an arm's length of distance between them. The men raised their guns, but Martin waved them off.

"Dera," he said, his voice taking on a softness Eryna hadn't heard him use before. His eyes glossed over, swimming with what looked like longing.

"I thought I made it perfectly clear what would happen if you ever set foot in the Thornewood again, Martin Blackwell. Or were your hundreds of fallen men not enough?" Dera asked as she gazed down her long lashes at him, her head high, her chin tilted up. He smiled.

"I always know when I have the upper hand, my love," he cooed. Eryna's mouth fell open. She couldn't comprehend what she'd just heard. Martin Blackwell and Dera? Was she the sister he'd fallen in love with?

Martin reached out to touch Dera's face. She slapped his hand away. The men cocked their guns this time but he waved them off again.

"You lost my love the moment you killed my realm and my kind," Dera accused, eyes lit with rage. Oihane pulled Dera back before she could do anything stupid. Martin was right. He did indeed have the upper hand.

He sighed, gave a sad smile, and shrugged.

"Yes, well, collateral damage, I suppose," he said nonchalantly, though Eryna could taste the bitterness in his words. His eyes dragged over the Dryads, over Derrick and Jenin and Eryna and Brody. Then he looked back at his men. He pursed his lips.

"Tie them up," he ordered, nodding toward the Dryads. "Actually, gag them too, just for fun." He smiled.

"You heard the man," Damian called out. "Round 'em up!'"

He took several confident steps toward the action but was clearly too afraid to stray from the cars. His eyes fell on Jenin, and he grimaced.

"Come, Jenin, dear. Let's put you in some decent clothes," he said.

"Fuck you," Jenin spat. Damian raised his brows but said nothing. He looked at Derrick.

"Let's go, son. You've had your fun. Martin and I did, too, once, but this isn't the world for you. I raised you better than this. Get your sister and let's go."

Jenin and Derrick looked at each other. Then Derrick looked at his father.

"No," he said flatly. Damian's hackles went up.

"Did you just say 'no?'" he asked, brows so high Eryna thought they might float off his face. Derrick widened his stance and crossed his arms.

"Yes sir. I said 'no.' We're not moving," Derrick said proudly. He flashed a brief smile at Eryna, and she couldn't help but smile back at him. Damian ground his teeth and seethed. He inhaled sharply.

"Fine, then," Damian said. "We'll just have to move you ourselves."

Damian looked at a few men lingering nearby and nodded. They converged on Derrick and Jenin, who protested and writhed in their arms but couldn't break free. They were shoved into one of the cars, and the last thing Eryna heard was Derrick calling her name before the door shut tight behind them.

"What's happening to them?" Eryna called out.

Damian's eyes slid to Eryna, and he pointed at her, his smile sharp and sinister.

"Don't forget this one, but be careful," he ran his fingers across his bandaged nose, the back of his hand scraped and red. "She's feral."

As two men approached her, Brody finally lowered the gun.

"I'm sorry," he whispered to Eryna. She glared at him furiously, concentrating all her heartache and anger and disbelief into her gaze. The two men grabbed her, their fingers so tight on her arms they left immediate bruises.

"Hey!" she protested and twisted to shake them loose. A palm flew up and her cheek burned with firm contact. Her sisters wailed and grunted angrily behind her, their noises muffled by their gags. The man who'd slapped her smiled.

"Watch it!" Brody warned. The man side-eyed him for a moment then gave a small scoff as he marched Eryna forward to where Martin and Damian stood over a large piece of paper laid out on the front of a car. Eryna scanned it, her eyes following roughly sketched trees and bushes and terrain marked with large "X's,", all surrounding a drawing of a colossal, sprawling oak.

It was a map of the Thornewood.

"Show us where the last Heart is," Martin demanded, pointing at the paper. Eryna silently stared at the map. If the Heart wasn't in the Mother Oak, then she had no idea where it was. If it had moved, no one had told her. The Thornewood sprawled for over two hundred thousand acres.

It was like asking her to find a teardrop in the ocean.

Damian lowered his face to hers and Eryna resisted the urge to thrust her head into his nose again, though maybe if she did, she'd completely shatter it this time.

"Tell us where the Heart is or I'll slaughter your sisters in front of you," he muttered in her ear. "Though, let's be honest. I'm going to do that anyway."

Eryna looked back at her sisters bound against the Mother Oak. She made direct eye contact with Dera, who had tears in her eyes. An unending pit of helplessness gaped open beneath Eryna. If she didn't tell the men where the Heart was, her sisters would die.

If she told them where she thought it may be—which, she had no idea where that was—they would still die.

There was no winning here.

Eryna nervously shifted her weight between her feet, the damp earth squishing beneath her.

Her heart stopped. She suddenly had an idea, but she needed to buy time. Eryna looked at Damian, then at Martin, and gave a short, breathy laugh.

"Why are you so sure I know where it is?" she asked while slyly digging her toes into the ground. She called on the rabbits and the mice and the squirrels of the Thornewood for help, begging them to find her sisters and chew through their bindings. So far as Damian and Martin were concerned, Eryna was simply widening her stance, standing her ground.

Damian crinkled his nose in disgust, then winced as the stupid expression irritated his tender nose. "Tell us or they die," he threatened. She clenched her jaw and brought her face within an inch of his.

"I. Don't. Know," she said each word like a sentence. She dug her feet in harder and could feel the forest listening to her. Her message was almost through.

Save my sisters, she begged. *Free them, save them,* she repeated in her mind. Then Damian grabbed her head and slammed her cheek against the car. Eryna involuntarily whimpered, and her feet slipped from the ground, the connection severed.

"Back off, Damian!" Brody shouted. He looked at his father. "You promised you wouldn't hurt her!"

Martin raised his hands.

"Do you see my hands on her?" he asked. Brody's eyes went wide, his jaw tight. He looked down at Eryna, intensely worried. Eryna looked up at him through the pounding pressure in her head.

"What's wrong, Brody? Surprised your father lied to you?" she bit, and he shrank from her words. She had to admit, it felt good to see him squirm. She dug her toes into the ground again, attempting to re-establish connection. She was so close. She only needed one more minute.

Free them, save them. Free them, save them, she begged.

Martin sighed.

"Damian, you've upset my son, and clearly Miss Thorne isn't willing to cooperate. Let's take her with us to where we think it is."

Damian begrudgingly nodded, and she was scooped up.

"Wait, no!" she cried out. She hadn't had enough time. She hadn't heard the forest's reply. The help she'd asked for might not have heard her. She bucked and tried to wriggle free, tried to break out of the man's arms but his hold was too tight. He tossed her into the back seat, and she landed face first against the leather. She scrambled for one of the doorhandles, but the car locked around her like a cage. She raged and screamed and kicked at the windows and punched the ceiling, hoping something would give, but it was a mobile fortress.

She gazed out the front window watching as Brody placed the spheres in Martin's hand. Martin clapped his son on the shoulder, smiling like he'd just been given keys to the paradise of Elysium. Then Martin gave one of them to Damian, and they chatted and laughed as they put the Hearts in their pockets.

Martin got into his car, but before Damian did the same, he pulled a young man aside and handed him a red plastic canister and small metal object. He said something to him, and the man nodded.

Eryna watched as the man walked up to her sisters, doused them in whatever liquid was inside the canister, and saturated the ground around them. They kicked and screamed, and the man laughed. He flicked open the metal object.

Just then, the front doors of Eryna's car opened and two people got in. Brody slid into the passenger seat. He looked at Eryna, but she ignored him, her eyes on her sisters as they struggled against their bindings.

Eryna's call for help was never heard.

Help wasn't coming.

The man struck his thumb against the metal object, and it sparked with a small flame.

No. Eryna gasped.

The car roared to life and drove away from the *Domecowé*, and as her sisters were about to fade from view, a large fire suddenly blazed in front of Eryna's eyes.

Pain ripped through her body, and it took several seconds for her to realize the earth-shattering scream in her ears was her own. She clawed at the window, the door, anything to try and escape and put the fire out, to save her sisters.

"This wasn't part of the plan!" Brody protested. "Turn around, now."

The driver simply laughed.

"This was always the plan, boy," he said joyfully. "And you aren't my boss. Your father is."

Brody continued to protest, but Eryna covered her ears to block him out. Her heavy body sank into the seat. Her tears pooled on the leather. She sobbed so loud, the driver shouted at her to "be quiet or I'll come back there and silence you myself."

"How about you shut your damn mouth or be out of a job," Brody warned him. The man scowled but said nothing more. Eryna folded herself deeper into the seat and crossed her arms to keep herself from splintering to pieces.

But what was the point now?

Maybe she *should* let herself fall apart. Maybe she *should* let herself completely shatter. Maybe she would simply die of a broken heart.

Without her sisters, there really was nothing left for her.

Chapter Forty-Five

The car jerked over the rough terrain, lulling Eryna into some form of grief-stricken meditative state.

She was in the car, but not really.

Her mind was at the *Domecowé* with her sisters, going over what she could have done differently. She should have stepped away from Brody, grabbed the Hearts from his hand. He wouldn't have pulled the trigger. She realized that now.

A light touch landed on Eryna's leg. She looked up. Brody stared at her from the passenger seat, tears in his eyes. She pulled her leg from his grasp and turned away, putting as much distance between them as possible.

"I didn't think they would..." Brody started, but his voice trailed off. He sighed, his breath shaky and brittle.

"Of course, you didn't," Eryna scoffed. Martin had consistently lied to Brody, and yet Brody was still surprised each time it happened. He was either blind and naive, or just too devoted a son to believe in the truth of what his father really was.

"I feel sorry for you, Brody," she said, brushing away a tear. "You will forever live in the shadows of Blackwell Manor, paying for the sins of your father while he keeps everything for himself. It sounds so awfully lonely."

A rattling inhale signaled to Eryna that her words had hit their mark, but she wasn't done. There was one question she needed the answer to, though it wouldn't change anything now.

"Was any of it real?" she asked. "What you said to me in the loft?"

Brody remained silent, taking three long, lingering breaths. Eryna glanced over her shoulder to find him staring at her, his cheeks stained with tears. He nodded.

"All of it," he said.

Eryna closed her eyes against the wave of pain that choked her. She wasn't prepared for that answer. She was ready to hate Brody for his lies and games. It would've made this betrayal so much easier to bear. But now she didn't even have hate to cling to. Just grief, and grief was much less stable ground to stand on.

The car stopped. Eryna's door flew open, and she was thrown to the ground.

"We're here," Damian said down at her.

Brody clambered out of the car and helped her up, but she pulled away from him. Disoriented, she scanned the forest. As she got her bearings, she froze.

She looked up.

They were parked just beneath her redwood.

"Why here?" she asked, looking between Damian and Martin.

"This was the last place our technology picked up an energy spike, which is unusual for Euryalea, unless there's a Heart around. So where is it?"

Eryna shook her head.

It couldn't possibly be here. This was a distant place in the Thornewood that meant nothing to anyone besides her.

"I don't know."

"Lies!" Damian screamed, but Martin put his hand on Damian's shoulder. Martin sighed, clearly exhausted.

"Then let's settle this the old-fashioned way, shall we?" he said, looking between Eryna and Brody. They looked at each other, confused.

Martin looked over Eryna's shoulder and nodded. It was a signal.

Fear struck her heart like a lightning bolt, but before she could run, she was restrained and forced to her knees. Martin grabbed Brody, put a gun in his hand, and pointed it directly at Eryna's chest.

"No! You can't make me," Brody protested. But then Martin took out a gun of his own and pointed it at his son's head.

"Sure I can," he replied. Brody looked utterly, thoroughly shocked and disgusted. Eryna wasn't in the slightest.

"Now, tell us where the Heart is, or my son will pull the trigger. If he doesn't, I will," Martin said coolly.

"I swear to Gaia, I don't know," Eryna cried.

He sent a warning shot into the sky and the two of them flinched.

"Wrong answer. Try again," he said. Eryna's throat tightened as she looked into Brody's frightened eyes, his hand trembling.

"You have thirty seconds," Martin encouraged.

"Wait, I want to make this interesting!" Damian interrupted, his voice uncharacteristically excited. He opened a car door. There, sat Derrick and Jenin, bound and gagged. They took in the scene in front of them and started screaming, their voices muffled. Derrick violently thrashed against his restraints and managed to break free, scrambling from the car toward Eryna, but one of his father's men held him back.

"Twenty seconds, Miss Thorne," Martin called.

Eryna had no idea where the Heart was, and even if she did, there was no point in telling them. She was dead either way. With her sisters gone, she had nothing left to live for besides Jenin and Derrick. But she didn't belong in their world. They would be fine without her. They would move on. And no matter how angry she was with Brody, she couldn't drag him down with her.

She looked up into his eyes and laughed at the irony of how their original roles had reversed.

"Do it," she said. He shook his head.

"I can't...I can't," he stammered.

Derrick screamed and kicked in the man's arms. Eryna caught his eye and shook her head. He stopped fighting.

The conviction in her choice must've been clear, because as he looked at her, his eyes turned sad, and a tear streamed down his cheek. His chest stuttered. He made a noise that sounded like three short words. Eryna she knew exactly what he meant.

Me too, she mouthed. He closed his eyes.

"Ten seconds," Martin called out. Eryna looked at Brody again.

"Do it, Brody," she urged. "It's okay. Just do it."

She stuck her chest out and closed her eyes.

"3..." Martin counted. "...2...1..."

The last thing Eryna heard was a loud metallic rattle that echoed through the forest, birds fleeing through the trees, and critters rushing from the bushes.

Then all she saw was sky.

Chapter Forty-Six

Eryna stared up at the canopies. Branches swayed overhead like hundreds of hands waving at a friend, asking her to join them.

Was this Elysium? Was this where the physical world ended and the spiritual one began? If she got up now, would Gaia be there to greet her as a daughter?

Eryna tried to move, but couldn't, like her entire body had been paralyzed, save for her eyes. Panic welled up inside her as she realized she wasn't dead, but that maybe her fate was much, much worse. She was half-dead, her body gone, but her mind still very much alive.

Her gaze slid to Brody, who stood over her, a smoking gun in his hand. He looked at the weapon in horror, like he couldn't believe what he'd done. Because he had, in fact, done it.

He'd actually pulled the trigger.

She wanted to laugh at the fact that he'd done what she once could not. She'd encouraged him to do it, after all, but some small part of her doubted he truly would.

Except, if he'd shot her, how was she not dead?

Before Eryna could follow that thread further, two things happened at once.

First, a loud *boom* sounded, like a large tree falling, though Eryna couldn't move to see the source. The gun landed in the dirt next to her, and when Eryna looked up, Brody was gone.

Then, there were shouts. Men scattered around her like fish fleeing from a predator. Her sisters came into view, their long legs striding as they chased after the men, weapons of all sizes clutched tight in their hands. Eryna closed her eyes in relief.

Her call for help had been heard after all.

The forest had saved her sisters like she'd pleaded. Many of them had long, blistering burns on their arms and legs and faces, but burns were nothing. Eryna could heal burns.

Frantically, she tried to lift her hands, to wave a sister down to show that she wasn't quite dead yet. She tried to shout, but all that came out was a soft grunt.

Seconds later, several arms pulled her to a seated position and propped her up against something warm and solid.

Dera's face hovered in front of her. She said something to Eryna, but Eryna still couldn't hear through ringing in her ears. Then Jenin pushed her face into view. She exaggeratedly mouthed something, but still nothing registered for Eryna.

Then Sierra popped her head in and—

Wait.

Sierra?

That can't be right. Eryna *had* to be dead, or at the very least, hallucinating. There was no way Sierra was in Euryalea.

Or maybe Eryna wasn't in Euryalea or Elysium.

Maybe she was in Hades.

That had to be it. This was some nightmarish welcome at the gates of Hades with a manifestation of Sierra to greet her.

But then Parvati pushed through all three of them and shook Eryna's shoulders violently. Ever so slowly, sensation crept back into Eryna's limbs. The ringing in her ears lessened, and her healing powers scurried to work inside her body.

"She's in shock," Parvati said, the first clear sound Eryna heard. Eryna blinked several more times.

"Wh…what's happening?" she croaked. Then her cheek stung with the second slap she'd received that day.

"Sierra, what the Hades!" Jenin spat.

"What? My mom said she was in shock. Thought I'd help her snap out of it." Sierra snickered. Parvati hissed at Sierra, saying something in a non-human language Eryna recognized but couldn't place. The warmth behind Eryna jiggled, and the soothing sound of Derrick's laugh rippled through her. His heart beat steadily at her back, each thump like a small, excited greeting. Eryna looked up to see his mossy eyes smiling down at her. He wrapped his arms around her and kissed her on the forehead, on the temple, on the cheek.

"I thought I'd lost you," he said into her skin. When he squeezed her again, her chest burst with excruciating pain, and she inhaled sharply, nearly toppling over.

"Easy, *faémona*," Dera said, steadying her. Eryna looked at the faces around her and didn't see Oihane.

"Is Oihane…?"

"She's fine. A little crispy like the rest of us, but fine. Before they lit the fire, our ropes had been chewed through by a mob of bush rats. You could have at least sent something cuter." Dera laughed, and Eryna chuckled. Another burst of pain bloomed through her chest, and she gasped, unable to catch her breath.

"Are you going to tell her, or should I?" Parvati asked Dera flatly.

"Give the girl a minute, Pari," Dera grumbled.

Had Dera just called Parvati, "Pari?" Did they know each other?

"Tell me what?" Eryna asked, unable to keep that question inside. Dera and Parvati looked at each other, deliberating.

"Well…" Dera started, then paused to gather her words. She started again. "Well—"

"There's a giant hole in your chest," Sierra cut in. Dera, Parvati, and Jenin all hissed at Sierra. Parvati lectured her more in that other language, something about being grounded for a century.

"Rude, Sierra. So rude," Jenin chided. Sierra rolled her eyes and shrugged.

"Someone had to tell her."

Hesitantly, Eryna looked down.

On the left side of her chest was a large hole where the bullet entered her body. It should have killed her instantly.

But as she examined the wound, the skin already knitting back together, she understood why she was still very much alive.

There, in her chest was a small steel sphere.

There, in her chest, was the third Heart.

Chapter Forty-Seven

All this time, the Heart of the Thornewood Mother Oak had been inside her.

She was the Heart.

"H…h-how?" Eryna stammered, clawing at her chest, the skin now completely sealed and healed. There were no words that could encompass all her questions, but this was the most pressing one. "Just…*how?*"

Wouldn't she have remembered them putting it inside her? Or had she always been this way?

Dera and Parvati looked at each other. Dera gave Parvati a nod, and Parvati pursed her lips, then looked at Eryna.

"It's a long story. But we'll start here: Prior to my marriage to Jerry, the human world knew me as Parvati Prolî. But to my family—my sisters—I am Parvati of the Polaris Range."

"Oread," Eryna breathed. Parvati nodded. Eryna realized why she recognized the language her and Sierra spoke. It was a different nymph dialect; the language of the Oreads.

"After the humans took the first Heart of Euryalea, all nymphs on Tegadona gathered to find a way of protecting the remaining two

Hearts, as well as the ones in our own realms. We tried everything: rituals, spells, enchantments, contraptions, but nothing lasted more than a quarter century. It was taking too long. Then we caught wind of Martin's plan to get his hands on the second Heart, and—"

Martin.

At the sound of his name, Eryna leapt to her feet and wobbled a little, her body not quite healed.

"You should sit," Derrick urged, but she didn't listen. She scanned the empty clearing around them. Martin, Damian, and Brody were nowhere in sight.

"Martin and Damian still have the other Hearts," Eryna said frantically. "We need to get them."

Eryna could listen to Parvati's story later. As long as the third Heart was in her chest, it was safe, and how it got there was suddenly not as important as getting the other two back. A tug on her hand pulled her out of her thoughts. Eryna looked down to see Dera staring up at her seriously.

"We will get them back, but Eryna you need to hear—"

"We'll have time for stories later. Right now, the other Hearts are all that matter. I'm going after them," she said. Her eyes caught on a set of tracks that started around where Martin stood earlier, and before anyone could stop her, she took off through the bushes.

"Eryna, wait!" Dera called.

"Eryna, don't!" Jenin shouted.

"Eryna, stop!" Derrick begged.

She ignored them all, their cries fading into the distance as she leapt over roots and rocks and barreled through bushes, sprinting through the muddied forest. If they wanted to stand around trading history lessons, that was fine, but Eryna wasn't about to let Martin and Damian get away with the Hearts again.

Martin's tracks carried her for nearly a mile until they came to a stop in a patch of moss. Eryna cursed.

She'd have to do this the hard way.

She dug her hands into the ground, asking the trees to find Martin for her. The trees sent her images of him running, his face scratched, his arms slashed and bleeding. But she couldn't pinpoint where he was, what direction he was headed.

Then a small, furry orange body appeared in front of her. It tilted its head, its dark eyes burrowing into her. Its large ears twitched.

"You again," Eryna said as she stared at the fox. She smiled. "Time to return the favor."

The fox barked as if to say "follow," then took off on quick feet. Eryna tracked it closely as it led her up small hills and valleys, her quick steps catching the same rhythm as the Heart that beat heavily in her chest.

"Eryna!" The distant calls of Dera, Jenin, Derrick, Parvati, and Sierra echoed toward her, but she blocked them out, following her fox as it guided her toward Martin Blackwell.

He couldn't have made it that far. He was human, albeit one that'd been living off magic for centuries. But she was certain she was faster than him and wondered how he'd gotten so far without being stopped by one of her sisters.

Eryna's foot suddenly snagged on something that sent her toppling to the ground. She slid across the dirt, scraping her palms, but righted herself quickly. As she did, she caught sight of what tripped her up.

Her sister Maya stared blankly at the canopies above, not breathing. There was a single bloody hole in her forehead.

Eryna knelt, bowed her head, and allowed a tear to slip down her cheek as she closed her sister's eyes and said a prayer to Gaia. As Eryna stood, she clenched her fists so hard, her knuckles nearly burst through the skin. There were so few Dryads left. Eryna wouldn't lose anymore sisters.

She let out an earth-shattering, primal scream and hoped it found Martin Blackwell's ears. She wanted him to know she was coming. She hoped Damian heard it too because he was next.

"Eryna!" The group called out as the fox barked at her several times. It stamped its feet, as if saying, "we're close." Eryna ran faster, harder than before, fury hot in her steps. She looked down to see a fresh set of human tracks. And then brown hair and broad shoulders came into view.

She'd found him.

Just in front of her, foliage rattled and swayed as he ran like he knew his life depended on his speed.

He briefly glanced back, pure panic in his eyes.

Eryna smiled.

With all she had left, she pushed herself until her legs nearly gave out, her lungs nearly collapsed, and every muscle in her body burned with the heat of five thousand bonfires. With a final breath, she launched forward and latched onto his shoulders, pulling him to the ground.

But when she looked down at Martin, she realized it wasn't him at all.

It was Brody.

He looked up at her with frightened eyes, panting heavily.

"I'm sorry, Eryna. I didn't..." he paused to breath, tears filling his eyes. "I didn't think I would do it. I didn't want to shoot you. I didn't want you to die. I'm sorry. I'm sorry," he repeated, but Eryna barely listened. Why would the fox send her after Brody instead of Martin? Eryna shook her head.

"Brody, shut up!" she ordered. He went silent. "I wasn't coming after you. I was trying to find—"

"Me?" Martin asked, smiling as he came into view. "It seems we finally know where the third Heart is."

Brody slid out from under Eryna and shoved himself between them.

"No more," he ordered. "You won't hurt her anymore."

Martin clicked his tongue as he drew closer, his smile growing feral as he eyed Eryna.

"Oh, my boy, I couldn't hurt her now even if I wanted to. She's become suddenly invaluable."

Brody pushed her behind him, but she moved right back to where she was. She refused to hide like a coward.

"You mean *you* need her," Brody corrected. "I don't want what you have. I don't want to live forever. Not after what it's done to you."

Martin looked at Brody sideways, his tongue pressed to his cheek.

"Disappointing," he remarked. He squinted assessing eyes at his son. "I really hoped you'd be different than the others. You showed so much promise."

Brody stiffened. "Others?" he asked, his voice breaking. Martin lifted a brow and smirked.

"Did you really think you were the only son I've had? Dear boy, I've been alive far longer than you know, even before coming to this island. I've had many sons, though you're easily one of my favorites. Top five, at least."

On reflex, Eryna stepped closer to Brody offer some comfort. He was a devoted son who loved his father, and if Eryna could feel the sting of Martin's words, she could only imagine how Brody felt. He stayed silent. Martin approached them again.

"I really thought you might be the one," he said, his lips turning down in exaggerated sadness. "Many of the others were just so…weak. They couldn't see the beauty in eternal life. The money. The fame. The power. The women! Or men. Or both, honestly, with that much money and fame, who cares. But no, they wanted families. They wanted love. And who needs love when you can have the world."

As Martin spoke, Eryna noticed him fiddling with something behind his back. As subtly as she could, she planted her foot deep in the ground and let Martin continue.

"I thought you saw the long game, my boy. I thought you saw

the enjoyment you could get out of it, that you wanted to change with the world like I did. But you're just like the others. It pains me really. Because now I have to start all over again."

Martin pulled a gun from his back pocket, but Eryna was quicker. Thick vines sprung from the ground and wrapped around his limbs, forcing him to drop it. Brody kicked the gun out of reach, and Martin's eyes went wild, his jaw tight. He tried to yank himself free, but the vines overpowered him.

Martin shouted and cursed at Eryna.

"Get the Hades off me you disgusting savage!" he spat.

Every ounce of ancestral rage and anguish pooled in Eryna's chest until all she saw was red, all she felt was white hot heat in her blood. She tightened her hold on the vines. Hard. They squeezed the air from Martin's lungs. He gasped like a fish on dry land.

She pulled tighter.

Her eyes landed on the soft, exposed skin of his neck. A vine grew from the ground and slipped over the knot in his throat. Her fists clenched, and she squeezed.

A rasp escaped Martin like the hiss of dying coals.

"Eryna, stop," Brody said softly. "You don't want to do this."

But she did. It felt too good to have that kind of power over him.

If she just squeezed a little harder, it would be over in seconds; *all of it* would be over in seconds. No more chasing the Hearts. No more fearing Martin would steal them again. If she only squeezed a little harder...

Two hands cupped her face.

Brown eyes met her gaze, drawing her attention away from Martin.

"Don't do it, Eryna. You're not me. You're not a monster," Brody whispered against her lips as he pulled from her furious trance with a kiss. "Come back. Come back."

Slowly, Eryna released her grip on Martin's throat and retreated from her rage, grounding herself in the feel of Brody's lips. For a moment, she let herself enjoy it. She let herself memorize his familiar rhythm, his sweet taste, and as tears slipped between their lips and salt coated their tongues, Eryna used that kiss to say, "goodbye."

She broke from Brody and, with her thumb, wiped a tear from his cheek. He placed his palm over her hand like he could hold her there forever. He looked at her, eyes pleading for her to stay. But his betrayal reached far too deep for her to forgive him. At least for now. Eryna shook her head. She slipped through his fingers as Brody closed his eyes, another tear falling from his long lashes.

Eryna walked to Martin, who was gulping down air, and pulled the Heart from his pocket.

"Open it," a voice said. Eryna turned and saw Parvati breaking through the bushes, Dera, Jenin, and Sierra on her tail. Parvati nodded toward the Heart in Eryna's hand. "Ask it to open in your mother tongue."

Eryna glanced down at the steel sphere. "*Arbo,*" she said, and the small sphere split in half like a walnut. Eryna opened it.

It was empty.

"What did you do to it, you mountain troll?" Martin accused in Parvati's direction. She ignored him but looked at Eryna and answered.

"I've done nothing to it," Parvati said. Her eyes slid to Brody at Eryna's side. They landed on his chest. "That container has been empty for nineteen years." Then Parvati's eyes moved to Derrick, who'd just joined them. "Both containers have," she said.

Derrick took in everyone standing around, staring at him. He looked at Eryna, his brow deeply creased.

"What'd I miss?" he asked.

Chapter Forty-Eight

Eryna looked at Brody, then looked at Derrick.

She looked at Brody again, then at Derrick once more, unable to wrap her mind around what Parvati was implying.

She looked at Brody a third time. Her eyes fell on his chest.

He followed her gaze and touched it, closing his eyes as if to block out everything except the feel and sound of the Heart that beat there.

"Wait, I'm so confused, what's going on?" Sierra asked. Jenin elbowed her and silently signaled for her to be quiet.

Eryna pointed at Brody.

"So, if…" she started, but trailed off. She pointed at Derrick. "Then…" For the life of her, she couldn't finish a damn sentence.

"Yes," Parvati said, lifting a stern brow. "And if you had let me finish my story, we would have gotten there."

Eryna winced a little. She pursed her lips and nodded.

"You wouldn't happen to feel like finishing that story now, would you?" she asked, heat climbing her face. Parvati pressed her tongue to the inside of her cheek and sighed.

"Once Martin and Damian—known as Orion in his earlier

centuries—finally got the two Hearts, they synthesized a way of using them to not only create new technology like the tonics, but to significantly delay aging. But after some time, the magic stopped working. They tried housing them in living vessels as a way of preserving the magic, but all it did was kill the vessels in days, weeks at most. The human body isn't built to withstand such raw power."

Eryna's mind flashed back to the wall of women. "Their wives," she murmured. Parvati nodded.

"Us nymphs heard what they'd done and decided to intervene. We couldn't send a Dryad into their world as they're too easily spotted with their bark skin. Brilliant idea using the Beauty Tonic, by the way. It was made from Heart magic, which is probably why you took so well to it."

"My idea, thanks," Jenin chimed in. Parvati threw her an approving nod.

"Some of us Oreads, however, have smooth skin like humans. They'd hardly seen our kind before, our mountainous terrain too much for them to handle. It made sense that one of us should go, so I volunteered."

Parvati approached Eryna, gently picked up the sphere and examined it.

"Decades before that, I'd created these shells for our own Hearts of Thessalia. They're contraptions of ancient magic, meant to prevent anyone from accessing whatever power lie inside. Very difficult to create. It hadn't been done in millennia. I offered them to the Fiddlewood and Thornewood Dryads as protection. The Thornewood Dryads accepted, but the Fiddlewood Dryads were too set in their ways, and severely underestimated Martin's ambition. I brought these shells into the human world with me, and after I'd weaseled my way into Blackwell Technologies, I was able to convince Martin to use the contraptions for the other Hearts. I told him they would concentrate their magic. All they did was stifle it," Parvati scoffed and looked down at Martin, who was rippling with rage.

"Why, you scheming, lying, venomous—"

"Enough out of you." Parvati spit on the ground next to his face. "I've had a century of it, and as far as I'm concerned, that's a century too long." She looked at Eryna. "Would you mind, dear? I think we could all use some peace and quiet around here."

"My pleasure," Eryna said. She commanded a vine to grow over his mouth like a muzzle. Parvati smiled at Eryna, satisfied. She looked at the sphere in her hand once more, and her smile fell.

"After we encased the Hearts in the vessels, I tried to smuggle them out of Aponyx, but it was just too dangerous. Then they decided to put the Hearts inside Gen and Marisa. I urged them not to. We didn't know what putting the vessels inside a person would do, and Gen had just had Jenin. She was a new mother, and the thought of putting her at risk, of maybe killing her and leaving her four-month-old baby girl with no mother…"

Parvati looked at Jenin, whose lips were quivering, tears brimming her eyes. Eryna reached out and grabbed Jenin's hand, holding it tight.

Parvati swallowed. "It broke my heart, but they did it anyway. And Gen and Marisa lived. They lived long enough to have the boys, to see their children into adolescence, and I started making plans to get them out of Aponyx and into Euryalea to turn the Hearts over."

"You wanted to kill our mothers?" Jenin asked harshly. "Is that why they got sick? You took the Hearts away? You were their friend!"

Dera put her hand on Jenin's shoulder and shook her head.

"Not kill. The Hearts aren't truly 'hearts.' That is just the human translation. They are *cowé* in our language. 'The spirit of the heart.' They are a life source. Pure energy and magic. Removing them would not have killed your mothers."

"Then why'd they die?" Derrick asked quietly. Brody leaned in, awaiting the answer as well. Parvati sighed. She looked thoughtfully at the vessel in her hand, then closed her fist around it.

"They started showing signs of sickness a few years before they passed. That was the first time I'd suspected that the Hearts might..." she paused and glanced between Brody and Derrick. "Might no longer be in them. After Gen and Marisa passed, the medical examiner found these still in their chests. When I opened them, they were empty. That's when I knew for certain."

"I'm sorry, hold on," Jenin said, shaking her head. "Are you saying that when my mother had Derrick, she *passed the Heart* into him?"

Parvati nodded.

"And Marisa to Brody. Because your mothers were human, the Hearts still took a toll on their bodies. It was just a delayed reaction due to the containers. My guess is that the boys' bodies can withstand the Hearts because they were built around them. They were made from their magic."

Eryna looked at Brody, who paled, still clutching his chest. Then she looked at Derrick, but his stoic indifference was impossible to read. She needed to know what he was feeling. Desperately.

She walked up to him and placed her palm on his chest. She closed her eyes and decided to try something. *Speak to me*, she asked the Heart, and the moment the thought left her mind, it bloomed beneath her touch like a morning lotus.

She felt everything he did.

His shock, his skepticism, his curiosity at what he was being told. She felt his anger and resentment toward his father, his sorrow for the loss of his cousin and for the loss of his mother. Eryna felt the deep, deep love and reverence he had for his sister, wrapping around her like strong arms in a comforting embrace.

There was even an emotion in there for Eryna. She couldn't distill it down to a single word, but it felt like breathing in the fresh air of spring or basking in the first light that breaks through the clouds after a long, dark storm.

Eryna smiled warmly, then tried something else. She pushed a feeling back.

She thought of how it felt to be one cup of berry wine deep, light and giggly, the urge to dance pulling at her edges; she thought of cozying up beneath her favorite pelts in the shelter of her hollow as a heavy rainstorm lulled her to sleep, safe and secure; and she thought of how it felt to run through the Thornewood on early summer mornings, free and exhilarated.

Light. Safe. Free. Those were all the ways he made her feel.

Eryna looked up to see him smiling down at her, light bursting in his eyes. He placed his hand over hers and gave it a gentle squeeze.

Sierra cleared her throat, shattering the sweet moment and calling everyone's attention her direction.

"I don't understand why forest freak over here still has the vessel inside her, and these two don't," Sierra said, pointing at Derrick and Brody.

Dera approached Eryna on slow feet. She looked down at her little sister and softly touched her chest.

"Us Dryads aren't born from a body. We are born from our Mother Oak, from the same cavity where the Heart lives. It seems when Eryna was born, our Mother had built her body around the vessel. We didn't know until Althea checked the Mother Oak nearly a decade later." Dera cupped Eryna's cheeks and smiled at her.

"That's when we knew you were different. Dryads have always been able to commune with nature. We've always had magical abilities, and healed quicker than humans, but you...you speak to the animals and the trees, and they *listen*. We used to find you sitting with the fox kits, sharing your toys, or trying to teach them how to forage so you wouldn't have to." Dera chuckled at the memory, and Eryna did too, barely recalling it. "You can mend broken bones or deep cuts in seconds. You are spirited and defiant and free-thinking and one with the world around you and everything it means to be a Dryad. Our sisters got sick while you were gone because the humans had finally gotten what they were after all those years. They'd taken the third Heart. *Our* Heart. While you were in Aponyx, they had all three of you together and didn't even notice."

Dera's eyes slid to Martin. She walked to him, knelt, and placed her hand on his face. They looked at each other softly, painfully, the look of two people who have a long and complicated history.

"You got what you always wanted and couldn't see it right under your nose," Dera said to him. She lingered a moment longer, a few more strokes of her thumb, then stood. She looked down at him through lowered lids and a clenched jaw. "You never could."

Just then, a rustle sounded in the bushes nearby. Everyone stopped breathing.

"What was that?" Jenin asked, leaning into Sierra.

"Jumpy, much? It's probably just a bunny. We are in the forest, after all," Sierra snorted. Eryna shook her head.

"That's not a bunny. That sound was too big to be a bunny—"

"No!" Derrick and Brody shouted at the same time, rushing toward her, their cries drowned out by a metallic rattling Eryna recognized far too well by now.

Eryna turned toward the sound and saw Damian at the edge of the tree line, gun in his hand. Then as quickly as he'd appeared, he disappeared into the bushes.

Suddenly, Eryna was on the ground pinned beneath a frantic Brody. He searched her. "Are you hurt?" he asked repeatedly. Eryna scanned her body and found nothing amiss. She shook her head.

"I'm okay. I'm okay," she assured him as he looked like he might splinter into a thousand pieces.

Then a pained groan came from her right.

Her and Brody turned to see Derrick horizontal, blood quickly staining his shirt.

"Derrick!" Jenin screamed, her voice breaking with the force.

"No," Eryna gasped and scrambled from beneath Brody to

Derrick's side. Her assessing hands fumbled around his body. He hissed at her touch. Jenin fell to her knees, her breaths coming in broken gasps.

"Help him. Eryna help him!" she begged, but Eryna was already ahead of her. Hands on Derrick's chest, she closed her eyes and felt around. She inhaled sharply.

She'd found the wound, and it was big.

Too big.

Gathering herself, Eryna took a deep breath and tried again, approaching his body like she would an animal and not a person she deeply cared for. The bullet had shattered his ribs and ruptured his stomach, a lung, part of his intestine, and his spinal cord.

The damage was overwhelmingly serious, and Eryna had to work quickly. She pulled on his spinal cord and fused it back together, but when she did, his intestine hemorrhaged. She tried to stop it, but then his breathing failed. She tried to heal his lung, but lost hold of the intestine. The wound reopened and he lost more blood.

Then there was the stomach, which was blown to bits. She mentally grabbed each part, trying to piece it back together, but then the other wounds worsened while she worked, and she couldn't keep every broken bit of him together at the same time.

"Come on!" she screamed at herself, tears rolling down her cheeks, on the brink of hyperventilating.

She got the spine, then the lung, then the— "Dammit!"

The ribs. The stomach.

Then blood. More blood. So much more blood.

She pulled with everything she had, trying to keep him together like a single piece of twine trying to bind a shattered rock. He was slipping quickly.

Far, far too quickly.

A hand touched her face, and Eryna opened her eyes to see a pale Derrick staring up at her through knowing eyes.

"I can feel it, too," Derrick said. He smiled at her. "It's okay."

"No," she replied. She wouldn't stop. She wouldn't let go of him. Not until he was healed. Not until she could put him back together.

"Eryna," he said. "You can't save me."

"Stop it, Derrick!" Jenin shouted, slapping his leg. "Stop it! You can't give up! Eryna will save you and everything is going to be fine. It'll be fine. It'll be fine."

Jenin's tears coated her red cheeks as she rocked back and forth, sobbing. Sierra knelt beside her and wrapped a tight arm around her, pulling her into an embrace. Jenin didn't pull away.

A light hand touched Eryna's back, and Dera knelt next to her.

"We need the Heart," she said. Eryna looked at her, appalled that she was saying such a thing right now. Dera read her expression and stroked her back. "If he dies, the Heart dies. It's keeping him alive, but only just."

"Then you can't have it! Not if it's keeping him alive," Jenin said through broken sobs. Parvati embraced her from the other side.

"I'm going either way, Neens. Might as well go out doing something heroic," Derrick laughed, then coughed, then groaned. Eryna followed his eyes as they fell on Brody, who was kneeling some distance away, watching it all through tears.

Brody frowned at him and nodded. In some unspoken language between male friends, Derrick smiled at Brody and nodded back.

"I know, man," Derrick said. "I know."

"Stop saying goodbye, you're not going anywhere," Jenin growled at her brother. She looked at Eryna with pleading eyes. "Eryna, come on. Keep trying, you need to keep trying."

Eryna studied Derrick's face, trying to memorize it. He pinched her chin and pulled her down to him. His soft lips found hers, and he gave her one slow kiss filled with all the words they no longer had time to say, the life they never got to build. He pulled back, brought the tips of his fingers to his mouth, then touched his chest. Eryna did the same.

"Take it," he said, nodding to his chest. "It was already yours, anyway."

Eryna felt herself crumbling, her resolve breaking. She was seconds from coming undone, and if what Dera had said was true, if they needed to get the Heart before Derrick died, then she needed to do it now.

"How?" she asked, looking at Dera, then Parvati. Parvati shrugged.

"Just like the vessel. Ask," Parvati said. Eryna nodded, then placed her hand over Derrick's chest.

"Wait, what are you doing?" Jenin cried out. She lunged forward and tried ripping Eryna's hand off Derrick, but Sierra and Parvati held her in place. She squirmed and cried, and it was all so unbearable, but Eryna shut it out. She had to. She focused on Derrick's chest and breathed.

Come, she beckoned the Heart. *Come to me.*

A small gasp escaped Derrick, and when Eryna opened her eyes, a small purple orb hovered in her hand. It was so small, so warm, like a tiny, violet sun. Parvati reached out with the vessel, and Eryna gently tipped it in. The lid shut tight over it, and Parvati handed it to Dera, who tucked it into a satchel.

A dry rattle came from Derrick's throat, and Eryna looked down. His eyes fluttered.

"No, please. Please, please, please," Jenin begged as she curled over Derrick. Then she looked at Brody and pointed an accusatory finger.

"This is your fault! This is all your fucking fault! If you hadn't betrayed Eryna, if you hadn't brought them here, none of this would've happened. He wouldn't be dying," she shouted, and Brody's face crumbled in agony. Jenin looked at Eryna and clutched her hands.

"Please help him. Please save him. I need him. He's all I have, Eryna, please."

Through burning eyes and quivering lips, Eryna simply looked at her friend and shook her head.

"I'm no match for death, Jenin. I'm so sorry."

"Well try to be! I need him!" she cried.

"Hey," Derrick said, tugging on Jenin's arm, his voice barely a whisper. She looked down at him. He smiled up at her. "I love you. No matter where I am, or what I am, I will always love you. And I'll make sure to tell mom how proud she should be of you, okay?"

Jenin nodded, clutching his hand.

"I love you too. Always," she replied.

And the same way Eryna felt as Tyler's soul slipped down into the earth, so she felt Derrick's go.

A final breath escaped him, and then silence.

The women watched him for a moment, waiting for another breath.

It never came.

Jenin collapsed onto Derrick's chest and shook with sobs. Eryna, Sierra, Dera, and Parvati embraced her and held her through the pain as she cried and whispered, "Come back, come back, come back, please come back."

A ripple of movement in the ground caught Eryna's attention. She stiffened.

Then Sierra saw it, too. Then Parvati. Then Dera.

Thick vines started wrapping around Derrick's legs, his arms, his chest.

"Wait, what's going on?" Brody asked, startled.

"Eryna, what are you doing?" Sierra accused, but Eryna shook her head.

"I'm not doing that."

The vines grew thicker, slipped under Jenin's crumpled body, and wrapped around more of Derrick.

"Stop it!" Sierra frantically tried to pull a vine off him, but Parvati stopped her.

"Let it happen," she whispered, and in that moment, Eryna

realized what was occurring.

The Gods had heard Jenin's plea.

As the vines covered the last of Derrick, they melded together into one large mass, the skin quickly turning to rough bark. It moved until it stood upright like the trunk of a tree, and Jenin slowly slipped off him into the dirt. One by one, thick branches extended from the trunk, sprouting fresh green leaves. It grew thicker and thicker, higher and higher until it was a beautiful, solid elm.

"Like Ardian's love," Eryna muttered. Dera nodded and patted Eryna's thigh.

"Love, no matter what kind, is a magic all its own," she said, and hugged Eryna tight.

Jenin's cries quieted as she placed her palm against the tree and stared at it. Then her eyes floated toward something in the tree line, and she tensed.

"You," she growled.

They all turned to see Damian standing there, the third vessel in his hand, tears in his eyes. Jenin stood and stared at him as if she could kill him on the spot.

"You did this," she said, pointing at him.

"I...I...," he stammered, his eyes wide, frightened. Jenin took a step toward her father. He took one back on instinct. Jenin took another step toward him. And another. And another.

But then she stopped.

Her hands clenched into fists, her knuckles white as the moon, and her mossy eyes turned black as a starless night. The forest air turned hot, dry, and impossibly heavy.

Worry for Jenin broke through Eryna's chest.

"What's wrong with her?" she asked Dera, but Dera simply shook her head.

"I don't know," she said.

"Jenin," Eryna called, but she didn't move. She barely breathed.

Then the ravenous growls of wolves and cougars and bears suddenly echoed around them.

Damian, eyes intensely panicked, dropped the vessel and ran. He didn't get far.

The vicious howls and growls and the sound of sharp teeth puncturing skin came from only a hundred yards away.

"Help me, Jenin, please!" he screamed in torment. "Help! Help, please! Please!"

Jenin's mossy eyes returned, her hands slackened, and the damp, cool forest air settled. She stared in the direction of her father's screams, her legs stiff, like she couldn't quite decide whether to run toward him or away from him.

But then she closed her eyes and didn't move until the last cry of her father died out, and the Thornewood was silent. She opened her eyes, knelt at the base of the elm, and whispered, "He's gone. He's finally gone."

Brody, who hadn't moved since Derrick had passed, stood from where he was kneeling and picked up the vessel Damian had dropped.

He closed his eyes, placed his hand over his chest, and moments later, the vibrant Heart was in his hand. He stared at it for a breath, and Eryna worried he might take back his decision. But he placed it in the vessel and shut it tight. He met Eryna where she stood, lifted her hand, and closed her fist around the sphere.

"I'm going to fix this," he said, though Eryna wasn't sure how he could. The mess he'd made was far past the point of cleaning. He then knelt next to Jenin and put a hand on her shoulder.

"I'm going to fix *all* of this." He said the words like they were the most serious promise he'd ever made. Jenin didn't even look at him. He stood and looked at Eryna once more, resolve burning in his eyes.

The last Eryna saw of Brody Blackwell was his dark hair fading into the distance as he moved in the direction of Aponyx, the Thornewood swallowing him whole.

Chapter Forty-Nine

Six Months Later

A biting chill nipped at Eryna's nose and cheeks as she inhaled deeply and leaned her head back against Derrick's elm.

The winter air was so crisp and cold, it burned as it entered her lungs, but the burn was better than the alternative. It was better than the sorrow that still lingered in her chest with every beat of her heart.

"I miss you," she whispered, closing her eyes to listen to the sounds of the jays and the cardinals, the last of the birds that hung around for the season.

The Thornewood was always quieter in the winter. It used to be Eryna's least favorite time of year, but with how much calmer it was, she swore that if she listened hard enough to the birds and the breeze, she could hear Derrick talking back to her.

And ever since she made the decision to put the Thornewood Heart back in the Mother Oak, the birds and the breeze were all she had to go off of.

"You're sure you want to do this?" Dera had asked, looking

Eryna squarely in the eyes when she told her her decision. She'd never felt pressured by her sisters to put the Heart back. No one had even suggested it. But with how few Dryads there were left, Eryna felt it was time for there to be more, and that couldn't be done without the it returning to the Mother Oak.

It was uncomfortable at first, not being so connected to the forest and not being able to heal in the ways that she used to. Some powers lingered, but nothing like what they once were. Still, for the future of her people, it was worth it.

Overhead, a few jays sang in sync, their short tweets and whistles sounding an awful lot like *I miss you, too.*

Eryna sighed and opened her eyes. Snow fell around her in a steady drift, whispering softly as it layered on top of the already blanketed ground.

"It's a big day today. I'm finally becoming a big sister," she told Derrick, smiling, though worry welled up inside her.

For one hundred years, Eryna had been the youngest Dryad. For one hundred years, Eryna had been *faémona,* and she was ready to be so much more. She only hoped she could be as caring as Oihane, as smart and steady as Dera, and even as commanding and wise as Althea.

"I hope I'll be good at it," she spoke the wish aloud, as if saying the words would increase the chances of it being true.

"You, my sweet *faémona,* will be a great big sister," Oihane said, coming into view, her thick pelts glistening with fresh snow. Just behind her were Jenin and Sierra. Oihane knelt and kissed Eryna on the forehead, then stood and stretched out her hand.

"It's time," she sang, smiling brightly. Eryna's chest fluttered. She wasn't expecting it to happen so soon, so early in the morning. Oihane's smile widened, and she winked. "You'll do great, I promise."

Nodding, Eryna sighed and took Oihane's hand, pulling herself to a stand. She walked to where Jenin and Sierra stood and joined them. Jenin reached out and brushed a stray hair from Eryna's face, then hugged her tight.

"Anything change today?" she asked, looking at the elm. It was a question she asked every day, and every day, the answer was the same.

Eryna shook her head and patted her on the back.

"Your turn," she said. Jenin sighed, nodded, and made her way to the base of the tree. Eryna walked a few steps away with Oihane and Sierra to give Jenin privacy. She looked at Sierra.

"How's Aponyx?" she asked, bracing for some sort of snarky response. While Eryna had warmed to Sierra a bit, she still found her incredibly annoying and abrasive.

"Mom's finally convinced the board of Blackwell Tech to promote her to CEO, and has been slowly building a plan for getting humans off the island and back to the Mainland," Sierra replied, studying her nails, picking an invisible layer of dirt from them. "And Alexander Blackwell's...*retirement*...has officially been announced. They told the public he's retiring to some small community on the Mainland, but where he actually is, I'm not sure. I heard something about a maximum-security prison on a hidden island in the South."

Eryna nodded, then asked the question she'd been avoiding for months, finally giving in.

"And Brody?"

Sierra pursed her lips and shrugged.

"No one's heard from him, but rumor has it he was last seen boarding a ship to the Southern Continent."

"The Southern Continent? Why?"

Before Sierra could reply, the crunch of snow beneath boots called their attention toward Jenin as she rejoined them, a large duffle bag that Eryna hadn't noticed earlier slung over her shoulder. Eryna eyed it. Besides shopping bags, Jenin never carried anything larger than a clutch, let alone a duffle bag.

"Ready?" Jenin asked the girls, and they nodded.

As they walked in silence for several miles, Eryna couldn't stop eyeing the duffle bag. Jenin looked at her and lifted a brow.

"Yes?" she asked, clearly annoyed by Eryna's stares. Eryna bit her lip.

"Going somewhere?" she asked. An insecure fear welled up inside her at the possibility of Jenin going somewhere without her. Eryna had her sisters to keep her company, but she would miss her best friend. Jenin silently looked at the ground as they walked, then glanced at Eryna from the sides of her eyes.

"Dera told me about a witch on the Southern Continent who might have a way of bringing Derrick back," she said, gaze straight ahead as if she was too afraid to look at Eryna while she spoke. Eryna froze.

"Jenin—" she started, but Jenin held up a hand, cutting her off.

"I already know what you're going to say," she said, her eyes sharp and serious. "Death is death. I know. But I don't want to hear it. I cannot exist in a world that he is not in. I *will* not. If there is even a fraction of a sliver of a hope of bringing him back, then I will follow that to the ends of the earth, or die trying." Jenin reached out and placed a hand on Eryna's shoulder. "You did it for your family. Now it's my turn."

It was the most deranged idea Eryna might have ever heard, especially coming from Jenin. The Ekatan was a perilous place, specifically for humans. But Jenin's eyes held a firmness that said she would not be dissuaded from her plan. There was only one thing left to do, and as much as Eryna didn't want to leave the Thornewood again, especially with new life on the way, there was no way she could let Jenin go alone.

Eryna placed her hand on Jenin's shoulder and sighed.

"Fine. Then I'm coming with you," she said. Jenin's face lit up.

"Really?" she breathed. "But what about your new sister? What about your growing clan?"

"We've raised many young Dryads before. Eryna has plenty of time to learn how to be a big sister," Oihane said, cutting in. Eryna smiled at her sister, then narrowed her eyes at Jenin.

"You didn't think I'd let you go to the Southern Continent alone, did you? You'd die immediately."

"Hey!" Jenin chided, shoving Eryna, the two of them laughing.

"Wait, I want to come," Sierra whined.

"No," Eryna and Jenin answered in unison. They looked at each other and burst into a fit of giggles. Sierra huffed and puffed the rest of the way to the Thornewood Mother Oak while Eryna and Jenin laid out their plans.

As they drew nearer, the steady beating of drums and singing pulled them in, Eryna already itching to dance to the rhythm. Oihane didn't have as much self-control, skipping the last stretch of the walk and excitedly pulling Eryna along.

They broke through the tree line of the *Domecowé* and were immediately greeted with cups of berry wine and flower circlets. Dera approached them on quick feet, embracing each of the girls, and ripped the wine out of Eryna's hand.

"Hey, I was drinking that," Eryna pouted.

"Soon, but not yet. You need a clear head," she said, taking her hand.

"Clear head for what?" Eryna asked. Just then, the Mother Oak began to glow with a bright purple hue and let out a loud, rumbling *boom*, and the Dryads all squealed with excitement.

Dera picked up her pace, dragging Eryna with her. They stopped in front of the Mother Oak, where Tera replaced Eryna's flower circlet with a crown of laurel leaves.

Laurel leaves, Eryna realized. This specific circlet was reserved only for those leading special ceremonies.

Dera squeezed Eryna's shoulders, gave her a reassuring nod and pressed a soft kiss to her cheek.

"You'll do great," she whispered. Then she gave Eryna a light push toward the Mother Oak. Her blood warmed in her veins and her heart hammered in her chest with the speed of a thousand hummingbird wings. As she stepped closer, she could hear the soft cries of a tiny being wailing from inside the trunk. The Mother Oak let out another rumble, and the glow died. The drums stopped. The Dryads fell silent. All that could be heard were high-pitched cries.

Eryna looked over her shoulder at Dera, Oihane, Jenin, and Sierra. They nodded and smiled at her, easing a fraction of her nerves. Eryna turned back to the Mother Oak and a large opening formed in the trunk, the cries growing louder and shriller the wider it got. She lifted high up on her toes and reached inside.

Her fingers met warm, textured skin, and the cries stopped instantly. A tiny hand clasped around Eryna's finger, and her stomach leapt to her throat with excitement. She scooped up the small, fragile body and pulled it to her chest, wrapping it in one of her pelts. When she looked down into her arms, she saw warm brown maple skin, dark curly hair, and the tiniest, widest green eyes she'd ever seen. The baby girl smiled up at her, the expression joyful and gummy. Eryna couldn't help but smile back. She turned around and held the baby up, and the Dryads cheered, tears of happiness streaming down their cheeks.

"What's her name?" Dera called. Eryna hadn't even thought of a name, though one stuck out in her mind. She brought the baby to her chest and looked down at her again.

"Genevieve," Eryna said, and all her sisters nodded. Jenin gave her a wide, approving smile with tears in her eyes. She touched her chest in gratitude.

"*Osea yao faémo*," the Dryad sisters chanted as the drums and the singing started up again.

"*Osea yao faémo*," Eryna repeated quietly for only Genevieve to hear. "Welcome to the world, *faémona*," she whispered. Then she kissed her on the forehead, promising her a world that was vastly different than her own.

And for the first time in one hundred years, a new Dryad was born.

Enjoy this book?

Please rate it and leave a review.

This is the best way to show your support for indie authors, like me :)

Acknowledgements

There are far too many people who deserve a big ol' thank you for helping me along the journey of getting this book published, and I'm certain I will forget someone along the way, but I'm sure going to try my best!

First, a big, big thank you to my husband, Jake, for not returning the ring when I told you I wanted to be a full-time author six years ago. I'm glad we've come so far! In all seriousness, thank you for all your love and support along this journey, and for the many nights spent going to sleep alone while I write, or taking the bath and bedtime shift with the girls so I could finish a chapter or hit my word count. I love you!

A thank you to my two precious, feral daughters for always making mama smile, being constant inspirations, and for filling my heart with so, so much joy. You are the lights of my life. All that I do, I do for you. And to Becca for being the best second mom to our babies, because this book would never have been written without your help!

Thank you to my parents for their constant support, and for being my forever cheerleaders. Even when I thought it wouldn't be possible, you told me to keep going, and have believed in me since the moment I told you I wanted to become a writer. I love you both so much.

A big, big thank you to my amazing beta readers Ashley, Alex W., Alex B., Tally, Hillary, Maddie, Harlee, and Leslie. Without your insights and feedback, this book wouldn't be what it is today. Thank you, thank you, thank you!

To Jacquelyn for the incredible cover art! The detail, the artistry, the love and thought that went into it. You took my vision and ran with it and created the most beautiful book cover I've ever seen, though I might be a little biased. And to Nel for the amazing interior art. You brought my city to life. I will never be able to thank you enough for that.

Thank you to Jill and Tarah for being my own little PR team, and for believing that your friend's hard work is worthy of celebration, no matter how much she may feel like an imposter.

To Urk and Al. My hype gals. My conspirators. My soul sisters. My first responders. I truly, truly could not have done it without you and your constant support and validation (or critique!). Thank you for loving my story and my characters as much as I do.

To Caitlin a.k.a. Sauron, for your sharp eye and gut reactions. I will never trust an early draft of my book any anyone else's hands again, except your sister's. I would also like to extend the offer to pay for any therapy sessions I may have induced.

To Aleshka, for falling in love with my characters and story, and for shoving me down the publishing path even when I dug my heels in.

To Angie, my hummingbird sister, because I wouldn't even have pursued the publishing path if it wasn't for you. You saw something in me that took me years to see in myself. I will forever be grateful.

Lastly, to my critique partner Lindsay, the sister of my soul! This book wouldn't—couldn't—exist without you. This story and its characters are as much mine as they are yours, and I couldn't imagine working with anyone else on the sweet little story that sprouted deep in my heart. Thank you for handling it with care, but also giving me a strong metaphorical backhand when needed. And thank you for dragging me by my ponytail through the publishing and postpartum trenches. You will forever be the first and last eyes on my projects. Thank you, thank you, thank you!

About the Author

Maxine writes whimsical fantasies set in stark contemporary worlds, and characters you'd either follow to the edge of the earth or toss over it. Born and raised in the Pacific Northwest, she lives in a menagerie with her Husky, Samoyed, three cats, two preciously feral daughters, and her co-wrangler husband.

www.ingramcontent.com/pod-product-compliance
Lightning Source LLC
Chambersburg PA
CBHW030350120726
47901CB00007B/1967